A STRANGER'S LOVE

Anne-Marie came to full consciousness in the arms of a man weary from love-making, a man she had never seen before.

"Who is Bart?" he asked. "Who is the man you make love to so passionately?"

"My husband," she replied. "Where is he?" A look of instant remembrance and utter panic crossed her face. "What am I doing here?" she cried, sitting up, looking at the man.

"I picked you up on the beach several days ago. Since then you have shared my bed, calling me 'Bart.' You have been frightened out of your mind. I was afraid you would never be sane again. I had hoped that by my love-making you would be comforted and come to your senses—as you have."

"And my husband's ship?" she queried.

For a moment he was silent. "She was lost at sea."

Wave of Destiny

Martha Melahn

AVON
PUBLISHERS OF BARD, CAMELOT, DISCUS AND FLARE BOOKS

WAVE OF DESTINY is an original publication of Avon Books.
This work has never before appeared in book form.

AVON BOOKS
A division of
The Hearst Corporation
959 Eighth Avenue
New York, New York 10019

Copyright © 1981 by Martha Melahn
Published by arrangement with the author
Library of Congress Catalog Card Number: 81-66486
ISBN: 0-380-79152-8

First Avon Printing, December, 1981

AVON TRADEMARK REG. U.S. PAT. OFF. AND IN OTHER COUNTRIES.
MARCA REGISTRADA. HECHO EN U.S.A.

Printed in the U.S.A.

WFH 10 9 8 7 6 5 4 3 2 1

AUTHOR'S NOTE

All major characters in this book—Anne-Marie, Bart, Don Miguel, Consuelo, Tim and their families—are fictitious. A number of minor roles are also, such as Wooleye, Captain Stiles, Shuttele, Mr. Leeds, Dr. Burbury, Pearl, Mimi and the sheriff. As I doubt that a corruptible sheriff existed in Key West during the whole of the nineteenth century, it became necessary to invent one and he is purposely unnamed. However, a number of minor characters—colorful old-timers—did live in this intriguing city at the time and are portrayed as local chroniclers remembered them.

Some of Dr. Samuel A. Mudd's conversations with Bart spring from letters written to his wife; others are pure conjecture. It was not until 1869 that Mudd was pardoned by President Andrew Johnson. In 1979 President Carter endorsed the wording of the pardon spurred by efforts of Mudd's descendants to completely clear the name. Unfortunately, the saying, "His name is Mudd," still survives as a play on words in the language even though it should remind us of this injustice.

The *Catherine* (later called the *Greyhound*), the *Dasher*, the *Annabelle*, the *Sea Witch* and the *Pretty Lady* are common ships' names and should not be attributed to any real vessels in use at the time.

Also, no hurricane struck Key West directly between 1864 and 1868 when this story is set. But, because hurricanes have always been a threat to the area (hitting in 1835, 1846, 1876, 1894, 1909, 1910, and so on, with a number of minor-intensity storms during the intervening years) one was included as an important aspect of the life.

Most of the buildings existed as described, except Consuelo's home. This is depicted as a prototype of many of the lovely old Key West dwellings unique to this area. Don Miguel's development on a fictitious key, Cayo de las Matas, is an embellishment of a wrecker's compound and pure fantasy, although the animals and plant life are not.

With the above verisimilitudes in mind, the reader should recognize that which is a matter of history: the events of the Civil War, the construction and use of Fort Jefferson and the yellow fever epidemics.

MM

CHAPTER ONE

April 1864

Land and sea not only met but intermingled on the southeast New Jersey shore. Inviting harbors had harbors-within-harbors, and harbors within these joined a lacy network of waterways that, woven into one river, drifted lazily eastward; intricate foldings and counterfoldings of the Egg River, unspanned by bridges, provided sheltered and tranquil ship havens. Shielded from the sea, ramified coves met unpebbled streams until finally further inland the earth sank into placid marshlands. Green and purple grasses, gaining a foothold, held more stable sand supportive of piney woods. Here people settled, making a good living from both timber and sea. Scattered farms and marine industries fed their children and their needs.

Among the more prosperous inhabitants were the Ramsdens and Fraziers. This day the families would be united in a long-awaited marriage. Still, a sullen sky, a sultry sun, and capricious breezes caused concern in everyone.

Anne-Marie Frazier stood in her bedroom, adjusting her veil; like most articles of clothing worn infrequently, the veil did not hang exactly right. Perhaps her grandmother or her mother had used a few more hairpins to keep the exquisite

Alençon lace in place, but Anne-Marie, beset with humidity, could not get the fragile heirloom to behave. Downstairs she could visualize her father consulting his gold watch, ever mindful of the hour and cognizant of the fact that they were due at the church. Her mother and the rest of the family were already under way in another carriage. Only one maid remained to assure her the veil was, indeed, absolutely perfect. Finally acquiescing, the young bride-to-be descended nervously to join her impatient father waiting at the landing.

"Don't worry, Father, the wedding won't start without me," said Anne-Marie, managing a wan smile.

"I promised your mother I'd have you there on time," replied Jason, scolding mildly as he opened the front door.

There at the portico, a hand raised obviously ready to knock at the door, stood a gypsy, and behind her, next to their carriage, a scruffy pony. Startled by her presence and resentful of any intrusion, Jason hastily reached for a coin in order to be rid of the woman. To his dismay, he found only a half dollar, a considerable sum for a beggar. Reluctantly, but bound by the spirit of the day, he pressed the coin into the woman's hand and ushered Anne-Marie toward the carriage.

"Thank you, Squire," said the surprised and delighted gypsy, her dark eyes flashing in gratitude.

"You must let me tell the beautiful bride's fortune."

"I'm sorry, we have no time. We're already late," replied Jason, anxious to be rid of the dowdy character. Unlike the typical banker, Jason was not austere and, although he was extremely shrewd when it came to lending money, his friendly mien disguised a hard practicality.

"It will only take a moment, and you have been so generous," pressed the woman, now looking to Anne-Marie. The gypsy stood before them, blocking their way. A bright red scarf wrapped her hair and a blousy print dress, dirty and stained, danced in the wind. A tattered shawl bunched about her shoulders, contributing to the bizarre effect. Although small tribes in caravans occasionally moved about the countryside, Anne-Marie had never been so near a gypsy. "Count the children, the gypsies are in town," joked the townspeople. So Anne-Marie stood on her first day of adulthood more curious than frightened. This day was sacrosanct, the most important day of her life and on this day no harm could possibly come to her.

"Father, I've forgotten the prayer book," said Anne-Marie, looking at her father with pleading eyes. "It's on my dresser. Please, while you're getting it she can tell my fortune." Anne-Marie had never failed to move her father. Seventeen years of marveling at her beauty and winning ways had not ended. Dutifully, but obviously exasperated, Jason dashed into the house as Anne-Marie offered the woman an upturned hand.

"I see you will be married today," said the gypsy.

"Yes," replied Anne-Marie, smiling placidly, "and I hope it will be a good marriage."

"You will have a good marriage, but you should not marry today! Another day—many other days would be better. I see danger. No! Today is not a good day for your marriage. I must warn you, you have a mortal enemy in a dark-haired man. Be careful."

The unexpected prophecy startled and repulsed Anne-Marie, who stiffened visibly and looked toward the door, but Jason hardly had had time to reappear.

Sensing the girl's discomfort, the gypsy ameliorated her reading, raising the tone of her voice. "You will travel far. You will be rich. Oh, I see great wealth for you! You will wear magnificent jewels—you will know rulers and noblemen." Her eyes sparkled and she squeezed Anne-Marie's hand as if to draw some of the wealth upon herself.

What a strange woman, thought Anne-Marie, placated somewhat by the brighter future and daring to look into the gypsy's glowing eyes. A short, crisp gust of wind gathered at Anne-Marie's veil, but the gypsy paid no heed. She closed her eyes for a long moment and when she spoke again Anne-Marie noted that her eyes had dimmed. "I fear for your firstborn," she said distantly, and then gathering force added, "I fear for your husband's children." The perplexed look on the gypsy's face was almost as startling as her words. Anne-Marie shivered and tried to withdraw her hand, but the woman continued. "No. Do not be afraid. You will have an outrageous fortune. Your beauty is both a curse and a blessing."

Anne-Marie looked up to see her father breathlessly clutching the needed prayer book. Thanking the gypsy, she allowed herself to be helped into the carriage.

"She promised me an outrageous fortune," said Anne-Marie. "Riches, jewels, but then a lot of poppycock..."

"A gypsy tells the truth once in a lifetime and immediately repents," scoffed Jason, extracting his watch. "Barring any further intrusions, we will only be a few minutes late." As the carriage left the long driveway and gained the turnpike he added, "Frankly, considering what she got from me, I see more riches in her hand than I do in yours for a long time."

Anne-Marie concurred, smiling. Dismissing the prophecy as preposterous, once again she turned her attention to the veil.

The simple ceremony proceeded, unimpeded by the gathering thunderclouds. It was not until Jason Frazier's family was safely once again at home that the heavens delivered a promised storm that only slightly delayed the arrival of the groom, Captain Bartholomew Ramsden, his best man and his parents.

Emily Frazier stood looking out of the window of her bedroom, thinking of her daughter Anne-Marie, just turned seventeen, the baby of the family and now a bride of one hour. Outside, fresh leaves glistened as a shy and reluctant sun struggled to break through the rain. Wagon ruts, looking like little rivers, creased the elm-lined drive leading to the house.

"What kind of a marriage does this weather portend?" asked Emily of her husband.

"Bart's a good boy," replied Jason. "A bit daring, but that's what it takes today. It is only three years since he got his papers and his first ship. Of course, the war helped, but he's a man of property at only twenty-four."

"It's just that she's so innocent and lovely," replied Emily. Unconsciously she had worked a fine lace-bound handkerchief into a twisted limp wad. "It's hard being married to a sea captain. She'll be alone so much."

"Come now, wife," said Jason, slowly rising from their four-poster where he had stretched out for a few minutes' rest. "She'll keep the home fires burnin'. A little absence does no harm. Bart's had his eye on her since she was a tiny girl. The fruit was ripe for the pickin'."

"I suppose so," said Emily, who also had noticed the rounded curves of her young daughter's breasts that seemed ready to explode from her tight bodices.

"Bart's either awfully smart or awfully lucky," added Jason. It was then he remembered the prophecy of the gypsy that Anne-Marie would enjoy great wealth. He decided to say nothing of that to his wife, not wanting to add credence to a charlatan's quackery. Besides, his largesse now seemed foolish.

As a banker, Jason was keenly aware of Bart's finances, which, of course, were confidential, but hardly so in that everyone knew of his rising fortune. Through three years of the Civil War Jason had watched his future son-in-law take to sea in one ship after another, often returning with a bigger and better ship. There was always a highly profitable commodity bulging in the hold. He seemed to have a knack for anticipating what would be in greatest demand by the Union armies at the time he returned.

Bart, like Jason's own two sons, had not enlisted, but had paid the three-hundred-dollar bounty to avoid the draft. This was not through cowardice or a lack of patriotism; they simply felt that their particular talents and training—as merchant seamen, shipbuilders and students—were more valuable to the Union than their marksmanship and marching ability.

Jason was also certainly aware that there were two Bart Ramsdens—one a quiet young man who adored his daughter and the other a demanding driver of men. But his daughter might never see that other side, just as he, the banker, never discussed loans and bitter foreclosures with his own wife. It was hardly talk for women's ears—at least not his sort of women.

The men in Jason's family had circled the globe, but his own travels had taken him no further from the hearth than to his great mahogany desk two miles away at Great Egg Harbor. From his many-paned windows he could gaze at the forest of masts, chockablock in the harbor, jibbooms rigged so as not to poke the windows out of warehouses. The spicy tang of Eastern merchandise mingled with whiffs of tar, tobacco, fish and oils. Here were the varied cargoes of the seven seas—the perfume of tea from China, spices from Java, dates from Arabia, coffee from South America mingled with the pungent West Indian fruits. Now tobacco from Turkey and cotton from Egypt supplanted that which once had come from the Southern states. In the end, to this family it all added up to the sweet smell of money.

Throughout the first three years of the Civil War the battles and losses had been discouraging. "Our leadership is so poor compared to that of the Confederacy," Jason had ranted. Indeed, few Union officers were career men or West Point graduates; instead, most were political appointees—some even unsympathetic to the war. Not until 1863 did President Lincoln put together the competent and reliable team of Ulysses Grant as chief field commander and Henry Halleck as chief of staff to turn the tide. "If I'm going to finance this damn war, then I want to win it," said Jason. The money to finance the Union armies had come from excise, custom and income taxes as well as loan and treasury notes. Consequently, the activities of both the Frazier and Ramsden families—and many like them—were in their own way contributing considerably to the war effort without soldiering.

During July of 1863 Grant had engineered the surrender of the Confederate stronghold of Vicksburg, clearing the way for the Northern control of the whole Mississippi Valley. General Lee's bold thrust to put the North on the defensive at the Battle of Gettysburg had cost the Rebels. Lee would never again be strong enough to mount an offensive. By 1864 the way to Georgia was clear and the end of the war in sight. The time had seemed right for the marriage, Jason reflected.

"Come, Jason, let me help you dress so that I can go to Anne-Marie. Our guests will soon be arriving," Emily said with a tender gaze toward her husband, stirring him from his reverie. After thirty years of marriage they could almost read each other's minds. There was no time to watch the rain drip from the eaves in long thin streams or worry about a war. Besides, the rain clouds were already scudding across a sky blown by the wind that was slowly clearing a path for the sun.

"Get on with you, woman," replied Jason playfully. "Just because your baby will soon be leaving, you don't have to start babying me. She needs you more than I do. I hope you've had a talk with her."

"As a matter of fact, I haven't. . . . But if she's half the woman I think she is, it won't be necessary," Emily chirped as she left him. . . .

Emily's instincts were right. Anne-Marie stood before her mirror more disconcerted over the *pit-a-pat* of her mother's approaching footsteps than what the night would bring. Were wedding nights always so embarrassing? She and Bart had waited so long for this day and night; now that it was here, it was awkward. There had been a few brief, stolen, rapturous meetings, but in a town where they were both known to everyone, little more than a few furtive kisses and promises were possible. Had she not been away at school and had Bart been more at hand, controlling their passion might have been more difficult. Bart had spent most of his time at sea, all the sooner to marry her. When they were together, even the walls seemed protective of her virginity.

Most alert of the watchdogs had been Brian Delaney, Bart's first mate and closest friend—almost Bart's shadow.

Anne-Marie didn't know quite what to make of this association. Brian seemed to idolize Bart, by far the handsomer, more charming, warmer and quicker of the two. Certainly Bart trusted Brian implicitly and relied upon him as one would a brother. As young boys playing together in Great Egg Harbor, once Bart had slipped between two boats and could have been crushed had not Brian held the boats apart and cried for help. The act, as described by Bart, had called for extraordinary strength and quick thinking. But Anne-Marie tended to discount this act of valor, and even surmised that, through the years, in Bart's mind the degree of danger had been magnified, as well as the extent of Brian's heroism. Surely, in that precarious position, Bart had been frightened. But Anne-Marie often noted that her own brothers boasted in later years of risky escapades that she herself had witnessed as a child and such recollections never lost any fat in the telling. Embellishments, like the size of the fish that got away, added drama and color to life that was too often dull and restricted, especially for the young.

Anne-Marie could not discount the lifelong friendship between Bart and Brian that became a working relationship when Bart got his own ship and signed on Brian as first mate. Sometimes Brian seemed to be an extension of Bart—like a hammer in his hand or a plow. But to Anne-Marie there seemed something untamed, almost cruel or uncivilized about Brian that she could only sense. Certainly she could never fault his manners or his loyalty to Bart; Anne-Marie recognized that she was jealous of this man who shared everything with Bart except herself, but there was more to it than that. For no demonstrable reason she felt there was something sinister about Brian, something Bart could not see. Had Brian had a family he could return to, his presence would somehow not have been so oppressive or disconcerting. It will be different now that we are married, Anne-Marie told herself, half aware that she was fooling herself. Now, the longed-for ceremony had taken place and her mother stood tapping gently at her door.

"You were the world's most beautiful bride," murmured Emily, feigning a cheerfulness that had suddenly disappeared in the hall outside her daughter's room.

"Everything did go all right, didn't it? The rain held off, Brian didn't lose the ring and you managed not to weep," said Anne-Marie, smiling to soften words that might have revealed her irritation. "Now if only the war were over, wouldn't everything be perfect?"

Emily stood gazing at the soft light dancing about her daughter. "That dress is perfect...perhaps cut a bit low, but I suppose for a married woman..."

Anne-Marie pirouetted, her wide skirts swirling, rustling to music only she could hear, but was suddenly interrupted by footsteps on the walk below. Her face looked flushed now, her eyes sparkling. "That's Bart and his parents—and Brian," groaned Anne-Marie, moving to look down from her window. "You'd better go greet them before Brian starts tormenting the dog."

Bart's golden hair, shining like a sun, stood out between the leaves and branches of an apple tree that bent toward the house. His hat was in one hand; in the other he clutched a small package that prophesied a gift—small and costly—from some place far away. A gift that, one way or another through his absence, she had paid for.

A few minutes later, downstairs in the spacious entry, Bart turned his bride toward a large gilt mirror and stood behind her. "Don't we make a handsome couple?" she murmured, nestling against him with a thrill of strange elation.

"Well, your half anyway."

As she stared at him, he reminded her of the young Hermes in a print on her mother's bedroom wall. His blond hair reminded her of wheat. His hands pressed against her arms, holding them tight to her body, helping to contain her palpitating heart.

Anne-Marie's wavy coppery hair was pulled back from her face, revealing a long queenly neck and a slightly jutting chin. Her vibrancy, her knack of sharing magic moments with others, like a spirit-flame flowed steadily toward him. Large eyes, under strong eyebrows and long thick lashes widened, encompassed and caressed. On the console table before them rested a small black velvet box. Reaching around her, never losing her gaze, he opened the box and fastened a glowing emerald on a gold chain around her neck. "So that you will always have something special from me with you."

"It's perfectly lovely," she whispered. "It's like the sea—the most beautiful jewel I've ever seen. I think I'm going to perish with happiness," she said, commanding the same thought from him.

He drew nearer to her. "Come," he said, forcing an invisible chain of propriety to pry them apart. "We must join the others."

"I suppose they are waiting . . ." Her voice trailed off, her eyes returning to the mirror for one more look at the magnificent touch of green between her breasts.

"I have several surprises for my beautiful bride. One secret has been very hard to keep. I couldn't have managed it without Brian, so don't be short with him. But you shall see . . ."

"I certainly hope I will. Do you remember, I don't even know where we are spending the night? Is that your secret?" she asked with a toss of her head. A small tone of hauteur crept into her voice, which she tried to erase with a smile. Nevertheless Bart had noted it.

9

"My dear girl—sometimes my *little* girl—when I'm away you will have complete control of your life. You will have to make all *our* decisions. But you must be prepared for the fact that I love surprising you. I can't help it. Allow me my peccadilloes, my foibles, and I will honor yours. Happiness and understanding come through little things, never big things—at least, that's what people tell me." He smiled unsurely.

"Little things like emeralds!" she corrected, holding his hands, swinging his arms as if in a dance.

"Perhaps I've set a difficult precedent. Let's join the others," he replied, mollified.

"No, wait. Let me take another look in the mirror. I look so elegant! It is beautiful and I will never take it off! I promise. Oh, Bart! You want to join the others and I want to kiss you," she said.

"You do manipulate me," he said, wrapping his arms about her. She looked up into his eyes. They seemed bluer than forget-me-nots. Then pulling down his head, she kissed him fiercely. Finally, pulling from him and taking a deep breath to still the beating in her heart, she said, "They are surely running out of patience by now." Without doubt, it seemed that was the way married life would be.

Extended with leaves, the mahogany dining table sat eighteen. Emily Frazier's silver and crystal rested upon an exquisite Belgian lace cloth; her family treasures emerged only for holidays and important occasions. The gleaming candelabra would illuminate a procession of courses. Oysters and cherrystone clams were followed by soup. Then came Emily's "Star Gazy" fish pie in which small whole fish were baked. The inevitable turkey and ham were accompanied by silver tureens of steaming Brussels sprouts and chestnuts, creamed corn, baked onions, puréed parsnips, green wild asparagus, escalloped potatoes and tomatoes. Crystal celery glasses held celery hearts, sculptured and curled. A magnificent "Bride's Cake," frosted with fluffy icing and garnished with candied crystalized rose petals, had been two days in the making. Coffee and cognac provided the finale.

At Anne-Marie's request the dinner was to be an elegant

10

family party—excepting Brian—with adults seated in the dining room and children attended to in a smaller breakfast room. One of Anne-Marie's older sisters, whose husband commanded a Union ship enforcing the naval blockade against the Confederacy, was not present, but two aunts and uncles had come from New York by coach. Jason's grace before the meal asked, therefore, not only for the blessing of the Lord upon the marriage, but also for the protection of those not present, for the rejoicing in the joining of the two close families and an offering of thanks that they were joined by loved ones from afar. "I realize, dear Lord, that I have asked you for a great deal in these extraordinary times. Your benevolence and mercy have blessed this family and our hearts overflow with gratitude. May it continue to be so," said Jason in conclusion.

"That was one of father's better prayers," whispered Anne-Marie to Bart.

"Short."

The end of the prayer was a signal for champagne to be served. Jason then offered a toast to the bride and groom. "Kind hearts and gentle people, please join me in a toast to our lovely daughter and her fine husband," said Jason, rising, his face beaming.

"He seems frightfully happy to be rid of me," whispered Anne-Marie, happily.

"Think of the expense he's out from under," replied Bart, shaking his head in reaction, but without thought of his own undertaking.

Most of the inhabitants around Egg Harbor would not expect to be invited and were not, they being families of sailors, merchants, traders, fishermen, ropemakers, small farmers, lumbermen and simple people—a crude lot whose numbers, in any case, sharply declined with the war. One small schoolhouse served the town and anything more than the bare rudiments of culture had to be obtained elsewhere. Boys and girls of the more prosperous families were widely scattered and attended prep schools and seminaries. Anne-Marie had finished at Bishop Douane's school—St. Mary's Hall—in Burlington, New Jersey. Had it not been wartime her friends would have been invited and would have come to the wedding from all over the country. Nevertheless, the two families made a festive group because they were all pleased with the match. The women chatted about losses and shortages due to the war and about their children. The war, politics and business absorbed the men. Their words were now washed down by Jason's hoarded, aged and decanted Madeira saved for this occasion. The wine loosened everyone's tongues and even produced an occasional risqué innuendo.

"It would be nice if the old man offered you some champagne for the ship," whispered Brian to Bart. Only Anne-Marie overheard the remark and flinched slightly. It was the sort of thing that Brian would say. If she called him on it, he would say that he was, of course, only joking, which would leave her feeling silly or at least juvenile.

"We can deplore the war," Jason was saying, "but it certainly has meant change. The miles of new railroads with railroad artillery, armored ships and torpedoes, machine guns, aerial balloons, rifled shoulder arms and more accurate cannon, breech-loading and repeating carbines and revolvers, wire entanglements and the telegraph make this unlike any war that was ever fought before—and worse!"

"It has certainly changed shipping," said Bart.

"What do you think of the new oceangoing steamships?" queried Jason, at the same time giving a knowing, enclosing glance toward Bart's father, Caleb Ramsden, also a shipmaster.

"They're coming, and they're coming fast. Labor costs are rising. Only the great influx of immigrants replacing the manpower that has gone West and to war has kept us going. Steamships use fuel and that is costly, but it doesn't equal the payroll of fifty men needed to keep a square-rigger afloat," said Bart, with Brian nodding his assent.

"Do you agree, Caleb?" asked Jason.

"Wind's free," replied Caleb, "and that's hard to beat. I think if we go back to schooners instead of square-riggers, where mainsails are not hung off those damn—excuse me, ladies—fixed horizontal yards, but run up masts from the deck, all that's necessary are a few strong backs on deck. From a gang of fifty sailors scrambling over a square-rigger, only a dozen are needed on the same ship converted to schooner rig."

"What you say is true, Father, but you don't put out to sea any more. I do. Steam is coming fast—much as I hate to see it." Looking down at the table he continued, "Father's solution is only a temporary one, but economically, probably necessary." Suddenly Bart was conscious of having ignored his quiet and watchful bride, and reached for her hand, but the talk of ships was too great a pull.

"I want to make it clear," he said, leaning forward, an elbow on the table, "that I don't think schooners have had their day yet and I'd lend money to build them tomorrow, but not the day after." He paused. "It's sad because schooners are so versatile. They'll take a course independent of the prevailing wind. They can slip into a harbor and be gone in no time. Not long ago, I took a schooner into Fort Myers, bought beef and salt, and then shot for New Orleans in one of the most profitable runs I've ever made."

"But, Florida is Confederate. That had to be dangerous!" said Anne-Marie, her eyes wide in protest.

"Confederate it might be, but there were enough Unionists wanting United States dollars or gold to make it good. We are going to have more and more perishable cargoes. When there's no wharf available you can beach a schooner on a high tide, unload her, and when the tide is back, off you go. They'll carry four masts—maybe even up to seven. A wide beam compensates for a deep hold," said Bart, turning to give Anne-Marie a knowing wink and at the same time squeezing her hand.

"And in a high sea they wallow like a bathtub," said Caleb.

"Design can change that," replied Bart. "I tell you, we must look today for speed. Design for it. Build for it. Personally, in fifty years I think sailing will be only a rich man's hobby."

A series of arched eyebrows and restraining glances circulated around the table. Bart looked at his bride and, deciding that this was a good note on which to leave, he rose. "Ladies and gentlemen, we will leave the war and shipping world in your good hands for the day. Squire and Madame, thank you

13

for the wonderful day you have given us. It has been a memorable feast. Now, please excuse us. We must be on our way."

Hand in hand the bride and groom departed, flushed and suddenly desperately happy to be free of the group. They took the brougham down the turnpike for only a mile to a white clapboard cottage that had long stood empty. Bart descended, admonishing Anne-Marie to wait. Soon a glow from the windows lit his return.

"Madame, your future home," said Bart, who led her a few steps and then swept her into his arms and carried her over the threshold.

"So this is your secret? I can't believe it! How did you fix up this old cottage?" Disbelief and happiness shone from her eyes.

"By neglecting my ship," he replied, a grin flitting uncontrollably across his lips as he took her in his arms.

"Let me look," she replied, wriggling free and pulling the hood of her cape from her hair.

"Come," he said, leading her into the adjoining room where their bed stood. Suddenly, self-conscious, she turned to face him. He stood tall, slim-hipped and hard-muscled, with his suntanned face above wide shoulders gazing down at her. An irrational panic gripped her. Instinctively her eyes dropped downward. She reached for her hair and pulled loose several pins, shaking free the luxurious russet mane. Then she felt him move toward her and heard him murmur, "Don't be afraid." Then she felt herself clinging to him as if she were falling. With his lips pressed to hers, she felt his hands gently and carefully undoing the buttons down the back of her dress and then she felt him lifting her out of it, placing her on the bed.

He left her for a moment, hastily discarding his clothes, his urgency clearly apparent in the flickering light. Then suddenly he was upon her, devouring her with kisses in a way he had never kissed her before. What was this strange instinctive behavior that so transformed a man? She would have to learn. She looked up, and in the darkness saw his face above her. There seemed a wild, ferocious energy about him, almost alien. She reached up, touching his face with her delicate fingers, to gather him in by touch and at the same time to calm him, to

14

control the fire that was about to scorch her. She felt his knowing hand traveling about her thighs, finding the source, the well, that would quench his need. How foreign were these satisfying gestures. Then suddenly she felt herself swept away, caught in a whirlpool of fury that matched his own.

"It is all right," she cried. "Now you must take me."

"You cannot know how much I love you," he whispered. Their velvet faces touching, he entered her after what had seemed an eternity to him. Easily her body rocked with his until the penetration and utter abandon overcame them. Exhausted, they slept.

She sat up, wide awake and gasping, as a sudden rattle of thunder seemed to shake the whole cottage. "What was that?" A storm had descended upon the house like a beast. Rain swept down in torrents, while lightning cracked open the sky.

"Can it be a nor'wester?" he asked, shaking himself awake. Suddenly, he was on his feet, grappling for his clothes. "I've got to get down to the *Catherine*. That sounds like a hard wind coming up. Your day has distracted me!"

Bart moved too fast to see the look of utter disbelief on her face. She was only beginning to realize that he was actually leaving her alone on their wedding night.

"I'll be back as soon as I can." With that he left the house, stopping only to secure the front shutters.

A second blinding flash of lightning followed with an explosion of thunder so loud she thought the cottage would crumble about her. The rain hammered at every window, whipped by a wind that whistled through the house. For a minute or two she sat terrified, left alone, deserted in a strange, screaming house with one flickering lamp and a dying fire. Spidery shadows danced about the room. The warm and hospitable cottage became a house of horror as macabre shapes came and went with the dancing drafts. Tears of anger welled forth, blurring everything in sight, while outside strange noises cracked over the steady roar of the storm. With difficulty she lit a solitary candle. Then, slowly gathering her wits, she arose and began moving about the room, retrieving her crumpled gown and unpacking her baggage, welcoming any activity to occupy her mind.

So this is what married life will be like, she thought. Meeting storms alone, making *our* decisions, adjusting to little surprises as to where I will live. I must be balmy... The light flickered and died.

Suddenly, an excruciating scream filled the house, paralyzing her with terror. Instinctively, with one great leap she sprang into bed, burying her head under the covers, reliving every childhood fear. Her heart beating wildly, she waited for some terrible onslaught that never came.

"Come murder me if you will," she sobbed. "Oh, Father, Father, where are you? Why did I ever leave home for a brute who has deserted me on my wedding night! I've been left to die..." Eventually, rage subdued her fears and finally she thought again of the sound, the screech that had sent her into paroxysms of terror. Bart's parrot! Of course, she thought, looking around the room. Bart had moved in first! All his things, including the parrot, were here. His clothes hung neatly in the cupboard. His shaving mug and shaving stand stood by the window. His books and charts, now visible only with a burst of lightning, were in the front room. The devil!

"Why didn't he tell me?" she cried. "He put me out here in a house without gaslight... he could have warned me..." In time, a sleep of utter exhaustion overcame her.

With the dawn a sense of someone stirring about the room disturbed her and she awakened with a start. She looked up to see Bart—wet, disheveled and gaunt. Like a flash, the horror of the night returned and she sprang from the bed, now fighting mad.

"How could you leave me?" she screamed. He stepped toward her to quiet her. "Get away from me!" she cried.

"Anne-Marie, there were things I had to do. You don't think I liked leaving?" Again he moved.

"Don't come near me!" She stood still, her face flaming and swollen from the night's tears.

"All I'm doing is taking off my wet clothes. Maybe I can get a fire started," he said meekly.

His calmness provoked a blind fury that propelled her toward

16

him and made her hammer his chest with her fists. He grabbed her hands and held them down tightly. "Damnation, woman, shut up! You're safe. I don't want to slap your hysterical face, but I've had a hard night and I don't like coming home to this."

His rough words stopped her and in despair she threw herself on a pillow and sobbed. Then he began speaking more softly. "What do you take me for? I thought it was for better or for worse. Had it not been for Brian, who had almost everything in hand by the time I got there, we might have lost everything. I knew you were safe in a house that has stood every storm to hit this coast since before you were born. The case is not so of my ship—our ship. I came home aching for the comfort of your arms and I find a screaming shrew—or are you just a spoiled brat?"

Suddenly she was ashamed. Painfully, she closed her eyes and blindly reached for him. "Oh, Bart, I'm sorry, but you don't know how terrified I was. Forgive me . . ."

He took her into his embrace and stroked her tenderly, soothing her like the child she was. "I'm so ashamed. You must think me a dimwit. And surely an ugly one—my face puffed, my hair matted, my eyes red . . ."

"You're a woman, a beautiful, passionate woman, and I, too, am sorry I was so rough on you." With water from a pitcher on the dresser he wet a washcloth and bathed her face. Then she saw the cuts on his hands, the rips and stains on his shirt, the vestiges of a colossal struggle.

Within moments they had returned to their own private world. Her long, uncertain fingers moved about his body as if to memorize it and gently rouse new memories. Knowing the need of his hands, she moved closer to him. Now her soul thrilled with complete knowledge. The earlier fears were gone; she knew the power in her fingers. She felt him quiver and knew herself to be quivering also. For the moment, it was all that she could bear. For racing moments she felt herself destroyed, utterly rent, disheveled, tossed about by uncontrollable forces that she was powerless to combat even if she wanted to.

She awoke to a raucous voice, strangely similar to Bart's, cawing, "That damn bird. That damn bird."

Bart cocked one eye open in silent inquiry.

"We have survived a wedding, a wedding night, and our first quarrel. That's pretty good," she said, shaking him. "You know that kitchen better than I. Come show me where I can make you coffee. I feel you may need it," she said, kissing him and scampering away before he could reach her. . . .

A few minutes later, as she stood gazing at the strange black monster of a stove, she remembered the gypsy and the prophecy. Without doubt, Bart had been in danger, but he had survived. The gypsy had been wrong.

CHAPTER TWO

The next two weeks were spent putting the new household together. The transformation brought by a woman's touch could be seen in every room. Anne-Marie's hope chest was brought in from her parents' house. Sheets, pillowcases, tablecloths and sturdy Irish linen towels so filled the only cupboard that another had to be ordered. Wedding gifts, simple and practical, stood about to be admired by tea-sipping ladies who came to pay their respects. Now curtains fluttered at the windows; rugs softened the waxed and polished floors.

Anne-Marie had been well instructed in the art of home-making—Emily had seen to that. She was not a bad cook, but not as good either as the one on her husband's ship. Bart was careful to make no unflattering comparisons, but instead pride-fully brought Brian home to dinner often. Brian gladly helped with tasks that Bart had taken on such as putting up shelving, installing needed hardware and clearing the small garden. "I'm a carpenter," said Bart. "Brian's a cabinetmaker. There's a world of difference."

Now, as Bart's wife, Anne-Marie felt secure, resenting Brian less. Not to appreciate Brian's help would have been ungrateful. The ground had shifted and Anne-Marie could afford to be cordial. Besides, Brian did serve an important purpose. Bart was not inclined to discuss much of anything to do with his ship with her. But when Brian was present, their conversation often drifted into the world of ships. By listening to what they said, she became aware of what was going on in that part of her husband's life.

"Captain Ledbury just pulled a smooth trick," said Brian.

"What was that?" asked Bart, tightening a screw in the kitchen to hang a shelf.

"He had a carton of fine French gloves—beautiful leather gloves—all for the right hand. 'They're worthless,' said Ledbury to customs. 'Those French have cheated me again. That's the last time I'm dealing with them.' So he refused to pay the duty. When the gloves were auctioned for unpaid duty, he picked up the right hands for a pittance. Meanwhile, the left hands had arrived in Boston, where his agent did exactly the same thing. He ended up with a couple of thousand pairs of beautiful French gloves almost duty free," said Brian, laughing.

"Brian, you can get away with something like that once. I wouldn't be bothered. Once you're caught in some fishy operation you can lose hundreds of hours while they go over your records with a fine-toothed comb for years afterward. It's not worth it. . . . But as you say, it's a good story," replied Bart.

Still, much to Anne-Marie's consternation, this was the way Brian thought. Fortunately, Bart held the reins and insisted on running a clean ship. One day Brian's lack of ethics would cost Bart, she could feel it. It was frightening, but she knew there was nothing to be done. . . .

Within a few days, Bart announced that he was shipping out. "I think you'd better go stay with your family. I don't want to leave you here alone." He was obviously pained.

"I want to stay here. This is my home. I'll be fine," she told him, a forlorn note creeping into her voice despite the best intentions.

"I wouldn't think of leaving you here alone. Anne-Marie, don't make my leaving harder."

She came down involuntarily toward him, fighting for composure, not wanting to poison things for them both. This was only the first of many partings, she knew, and she must learn to let him go bravely. Yet, she thought, there is so much more of him to know. With him gone, the days will be meaningless; the nights will be empty.

"I don't want to leave feeling like a cad, guilty for leaving you."

"I understand, which should make it easier, but perhaps I'm greedy—and childish enough to want everything now. The everything is you," she said simply.

Bart had only a small satchel, a few books and his parrot to carry, since many of his clothes remained aboard the ship. Sad-hearted, Anne-Marie accompanied her husband to Great Egg Harbor to see him off and wish him godspeed. When they arrived at the port the harbor was full. Despite her mood, Anne-Marie could not help but be fascinated by the busy scene: West India traders, brigantines mostly, loading dried fish and staves and discharging sugar and molasses. Colorful, fragrant schooners, speckled with yellow lemons, green bananas or golden oranges, spilled their contents across the wharves. Black deckhands in bright scarves and earrings, with gleaming teeth and lumbering gaits, laughed and chatted unintelligibly. The spicy tang of exotic Eastern merchandise—ginger, pepper, cinnamon, nutmeg—mingled with whiffs of tar, whale oil and strong tobacco. Great hawsers snaked like giant feelers. Pulley blocks and tackle creaked above the shouts of the laborers; gulls circled above while pigeons scurried for pickings below.

Anne-Marie welcomed the distractions and then, abruptly, it was time to give one last kiss to Bart—who was now busy with other concerns—and turn from the harbor.

She would have to face the fact that most of the time, and especially during the loveliest time of the year, the summer, he would be gone. Only in the dead of winter, when traffic over land slowed to a crawl, could she expect to see much of her husband.

She clutched the emerald that hung between her breasts, a constant reminder of Bart and the sea, and returned to the home of her parents. Her status had been changed. In the eyes of the world she was now a woman, a person to be reckoned with, but strangely, she felt like a little girl.

She had no idea how long Bart would be gone; he refused to be pinned down on this point. For one thing, since he had his own ship he was free to shift course whenever weather, economics or any number of exigencies demanded that he do so. On delivering one cargo, he was free to pick up another—not necessarily bound for his home port. Once, he said, he had even sold his ship in a foreign port at a large profit and bought another cheaply before returning.

Above all, he believed that a timetable would only engender worry. "I'll get back as fast as I can, believe me," he had said. Still, it was hard not to worry and harder not to feel lonely back in her parents' home.

It was a large old white frame house, a sort of manor with its own charm, standing high and noble. It was crowded now with family, there being three married daughters in the house on extended visits with their men away, and a string of women's voices ran from room to room.

Anne-Marie wandered about, distractfully mindful of her mother's dominating voice calling, "Kate, come here a minute," "May, your child seems to be crying," "Anne-Marie, did you order a package from New York?" A romping niece or nephew invariably cluttered the stairs, a good vantage point from which to view the life within the house. Now the place was a hotel for women and children—all waiting. Sisters no longer fought over beaux or misappropriated clothing, and chores were genially shared, as the girls were considerate of one another—and yet bored with one another.

The coming and going of Jason marked the days. Doting daughters did their primping for him. Grandchildren vied for his attention. Only he enjoyed the state of affairs, being the sole adult male in the household on whom they all depended upon to settle the weighty—and trivial—questions of the day.

Anne-Marie felt frightfully lonely, wondering at what stages her sisters' marriages had slid from the vibrating, passionate pitch that marked her marriage into the muted, almost mechanical, passivity that seemed to mark theirs. They did not seem to feel as she did. With heavy-lidded eyes she could see Bart, always sailing further away. Waves of loneliness broke over her and only her deliberate attention permitted a few co-

22

herent remarks—so different to what she was thinking. She felt lost in rooms she had known all her life. To survive was to retreat into silence, allowing mindless distractions to seep into her consciousness a drop at a time. . . .

Several others in the family knew she was pregnant before she did. Bart had been gone for six weeks when her mother's laundress remarked to Emily that she had washed no napkins for Anne-Marie. "She's had no period, ma'am, and I've thought she was looking peaked."

"I have too," replied Emily, "and thought it was only loneliness. But this should be her news to break, so don't say a word about it."

Characteristically, Emily had worried about all her daughters' pregnancies more than she had her own. There was so much that could go wrong in bringing a new life into the world. That night she confided her news to her husband.

"The laundress told me," she said, feeling as if she had somehow been spying.

"Well, I suppose that's natural," replied Jason. "Aren't you glad?"

"Yes, of course, but it might be a little soon." A mother's natural concern for her youngest child overshadowed the joy of an unknown entity, a new personality to be discovered.

"She'll be all right," counseled Jason, and within a minute he began to snore.

"Men!" exclaimed Emily—to her pillow.

A few days later Anne-Marie did not appear at breakfast. Emily found her in bed, sick to her stomach. "Mother, I'm sick," she moaned. "I've been retching. Do I have a fever?"

"No dengue for you, dear. My diagnosis will prove as good as Dr. Macy's. You're going to have a baby."

Anne-Marie disappeared under the covers. A loud groan drove Emily from the room. "Poor little heart," she murmured, shaking her head. She descended the stairs, slightly nauseated herself.

During the next few weeks Anne-Marie digested the idea of motherhood better than the three meals presented to her each appalling day. One consoling thought—how pleased Bart

23

would be—carried her through. "That man will kill me," she told herself. "First with loneliness and now with this . . ." Her morning sickness was so severe she was relieved that Bart was not home, which would have required rising, cooking and certainly some housecleaning. In more rational moments she knew that he would be understanding and helpful. He always had been. He would have had only to look at the dark circles under her eyes and to see how drawn she had become to realize her difficulties.

Bart's return came unexpectedly. Instead of coming in on the *Catherine*, his ship, with his crew, he arrived on a small sloop with only one sailor.

Anne-Marie was lying on her bed, dressed, when she heard the downstairs chatter draw to a hush followed by leaping footsteps on the stairs. Suddenly, she was looking at him astonished, her heart leaping. "You certainly are a man of surprises," she cried, choking with happiness. He sat down on the bed beside her, pushing her over and smothering her with kisses.

"I bought a sloop cheaply—practically stole her—and wanted to get her out of Boston before her previous owner woke up," he announced, laughing. "At least, that's what I told the crew. Actually, I wanted to see you—desperately." But there was no mistaking the concern in his eyes when he saw how thin she had grown. "Aren't they feeding you?" he asked, poking at a rib that he could not help but feel as his hands moved to her waist. "Come, let's go back to our home— if only for a day or two." He ached to caress her, to hold her thin little body and to ease the lusting ache that gnawed his loins. Desire for her besotted his senses. In her excitement she noted that the waves of nausea had ceased, and she hurriedly fished for a few articles of clothing. Teetering as on a seesaw, she moved about the room and then down the stairs. Flushed and vibrant, she let herself be led joyously from the house. Breathing the exuberant air, feeling supported by the warmth of his body, she moved as one with him into the waiting brougham. Once on the road she gripped his thigh in order to steady herself as the carriage shook and lurched with every pock and rut. The pressure of her hand proved too much and suddenly Bart pulled off the road. Tense, quivering with passion, he turned to embrace her. His hand ran up her skirts, frantically groping.

"Bart, someone may come along," she whispered, a feeble protest in the face of a rising intention to take her then and there.

"If you had more fat on your bones, I would rape you on the ground. Anne-Marie, I'm on fire. Feel me. Straddle me. I cannot wait. Come to me now," he begged, his words almost lost in panting pleas. Mounting him like a pony she rode him on a journey of ecstasy until, at last, spent and momentarily quenched, he eased her back to the seat.

"I'm sorry I could not wait. I will fill you until you overflow with my love."

"Indeed, you have, Bart, and in a way perhaps you haven't dreamed of—because we're going to have a baby. That's why I'm so thin. I've retched and retched again until I think the baby is all that's left inside of me."

The expression of unmitigated joy that spread across Bart's face made it all seem worthwhile.

Later, back at the cottage, he paced off where he thought a large addition should be built and advised: "Sell the sloop that I bought. You'll be able to get a good price right now. I'll take the train back to Boston. You need something to keep you busy—to take your mind off things. You need to be doing things yourself instead of having everything done for you—as I know is the case at your mother's. I will draw up some plans before I leave and you can get a mason started with the foundation. I'm sure it will be good for you." Bart's energy was infectious.

"I feel better than I have in months," Anne-Marie said, thinking of his power, the intense masculinity, the life that seethed through his veins, a rambunctious lusting stream that spread to every inch of his body. Like a resurging current, it caught her, propelling her along with him at neck-breaking speed. No wonder he's in command of a ship, she thought. He

25

was born to direct. But how does one ship contain him? A ship could, but with difficulty.

Characteristically, he paced the decks. Bart ate fast, walked fast, talked fast and thought fast. His speed and intensity awed his tranquil wife.

During the following months Bart came and went. Both additions took shape—that of the house and the family. Bart had been right. Overseeing the construction of the addition to the house was good for Anne-Marie. She hired and paid the men, drove back and forth to the suppliers for this or that sort of nail or lumber or tool badly needed to speed the progress of the work.

Concordant time passed until finally a tiny girl was born before Christmas, premature by almost a month. Anne-Marie had moved into her parents' house for the event, and considering the difficulties in caring for such an infant, she was relieved that Bart had not been there. Maintaining a necessary warm temperature in the crib took constant surveillance. The birth had not been particularly difficult, but the period that followed was. The midwife had done her work well. The task that fell to Dr. Macy—that of keeping the child alive—was harder.

"A baby slips away quickly," he warned, "but with each day there's a better grip on life. I do what I can, but it is all in the hands of the Lord."

Dr. Macy also had another warning for Anne-Marie. "When Bart returns, keep him out of your bed for a while, dear girl. You need a little building up before another little one comes along." Anne-Marie lowered her eyes, knowing that, indeed, Bart might be a problem.

"When he comes in, perhaps you should talk to him," she suggested.

"I'd be glad to," he replied, packing his satchel and beating such a hasty retreat that Anne-Marie decided that somehow he had not spoken his full mind. Was he concerned with containing Bart or was it the child's health? Newborns had always seemed frail to Anne-Marie, but now and then it seemed to her that her mother had shot a desperate look to her older sisters but

26

not to her. As the gypsy had said, "I fear for your firstborn," so did she.

Bart's first return indeed proved awkward. He did talk with Dr. Macy and the strain of abstinence grew on them both. The child was still too frail to take to the cottage, away from the care of many hands and eyes at the big house and away from the great kitchen oven's warmth that spelled survival. On the whole the baby was silent except for an infrequent thin wail that sounded like a protest at having been born.

"Almost too delicate," said Emily to Bart. "Is she not angelically lovely?" Bart bent over his daughter, giving her one long look, and then moved to wrap an arm around Anne-Marie as if to bolster her.

On that first visit he spent most of his time in the port talking with the men or at the cottage working on the addition. Both activities excluded Anne-Marie; on one hand she felt left out, but on the other, she was too anxious about the baby—now christened Samantha—to be concerned with his problems.

His next return was easier. The baby had gained weight—although slowly—so that Bart could gather his small family together and take them home. The house now had central heat; a large living and dining room had been added and on the second story were two large bedrooms.

Dr. Macy often dropped in, keeping a watchful eye on his tiniest patient. On one particularly cold day he said to Bart, "If I were you, as soon as the weather breaks, I'd take that baby girl and Anne-Marie to Key West, where it is warm year round. It is a Union outpost, you know. A setback now and we'd lose the child. A wet and windy spring is often worse than a hard winter. The sunshine would do them a world of good. Give it some thought..."

The doctor's recommendation took both parents by surprise. To Anne-Marie, Key West seemed like the end of the world, although a few girls from Key West had attended her school. Bart had been there many times carrying machinery, lumber and granite to nearby Fort Jefferson. The doctor's suggestion struck Bart as unusual but not preposterous.

Brian was visiting that day, helping Bart put down carpeting in the baby's room. He was the only one to veto the idea.

"Remember, skipper, you're taking them away from Dr. Macy, who so far has taken good care of them," he remarked. "There's been yellow fever in Key West."

"That's true," replied Bart, "but only in the summertime. There are capable doctors in Key West."

"I wonder if any of my old friends are still there," mused Anne-Marie. "Girls have a way of marrying and going off."

"I remember one harrowing trip," said Bart, "carrying granite in a leaky ship. Had we had a storm, I wouldn't be here now. It can be a rough trip."

"The older a ship is, the more lumber she carries," said Brian knowingly.

"Well, lumber floats," said Anne-Marie. "Can't you deliver a load of lumber, Bart?"

"Oh, we could deliver any number of things—ice from Maine, for example," he replied, at that moment thinking more about the nails he was driving to hold down the edges of the carpet than anything else. "There's a good marine railway at Key West. Browne and Curry built it and it will carry—with steam power—up to five hundred tons.

"Our bottom could do with some work," said Bart, looking at Brian.

Bottom-cleaning was a familiar sight at many ports along the coast. A marine railway pulled the ship out of the water, then the vessel was hove-down alongside a wharf, first one side and then the other. This was done by ropes attached to the top of the masts and run through heavy blocks on the dock. The vessel careened first with one bottom out of the water and then the other. This was hazardous because a little mischance in righting or a sudden squall might endanger those working on her or injure the vessel.

"Then it would be good for you to go to Key West," said Anne-Marie, her eyes alight.

"Now that you mention it—yes," replied Bart, giving her cheek a pinch.

"Such costly work is probably a bit premature, sir," cautioned Brian. "The *Catherine* is in pretty good shape."

Anne-Marie resolved to say nothing more until she and Bart were alone. She sensed that perhaps this would mean the first of many such trips for her and the baby. Perhaps for this reason Brian had objected, feeling that a woman aboard ship meant bad luck. Still, Brian's disapproval was both irritating and provocative. It was not yet an open declaration of war, but two sides were aligning.

That night in bed Anne-Marie plied her advantage. "I'm sorry to disagree with Brian, but he should not make gratuitous remarks about our personal plans. Our child doesn't mean anything to him." She tried to see Bart's face. The bedroom was filled with a soft-colored light from the hall and he lay on his back with his hands locked under his head, his elbows emerging like wings, thinking.

"I'm trying to put everything into perspective. Your dislike of Brian would not make an easy voyage, you know..." said Bart, now looking at her.

"Sometimes I am downright naughty, but I promise you that in the close confines of your ship, you will have no problems with me. Oh, the baby may cry—that I cannot help—but I won't in any way interfere," she said, looking into his questioning eyes.

"Brian is a very valuable employee. He makes money for you. I know the men don't like him—he makes them work—but I run a business. Brian loads a ship exceedingly well. The weight is always perfectly balanced, which gives us speed. I don't care whether people like him or not, he pleases me and he is dependable—and I don't want to lose him. If you knew how much he spares me, you'd be more tolerant."

"I've given you my promise," said Anne-Marie. "If you really feel I won't keep it, we can take a packet—"

"Oh, don't be silly," he interrupted. "I wouldn't think of that—nor would you, had you seen as many of them as I have. I doubt the baby would survive. I'll take you, but you must not interfere with the running of the ship. The *Catherine* is our livelihood and there's a fortune right now to be made in shipping. It's a rough business, but I see no other way of making the money to give you all the things I want you to have."

Their kiss was the beginning of a magnificent night. An inheritance of deeper understanding with a promise of halcyon days and even more glorious nights was left to them. Hopes spun through their heads, sending them flying on flights of anticipation, an ever recurrent miracle of love.

The following day Bart announced that Brian had reversed his position on taking Anne-Marie and the baby to Key West. "Now he thinks it's a good idea," reported Bart, much relieved.

Anne-Marie wondered what had changed the man's mind. Surely it was for no good reason as far as the young Ramsden family was concerned. . . .

CHAPTER THREE

As a bride Anne-Marie had been a pretty young thing; as a young mother she was ravishing. Her bustline filled out; her waistline lost its adolescent bulge, her hips slimmed. There was a new litheness about her figure that was both sensuous and elegant. In the space of one year she had become a woman and a lady. The metamorphosis was that of a pert bud into a full-flowered bird-of-paradise. The alteration would not have disconcerted Bart had he been in a different profession, one that held him in port; he had only to walk the street with her to note the way heads turned. Like any handsome and proud young man, he had desired a beauty, but so much beauty was threatening. Those with nothing are not frightened of thieves. Now with something so obviously precious and desirable, he felt intensely possessive. He thanked his lucky stars that he had so easily acquiesed in the suggestion to take Anne-Marie with him, because he would have regretted another decision. He could do a bit of hauling between the West Indies and New Orleans with Key West as a midpoint, regardless of the repairs. Anne-Marie's presence certainly would make the voyage pleasanter.

His profession preordained a lonely life. As captain, his decisions were law. He stood no watches, came and went when and where he pleased and was accountable to no one. He was to be obeyed by everyone without question; he had the power to make officers, and—if he chose—to break them. Most captains had no companions but their own dignity and the proud consciousness of their supreme power. Bart enjoyed a rarity, a close friendship with both his mates, but both these men knew their places; neither presumed upon his authority.

Anne-Marie considered Brian Delaney, the first mate, the prime minister of the trio that governed the *Catherine*. Bart told him what he wanted done and left to him the care of overseeing the work—and also the responsibility for its being well done. Brian had charge of stowage, safekeeping and delivery of the cargo.

On most vessels the second mate's position was generally regarded as a dog's berth. He was usually not respected as an officer and was obliged to go aloft to reel and furl the topsails and to put his hands in tar and slush along with the rest of the sailors. Bart's second mate, however, was a young Englishman named Tim Clayton, and Bart liked him and did what he could to make his life less difficult. Much was required of Tim as he had to be on deck nearly all of the time. Because of the no-man's-land status of the second mate, Bart had looked for a man with an unusually sharp wit. A quick mind and a barbed tongue soon commanded an unwritten respect. Although Tim slept in the cabin, he took his meals at the second table—in other words, he got what the captain and the first mate left.

Despite his English birth and slight reserve, Tim had an easy manner. This evidenced itself in a lopsided grin that broke down all barriers. A funny remark and the twinkle of his dove-gray eyes often cajoled the men into doing a nasty job well, simply because they liked him.

"Tim Clayton has a soul," Anne-Marie told Bart.

"Everyone has a soul," he replied.

"But some have better souls than others. Some souls shine, like Tim's. Some are pure—others are soiled."

"And, out of curiosity, just what sort of soul do I have?" asked Bart, relaxing with her at the bulwark as they entered the open sea on a southerly course, the goodbyes and tears behind them.

"Oh, Bart, I don't know about your soul. I only know your

body, and that is beautiful. But *there* is an impoverished soul," she said, nodding toward the steward, Roger Bains. She spoke softly but without fear of being overheard as their voices were instantly carried off by the wind.

The steward had charge of the pantry, from which every-one—even the first mate—was excluded. This distinction displeased Brian, who like most chief mates, resented anyone on board who was not under his control. The crew did not consider the steward one of them, so traditionally the steward was very much at the captain's mercy. Bain's weaselly expression contributed to his lack of personal appeal, but Bart felt sorry for the young man. "Bains has a hard time," said Bart, "but he does a good job and he pleases me. He's something of a gnome, isn't he?"

"A little kindness would make him your slave for life—that's the way he is," she replied.

"Don't wish that sort of touching devotion upon me, please. Give me an adoring cook."

Regardless of Bart's wishes, the cook in fact was the patron of the crew. Like the carpenter and the sailmaker, he stood no watch. Because this trio was busy all day, they "slept in" at night unless all hands were called. The cook could easily favor those he liked, not only with bits of extra food, but by drying their wet mittens and stockings near the fire or lighting their pipes in the galley.

These distinctions and the chain of command were important even on short cruises because of the constant danger of wind and sea. Even small negligences could mark death for all.

"On cruises of a year or more, the harmony aboard a ship results in orders being speedily carried out. A disorderly ship can cost unnecessary weeks—and time is also money," said Bart. Indeed, Anne-Marie could see that petty grievances in such a small space were easily magnified and could be disastrous. Constant work was the only antidote and no-talk-at-work the necessary rule. "It seems unnecessarily harsh," Bart continued, "but that is not the case. Customs at sea have evolved over hundreds of years and basically, man hasn't changed. The system works."

Convicts couldn't be watched more closely, thought Anne-

Marie. "I'm amazed," she replied, unwilling to rap any knuckles.

At first, she supposed the intense work aboard the *Catherine* was simply getting the ship in trim and it would soon be over, with little for the men to do but sail the ship. She was mistaken. Many of the small things—spun yarn, marline, seizing stuff— were made onboard. All the rigging was examined and any that was found unfit was hauled down and new rigging rove in its place. Taking off, putting on and mending the chaffing gear alone usually took the constant employment of several men during the entire voyage.

Because Anne-Marie and the baby were now occupying the captain's cabin, Brian—of his own choice—took his meals with Tim. She knew this to be a significant change in the ship's routine, but a necessary one due to the cramped quarters. She made up her mind to keep out of everyone's way. While no one had said anything about the voyage being a test run, Anne-Marie knew that this was so, and was determined to pass with flying colors. Often, Bart seemed tense, and their joint concern over the baby cast an ever-present shadow over their daily routine.

"The baby doesn't cry," said Bart, feeling that to be a good thing. "I didn't know babies could be so good."

"You don't know how I would rejoice over a good lusty bawl," murmured Anne-Marie in desperation. "Her little whimper is pathetic."

"The ship is soothing. Don't you think that could make a difference?" he asked, his brow furled, helplessness on his face. A great compassion for his wife crushed him, squeezing his heart.

"No, I don't. She gains so slowly. I have a lot of milk. If I even think about nursing it flows like a river. Still, she may not live, Bart," said Anne-Marie sadly, taking a little hand in her own. "You don't have a good broodmare for a wife, I fear."

"Don't talk that way—don't torture yourself." He wrapped his arm about her, his compassion now filling the cabin. A blazing pink light from the polished mahogany made the room seem afire. He then took his wife in his arms, doing all he could to comfort her, holding her, caressing her, desperately

34

trying to be strong while she floundered. "I've neglected you," he said. "I haven't appreciated your burden."

"No, dear, not at all. Sometimes—I see now—we're in different worlds."

"You mustn't expect me to talk to you or pay too much attention to you when the crew is around. Please, don't take offense where none is meant."

"I understand. I really do."

Indeed, she knew that no man had more to do with the reputation of a ship than its captain. Daring, enterprise and endurance had to be combined with steadiness, caution and prudence. These characteristics are seldom found in conjunction, and Bart had an excellent record. He never would have sailed a slaver—or a whaler, for that matter; his sensibilities would have been too offended.

It was common knowledge that Bart's family fortune had its origins in blockade running during the Revolutionary War. It had been a risky enterprise, but one that fostered courage. The Civil War was another matter. Bart's sympathies were strongly with the Unionists. He would not—for any price—run guns to the Confederacy. But he would have run guns elsewhere, at another time—legally or illegally—for other governments friendly with the United States—for a price. Anne-Marie understood this because she was something of a pragmatist herself; she would not short her knight in shining armor, even though he was not Sir Galahad.

Because Bart's berth had been built to sleep one person comfortably, she tried to alternate her hours of sleep with his so that each would be assured of a few hours of good sleep each night. Nursing the baby imposed its own "watches"—a timed regularity not unlike those of the crew.

Brian commanded the larboard watch and Tim the starboard with the crew fairly equally divided between the two. Hence, time was divided between the men being on deck or below every four hours. It was a strange sort of time, a series of miniature days in which she looked forward to whatever might happen in a miniature future. Even time is pigeonholed, thought Anne-Marie, looking about the tightly organized cabin. I should be thinking about the real future, but instead I'm only wondering about the next few hours. When the baby will awaken or what I would like to eat or when we will pass another ship. How trivial. . . . I spend my time thinking of things no further away than my nose.

She went up on deck, and such thoughts were immediately dispelled as she reveled in the infinite expanse of ocean and its canopied sky. The world with all its majesty opened before her; here was another reality, the antithesis of the cabin's microscopic view, and she fought for some sort of mental bearing. They were making better than eleven knots, and the sensation of forward movement was one never to be forgotten. The ship seemed driven by some tremendous irresistible force. Water hurled alongside; the wind hummed in the rigging and they seemed as uncontained and free as some Greek god in a chariot flying across the heavens. She stood feeling it, drinking it in as a smothering man would gulp air, insatiably gathering the pulse and momentum of freedom as though her mind and body could contain it.

That night at dinner she looked at her husband with new eyes. "Your world exhilarates me. I can't express it—it's a world of change and especially of motion. When you're on land and the motion stops, don't you have to pinch yourself to find out whether or not you're still alive? The world must seem dead—still."

"When the wind dies down—and it does—you sit and drift and you know *real* stillness," he replied. "Honestly, you feel you're going mad—and sometimes that's the *only* place you're going for days at a time," he continued, drawing a nightmare to rival a dream. "The crew gets nasty. It's like a sickness. And then there's real trouble as the men break down. Then the world is not a very nice place."

"It seems wonderfully nice right now," she said, a smile curving her lips.

"When there's someone around like you, Anne-Marie, it's a beautiful place, otherwise it's just bearable." Gently he caught her hand and pressed a brief light kiss upon her slender fingers.

Three times they were stopped and boarded by Union warships with requests to show their papers. Each time Anne-Marie and Bart hoped they would be met by her sister Kate's husband or a friend, but this was never the case. The time lost—often an hour or more—was chiefly spent in jawboning. They are like old gossips meeting in the street, thought Anne-Marie, listening to the men talk. Who had been seen where and with what was gleaned from each boarding officer and this would later be chewed over by Bart and Brian. "That blockade has to be working," said Bart. "We're never very long out of sight of a Union warship, and if you don't stop, they'll blow you right out of the water."

They rounded Hatteras, infamous graveyard of ships, without a gale. Still, the water here was rougher than it had been. Every man on board had a weather eye out and seemed more at ease when this milestone was behind them.

"I'm going to ask Brian to eat with us tonight," said Bart. "It will give me a chance to pick up a little scuttlebutt on the crew."

Suddenly, Anne-Marie realized that Bart had been feeling cut off by her presence, since mealtime normally afforded the two men time to talk privately.

"Oh, by all means," she replied, her expression clearly conveying this was to be expected.

However, when Bart extended the invitation, Brian declined. "It's all right, sir. Thank you, but I would crowd the cabin," said Brian. His tone was friendly, but he avoided Bart's eyes.

"No, that's an order," said Bart, laughing, but still meaning business.

"Then, of course, I'll be there," said Brian patly.

He was, but despite several openings on Bart's part, he remained relatively uncommunicative.

As always, they were served by the steward, Roger Bains. It was difficult serving them properly in the crowded cabin. Bains had always been adept at handling the hot liquids when only Anne-Marie and Bart were served, but she noticed that when it came to serving Brian, Bains was all thumbs. Clumsily, he almost toppled a glass of wine, causing Brian to glare at him. Bains fairly shriveled. After that, Anne-Marie saw it was all he could do to keep from trembling. Compassionately, she smiled at Bains, but he was obviously terrified of Brian. Bains was hardly out of earshot when Brian started in on him. "I don't know why you put up with that wharf rat," said Brian. "He's the worst steward I've ever seen in my life."

Anne-Marie was about to come to Bains's defense when she remembered her promise to keep out of things. She held her tongue. Bart laughed it off, but Brian was not to be stopped. "He's also a lying weasel." Aware that Bart did not agree and that the situation was awkward, Anne-Marie finished her meal with dispatch and excused herself for a little air.

The deck was quiet, but to her surprise Brian was on her heels within a few moments. He might have been dismissed by Bart or he could have been playing a little game, snubbing him; she did not know which. Feeling a certain coldness in the knowledge that such intrigues between men were dangerous, she started back toward the cabin. Passing Brian, she looked steadily at him as if to say, *I see right through you, Brian Delaney*, but his eyes in smug indifference avoided hers.

Within a few minutes Bains returned to finish tidying the cabin for the evening. Without Brian present, the steward was composed, his usual timid, attentive self. With obvious dexterity he handled the dishes and tray. Roger Bains was not naturally awkward, in fact quite the opposite. Without doubt, the animosity between Bains and Brian was serious, but she did not mention her impressions to Bart. The *Catherine* was his ship to run. The ill will between the two men was probably not unusual. Eventually, she told herself, one of them would leave. Saying little beyond good night, Bart smothered the irritations of the day while she did her best to allay hers.

The following evening Bart invited Tim, his second mate, to dine with them. Anne-Marie liked Tim as instinctively as she disliked Brian. He was amusing and his accent made him seem to be a well-bred young man. When Bart questioned him about various members of the crew, his remarks were always surprising. "He owns and operates a ferocious temper, sir, but he's a good man," or "That man's silence is wonderful to listen to." He turned to Anne-Marie and said, "Sometimes you can tell by watching a man what kind of a past he's going to have."

He described a previous ship Bart knew of as "a packet of miseries," but he could still laugh about it.

Tim had sailed on British and French ships and could discuss their designs—the advantages and disadvantages—intelligently, and his observations and opinions earned as a sailor were obviously reliable and of great importance to Bart. "I'm interested in speed and reduced crews," he said. "That's where the money is, and, frankly, that's what I'm working for. I don't love the sea. It's a hard master—and those of us who survive are just damn lucky. You know as well as I do that in time your luck runs out."

Inwardly, Anne-Marie shuddered and desolation crossed her face. Noting her expression, Bart reached for her hand. She removed it, feeling suddenly irritated with him for regarding her as a child who must be reassured. Usually she let this pass, but now in the presence of a guest, she found it irksome.

She was now aware of a gnawing uneasiness regarding their relationship—a slight discomfort that came and went like an annoying mosquito that fails to bite, yet does not fly away. It was not due to their shipboard proximity, because there actually was little of that. It seemed to her, in fact, that he had been avoiding her, spending time in parts of the ship where she did not go.

The following day she remarked about it. "I've hardly seen you today," she said, with a toss of her head and a tone that carried cool detachment, now allowing the baby her full attention.

"Every moment that we are alone in here, do you know what the men think we're doing? Just what *they'd* like to be doing," replied Bart wryly. "I see no point in titillating them." He paused. "At the same time, I'm the captain of this ship," he said, taking her into his arms and bearing down upon her lips.

Later that night Anne-Marie went on deck and stood admiring the beauty before her. As a novice at sailing, she could consider the ship as a separate entity. There rising from the water, supported only by the now gray hull, pyramids of canvas towered toward the clouds. The seas were not heavy and the wind was steadily breathing from astern. A thousand stars studded the dark sky, leaving space for an unjubilant moon. The sails were spread high and wide, stretching far beyond the deck. The topmast studding sails reached skyward like kites, winging to the topsails. Above, the little skysails seemed to touch the stars. There was no sound except the rippling and gushing of water. Anne-Marie stood gazing upward at the sails, motionless as if they had been cut from marble. So perfectly were they distended that there was not a ripple or a flap; not even a quivering stirred the white canvas. Suddenly she saw Tim, who was half hidden in shadow.

"How quietly they do their work," he said softly as he moved back into the shadows.

Indeed, what a marvel was this intricate harness of power and how well had these sails both freed and enslaved man. Anne-Marie stood motionless, staring into the darkness. She could see in her mind's eye the hidden waves breaking on a long, gloomy, war-torn Georgia shore, breaking under the rhythm of fate that came with Sherman's army and his measured blasts of heavy artillery. For the first time she felt an overwhelming tenderness toward the doomed Confederacy. The United States, an endless land, must be preserved. This night the coastline seemed to stretch to eternity, beat upon by waves sullenly and relentlessly pounding from all directions, while the land quaked and shuddered under a fury of guns. A pink light of distant fires, fueled by burning homes, ribboned the horizon.

She wrapped her cloak about her, tightly holding in the night, and moved toward the cabin. In that moment, the watch changed and Brian Delaney, intent and wide-eyed, marched toward her. So cold and calculating was his manner that for a moment she felt frightened. Then, quietly again, Tim stepped from the shadows between them. Instantly, Brian's manner changed and, smiling, he greeted them both.

Could she have been in danger? The thought was preposterous. Her mood and imagination had combined in a ridiculous conjecture. Ashamed of such an evil judgment, she entered the cabin.

40

CHAPTER FOUR

The following night Bart again invited Brian to dine with them. This time he readily accepted, causing Anne-Marie to wonder whether or not he feared Tim would be asked in his stead. It was the Sabbath and to increase the value of the day as many men as possible were relieved of their work. On some ships it was a day that included religious instruction and exercises, but Bart, having a good control of his crew, never needed threats of hellfire and brimstone to bring his men to heel. "Probably the Father, Son and Holy Ghost will make me pay for this one day," he told Anne-Marie, "but for one thing, I don't feel competent to take on the instruction or conversion of anyone. If I can gladden their hearts with a bit of pudding, that's it."

Brian was more communicative, now willing to discuss work that should be done and the general atmosphere among the men. Wisely he ignored Bains.

"Keep the lazy ones and troublemakers apart from one another," admonished Bart, his eyebrows bristling and his fist coming down emphatically upon the table. "It takes two to breed. Now and then we can't help getting a rotten apple, but if they are not with their own kind, they can't do much damage."

"As you say, sir. It being Sunday, the men aren't busy so I can observe them," said Brian. curling his mouth into a wan smile.

"You can learn a lot about their colors while they loll around. Put the punks on different watches and on different parts of the ship and we'll have an easier run," added Bart in a much calmer tone.

"Right away, sir," said Brian.

"What do you mean 'Right away, sir'?" asked Bart. "I said observe them today. That's not right away! I don't think you were listening to me." Bart was obviously irritated. "I expect rain tomorrow. It won't do to work on the rigging, but the men can pick oakum, pound the anchors and scrape the chain cables until the weather clears."

"I'll handle it," said Brian, ignoring his mistake.

Anne-Marie wondered if Bart had seen Brian's eyes turn steel-cold at her husband's rebuke. That Brian would handle it—and in a bullish way—she had no doubt. Then, in his own tidy way Bart dismissed Brian with an order to check the watch.

With Brian gone, their mood lightened. "I think he sometimes tests me," said Bart, "but I nip it in the bud. I know how I want this ship run—and you'd be amazed at how fast troubles can arise. I've seen decks washed down and scrubbed with seawater when fresh water would have frozen, when we had on our pea jackets and our hands were numb. Those are times when, cruel as it seems, men really need work. It makes the time pass faster."

Almost roughly he reached for her hand, giving it a firm squeeze and releasing it with a wave of understanding and trust. It was one of those candid moments when Anne-Marie felt suspended, observing Bart as a stranger, unhitched from the touch of his hand. He spoke as if he were totally sure of himself, and yet she could see an inner need for self-vindication—or perhaps justification—for his harshness. It was something tight and unfree, that something inside him. She seemed so separate; not estranged, but different—apart. As different as Brian and Bart.

Then Anne-Marie clearly saw a basic difference between the two men—in the way they used their power. Bart had both principles and scope, Brian did not. She wondered if her husband completely understood it. He felt that discipline was necessary to avoid trouble, a necessary evil. Flogging or any form of punishment should be a last resort. Every man deserves respect, even when he deserves—and gets—correction. Brian, on the other hand, used fear as his tool, and thus had to recreate it with frequent violent reminders, no matter how humiliating. So he was less prone to avoid trouble and instead handled it harshly when it occurred. Anne-Marie realized that Bart was not a cruel man, but Brian was. "Brian was out of sorts tonight," is all she finally said.

"It takes many different sorts to run a ship," Bart said gruffly. Understanding him, she did not argue. Brian's way was a backup when his own way failed, a necessary backup that Bart only sometimes acknowledged even to himself. Brian's arrogant swagger around the crew, his avoidance of eye-to-eye contact with peers and his smirking smile were all part of a language, a foreign language, that she alone seemed to recognize and understand. On ship, small irritating mannerisms were magnified. But Anne-Marie could only conclude that Brian suffered from inherent meanness. He is really a moral pirate, she thought. I would put nothing past him. He cares as little for me as I do for him. They did not, however, share the sort of mutual dislike that sometimes ripens into a passion. This was a basic aversion, forever unbridgeable; Brian jealous of Bart's love for her; she despising him for using Bart for his own selfish purposes.

Three days of rain followed. Because they were in waters off Florida, they did not suffer from the kind of penetrating cold that numbed men's hands and draped long slivers of ice from the lines as Bart had often described. Still, the gales that came and went made giant waves that came washing down the decks, tossing the *Catherine* like a bobbling cork. The brilliantly colored tropical birds, which Anne-Marie had heard described and had looked forward to seeing, were conspicuously absent—having sought shelter inland.

To avoid the perilous reefs they sailed far off shore, and were pounded by the powerful north-flowing Gulf Stream, at odds with the buffeting northeasters which pushed them south. They could only wait it out, caught in this vise, with hard maneuvers to avoid being swamped. Nor could they come too close to the reefs, lest they fall into the hands of the notorious Florida wreckers, the worst of the whole South Atlantic lot. On the upper keys, these plunderers were not satisfied with the salvage proceeds from ships already foundered, but went themselves into the business of wrecking, employing any number of tricks. On stormy nights they laboriously drove cows up and down the beaches with lanterns dangling from long poles strapped across the animals' heads. These lights appeared to be bobbling channel markers confusing the helmsmen into disastrous courses—straight onto the reefs. It was, then, legal piracy to claim salvage from a wrecked ship.

Late in the afternoon the squalls seemed to have subsided. The sun shone magnificently. Thinking that Bart would rest better if he were left alone—quiet as Samantha was and as she tried to be, the quarters were claustrophobic for three—she decided to take the baby out for a bit of fresh air. Wrapping her cloak about them both, she went up on deck.

Beside the vessel, vast numbers of gliding dolphins accompanied them, leaping and falling in tandem, a symphony of motion. Occasionally they deviated in pursuit of flying fish or bonita. When approached by the dolphins, the flying fish spread their broad finlike wings and sailed through the air, but often too late, the dolphins having also leaped, catching their prey as they hit the water. A nearby sailor, also watching, offered, "They bring good wind, ma'am. We'll have fair weather." Together they admired the school. The dark upper fins, reaching from forehead to tail, cut the water like so many sequined blue fans. Anne-Marie turned to tell the sailor that another school was approaching and found him gone, but she was not alone. Brian was now at the wheel and she threw her attention back to the fish.

The wind was fair—manageable but brisk; the ship was riding well, rising and falling with the swells. To enjoy the air she sat down, drawing the baby close to her, enfolding her warmly in the folds of the cape. Suddenly, a gusting wind came up harder, nearly sweeping them from the hatch. Bart would scold her for staying on deck under those conditions. It was frightening, but in a thrilling way, so she lingered. Besides, for the moment there was nothing to do but sit tight and wait for the roughness to subside. She saw that Brian was watching her. He must know she was uncomfortable. Only one other man was then on deck; Brian remained at the wheel. No *real* emergency existed to make him leave his post, she told herself; it was only a momentary aberration in the weather, she supposed. Fault, if any, she conceded was her own. Still, she hated Brian, hated him with all the force she could spare from the strength needed to hang on to her perch. Her distress was written across her face, she knew, but his face wore only an expressionless stare. He could lash the wheel and help me, she thought, but he will not. I can wait and manage by myself.

After a few minutes the wind seemed to be steadily worsening. She decided to take the next slight lessening and make for the leeward side of the ship to work her way to the cabin below. Brian stood motionless, cast in steel, glistening in the new mist like the blade of a knife, his eyes two fiery slits. Hatred met hatred. With a lull she rose. Suddenly the cook's firewood came loose, rolling about the deck, and in the same moment—outside her range of vision—a giant wave came up from the sea, rising from the depths, a sudden tower of water forming a great blue wall roaring toward her. Unaware, she moved toward the lines, then turned. Terrified, she opened her mouth to scream, but no sound came, nor could she move, the baby clutched in her hands. Steadily in a sweeping course the wave approached, growing taller with every second. Then like an enormous Herculean arm it hit, thrusting them toward the bulwark, then lifting them and tossing them both over the bulwark into the sea, but apart, the baby torn from her arms. Down into the depths she plunged and then was lifted again, now free of the ship. The monstrous wave bore on and on, taking her with it until it threw her and dropped her. To her amazed consciousness, her feet touched bottom. Still, she was far from shore and the disappearing ship. Choking, gasping for breath, salt water streaming from her throat and nose, she staggered over the white sandy bottom frantically and futilely searching for the child she would never see again. How, she

45

did not know, but she made her way to the beach. The *Catherine* had sped on, now out of sight. Reaching dry land she collapsed in shock.

Anne-Marie came to full consciousness in the arms of a man weary from lovemaking, a man she had never seen before.

"Who is Bart?" he asked. "Who is the man you make love to so passionately?"

"My husband," she replied. "Where is he?" A look of instant remembrance and utter panic crossed her face. "What am I doing here?" she cried, sitting up, looking at the man.

"I picked you up on the beach several days ago. Since then you have shared my bed, calling me 'Bart.' You have been frightened out of your mind by the sea. I was afraid you would never be sane again. I had hoped that by my lovemaking you would be comforted and come to your senses—as you have."

She understood him fully. His voice was kind and reassuring. He was an older man, perhaps in his mid-forties, yet still trim and handsome. His hair was gray around the temples, his skin bronze, his hooded eyes like those of a tiger with tiny flashes of yellow in flickering brown pools.

"And the *Catherine*?" she queried.

For a moment he was silent. There was only one reasonable and conceivable answer: the reefs. "She was lost at sea," he said pensively. Then he knew that he wanted her to remain with him and that he had gambled unwittingly that with all else lost, she would stay.

Anne-Marie visibly withered and closed her eyes. She turned away from him as if she could that way escape his gaze. She felt as if her heart had physically cracked open, so great was the pain in her chest. Grief swamped her. Great waves of sorrow came and receded, but in a moment of remembrance, they rose to crush her again.

"If only I had died too," she cried, looking straight at the man, but not seeing him. She looked through him and beyond him, feeling only intense loneliness and isolation like a great fog closing down upon her, and slept.

He gazed down at her and the huge glowing emerald on a chain about her young throat. The stone had slipped back from its resting place between the curves of her breasts, finding an indentation at the base of her throat.

"Sleep, pretty one," he said softly. "Only time can help you."

When she woke again she was in a room filled with sunlight—sunlight brighter than she had ever seen. She lay in a great carved bed encased in yards of white toile. Through the sheer fabric she could see dimly on the walls great oil paintings framed in heavy gold. Across from the bed stood a large carved desk with many small drawers, each dotted by ivory pulls. Steadily she focused her eyes, making out the intricate intarsia inlays in the pattern of carnations. At first they seemed to move, but then she realized it was only the fabric shifting with the breeze. The floors were patterned with Spanish tiles that also slowly wavered. Arched doors opened onto balconies. The linens on her bed were the loveliest she had ever seen, as ornately embroidered with carnations as a queen's banquet cloths. Only a wealthy man could own such a house; it reminded her of a castle.

Within a few minutes a rotund, dark-haired woman entered with a tray, which she placed on a table by the bed. Then without speaking the woman pulled up a chair, threw back the curtains dressing the bed and sat down, preparing to feed Anne-Marie as if she had done it many times before. As in a ritual, she unfolded a napkin and placed it about Anne-Marie's throat, picked up a large spoon and, lifting Anne-Marie's head, placed a spoonful of rich broth to her lips. When Anne-Marie, with eyes open, took it, the woman smiled and in an endearing tone spoke in some strange language. Her entire manner was one of gentleness and sincere concern, as if Anne-Marie were a particularly favored patient and she were a born nurse. When her ministrations were finished and the pillows tidied up, the woman took the tray and left the room, humming what might have been a prayer.

I should have thanked her, thought Anne-Marie, but I don't think she would have understood, and I might have frightened her. She has probably been taking care of me for a long time now. I smell sweet—and even my hair is clean. Everything

47

she did, she did as if she had done it many times. . . . I'm simply not up to talking. . . . I don't even dare think. . . . Somehow I must learn to erase every memory—to wipe out everything that has ever happened to me. If I don't, I will feel only my broken heart. It seems I was not meant to die . . . not yet.

She turned, closing out the light, and drifted off again.

She was awakened by her host's gaze.

"Who are you?" she asked.

"I am Don Miguel, the man who picked you up on the beach, limp flotsam and jetsam. I threw you over my horse and carried you to my home. Welcome. I've been happy to share my bed and board with such a beauty." He had pulled back the toile that tented the bed; a sea of whiteness engulfed him. Only his dark eyes and dark moustache remained steady and fixed as the whiteness wavered—white that was whiter than white—blinding her with its chalky brightness, rippling and swelling before her.

Finally, the milky cloud stilled and she could ask, "Just where am I?"

"Nowhere—and everywhere. At the end of the earth," he replied.

"You speak in riddles. I mean . . . are we in Key West?"

"Miles from it. Miles from anything. You are on an island that belongs to me. Cayo de las Matas—the Key of the Plants. One last little Spanish outpost, but you will find that you are not among barbarians. As soon as you are strong enough, I will show you this place. Come. Try to get up," he said, pulling back the gauze and lessening the whiteness so that flecks of red and green might fuse their primary glow into pictures and patterns. "I'll help you. If you lie in bed, your muscles will turn to jelly." Two firm velvety hands—too soft for a man's, she thought—grasped hers, pulling her forward.

Shakily, she managed to stand. Her body ached as if she had been hammered. By not moving for a moment, the pain subsided. Then she was conscious of wearing only a nightdress, and she modestly slipped back onto the bed. "Have you a robe?" she asked, aware that her legs were weak and trembling.

"Of course," he replied. "How clumsy of me." For a moment

he left her to produce a golden Chinese brocade. It was a man's robe, but it served. With his arm around her body they walked slowly toward the open louvered doors that led to the balcony. Her eyes needed a moment to adjust to the shimmering sunshine that engulfed everything. Sparkling hot, bright flames made little spears of light that danced from every surface.

From the balcony she could look down to what appeared to be a compound. Across the carefully tended garden lined with orange and lime trees were clusters of small, white wooden houses, all with many porches; shutters and unfamiliar flowers added brilliant spots of every color—purples, reds, yellows, blues, some speckled or striped.

Above, a clear blue sky was dappled with clouds like great cotton bolls, capriciously tossed aloft. A brilliant sun showed a world she had never seen. It was blinding in intensity, an immovable sea of light. Closing her eyes, she turned her head down; then, opening them, she saw the stone terrace below, shimmering as though paved with diamonds. Slowly refocusing, she saw a large and battered basket. She knew it at once. For a moment she thought she would faint. "Where did you get that?" she cried, pointing to the basket that had been her baby's bed, pain rushing back to choke her.

His arms steadied her as her knees failed, bones dissolving.

"It was picked up on the beach," he replied. Then he added, "Miles from here. Is it yours?"

Her stricken look gave him the answer. In an instant he knew. In her ravings she had mentioned a baby. Aboard the ship, this basket had been a baby's crib.

"I'm terribly sorry," he mumbled, feeling her pain sweep through him. "I had no idea. How could I?" He spoke as if it had all been his fault. Her eyes seemed to be blaming him, but then she withdrew them mercifully.

There it was. The proof. The *Catherine* had wrecked. The baby's basket had been in the cabin. How else could it have turned up on the beach? Now it held only a few oranges. She felt sick, desperately sick.

The exquisite red-haired lady struck Don Miguel as the

loveliest creature that he could have imagined. And, by some great stroke of fortune—some fortuitous wreck—she alone had reached his island home. Heaven only knew where the ship had gone down. . . .

CHAPTER FIVE

Bart awakened after a longer and deeper sleep than he had intended. The cabin seemed too still. None of the familiar noises—or rather the unfamiliar noises—had penetrated his sleep. Anne-Marie's moving about the cabin had not disturbed him, not even her turning the pages of some book. Samantha in her basket had not whimpered. The ever-present rocking and rolling of the ship—as constant as breathing—could be discounted. He knew instinctively that he had been alone for a long time, much longer than usual. The cabin seemed overwhelmingly empty. Seldom had he been so unaware of the passage of time. Usually he could tell himself: I'm going to sleep for ten minutes, and ten minutes later he would awake, refreshed and ready for the next activity. His sense of time was honed to the minute. "God, I must have been awfully tired," he said, shaking himself as if to loosen his joints and banish any lingering numbness.

Slipping into a jacket and mechanically buttoning it, he stepped into the dusk. Brian was motionless at the helm; otherwise the deck was deserted.

"Where's Anne-Marie?" he asked.

"Why, she's below, sir," replied Brian, his face impassive, intent upon his course, his body stiff and tight.

"She's no such thing!" said Bart, irritation coloring every movement. She never roved about the ship, and if she had, he would have forbidden it, nor would she ever have joined the men for company. The galley, perhaps, for a little warm something, but Brian would have noticed this. Whatever it was, Bart did not like it. A scowl marred his face, deepening lines and setting his jaw in a mounting anger.

"I've been here, sir, at the helm for an hour or more, relieved only for a couple of minutes. I don't trust these waters," said Brian with measured breaths. Bart's expression left no doubt that he was more than displeased and worried.

Like a storm he moved about the ship, overturning everything loose in his path, from forecastle to steerage, at first with a contained rage, later with the vengeance of a hurricane. His eyes flashed, illuminating his face like streaks of lightning, flashing their uncontained fire, searing every man aboard with their heat. The men jumped to join the search, scurrying about like frightened ants, getting into one another's way, stumbling and tripping, not knowing which way to go. None had seen her. There was nothing unexamined but the formless irregular tossing sea with caps of spewed foam—and nothing to hear but the constant murderous voice of the sinister great waters surging around them. Within it, the vast, teeming river of the sea—the Gulf Stream—churned on and on. In the distance a tiny ribbon of land appeared and disappeared as the *Catherine* took the swells and wells, plowing on, oblivious to the cares of men shuddering within her.

Anne-Marie and the baby had vanished. The second, third and fourth detailed searches revealed no trace. They must be overboard. When or where or how it happened was a mystery. In some unguarded moment as heads were turned dealing with the exigencies of the time, possibly when the cook's logs came loose, she had been swept away, the baby with her. Although there was no reason to turn back and circle, they did—seeing nothing but the close-mouthed sea. The two could not have survived its grip for long—and it had been long. "Lost at sea." Following his capitulation, Bart's expression of grief was to go down to the cabin and destroy all reminders of their presence. Into the sea he threw the baby's basket filled with tiny clothes, its blankets—everything used for her need, comfort or pleasure. Anne-Marie's belongings followed. Like a passel of rags—silks, satins, aprons, petticoats, underwear, nightshirts, every scrap of ribbon that she and the baby owned went ballooning off into the twilight's deep waters like giant lotuses.

Before the men, Bart was stoic while some openly wept. Their captain and his lovely wife had represented the best of everything. The fairy story before their eyes had become a tale of horror. None would ever forget it. The event was a flogging that left the hearts of the crew bleeding instead of their backs, which all would have willingly accepted if it would only have spared their captain. "Sometimes it is easier to take a loss one's self than to see it in others," said an old sailor, his head bowed.

Bart moved as a sleepwalker. How and why had it happened? If only . . . if only . . . things might have happened differently. Recriminations against himself, smothering in their intensity, haunted him. There had been no call of "All hands, ahoy. Man overboard!" Those words sent a chill through everyone. Every man would have sprung into action—lowering the quarterboat, coming about, scanning the sea. But here, no warning or action, until it was too late. . . .

While the cargo was unloaded at Fort Jefferson, Brian took complete charge. Bart suffered alone in his cabin, curled like a snail in his shell, quietly and desperately mad, all believed.

On arriving in Key West, many men left the ship. With eyes lowered they gave the captain one excuse after another with their goodbyes. Bart hardly heard their reasons. He knew. The luck of the ship had changed. No one wanted to be associated with a ship that had hit bottom. Sailors were a superstitious lot. "Troubles come in threes." They would escape the remaining two. Tim was among them, but not for their reasons. His was a compound of grief and fear that the captain might remain in his lethargy, leaving Brian in command. If so, the remaining two troubles would certainly occur, Tim was sure.

On foot, Bart made his way past the harbor area on the south and Gulf end of the island, leaving the townspeople gathered at the waterfront watching the sunset, a magnificent blaze of color. He knew that the accident aboard his ship was a topic of their careless gossip, hashed over in both Spanish and English. He passed the cheap rooming houses where the sailors bunked, the hoydenish bars and grog houses to reach a more sedate residential area and a house which he knew on the corner of Whitehead and Greene Street. He wanted to hide, to wrap himself in a cocoon so that no one could see him. Nor could he see people and their surroundings now as he walked. Small native dwellings and large two-storied balconied houses squared off by white picket fences hardly came into his focus. Houses were close together. Many roofs had cupolas or widow's walks used as lookout posts, some specifically to sight wrecks on the reefs and—as a matter of business—to be first on the scene to claim salvage. This he knew, but now it did not matter. Wretchedness hung about him like a heavy coat as he trudged along, an occasional chicken scurrying from his path. One or two dogs mildly protested his approach while sleeping cats monopolized the wooden rockers dotting the porches. From even these he would escape.

Numbly he approached a large wooden house—for Key West a mansion. Five steps put him on a wide porch containing a familiar slatted wooden swing accompanied by the usual wicker chairs and tables. A massive door beckoned; green shutters sealed out the dusk. Bart lifted the shining brass knocker and dropped it with a succession of bangs. Within minutes a small black maid appeared and recognized him; she immediately admitted him and went to fetch her mistress.

Before long a beautiful dark-haired woman gowned in rustling silk appeared. Her joyous expression faded as she saw the desolation in his eyes, the droop of his shoulders, the tightly drawn mouth. Still, he stood tall and took her into his arms. This was not a lover's embrace, but a coming together of old friends who would always be a source of solace and comfort to each other.

"What happened? You're so haggard. What in the world? ...I've never seen you like this." Anxiously she spoke, freeing herself from his arms to better see his face. Worry clouded her hazel eyes as she bit her lip and waited. It seemed to Bart an age before he could form the words and speak without weeping, so great was the tightness in his throat. Haltingly he told her briefly about his marriage, the baby and the catastrophe at sea.

"Oh, my God. Dear God," was all that she could say.

"I have said it myself, Consuelo—'My God, my God, why hast thou forsaken me?'—but there you have it. I want to hide."

"My house is your house. I know there are no words of comfort that can make one iota of difference, but my heart aches for you," she said, pain swelling in her throat. . . .

Consuelo Lamar had been born in Key West, a native of "The Rock." Five years ago she had been widowed; for almost that time she had known Bart, who casually and unexpectedly breezed in and out of her life. On his last few trips, instead of staying at the Russell House, Key West's finest hotel, he had been a guest at her home. Her husband, an older man, had been lost at sea, leaving her well provided for—as they said, "He was a warm man," meaning "well off"—and they had no children. Although Bart was ten years younger than she, he thought her a wonderfully attractive woman. Dark wavy hair rippled carelessly about her face. Her figure was pleasing to men and to fashion—curved, warm, soft and beckoning. He would not have chosen her to be a wife and mother of his children, first because of their age difference, but also—later— because of his love for Anne-Marie. Still, Consuelo would always have a secure position in Bart's life as a friend.

Bart was not the sort who had a woman in every port, but Consuelo was a woman in this port and in a singular kind of way he loved her. Naturally, he had never mentioned her to Anne-Marie; young Anne-Marie would not have understood, but Consuelo was the sort who did understand. She knew her place in his life—proper and discreet in the eyes of Key Westers—and she never crossed that place. His hesitancy in bringing Anne-Marie to Key West was not because of his affection for Consuelo; Bart had no conflict in his loves. There was a place for everyone. He could come to Consuelo wracked with grief and she would know exactly how to behave. She would not come tumbling into his bed believing sex to be consolation. Nor would she expect attentions. She would offer him closeness, advice, support and understanding, asking for nothing but acceptance.

That night they dined in the patio within her walled garden. A profusion of roses perfumed the night, and the twisted trunk, clusters of red blossoms and dark green leaves of a Geiger tree joined lacy tamarinds to shield them from the view of neighbors. They talked without interruption long after the candles guttered out.

"This is my first taste of death," said Bart. "As a child I remember waking in the night, fearing that something would happen to my parents, but I think all children experience this. Then I also worried about losing Anne-Marie before the baby was born and after—so many women seem to go with childbirth. But she surprised me and had the baby while I was away. By the time I got back it was all over and she was fine."

"Bart, is there any chance . . . any chance whatsoever that Anne-Marie might have survived? I doubt that the child could have, but could your wife swim? Could she have touched bottom?" Consuelo asked.

"She could swim a little, but now you are talking about a miracle. The sea was heavy . . . heavy enough to carry them overboard. I see no way . . ."

"Was she depressed?" continued Consuelo. "Sometimes young mothers have strange depressions."

"Not at all," he replied. "I'm convinced that it was an accident."

"And no one saw?"

"No one."

"You're still a young man, and you charted your course never stopping to think that you might have been living in uncharted waters. My dear, my heart bleeds for you."

"And my heart simply bleeds," he replied. "Forgive me if I talk about her all the time . . ."

"If that will help, please do," she urged, speaking from her heart and, indeed, she would have done anything in the world if it could have brought the girl back.

At the same time that Consuelo and Bart were dining that evening, Tim, the former second mate, rushed up to Brian, who was strolling about Jackson Square, walking off a particularly good fish dinner. "I'm so glad I found you, sir," said

56

Tim. "I've been looking for either you or the captain. I'm putting out early on the *Sea Witch* and I wanted to give you an odd piece of gossip I picked up."

"That's kind of you," replied Brian. "Pray, what have you heard?" Tim's words fell pell-mell from his mouth. "A darky down at the wharf said a young woman was picked up on the beach near Indian Key—alive—by a wrecker a few days ago. I just happened to overhear him. I broke into the conversation and pressed for details—what she looked like and so forth, but he didn't know as he hadn't seen her himself, he had just heard about it. When he could give me no more information, I hurried to find the captain or someone with the *Catherine* because it might have been the captain's wife. It is something to go on...a clue that might lead to a wild goose chase, but then it might not. The captain could run it down in any event."

"That's very kind of you, sir," replied Brian, doing his utmost to remain calm. "I've heard of stranger things. I'll certainly inform the captain. Have a good voyage," he said, turning toward the harbor and carefully escorting Tim toward his ship.

Tim was a man Brian had been glad to get rid of as he, being Brian, was certain Tim had an eye on his berth, and the captain liked Tim a little too much for Brian's comfort. His piece of information, however, was disturbing. He hoped that he had been cordial enough to disguise that fact. It was a piece of luck that Tim had found him and not the captain and a second piece of luck that he was about to shove off. His bit of news was going to die right then and there....

Bart remained at Consuelo's home for a number of days, but he returned daily to the ship, where Brian had things in hand. Of all those in the exodus Bart missed Tim the most as a highly competent sailor, officer and friend. Anne-Marie had liked Tim and Tim would have taken her loss hard, Bart thought.

Brian had picked up a good cargo for the *Catherine* from a ship that had limped in and would have to undergo a lengthy repair job before shipping out again. Sponges, cigars and pineapples would be added and the *Catherine* would sail for New Orleans—a short run, but one that suited Bart well. Home base had little appeal; he couldn't bring himself to think about it. The new crew was a motley bunch, but Bart found himself for the first time in his life not caring. The goddamn ship could sink.

Brian handled everything except Bart's inner rage. Grief was something he found himself unequipped to handle; everything had become inexorably shattered.

Bart cared little about his appearance or his dress—an oddity in Key West. One of the surprising things about Key West, an out-of-the-way, isolated small town, was the scrupulous elegance of the dress of its men and women of affairs. In summer the men all wore white linen duck of the finest quality and perfectly laundered. During the winter—and always on Sundays no matter how warm—the men wore frock coats and silk hats. The women were also stylishly attired, wearing hats and gloves every time they left their houses.

"Before you leave on your next voyage we must see that you get some comfortable attire for Key West," said Consuelo. "I think you will be spending more and more time here and you might as well be dressed properly to fit your station."

"I've been careless and I'm sure I've embarrassed you," said Bart.

"Of course not. I simply want you to feel better. White and Ferguson will have some ducks that can be tailored to fit and they would be ready for you when you return. One way or another we must draw you back into the human race," she said, reaching out to give him a hug.

"Have I been so bad?" he asked sheepishly.

"Not at all, but I doubt anyone knows you've been staying here—or you might have." At this stage, saying little was best and Consuelo sensed that she was on shaky ground. Bart was, after all, usually quite conventional, but he was now much more out of character than she had guessed. One day passed and then another. He was like a man hanging over a cliff. There was nothing to grasp, nothing to hold his interest. . . .

By the time he and Brian set sail, he had become a different man, mean and bitter. He was ready to flog anyone who crossed him. Even the slightest infringement provoked severe punishment. He drank heavily and swaggered about the ship, too bleary-eyed to know one watch from the next.

Brian, of course, was in his heyday in command. On Brian's orders, for the first time on Bart's ship, a man was thrown overboard to be dragged astern with only a line about his waist. Had they been in shark-infested waters, the man would have been human bait and eaten alive. Fortunately, he was not left dangling long and the man survived. His crime, Brian said, was insolence. Bart had not interfered. He allowed Brian to run the ship as he chose. Luckily, it was a comparatively short run to New Orleans and back. Bart might not have survived a longer voyage.

For the next few weeks Anne-Marie retreated into a world in which the curtains on the recent past were drawn. With equanimity and the clarity of a quartz crystal she remembered childhood events and scenes as if she were poring over an album that recorded her life prior to her romantic awareness of Bart. Then suddenly, the book ended.

Her mother's parents had been Quakers, and she remembered excursions inland to May's Landing on the Somer's Point Road to visit the quaint-sounding couple who said "thee" and "thou" even to children. They passed the Tuckahoe Inn, where for the first time the family took a meal in a public place; although Anne-Marie was hungry she was too intrigued by the strangers to eat. Then her brother Francis confided that food served in public rooms was always wormy, quashing her appetite further. Her uneaten food was then offered to Francis, who gobbled down the second portion with relish, saying that he didn't mind eating worms. She was almost grown before she realized she had been tricked. The trips ceased when her grandparents died of typhoid and rested at the burial grounds of the Catawba Meeting House.

She vividly remembered her first haircut, which took place in the barn at the mercy of Francis's unskilled hands using great rusty old shears, clippers, a dandy brush and even a currycomb. When Francis finished there was not a hair on her head over a half-inch long. Emily's screams at the sight of her scalped daughter brought the household running, and Francis received a good thrashing with the willow stick kept in the kitchen. For months afterward Emily kept her in a bonnet. But, finally, when new hair grew in, it was surprisingly curly and luxuriant. Emily said the scars and scratches had in some way changed the growth pattern, and that it was a good lesson in life. "What turns your hair curly is usually frightening," said Emily.

Another near disaster contributed to Anne-Marie's beauty. When she was ten, somehow she picked up an eye infection. Rather than consult the doctor, Emily employed a homemade remedy she had watched her mother make. But instead of a tenth of one percent of sulphur in petrolatum, Emily's memory failed her and she used either a tenth or perhaps even one percent sulphur in the salve. The eye infection was cured, but Anne-Marie was so badly poisoned by the mixture that her eyelids swelled shut for days and her eyelashes fell out with an erupting rash. Eventually, her eyes opened, but for days her vision remained blurred. When her lashes finally grew in again, like her hair, they were incredibly long and thick—and so they had remained.

Anne-Marie clearly remembered running through the pine woods near her home—woods that gave way to a deeper forest of cedar, maple, oak, spruce, elm, chestnut and sycamore. Deer and little foxes, startled by the intrusion, always scampered to safety. Once a storm came swiftly, first as a light rain and then a torrent. Savage streaks of lightning and world-splitting thunder broke the darkness while Anne-Marie prayed passionately for safety. Hours later she made her way home, drenched as a water rat. Her clothes were torn; her new brown shoes that laced past her ankles were ruined. Relieved to see her baby daughter but enraged over the protracted absence, Emily dragged Anne-Marie up the stairs and paddled the child's bottom with a stout wooden hairbrush. There was no supper for her that night, but later Francis—who also had feared for his sister with sickening anguish—slipped her a bowl of bread and milk. The gesture, engulfed with a child's love, so touched Anne-Marie that a second storm of the day swelled within her.

Other less turbulent memories were lived again or dreamed again, but the moment Anne-Marie's recollections approached the advent of Bart in her life, like a reflex action, her mind closed. As if her mind knew its limits, she could not push forward. Poems that she had memorized in school returned so that she could recite them word for word, but, strangely, the emotional content seemed missing. Sonnets lauded for their beauty, she could remember, but they no longer moved her.

Many times Don Miguel tried unsuccessfully to talk to her, to increase his hold upon her, but always when he felt she was close to accepting him, she left him holding nothing in his hands, hoping. . . .

"It is a beautiful day. Would you like to walk along the beach or go for a swim?" He stood, dressed in white duck pants and an open, loose white tieless shirt that moved slightly with the breeze, his back to her. Mechanically he combed his hair with his fingers, a gesture that was a cover for caring.

"I think I've had enough swimming for a while." Tearing out the words, she replied, wondering how he could be so callous.

"That was thoughtless of me, but there's not a lot to do on this island—that is, unless you enjoy nature." He spoke, extending a hand, which he let drop.

She turned from him, remote, but at the same time sensing his kindness. Yet, this was a man who had saved her life. She could not hate him. Slowly, she faced him. "I'm sorry. I do enjoy nature. At least I used to. I am not enjoying much right now."

"Is that my fault?" His eyes were soft and pleading over a faint smile.

"Oh, no, of course not. Don't think me rude. I'm stunned. Can't you understand?" She seemed to wither.

"Don't be self-destructive, Anne-Marie. I do understand. I'm simply trying to bring you out of your grief. You must let me help you."

She could not hate him, the man was too kind. "Don Miguel, would you mind if I asked a servant for a cup of coffee?"

Bart returned to Key West, and it did not take more than a few days for Consuelo to learn of the "bathing" incident on the ship and Bart's wretched conduct on the voyage. Waterfront tongues wagged. Gossips also remarked on Brian's increased arrogance and that Brian encouraged Bart's drinking. "They're like a gaggle of geese," said Consuelo about the gossipmongers.

In port, under Consuelo's protective guidance, Bart's former personality reasserted itself. It was Consuelo who insisted that he write his and Anne-Marie's families with the sad news. He had not been able to bring himself to the task. "Those poor parents have a right to know. It is not as if you had any guilt," she said. The look in his eyes told a different story; he had let Anne-Marie and the child make the journey. Consuelo helped him compose letters that expressed his grief, and although they would be some weeks arriving, it would be better than having to convey the story in person.

Also, Key West was the right place for Bart; the setting and the people so different from his home port and his memory of Anne-Marie there. Because of the few weeks that Anne-Marie had been aboard the *Catherine*, the ship grew to serve simply as a constant reminder of his loss, not a distraction.

Consuelo sensed that Brian's presence was a bad influence—not that she knew him well enough to make this judgment, but she had heard the gossip. From Bart she had heard only of how capable he was. It was easy to see that Bart was leaning upon Brian when he should not be doing so. Instead of being busy commanding, he was wallowing in self-pity and whiskey while Brian ran the ship. When Bart was with her, he was a sad but civilized man. But he had only to meet Brian for an evening or afternoon at the Gem saloon, presided over by Captain Jack, as its owner George Alderslade was known, and he returned drunk. The Gem was a favorite resort of the officers of the navy and army and Consuelo believed it was no place for Bart in his state. That fact that he had never drunk himself into oblivion when he was with her made her suspect that often he had been plied with rum. There was no proof, but gossips lent credence to this possibility. She had ways of finding this out, but to do so deliberately would be spying. One did not spy on one's friends. As long as he did not go off on a long voyage, she felt that time more than anything else would heal him.

Consuelo had an additional weapon, however, that now, all else failing, she resolved to use—her own beauty. The loss of Anne-Marie had imposed a state of celibacy on the man that was to be expected. A natural loss of libido came with his wretchedness, insecurity, and powerlessness; she was certain that the one thing that could restore Bart's male self-respect and well-being, he was being deprived of by his own choice. Often in the evening he had lain in her arms and simply apologized for his impotency. Once he had commented on the fact that she deserved a Lothario that would rise in his britches every time she entered the room, and that she must feel that he was a hopeless clod. This comment convinced her that he needed to be seduced.

Consuelo considered her plan of attack and decided that he would be most receptive to her charms early in the morning as he emerged out of a deep sleep. Then he might be taken unaware, perhaps in a dream state when he might assume that she was Anne-Marie and that the accident might only have been a nightmare. At any rate, the ice needed to be broken; after that, it would be easier.

My heavens, what would my friends think if they could read my mind at this moment, said Consuelo to herself, gazing appreciatively into her dressing room mirror, applying a touch of unobtrusive lip salve before attending the Ladies' Missionary Society of St. Paul's. Consuelo was known for her zeal in church work and all public enterprises. She was president of the Daughter's of the King—all of whom would blanch and instantly impeach her had they the slightest inkling of her intentions—or for that matter, even the presence of her houseguest. All right, so I'm a hypocrite, she admitted to herself, but I'm a friend too. I guess more importantly, I'm a woman. But I do feel a bit like a witch, she conceded to her absent judges, giving one more small adjustment to her hat.

Throughout the day and that night she was too full of her own intentions to think seriously of anything else. Shortly before dawn she slipped into Bart's room. He lay flat on his back, his hands crossed over his chest, reminding her of a marble figure adorning a tomb that she had seen once in Europe. Carefully, but not too quietly, she slipped under the white mosquito netting that hung about his bed, murmuring something about feeling alone. She did not want him to be frightened or think he was being attacked by some man, and fight her. Still sleeping, he moved, making a roomier place for her. As she snuggled near him his arms welcomed her, but still he slept. She lay as still as the pure morning air, hardly daring to breathe. After a moment or two she let her hands move slowly about his body, at first rubbing his back, for he was on his side now. Then firmly she pressed a hand between his thighs, which seemed to loosen under her touch, and soon her hand could travel freely up and down his leg; then she moved to more private parts. Very slowly she began a gentle massage, feeling the wanted stiffening and enlargement, even though he slept. By this time she so hungered for him that it was a struggle to restrain herself or else he might awaken to recognition and all would be lost. Slowly, sweetly and deliberately she kissed his face, finally finding his lips. When he responded to her kiss with a jerk of his tongue, she stepped up the tempo of the massage. Then she slipped onto him, driving him into her like a sword into a scabbard and pounding him into oblivion. The siege was successful. "Thank you," he murmured. "That was lovely," and slept.

Consuelo remained in his room, but she slept badly. A blue-gray dawn was seeping into the room and she had lain motionless too long. The deep and obliterating sleep that he needed was now an alienating and unending weight that she could no longer endure, so she disengaged herself with a careless heavy turn as one would in a natural sleep, oblivious of a partner. He did not awaken and her relieved bones rejoiced. The air on the other side of the bed was fresher, less drugged with maleness and his musk, less heady and ripe with sleep. A church clock struck the hour, calling the fishermen who pushed off in the dawn. A few early bird cries pierced the light and soon gathered company until a cacophony outside the windows made further sleep impossible. Then she felt his hand rest upon her waist, at first heavy and still, but soon it took on a life of its own, moving up to feel her breast, gently roving over the curves, ever gaining in awareness. She turned to face him, to meet his lips now needing hers. Steadily he went to work upon her, this time needing no tutelage. He rose, phoenixlike, with perfect motion enveloping her, devouring her with strong, sure, white-hot force just as he had years before when as a carefree young man he had strewn his seed from one far end of the earth to the other. . . .

Bart's lovemaking was different with Consuelo than it had been with Anne-Marie. A deep basic love with a sense of permanency unconsciously influenced his mating with Anne-Marie. He had sought a satisfaction, but coupled with it was a desire for oneness, a great feeling of cherishing and an over-whelming, mysterious need to impregnate. He dominated Anne-Marie despite her beauty that sometimes made him feel weak in the knees as he examined its perfection. Still, he was the master, and with almost childlike simplicity Anne-Marie made him feel powerful.

With Consuelo lovemaking was lusty. Their friendship made it something of a sport, a joyous celebration of two reveling bodies, romping, unwhipped by love, cavorting on an equal plane. He was not a master, but a sharing participant. Consuelo's soft little body was all curves, with the warmth of a bath in oil exotically scented, slippery and sensuous. Possession came easy and a delicious wickedness and carnality added a wild dimension to the excitement. Because so much less emotion—basic, loving emotion—was involved, he had the energy to make love with Consuelo several times in succession without feeling physically spent. His pockets remained full despite the giving. Only Anne-Marie took everything, even his soul.

Late in the day a brief dusk settled over the island and he decided to take a walk. Consuelo needed time to attend to some of her own activities unhampered by his presence, and so he set out, the twilight stretching before him, vacant as a plowed field. The most relaxing day that he had experienced in weeks was behind him, and he felt as if he could see a light at the end of a tunnel. The hell that he had been in burned less hotly.

He strolled along little lanes and alleys without thought of a destination, conscious only of a lighter heart. Outside a small house, not unlike all the others, a man lounged against a wooden post supporting the roof. Bart noticed the man suddenly stiffen and then remain motionless until he had passed. Bart

65

sensed only that he had been recognized. He walked on at the same pace, now hearing footsteps behind him. At the corner he turned, and the footsteps continued. Looking back, he saw the familiar outline of the man who had been on the porch and now recognized, because of his rolling walk, the man as a sailor, but one whom he did not know.

"Have you got a match?" asked the approaching figure.

"Sorry," Bart replied, suddenly aware that they had entered a blind alley.

He felt closed in, closeted in unfamiliar surroundings. Sharply turning, in the dim light he saw a knife glinting in the man's hand. "What the devil?" he grunted, addressing the rough figure, disheveled and dirty. He felt the first knots of fear, the pangs that turned on the adrenaline, and braced himself for an onslaught. The man lurched toward him, fairly springing through the electrically charged air.

Drawing on resources almost forgotten, Bart swerved and ducked, deftly seizing his assailant's wrist as he moved toward him, and shoved, throwing him off balance. Together they fell to the ground, falling as a tree falls, bouncing on impact. As they rolled, Bart heard twigs cracking under them, snapping like whips digging and stabbing into his back. Now the man was on top, his thick shoulder flattening Bart's nose, cutting off his breath. Gasping through his bleeding mouth, he struggled to lift the heavier man by digging his heels into the dirt seeking leverage, but it was soft, and gave way. Pivoting and twisting, Bart's boot found its place on an outcropping of rock that held firm. With one great lift he sent his knee into the man's crotch. The opponent shuddered and jerked his elbow into Bart's jaw, still holding his position, but less securely. Bart could hear only the man's hissing breath as it wheezed through rotten and stinking teeth.

Greasy perspiration seeping down his arms threatened his purchase on the other's wrists, but with fingernails dug deep, he held.

Spurred by the overwhelming stench of the unwashed body and foul breath smothering him, Bart tightened his viselike grip on the wrists. Then, tossing and turning, he maneuvered his thigh and with one great surge of power drove his knee again

66

into the opponent's groin, this time convulsing him with disabling pain. In that moment Bart found himself on top administering a final blow to the groin. The knife dropped. Quickly he flipped it out of reach. Now riding the prone but struggling figure, using both fists, he slammed into the man's face, grinding it to a bloody pulp.

When all resistance ceased, Bart raised himself from his knees to stand. Still trembling, filthy, bruised and bleeding, he hitched up his pants and left his unconscious foe. Staggering mindlessly through the now dark streets, he found Consuelo's home. Her scream and terrified expression roused him from his stupor. As she and the maid Pearl stripped his rags, bathed and dressed his cuts, he was able to describe the battle.

"I'm not really hurt," he said. "I don't think anything is broken, but God, how I ache! But who?...And why?"

"I doubt that this is an isolated incident—although it could be. You must have felt that his motive was murder—not robbery," said Consuelo. "You may have a mortal enemy, perhaps the man who was dragged behind your ship—or maybe his brother." She paused, feeling Bart stiffen. "I know that it was not your command, because I've heard the whole story, but if you allow such inhuman practices, you'd better protect yourself with bodyguards." Her level gaze and the husky tremor in her voice revealed her disturbed state.

Quickly he looked away. That incident had retreated into his darkened mind as if it were only a memory of a drunken nightmare. Apparently, it had indeed happened. Now Consuelo was turning up demons. Shame and guilt hammered in his throat and finally took form in rigid defiance. "Don't tell me how to run my ship," he snarled, his reproach a defensive attack.

His fury took Consuelo by surprise. Tightly she closed her eyes, trying to shut out how vividly she was aware of everything about him—his pride, his hurt, his anger. She understood perfectly: he had just roused such feelings in himself, but she shrugged and was silent. When she finally spoke, her words were considered and smoothly paced, but cold as ice. "I'm not telling you how to run your ship. I'm telling you that you *haven't* run it and perhaps this 'accident' tonight was a result."

The flame from a lamp cast a circle of light over the center of the table where the two women had been working on Bart's cuts. The edges of the room where now ominously dark.

Consuelo regretted having brought up the shameful incident while his defenses were down, yet she had wanted to strike while he would be sensitive to the rudeness of her rebuke and be jarred into the realization that he was responsible for Brian's excesses. His reformation was now threatened by her timing, she thought helplessly. Bart sat in stony silence. Consuelo lifted a hand to run shaking fingers through her hair. "Bart, clearly the man who attacked you was a real brute, the scum of the earth, and probably the world would be a better place without him, so let's think of that no more. Please, just promise me that you'll be careful." She looked at him with a long, slow, caring look. "Please," she echoed, maintaining her gaze until he was forced to return it. Her tender plea and gentle hand reaching to him asked his forgiveness. Ashamed, he melted.

In any case, it was impossible to stay angry with Consuelo. The brimming sincerity in her eyes, the caress in her voice and in every touch, her smile—so uncommonly nice—were totally disarming. And, no matter how outrageously candid her remark, she could always throw out a line to pull one back to her side.

"Could you have other enemies," she pressed on, "who could profit from your death?"

Little fears and suspicions flickered in her eyes that met his, scanning for an answer, begging at least for thought on it.

"No one I can possibly think of. Now that Anne-Marie is gone, my parents are my heirs and they've given to me with both hands. You've mentioned the only man I have truly injured," he replied, tacitly accepting her condemnation. She hastened to ignore his capitulation.

"I understand that other men could be jealous of you, but few would go to that length. Did you take Anne-Marie away from another man?"

"No, my dear. I'm afraid your romantic fantasies have taken over. But now that you mention it, I wonder if you have any discarded lovers around who would like to be rid of me? Own up . . ."

Relieved, she laughed, tossing back her hair. "That would be something! No, unfortunately no tempestuous young men driven insane for love of me walk this earth. My male friends have all reached an age—and a state of mind and body—that brings the realization that women are not worth fighting over. I'm sorry!"

He pondered this for a moment, doubting it. "I'm not ready to believe that, but right now I'll take your word for it," he said, a bemused and admiring light in his eyes, ready to change the subject.

Still unsatisfied with their review of possible instigators, Consuelo's mind rejected her unspoken thought. Brian's name was on the tip of her tongue, but she restrained it in fear that she might only anger him and again shatter their tenuous rapport. It was a dreadful tyranny, almost an obsession to query him further but she held still, her mouth open, frozen by discretion.

"What were you going to say?" asked Bart.

Her voice rumbled in her throat unintelligibly. "Nothing. Nothing important."

"I don't believe that." He frowned. "You look too serious and you almost said something."

"I shouldn't state a vague suspicion until I contact some friends. There are a few unsavory characters who owe me old favors. One of them may be able to get to the root of this."

"Then again they may not, and you will have used up your credit, which you may need yourself one day."

"No, I can handle this, but it will take a little time. Meanwhile, you must be very careful. Don't walk about alone and stay out of blind alleys. Whoever attacked you obviously won't be walking about for some time, anyway." She added, "Look at every man you see or meet, asking yourself, 'Could this be he? What could this man gain?' and watch his face and hands." She shuddered thinking of the fight and the way one's past comes back to haunt one. "One way or another old debts require repayment," she said. "No one gets off scot-free."

"And no one forgets where he has buried the hatchet," replied Bart, meeting her eyes.

CHAPTER SIX

The following day, to Brian's startled surprise, Bart appeared at the ship. "Good morning, sir," stammered Brian, eyeing a cut on Bart's forehead, the only visible wound. "You look as if you had a bad night."

"A small mishap," replied Bart. Then, to Brian's obvious consternation, Bart insisted that they track down the sailor who had received such rough punishment at Brian's hands on the voyage to New Orleans.

"We may be asking for trouble, sir," said Brian. "In fact, it sounds like a printed invitation to trouble. I had hoped to see the last of that one."

"Perhaps I haven't," replied Bart dourly. He had not wanted to discuss the attack with Brian. Mindful of Consuelo's suggestion that he suspect everyone and remembering Anne-Marie's persistent distrust of Brian, during the night he had decided upon a role of silence. His clothes hid the worst cuts and bruises and his pride the aches and pains. He would not let himself dwell on the possibility that Brian could have been involved and would not pursue it. Understandably, he did not want the incident discussed by Brian and the crew. He was ashamed of his behavior during the last few weeks and, although it hurt to admit it even to himself, he knew one way or another he had a beating coming. There was also the off chance that, cloaked in silence, he might pick up something, some hint as to who the culprit was.

A check of the *Catherine*'s log showed that the man Bart suspected was not a Key Wester. A further check at the shipping offices showed that he had put out to sea the week before; he could not have been in Key West on the previous evening. Obviously, he was not the assailant.

As he walked along with Brian, pursuing the inquiries, Bart felt a coolness in the first mate's manner. As he pressed on, Brian was pooh-poohing the search, impatiently humoring him.

"I can't for the life of me understand the reason for wasting a morning on this," said Brian finally.

Bart turned sharply to Brian, feeling the pain of the abrupt movement throughout his sorely battered body so that his face rightly showed pain. For a moment his eyes met Brian's squarely, but then Brian quickly looked away. Could he be afraid of me? thought Bart, struggling for an unhampered breath. In a fleeting moment until Brian gained composure Bart saw something he did not like, something as painful as his wounds. He would not explain the search to Brian. He could not say, "I wanted to vindicate you." Instead he said severely, "There is no need for you to understand what I do. You have only to carry out orders. Today my curiosity is in good supply. Let's leave it at that." Saying nothing more, he was happy to leave Brian.

That evening at dinner in the garden he told Consuelo about his investigation. "So, my dear, the trail ran cold. I can only assume it was an isolated incident, probably with robbery as a motive." It was what he wanted to believe. His face was so close, she had no difficulty discerning every detail beyond the healing cut on his brow. He was untroubled, she thought. Why? she asked herself. She had rejected robbery as a motive and he seemed to agree. Why did he now seem to accept it? Perhaps, she said to herself, he feels that the violent beating he suffered has purged the only guilt he can recognize. So he is done with the matter.

She could not know that this, in fact, was precisely his

thought, but that it was hastily born of a need to absolve Brian from suspicion. Nor did Bart know himself. He was saying, as she supposed, only, "I am free!" And his face reflected his serenity.

"By the time you return from your next voyage, my sources may have some information," she persisted, but, dissuaded by his nearness, her heart changed the subject and shivered with disturbing memories. The warmth that suddenly ran through her disrupted her composure and she turned away to disguise her feeling; she would miss him. She had not wanted a disturbing emotional commitment, but one was growing nevertheless; clearly, she was too aware of his presence, of his every gesture, of his flesh. Nothing about him escaped her attention. This awareness and sensitivity had become a tiring weight.

"I hate to think of your leaving, yet I feel you are safe on your ship," she managed to say, smiling wanly.

"Duty calls," said the young captain theatrically. "But I must confess, Consuelo, I go reluctantly. You have made life bearable again."

At first she said nothing, believing him, but his words unnerved her. She needed no encouragement, and truly wanted none. She hoped her face did not betray her quailing heart; for her future self-sufficiency she must remain staunch.

"I want to see you whole again, physically and spiritually. I want to see you proud—proud of your ship and yourself and happy with your life. You were, until grief drove it from your grasp, but you will find—are finding—it again," said Consuelo.

There was shock in his eyes, and puzzlement too. Was she rejecting him? He tried to cover his disappointment, looking up at the sky as if at the state of the weather. His hand slipped down to rest possessively on her knee, still begging for comfort and solace. "Right now I want to be 'best friend' to you— intimate friend," he said. "Can't you see that? I am slowly learning to take one day at a time. I can't think of the past and I don't want to think of the future—at least a future that is further away than the lovely fish that Pearl is about to serve. It is all I can manage."

They looked up to see the young black woman bearing a

silver platter of baked kingfish, pink with paprika, flaming cognac still curling the circling bay leaves.

"Men never cease to amaze me," said Consuelo, now pouring the wine. "You want everything settled, down pat, so that you can go about living as if it were a mercantile business." She sat playing with her fork. "Despite all our efforts, we seem to have so little control over our lives. We are buffeted about— me by you, you by me—both by killers who stalk the streets or the sea or a ship that must sail because hundreds need and want this or that. What is it that we really seek? Intimacy you say, and you say that now because you have just endured the ultimate loneliness. My dear, we come into this world alone and we go out of it alone. Learning to live alone is life's real challenge."

"You've learned your lessons well," he replied, fingering a small curl on her cheek, an obstinate escapee from her sleekly elegant coiffure. Suddenly his eyes were looking straight into hers, their strange blueness reflecting the candlelight. Distracted, she tapped his finger away.

"Hold still—it is difficult to see you and I must remember what an incredibly handsome man you are. The last few months have aged you—beautifully. People age in leaps and bounds, you know, not daily." She was warning him against herself, God help her. By lecturing him she managed to steady her own pulse, to quiet her longing heart and body. He was ready to grasp her, to woo her, to drown himself in her—even marry her, with the slightest encouragement. It was frightening. Saving him would drown her. "I am a brief interlude in your life. We must keep our emotions within sensible bounds. Don't let our feelings get out of hand. It is the only way that we can help and not hurt each other."

"Then you do not want me as a lover?" he queried pathetically.

"No, not permanently, because we could spoil things for each other by giving something that is not enough. A total commitment is impossible."

"I don't know why you say that," he replied sulkily. "As long as our age difference doesn't bother me, I don't know why you should care. . . . I'm sure this is why . . ." His voice trailed off.

"You might come back one day and find yourself married to an old woman—this I could not bear. Your parents deserve a house filled with grandchildren. My roots are here. Yours are elsewhere. I don't know how many reasons you need, but these are enough for me."

"There is only a here and now. Nothing else matters," he urged with his hands on her hands. A determination coursing through his veins nourished him, unsteadied her. "Let's not worry about a future now or put any feelings into words. Just let the night be."

Above, a thousand stars shone from which man could chart a course from one end of the earth to another, but not all men— and women. So Consuelo rose with the candlestick, the last item remaining on the table, and he followed her into the house.

Mechanically, they moved about the evening chores, winding the clock, extinguishing the lights, securing doors and windows. It was companionable, so cozily domestic that Consuelo silently wept. Fear and elation warred in her heart. He followed her up the stairs, once touching her waist as if she had missed a step and needed steadying. At the landing she turned and carefully took his face in her hands. He was standing a step lower, a lamp in one hand, his face almost on a level with hers. The light shone only upon his face, vivid and tense, throbbing with a fire of desire. To hide her face from his eyes, she kissed them closed, then turned and entered her room, leaving him to make his way to his own room while she sought the safety of hers.

Firmly, she closed the door. Without his presence, her room seemed empty—barren of love. Pearl had turned down her bed, and a nightgown and negligee rich with French lace laid flat at the foot, awaiting the curves and warmth of her body. Mosquito netting closed three sides of the bed like an Arabian tent in an arid desert, but it was also a secluded haven in which she could cry. Trembling, she unbuttoned her dress and tossed it upon a stool. Petticoats followed and finally a waist cincher and underwear. Layer after layer joined the heap, leaving her naked and free. Brushing her hair, which grew fuller and more luxuriant with every stroke, she halted to wipe a reluctant tear from her patrician nose.

Then she heard him at the door. Without leave he entered, his eyes upon her, the heat of his gaze ran the full length of her. Before her he stood naked.

With considerable effort and resolve, volatile Consuelo felt she had made her position patently clear. Obviously, Bart was ignoring her resolution, which was at first irritating. His arms moved to her, one hand reaching to caress her breast, his eyes lit with a rampant fever. She rose, slipping away from his touch, moving toward her bed and negligee. "Please," he whispered.

"How dare you come into my room like this," said Consuelo, straining to maintain an amicable tone. Bart ignored her admonition, firmly taking her into his arms and pressing a kiss upon unwilling lips. "Leave, Bart! I've said no as nicely as I can," she said, trying to pull loose.

"Please, Consuelo," he again pleaded, holding her firm and kissing her.

"Stop," she cried, freeing her face, anger mounting.

He ignored her command and tightened his grip, which only added to her fury.

"Bart, did you hear me?" she demanded, no longer making any effort toward civility, pushing him with all her might—persistently but futilely against his superior strength. Ignoring her struggles, he tossed her to the bed and fell upon her, confident both of his own prowess and that she really did not mean what she was saying.

"Stop this minute," she hissed, now in a rage.

Trapped in a maelstrom of desire, his passion heightened by her protests, he forced a thigh between her knees.

"You have gone too far with this!" she cried. His kisses cut off her words. Still, he persisted, amorously trying to subdue her with firm roving hands.

At this point Consuelo realized that she had no choice but to cooperate with him to avoid injury. Yet, she was outraged but not entirely powerless. Ostensibly, her struggles ceased, but only physically. She set upon a course designed to shame him.

Despite his opinion to the contrary, he was not an expert lover. He had marvelous good looks, youth and sex appeal, but when it came to actual performance in lovemaking, a good many men, interested in pleasing a woman, were more adroit.

Through the years a number of imaginative lovers had tutored Consuelo, and despite a Victorian upbringing, a Rabelaisian streak had made her a talented and inspired pupil. Consequently, when it came to lovemaking as an art, Consuelo was more skilled and experienced. With the expertise of a professional, while at the same time lacking the drawbacks of a demimonde or harlot, Consuelo went to work on Bart, calling upon every trick designed the world over to make a man crawl the walls in ecstasy. Coolly and calculatingly, drawing no real pleasure for herself, she plied the cunning artifices learned from older, proficient and knowledgeable lovers until with great heaving shudders his body exploded.

Indifferently, she then rolled over, pulling the linen sheet over her creamy white shoulder.

Physically satisfied, but now painfully aware of the frigidity in the air, Bart meekly slunk from the room, thoroughly chastised and utterly ashamed of his behavior. Then and there he saw that beside Consuelo, in many respects he was a child. He would never again presume upon her in such a manner.

CHAPTER SEVEN

Anne-Marie surveyed a world turned upside down within only
a few weeks' time. Everything familiar had vanished. Family,
home, all the minor routines that give life its continuity, had
been swept away. The known physical features of her world—
the rolling sand hills of New Jersey, the gray sea and grayer
skies, her cottage, the old gnarled trees—receded under an
unrelenting, blinding tropical sun and a panorama too brilliant
and lustrous for even the boldest artist's palette. There was no
need to retreat into unreality. She was already there physically,
uprooted and transported into a strange new world. The only
way to escape overwhelming grief was to accept the here and
now.

Obviously, for some days she had been living with a strange
man as his wife. He was feeding her, clothing her, and his
servants were tending her. Even though he helped himself to
her, he treated her with kindness and affection. Although he
was old enough to be her father, he had the body of a much
younger man. The graying hair at his temples gave him an air
of distinction which, combined with his charm and sophisti-
cation, made him attractive. Above all, he was protective and
gentle; for this Anne-Marie was grateful. It was easy to imagine

that she could have landed in worse hands, or—much worse—in no hands, where she would have starved to death.

Don Miguel was not a rapist, but an opportunist. Anne-Marie supposed that many women would have enjoyed being rescued by him. The fact that seafaring people were a somewhat impious breed saved her from overriding feelings of shame and guilt that might have accompanied her state. Still, her upbringing came to the fore, and she desperately hoped to escape this situation so alien to her sense of morality.

"Don Miguel, I think that we should sleep apart," she said one afternoon. "Surely there is some work that I can do here to earn my board until I can regain my strength and go home." The words, although carefully rehearsed, came haltingly.

Don Miguel stiffened. Pondering her words, he placed a thin knuckle against his lips. "I have a housekeeper, a cook, two cleaning women and a houseman. If we exclude these duties, what other services might you have in mind other than a wifely role?"

His reply shocked her, causing her to tightly grip the arm of her chair, which had been carefully placed for her in the shade on the terrace.

"I . . . don't know," she stammered, "but considering your circumstances, I surmised that I might also simply be a guest in your house until funds can be drawn from a bank to repay you. My people are not poor." She passed shaking fingers across her brow, knowing full well that on this island she was a prisoner at his will.

Don Miguel rose and stepped toward her, gazing down tenderly. "I'm afraid bank drafts are of little use to me, my dear. I know of no bank south of St. Augustine. There is nothing to buy around here. What would I want with more money?"

Anne-Marie shriveled. "I'm here because I had no choice," she replied, both angered and bewildered.

He turned her words aside. "Anne-Marie, forgive me for forgetting that." He reached for her hand, but she pulled away from his touch. Ignoring her withdrawal, he laid a hand on her shoulder. The gesture was not seductive but warm and sympathetic.

"I will try to respect your wishes," he continued, "but keep in mind that you need someone close to you right now. You have been through a terrible experience. Try to forget a lot of foolish things you have been taught that pay no mind to the human heart. You will continue to share my bed, but I will not trouble you unless you ask." Aghast at his attitude and suggestion, her heart thumped far too wildly to permit a reply, yet she felt she had gained a little ground. The impertinence of him!

She had, after all, been sharing his bed for some time now and his physical presence was not repulsive to her. What in the world can I do with this man? she cried to herself. He is absolutely maddening! Slowly she managed to curve her lovely mouth into a desperate smile, and the anxiety disappeared from her eyes. Nervousness prompted her to stand, but then he wrapped his arms about her, hugging her as a man would his daughter. Such disarming gestures were impossible to combat. In her distress, he was the only one she could turn to, and in a great way he was comforting. Besides, she liked him. If only I could hate him—but this . . . this is impossible!

"Thank goodness you are not a Southern belle," said Don Miguel.

"I take it that you are a Unionist," said Anne-Marie, wondering what prompted his remark.

"I deplore slavery," he replied. "But remember, you are in Confederate territory, so watch what you say. But I was not thinking of that. I was thinking of your untutored charm. You are genteel, but still natural and genuine."

At this point, Anne-Marie considered herself anything but sincere. Allowing a demure smile to cover her, she thanked him.

Anne-Marie had found the remaining rooms in the house as spacious and luxuriously furnished as the bedroom. Thick plastered stone walls supported massive decorated beams and ornately carved corbels, all carrying the design of the carnation. Heavy iron candelabra hung from high ceilings or jutted from the walls. Richly patterned Spanish tiles imparted a splendor, gaiety and exuberance to the solidity and security of the ma-

81

sonry. Tall, slender persiennes, doors with adjustable louvres, held out the heat and sunlight, but admitted playful tree shadows on the wings of sea breezes. It was elegant and opulent, completely unlike any dwelling she had seen before. She felt like a princess imprisoned in an ivory tower. The tower was called Los Claveles, meaning The Carnations. It was easy for her to understand why Don Miguel would want to keep her here. She told herself that he had to be very lonely here, with only uneducated servants and an overseer to talk to. As for work, he apparently had only a small citrus grove to run. The people within the house spoke only Spanish, so whatever she learned about the place had to come from Don Miguel or her own deductions.

That evening she was surprised when he presented her with a small Spanish grammar. "It won't hurt you to learn the language," he said. "It is beautiful—powerful—much more musical than English. Because you are so young, you may learn to speak it without an accent, although a little accent is charming in a woman." There was a slight twinkle in his eye and, as always, a manner of speaking to her that conveyed a gentlemanly appreciation of her mind as well as her body.

She said nothing, watching his eyes. He does mean to keep me here, she told herself, and slipping away will not be easy even with the language. Suddenly she realized that she had better speak or he might be able to read her mind. "That is kind of you," she murmured. "I do need something to keep my mind busy. I also want to be able to thank Concepción for her wonderful care."

"I have a few other things for you," said Don Miguel, leaving the room. "Wait." Within a few minutes he returned with several dresses over his arm produced from another bedroom. "I think they will fit. One or two may have been used, but the lady is no longer here."

A strained expression crossed his face and he seemed for the first time self-conscious, even awkward.

"She won't mind?"

"Where she is, she won't mind."

"Where is she?" countered Anne-Marie quickly.

Don Miguel turned to avoid her eyes. "She no longer lives.

I would have preferred not to tell you that these clothes were hers. It might distress you to wear a dead woman's clothes, but for the moment there is little choice." A bitter note entered his voice. "If you can bear to wear them, you would be doing me a great service. You could erase another face, not half so pretty or so gentle, but one that I once cared for very much. Surely, you are tired of the dress I found you in . . ."

"True, I am desperately tired of it. So I guess if you can bear it, so can I." A slight shudder rippled her shoulders. She dared not think. To think meant to feel and there seemed no place for that.

As soon as she was left to her own devices, she took the opportunity to explore the grounds. Once away from the house and its terraces, there was no lawn, but sickled-down brush which, on the near side, gave way to a tropical hammock, dense, dark and almost impenetrable. Here giant oaks dripped with gray, spidery Spanish moss and strange exotic trees majestically rose to scrape the sky. Orchids, bromeliads and bright, lustrous birds colored their limbs with strange forms. On the other side of this wood was the sea. To the rear were lime trees planted in gray rocky soil with even more rocks piled around their small trunks. "Rocks and more rocks," said Anne-Marie. "How does anything grow in this soil?" Where the soil appeared to be slightly deeper, there were rows of pineapples growing weirdly in the air atop spiny bushes. A few hundred feet away began a small village of wooden cottages where the workmen lived, and she saw what appeared to be a warehouse on an inlet.

The inlet ran diagonally from the sea to another opening on the Gulf. The middle of the inlet had been widened to a basin where a large ketch and a few dinghys were tied up. The basin was large enough to take perhaps half a dozen ships. It was the most secluded anchorage she had ever seen. Both ends of the inlet were lined with a heavy growth of mangrove; their twisted roots, like fingers dipping into the water, completely obscured the basin.

Anne-Marie had a long walk over rocky terrain to get to where the inlet began. She passed a grove of wild orange trees, elegantly raising their fruited tops into the open air to receive the unbroken rays of the sun. The rich perfume of their blossoms wafted about her, filling her lungs with their heavy sweetness, while beneath, the deep green glossy leaves waved with the breeze. The orange trees enjoyed a better ground so here the walking was easier. Raising her skirts, she picked her way until at last she saw an open path to the sea. The path, only a few feet wide, was a natural tunnel created by overhanging trees. Suddenly, the shade ended at a beach of coarse pinkish sand. Before her was the wide emerald sea, at first light with whitecaps, then dark blue.

Clearly, from either the ocean or the Gulf, no glimpse of the estate was visible. Ships could scoot in and out from the ocean to the bay on the other side. They would disappear as if swallowed by the earth. Standing on the beach, in the far distance she could see a large schooner sailing toward her, traveling northward. The sight of it made her heart leap. She could be saved! Up and down the beach she ran, back and forth, sometimes stumbling on masses of seaweed washed ashore. Wildly she called, "Here! Here! Come! Help me!"

Back and forth she ran as the vessel approached. Back and forth, stopping only to jump up and down. Gloriously, it seemed to be coming right to her. Then suddenly, the ship came about, changing tack and heading out to sea. No one saw her—or would have thought anything about it even if they had—and certainly they could not have heard her. Forlornly, she watched the schooner disappear, tears streaming down her cheeks. Then she saw. A change in the color of the water marked a perilous reef. Even if they had seen her dancing and prancing on the beach, they would have come no closer for fear of wrecking on the reef. Suddenly, a blinding revelation came to her: she was with wreckers. Don Miguel was a wrecker! The basin was the lair. Only a sharp diagonal channel permitted entry. Salvage from wrecked ships on the ocean could be hauled by mules to the basin where it could be loaded onto ships and then taken out to sea again, eventually landing in a port where the goods could be sold. Her heart hammered. Indeed, escape would be well nigh impossible.

The brisk ocean air soon dried her eyes and cleared her head. Slowly she made her way back to Los Claveles. She passed a few hands scattered about at work. Apart from giving her a quick glance, they paid little attention to her. Obviously, even they had not heard her cries. She must not reveal her deductions about Don Miguel's business, but certainly, sometime soon, someone would come in by ship to load from the warehouse. When they sailed out, she could be a stowaway. This might not be difficult at night. By day it would be impossible. And when she was discovered might they not throw her overboard? Possibly.... Schemes seemed to rattle her brains; the wheels of her mind spun like sheaves riven by ropes. She would have to bide her time, being careful, watching the coming and going of ships until the right moment.

That night sleep avoided her. Had she tossed and turned, she would have alerted Don Miguel, who, because of their earlier conversation, would have made any number of wrong assumptions. Consequently, she lay rigid. She tried counting sheep and when that didn't work she tried counting his breaths. That too became tiresome, but not tiresome enough. Finally, shortly before dawn she dropped off. When she awakened, he was gone....

A few days later, however, another discovery threw her into total dismay. She awakened early and sat up, but when her feet touched the floor she knew something was wrong. She felt queasy, the queasiness of pregnancy. This time she had no need of her mother's diagnosis.

"Oh, dear God," she moaned, falling back on the bed. "Please, not now!" It was a blow she had not expected.

"What is it?" murmured Don Miguel sleepily.

"I'm sick! Worse, I'm pregnant!" she moaned.

"Worse things have happened," he replied, now trying to digest the news himself. "I think, in fact, I like that news." He was actually smiling.

"How can you lie there and smile, you wretch," she screamed. "How will I ever get away from here now? What *you* have done is cruel, monstrously cruel! I hate you," she sobbed.

"There now, little one, don't fret," he implored, wiping her tears on the edge of a pillowcase. He got up and began dashing around the room looking for a handkerchief, opening all the wrong drawers. Finally, he found one and returned to the bed.

"Please, please, listen to me," he begged.

"Don't touch me! Haven't I gone through enough?" Then, burying her head in the pillows, leaving him only her heaving back, she wept.

"Anne-Marie, I love you. I've loved you from the moment I saw you lying half dead on the beach. I was crazy with fear that you might not regain your senses. I pounded the water out of you. I sat a vigil at your bedside. Please, please, don't carry on so." The pitiful tone of his voice slowly reached her. "I will give you everything you want. The world can be yours," he promised.

The explosion of the last few minutes subsided under both his pleas and promises—and her sheer exhaustion. There had been comfort in his words. At least he cared about her. He was promising her everything. She had wanted nothing except to get back to her home, and now this was impossible. Tiredly, she ran her fingers through her hair, trying to sort out a hundred impressions and numbly to gather her wits. Her cheeks smarted under the salt of her tears and her mouth felt dry and swollen. Now it would be a long time before she would be able to leave Los Claveles—a very long time. A year loomed like ten, an eternity. And even then, what? Being fed and cared for seemed like nothing in the face of a horrid pregnancy. "I feel dreadful, absolutely dreadful," she said. "Being pregnant is too horrible to contemplate." She looked straight into his eyes, not caring how she hurt him.

Don Miguel gathered his pride about him like a greatcoat and sat looking at her with large doleful eyes.

He had made a pretty speech, and at that moment Anne-Marie knew that he was sincere. But how would he feel in a few months when she was swollen like a cow—no longer slim and attractive? Don Miguel seemed a dramatist at heart, a man in love with being in love. Undoubtedly, in the course of his life he had loved many women. The Latin blood in his veins augured a turbulent stream of passion that would not, she knew, follow a smooth and quiet course for long. Finding her on the beach, rescuing her and keeping her would be grist for his romantic mill. And if he truly did care for her as he said, it would be the love of a middle-aged man grasping at one more insanely romantic interlude, a frantic effort to recapture his yesterdays, grasp his today and gain his tomorrows. She would be a pawn, the one who could, for a little longer, postpone the inevitable day when the fire of youth would die. She was trapped.

"Pull yourself together, my love," he said finally. "We will have guests for dinner tonight, and as mistress of Los Claveles you must be your most beautiful best. You will be the only woman present—and this I regret—but I'm sure you will enjoy the company." His voice was smooth, veneered with a clever blend of concern and apology. She stared at him. So that was that! Now we are on to the next topic of conversation. The devil!

His bright dark eyes enveloped her. Her mouth hung agape and finally closed as if she had at last discovered what he was talking about. Astonished, she paled. So, tonight they would be entertaining a collection of wreckers! She shuddered. "God, help me! What have I come to?" Immediately a crew of black-whiskered, stump-legged pirates wearing eye patches and with recollected murder in their eyes came to mind. She shivered at the thought. Gathering her wits, she decided it would be best not to speak her mind—not to betray what was to her a secret discovery by a display of revulsion at his mention of "guests." Her position during the coming months would be tenuous enough; envisioning the retching, the bloated belly, the constant fatigue, she would be wise to hold her tongue. In the end she managed a weak smile. "Then let me rest," she said, closing her eyes.

Don Miguel, pacified by her attitude of capitulation, tiptoed from the room.

One by one that afternoon, a number of ships entered the basin. Fine large sloops and schooners, obviously in first-rate order, put up. With each new arrival Don Miguel left the house to cordially greet each well-dressed guest, offering a friendly embrace. Then, arm in arm, he led them into the house. When they entered, Anne-Marie walked out on her balcony, ostensibly to brush her hair in the free air, but actually to try to overhear the conversation going on below while remaining out of sight. To her surprise the conversation was that of educated gentlemen discussing a wide range of subjects from the war and politics to ponies. Enheartened somewhat, she finished making her toilette.

Still inwardly angry, her first urge had been to embarrass Don Miguel by wearing her old dress, but the basic preparations soon made her realize that she would only embarrass herself. In the end, she wisely decided that by acting the lady she might find a valuable friend among these men, and certainly such an opportunity would not often arise. Prompted by discretion, she selected the finest of the gowns she had inherited from her predecessor. Anne-Marie was taller and thinner so the dress required a little taking in at the waist and letting out at the hem, but Concepción quickly worked that miracle. The soft green silk with darker bows of velvet fitted as if it had been made for her. Its low neck would display her emerald perfectly and compliment her coppery hair. Also the sewing and fitting had been a distraction that had softened her distress.

This Don Miguel saw with relief when he came to escort her. The light of appreciation in his eyes confirmed her own satisfaction with her appearance. Noting the emerald, he exclaimed, "One day, my love, I will hang emeralds upon your beautiful bosom and dainty hands that will be bright enough to light your way to paradise. Just wait!" Taking her in his arms, he placed a chaste kiss on her temple—light and airy as the evening's breeze—and just as quickly released her. Enveloped in her perfume, he led her from their room. . . .

All day the feast had been in preparation. In the back yard a pig was roasting on a spit, sending up occasional puffs of smoke, and the aroma of browned honey and orange peel filled the air. Enameled basins held a macédoine of chopped pineapple, orange, grapefruit, melon, banana and coconut. In the large Spanish kitchen a conch chowder was under way. Bread and cakes had been baked in the morning; now quail were in the ovens. There would be a feast for all. Tables and benches had been set up near the roasting pit for the crews and help. Inside, at the great refectory table, dressed as if to await the king of France, Anne-Marie and Don Miguel would dine in splendor with the captains.

Don Miguel introduced her as "my bride," causing her a moment's consternation, but because the gentleman was bending to kiss her hand, it went unnoticed. Each guest bowed and placed a proper kiss that almost touched her hand. Within minutes she decided that the guests were "perfect gentlemen," fashionably groomed, well-coiffed, honest-looking and jovial. One, called Ben Baker from Key Largo, had come in on his fourteen-ton schooner, the *Rapid*. He was a tall, gaunt, shrill-voiced man. There was also an old Captain Geiger, who mentioned his "buffalo"—as he called the top-floor cupola of his Key West house—where he spent much of his time watching passing vessels. He had arrived on the *Nonpareil*, his pet schooner. Sylvanus Pinder, a handsome and jolly man, struck Anne-Marie as a born politician. Their admiration was enough to be pleasing to her and yet not so immoderate that it offended Don Miguel, whom they all obviously respected. Their homage soothed her ego, making conversation less a chore than she had imagined possible, but the choice of topics was limited.

Just don't *think*, Anne-Marie, she told herself. None of this is real. It is only a dream from which you will awake.

The truth was, there was not much she could talk about other than the war, and even that was difficult for her, knowing they were all Confederate sympathizers. And she could not say, "I just lost my husband and my child. I am now living with another man who picked me up on the beach and I will now bear his child," though these thoughts were paramount in her mind. Nor could she discuss shipping, or its hazards—such as wreckers. And merely *thinking* of her family might have precipitated a tearful breakdown. An innocuous comment about the weather and her adjustments to it and her determination to learn Spanish had to suffice. Still, Anne-Marie's genuine interest in everything that the men had to say was charming in its evident sincerity, and she did learn that several men present were on their way to Key West to renew their salvaging licenses.

She was careful to hold her head high. Her upbringing, which fostered a prideful need to keep a stiff upper lip and show the world a smile, did just that. Such serenity eventually exhausted her, and she excused herself early and went up to bed.

Throughout the night, strains of music coming from the crews' party drifted through the house. A banjo, accordion, guitars and several fiddles accompanied an occasional rising chorus as the sons of Neptune serenaded the night and the females in the house. There were occasional bursts of delighted applause from the onlookers and she presumed there was even some dancing. Concepción had been in a dither all day and Anne-Marie could guess that she reigned like a queen with all the men present. Surely she had chosen some man for her favors by now. But Anne-Marie could dwell on this no longer and recollection of the events of the day could not be permitted. She closed her eyes and fell into a deep sleep. . . .

Early the next morning, long before the sun's rays slipped through the persiennes, awakening Anne-Marie, the visiting ships quietly slipped from the harbor and were on their way. A muted, groggy morning-after slowed the pace of the usual morning's activities to a shuffling, stumbling crawl. An occasional moan and groan from Don Miguel bespoke "a head the size of a bucket and a mouth of mohair," as he said. "Anne-Marie, we will die together," he groaned. "But please, let it be now."

She could not help but smile. A glass of lemonade and a few crackers on the night table beside her bed miraculously stemmed her morning sickness. Thoughtful Concepción! Don Miguel must have revealed her pregnancy, and even with all the attention Concepción had had last night, she had thought of her.

Late in the afternoon, when the pall of the wine had lifted, Don Miguel announced a will to live.

"You were marvelous last night. I don't know how you did it. You managed to charm everyone," he added sheepishly. "You're not just a pretty face and body. You have stamina—and above all you're a lady."

Compliments and kindness always overwhelmed her and Don Miguel was particularly adroit with his. Unless she were careful, she would awaken one morning and find herself totally pulled apart. "It was . . . a magnificent dinner," she stammered, trying to change the subject. "I never saw such a table."

"I don't want to talk about the food. I want to talk about you. I know a woman never forgets her first love or the man who made her a woman. I understand how you felt about your husband, but why spend one's life in only remembering? There can be only one *first* love, but there can be other loves. Take heart." He reached out, pulling her into his arms. She wanted to pry herself loose and push him away, but what was the use? She felt strangled by his kindness, but not revolted. Bitter tears rising, about to overflow, forced her to blink hard to stem their tide. In order to see her face, Don Miguel opened his arms and freed her. She looked like no other woman he could ever remember. But she was weeping now.

Before her he stood, blurred and wavering, washed in fuzzy light. His scrutiny was too much of an intrusion; she was still too defenseless, too vulnerable to pain. "Don Miguel, do not rush me. Let my wounds heal from the inside out. I don't want a lot of ugly scars." The trickle of tears ceased, and she determined they would be the last. Don Miguel looked pained, causing her to gather herself together and say, "Remember, I have a new language to learn." A note of tenderness in her voice erased the stress that ravaged his face, but the double meaning in her words was kind, if not entirely honest.

Resignation to remaining on Cayo de las Matas with Don Miguel in itself brought some peace of mind. Instead of scheming and hoping to leave, she would turn her attention to learning Spanish, making maternity clothes and infant wear and slowly taking on some of the responsibility of running the house. . . .

Because of the communication problem, Anne-Marie moved slowly when it came to matters of housekeeping. The servants were accustomed to doing things their own way, but clearly they welcomed her presence. She livened things in the household and Don Miguel spent more time at home, which meant more work for the staff, but less boredom. Even without much speech, her manner and her grace were appealing; they knew her troubles and opened their hearts to her. Perhaps most importantly, Don Miguel was happier than he had been in years and he showed it.

It was mid-April of 1865 when a ship came into the basin unexpectedly. Don Miguel, of course, recognized the vessel and her owner immediately, but he was taken by surprise and hurried down to the wharf. Anne-Marie stood on the terrace expectantly waiting for the two men to return to the house. When after a few moments they did not return, she too left the house, sensing that something extraordinary had happened to delay them. Don Miguel introduced Captain Jack Buckley, smack fisherman and incidental wrecker. "On April ninth, Lee surrendered at Appomattox in Virginia. The remaining Confederate armies surrendered soon afterward," said Don Miguel somberly.

Anne-Marie could have jumped for joy, but she also knew that Don Miguel was secretly a Unionist in Confederate territory. She also had no idea of Captain Buckley's loyalties and therefore remained stoic. But both men looked distraught. Then Don Miguel told her that Lincoln was dead.

"You cannot mean it? It cannot be true."

"He was shot in a theater by a Southern sympathizer," he added.

"The poor South! What vengeance will follow?"

At that moment she, Don Miguel and Jack Buckley became instantly a part of a national grief that would deify Lincoln and make him a martyr to the Northern cause—part of a wide and profound wave of emotion that would sweep the country and, in the end, have precious few signs of grace.

CHAPTER EIGHT

Bart Ramsden and Brian Delaney set sail on the *Catherine* with a fairly respectable crew. Bart had carefully supervised their selection.

Riding the Gulf Stream, they headed for Boston. "Just spare me the goddamned Florida Keys and the Jersey coast, and I'll be all right," said Bart. "I have no intention of getting blind drunk, but I don't want to look at either of those shores."

"I guess that's to be expected, sir," replied Brian. "It's good to be off again. I've had my fill of Key West—and I guess you have too."

"Not at all," replied Bart, wondering why Brian had made such a statement. As far as Brian knew, he had had a sweet berth with the exception of one incident.

"I'm happy to have my sea legs again," said Brian. "And now that we're off, will you share a toast with me to a pleasant voyage?"

"I think not, if you don't mind," replied Bart. "I intend to stay dry. I'm looking forward to seeing what the cook can produce."

"He damn well better produce. The galley is well stocked." Brian followed Bart into the cabin and opened a bottle of wine. "It's good to have you back, your old self, sir," he said, smiling.

"The Yankee dollar beckons. I'm willing to start over again, but I don't want to start poor."

"I know what you mean," said Brian. "When you think of those poor slobs below, you *know* you don't want to be poor."

Bart noted that his tone was laced with mockery, but let the statement pass. He never thought of his crew—collectively— in such terms. His men were a working force, an asset, and he was proud of them.

Much to Brian's disgruntlement Bart was not interested in the long, though profitable hauls, but instead wanted to get back to Key West again. He looked forward to seeing Consuelo, who could offer some measure of peace and affection. Nevertheless, it was two months before the *Catherine* put into that port again. Because the ship was at sea when the war ended and when Lincoln was killed, Bart missed the period of national mourning.

There was no need to approach Consuelo's front door cautiously. She would have had several hours' notice of his arrival. Old Captain Geiger, who had met Bart when Consuelo's husband was alive, would have spotted the *Catherine* from his cupola. Also a number of other wreckers would have had their eyes out. Each arrival was an event, and the word traveled fast.

"Who did you kick out of your bed this time?" joked Bart, hugging her so she couldn't breathe.

"A total of three men," she replied. "I told them that you refused to play musical beds and they scattered to the winds."

"Serves me right," said Bart, putting down his bag. "Now you've broken my heart."

"Not too badly. You look wonderful! What a transformation. You're obviously living right."

"What's right about two months at sea?"

"You tell me." Consuelo was equally glad to see Bart. However, one thing troubled her. After he had left, she contacted her informants as she had promised. Some days later she had her answer, and it was one she had not wished to hear. Brian, as she had suspected, was indeed the party who had hired the assailant who attacked Bart. She did not doubt her sources as they would have no interest in the affair, which included no reason to accuse Brian.

"The old place looks just the same," said Bart, looking around. "And you, you're a sight for sore eyes."

Strange lights danced in her shining jet hair and her shoulders gleamed with a soft creamy glow. The heady scent of her perfume enveloped him enticingly and the heat of his hunger for her spread like a brush fire. "Do I have to stand here burning or will you show me to my room?" he begged. His hand reached out to caress her silky shoulder and his eyes filled with yearning; his action was much more tender than his words.

"It is simply so good to see you yourself again. I'm overcome." She reached up to stroke his face and then led him up the stairs, her heart beating faster with every step. She had foolishly thought that all the fires quickened by his last stay would be cooled by now, but she was becoming increasingly aware that this had been a silly thought.

Once inside the room, he put down his bag and closed the door. "Consuelo, get out of that dress and lie with me. I cannot tell you—I can't even talk sensibly until I make love to you."

A silencing finger touched his lips. The old, unsure, shattered Bart was gone. In his place was a masterful, almost autocratic man. A deepening kiss touched off the passionate core inside of her, exploding throughout the softness of her body. She could feel the rapid beat of his heart, a wild serenade in tune with her need. Dropping her dress and petticoats to the floor as a child would leave discarded toys over which to stumble, she joined him on the bed.

"It has been such a long time," she whispered. "Months since I've felt like this."

Finally, they quieted down.

"You will never know the way I've missed you. When I floundered and fell back into grief, I could think of you and come out of it. You always understand, Consuelo. You never play games." He gave her hand a squeeze, emphasizing his words. "Thank you for not dallying through dinner. Thank you for responding in kind, for knowing my need, bandaging my wounds and for many things that I could not say before."

"Dear one, never accuse me of not playing games," she

said, caressing his face. "That dress, that heap on the floor, was constructed solely to entice you. It took four fittings to get that bodice just right."

"Your dressmaker is a jewel," replied Bart. "Hang on to her!"

Laughing like two children, they picked up their toys, combed their hair and descended the stairs ready to face the world, ready to slay dragons, to conquer greener fields—after dinner.

"How was Brian this trip?" asked Consuelo, thinking of her information about the beating, yet approaching the subject carefully.

"First rate," replied Bart, beaming. "I figure I made twenty percent more profit due simply to his expertise," he chuckled.

Bart's reply and obvious delight in Brian's work was enormously unsettling. Now she could not tell him what she had learned without a good deal of maneuvering. First, he would not believe her. Second, after rejecting her story he would not trust her. She would avoid the subject and hope that there would be no further incidents. After all, he had just spent two months with Brian and apparently nothing unpleasant had happened. She fingered the candlestick, then threw him a smile.

"Say, tell me something," said Bart, leaning back to ease his full stomach. "What did you find out about the ruffian who attacked me?"

"Nothing," replied Consuelo, with an open, innocent look, pressing her lips together to seal them against the truth. "The motive was robbery and the culprit will think twice before attacking anyone again. His face was thoroughly smashed."

"Really?"

Consuelo felt he was studying her, but she changed the subject and dismissed the thought as a product of her own guilt. She hated lying.

The following evening Bart went for a walk down to the waterfront. The *Sea Witch* had just come in and he rather enjoyed the business of watching another ship unloading. Freed of all responsibility himself, he found it interesting to watch crews other than his own. He tarried, hoping to see Tim, his former second mate. Soon the tall, familiar figure did in fact emerge. Bart waved and Tim's face broadened into a welcoming smile. "I'll see you shortly," called Tim excitedly. "Wait for me." Bart nodded his assent. . . .

"It is good to see you, sir," said Tim, heartily pumping his hand. "You look excellent."

"I must say the same," said Bart. "We've never had a second mate to equal you since you left."

"Those are kind words," replied Tim, "but tell me, sir, what happened after you got the message from Brian?"

"What message?"

"He didn't tell you? That's odd . . ."

"Start right at the beginning, Tim, because you've lost me somewhere. What message was I to get?"

"I was just about to leave on the *Sea Witch*. We were sailing at dawn and I had plenty to do. I was at Jackson Square when I overheard a darky talking about a girl who had been rescued on the beach on one of the keys. Right away I broke into the conversation and asked what she looked like and what her name was. The bloke didn't know. He hadn't seen her himself. He'd just heard tell of her from a friend who worked on a pineapple farm."

"And?"

"I looked all over for you. My time was running out, but I did manage to find the first mate, sir. I remember running after him. He promised to tell you about it. Of course, it might not have been your wife, but I felt it was worth an inquiry."

"I would have thought so too," replied Bart, his mind racing.

"Now, there's another thing I want to tell you. Do you remember the steward on that trip, a man by the name of Bains?"

"I remember a lot about that trip," replied Bart ruefully. "And I've read the log at least a hundred times. Yes, I remember Roger Bains."

"Well, I saw him in the West Indies. He was in his cups and talking freely. He said that you were the finest captain he had ever worked for, but he was scared to death of the first mate. He told me something that I've mulled over and over. He said that all the while that your lady was on deck, he had been standing in the companionway and—despite what the first mate said—she never went back to the cabin. She didn't pass him, sir. He was there all the time."

Bart had trouble hearing anything more that Tim said as his rage began to rise until it paralyzed him. He stood, planted like a tree, digesting Tim's disclosure. After a moment or two his vision failed, blotting out Tim's face and all about him. The hair on his neck ruffed as would a dog's. Lifting his feet like clumps of iron, hunched, clenched fists swinging at his side, he stalked off to begin a search for Brian, leaving Tim to return to his work. Bart entered bar after bar, scanning each room, murderously glaring at everyone and then departing, leaving a trail of quizzical faces.

On and on he plowed, thoroughly canvassing Front Street, until at last he reached the Louvre. The Louvre, an amorphous cluster of buildings, resembling the Parisian palace in name only, housed several clothing stores, barrooms and questionable businesses. There in a back room he spotted his quarry, seated with another man. Brian at first smiled and then, seeing the threatening expression on Bart's face, he blanched. Bart strode to the table and, violently grabbing his first mate by the shoulders, hauled him to his feet. With one massive stroke, a cut to the jaw, he sent Brian reeling. A second blow followed and then a third. Flying toward the floor, Brian's head struck the corner of a table that imparted a blow to the temple. As though swallowed by a fresh cavern in an earthquake, Brian's companion vanished into a crowd in another room. As Bart stared down at Brian, his flush face paled to gray. He knew then that Brian was dead. Deliberately and steadily he moved out of the building into the night. Inside he could hear women screaming. Turning his back on the shrieking figures bursting from doorways within the Louvre, he disappeared into the shadows of the night.

Consuelo waited for Bart for a time. Dinner was ready and, annoyed, she finally dined alone. This was unlike Bart, but then, Bart was a new man and she wondered if she would now have new problems to contend with. Pearl skittered around her mistress like a little black cat, fearful that she would feel the brunt of her mistress's ire. Eventually, hurt and angry and unresigned she observed to herself: Bouncing into bed with a man is always a mistake. I was stupid. Again and again she told herself, Men are all alike—only interested in one thing. And, having gotten it, he's probably now out drinking with the boys.

Feeling used and abused, she retired. However, one persistent little thought kept her from sleeping. Had he been attacked again? The chance was enough to allow worry to subjugate wrath. Perhaps he was behaving badly, but she had also lied. . . . Despite the excitement of the day, she spent hours tossing and turning.

Just as she was about to drop off, she heard men's voices outside, followed by heavy footsteps on her porch and an insistent rapping at the door. Snatching a robe and lighting a lamp, she hurried downstairs and unbolted the door. There stood the sheriff and two of his deputies. "Sorry to trouble you, ma'am," he apologized, "but we're looking for Captain Bartholomew Ramsden."

"He's not here," she replied. "What's happened? He's a friend." Her evident shock confirmed to the sheriff the truth of her statement.

"He's just murdered his first mate, Brian Delaney, ma'am. He's a dangerous man. Let us know if you see him or hear anything from him."

"That's impossible. . . . They're . . . good friends," she stuttered.

"We have many witnesses, ma'am. And, as I said, we'd appreciate hearing if you see him." With a tip of his hat the sheriff departed, leading his men—not regulars, but two men quickly rounded up for the hunt.

Oh, dear God, what has he done? He must have learned something about Brian. What? Her silent questions flew like birds as she paced without answers. Finally, she dragged herself upstairs. On only one point could she be thankful: she had not been one to fuel the flames by revealing that Brian had instigated the attack in the alleyway. From someone else Bart got incriminating information and acted upon it.

Almost immediately something struck her window sharply.

99

Then came another *clink*. Perhaps someone was tossing pebbles to draw her attention, possibly with word from Bart. Flying downstairs—this time in the dark—she again unbolted the door and Bart himself slipped in. "Come upstairs," she whispered. "We must talk. The sheriff has been here."

"I knew he would be," he replied. "I saw him and climbed into your big tree out there and waited until he left. They won't be back tonight."

"So, Brian is dead. Did you mean to kill him?" she asked fearfully.

"No, I didn't intend to, but I've never known such hatred for anyone or such anger in my life. I'm afraid I'd beat him again, but I didn't know his head would crash into the table. That was what killed him." Bart's head bowed, and closing his eyes he pressed his own forehead into long powerful fingers that for moments afterward left their mark.

"Tell me how it happened . . ."

Moving to sit at the foot of her bed, Bart explained the events of the evening, his meeting with Tim and hearing his story, then the search for Brian and finally finding him. "I knew the police would come here and so I waited. Christ, are they slow!"

They found themselves laughing, the nervous laughter of an anticlimax, but not for long.

"You realize the consequences are serious. If they find you, you could spend years in prison. You could even be hanged. Your ship will be confiscated at once, and even the authorities in New Jersey will be looking for you. I don't know how to help you—except temporarily."

"Don't think I haven't thought of all that. As I was perched in that damn tree, I thought of everything. You realize, don't you, Consuelo, that there is a remote possibility that Anne-Marie is alive?"

She had, and for a moment the possibility shook her, but soon reason prevailed. Had the girl been Anne-Marie, she would have appeared certainly in this length of time. "I fear you may be clutching a straw," she whispered sadly. "In the light of what you face now, we can't dwell on some faint, utterly remote hope . . ."

"I know," he murmured. Then, gathering force, he added, "I can't endanger you, yet I could not leave without explaining. I've stayed only for that and I shall leave at once."

Slowly, Consuelo gathered her reeling thoughts. This was no time to be swayed by emotions away from clear thinking. "I can hide you here for a while—until we find a way for you to escape once things quiet down. You will need to grow a beard and you'll need different clothes." Building a defense for this good man would take time. Careful planning was required.

"By tomorrow—in a few hours—they'll be back to search this place. They'll tear the place apart, Consuelo, and if they find me, you'll become an accomplice. I won't have that!" Bart frowned heavily, pausing for thought. Then he made a move as if to leave.

Consuelo grasped his shoulders firmly. Her eyes and her voice were determined. "No, listen to me," she hissed. "There's a place here in this house where they'll never find you. It's a hidden pit—underground," she added, visibly shuddering. "But you will be safe there. Whenever anyone, anyone at all, approaches the house, you must go down into that shaft and wait. The rest of the time you will be able to move quietly about the house. We must always be careful to keep our voices down and you must not light a lamp in your room. You're going to feel like a prisoner here, but it will be the most comfortable prison I know of."

"Do you really think that would work?" Bart asked incredulously. "I can't involve you—you've already been too good to me..."

His distress brought her to her feet, needing movement to quiet her concern. She must not break down. Bart was a motherlode of stubbornness and obviously he could be reckless. With every muscle strained and tense, his face now looked as if a mask had been dropped over it. He *must* put himself in my hands, she thought—and this meant that he had to feel he could trust her. Again she thought of what she had not told him earlier. Had he known that she lied, he would not have trusted her even though that knowledge might have reinforced his actions, and vindicated him somewhat. Time enough for that.

"Come, let me show you," she said, firmly taking him by the elbow and steering him into her late husband's bedroom across the hall from the guest room that Bart used. The dim light of early dawn filtered through the shutters, illuminating her goal, a small night table. In it, from a hidden panel behind a drawer, Consuelo extracted a flat iron key. Dropping to her knees, she ran her fingers along the floor, carefully inching her way along.

"It must be right about here," she said, looking for a tiny notch in the polished flooring. She moved her fingers. "Yes, here's the lock right under the leg of the bed. Help me move the bed a trifle." He did. Then, taking the key, she inserted it into the lock and made a small turn. "Now lift," she said, moving aside so that he could raise the invisible section of flooring that comprised the carefully carpentered trapdoor. A black hole appeared. The smell of cold, damp, dank air assaulted their nostrils. Drawing the lamp closer, Bart could make out a descending iron ladder built into a cement wall. The vertical shaft, just large enough to accommodate a man, ran down through the house into the ground.

"Not even Pearl knows that this is here," said Consuelo. "She will only know that you disappear." She looked into his eyes, seeking approbation.

For a moment Bart was silent in amazement. "I would imagine that many a gun has been stored here," he said finally, "and maybe slaves?"

"Guns, gunpowder, gold, silver, many things . . ." said Consuelo, now whispering.

"The passage is built into the wall between the dining room and the kitchen, where it is hidden on both sides by cupboards. Under the house it adjoins the cistern, which is not as big as it looks. So even if they search under the house, there is nothing to see. The house would have to burn to the ground to reveal it."

"It's damnably clever," mused Bart. "And I will accept your hospitality because I don't think the devil himself could find me here—or implicate you."

"In 1859 we had a terrible fire in Key West. It began in a warehouse owned by a Mr. Shaefer, who, people say, possibly

102

set it himself. It jumped to other warehouses and buildings, including a house that stood on this site. Finally, a Mr. Mulrennon saved the rest of the town. He got a keg of gunpowder from Fort Taylor and, entering his own house, with the fire raging beneath him, put the keg in place, laid a train of powder and blew up his home. This prevented the fire from spreading and burning the whole town. When my husband rebuilt this house he added the shaft.

"Be on the lookout for scorpions, roaches, possibly small snakes—and perhaps even a ghost. I don't think you'll ever have to be down there long, but it looks like an ideal home for such varmints!"

Her look of revulsion was ignored by Bart. "They'll just have to move over, that's all," he replied, still studying the shaft that looked awfully good to him. "And I promise not to scream," he reassured her in a falsetto feminine tone, and smiled.

Carefully he replaced the door, pocketing the key.

"We must be enormously careful," warned Consuelo. "The neighbors cannot be allowed to suspect there's a resident 'visitor' in the house. This means your clothes cannot be hung outside to dry. Sheets will be on the beds longer. Every detail that could conceivably give you away will have to be guarded against."

"How did the sheriff know to look for me here?"

"When you weren't at Russell House, the sheriff would have questioned a few old-timers like Captain Geiger, who may have suggested several known friends or even a house of prostitution. This is a little town, you know. Secrets are hard to keep."

"And Pearl, can she be trusted?"

"For a while, I'm sure. She has an incriminating past that I'm aware of. She knifed a man once. I've protected her and for that reason she's been grateful and loyal. But under real pressure she might break. Right now we'll have to take our chances with her until I can think of something."

"I have some money—fortunately here in my baggage— that I must give you because with all my things it will be confiscated as soon as the sheriff gets a few hours sleep. Use it as you see fit. You might pick up some used clothing for me. I'll also need some forged seaman's identification papers and that may be expensive. If you want to send Pearl on a vacation at my expense, do so. Do you have a lawyer you can trust?"

"You haven't mentioned anything that is impossible in this town," replied Consuelo. "You must not worry, but you'll have to be patient. For a few days this house will be watched around the clock. I don't know how you'll take the inactivity. I'll also have to move carefully."

"I hate this," said Bart, thinking of his isolation and dependence. "I hope you're not afraid." He scanned her face and saw only grim determination.

"I'm not," she said, speaking truthfully. The words came out with great conviction.

Bart reached into a small iron box and pulled out what appeared to be several thousand dollars.

"Don't put all that money in my hands," she whispered, aghast. "You know where you can keep it safely. Just give me money when I ask for it."

"There's one more thing," said Bart, "but I think that it's important. You must try to find Tim Clayton. He was on the *Sea Witch*. He's a witness. Explain things and get him to make a statement to the authorities. His testimony could substantiate several pleas."

Consuelo's blood ran cold. She thought Bart was going to mention the possibility that Anne-Marie might be alive, and that he might ask her to open this investigation. But he did not. The gulf that was about to spring between them never materialized. She was not averse to protecting Bart at great personal risk, but to search for his wife would be too much for her to bear.

"Tim's statement is almost the first thing," she said, "but not quite. First, I'd like to handle Pearl. I think an understanding friend can use her for a week or two. I can convince Pearl that she should be out of the house to avoid questioning on her past. Then I'll find Tim Clayton."

He wrapped his long arms about her, drawing her hair through his fingers. "How can I thank you?"

"I'm sure there will be ways. Lie down now on my bed and

try to get some sleep. I don't dare join you. The next few hours are terribly important. I need some coffee to help me think, and sleep would be impossible for me anyway."

Consuelo dressed quickly, driven by a nervous energy that almost divorced her from her normal self. Before she left the room he was, astonishingly, asleep. She stared down at him, shaking her head in disbelief, and slipped down the stairs.

In the kitchen she made a pot of coffee and then sat down at her desk to compose a letter to her oldest friend, a woman of French descent, Mimi Lacrosse. They often exchanged notes, the custom being part of Mimi's formal French upbringing. Suddenly she changed her mind. It would be better to have nothing in writing.

As soon as Pearl appeared, Consuelo explained the events of the previous evening. "Captain Ramsden has vanished, but I expect the sheriff this morning and I'm sure the house will be watched. I don't want them questioning you. They will ask a thousand questions and you may get nervous and act suspiciously, which would get you into trouble—if you know what I mean. Now have yourself a little breakfast and then come with me. I'm going to ask Madame Lacrosse to keep you for a week or so. You'll be safe there. You'll continue to get your pay, so don't be worried. I'll manage without you for a short time."

Pearl's eyes widened with fear and disbelief in everything that had happened and was happening. She admired Captain Ramsden. "Oh, the poor man," she moaned sympathetically.

"Now hurry and put a few things together," ordered Consuelo, allowing a frightened tone and anxious look to do their work. "I'll get you back here as soon as possible."

Together the two women walked quickly the few blocks to Mimi's. The earliness of the visit surprised the staff, but Mimi received Consuelo in her bedroom. There, propped by great square French pillows, Mimi was breakfasting from a tray.

"This is an intrusion," cried Consuelo, "but please forgive me."

"It must be an emergency to get you up at this hour," cracked

Mimi, obviously pleased to see her friend and to be a part of some excitement.

Making certain they could not be overheard, Consuelo explained that Captain Ramsden—unjustly charged with murder—had been a guest in her home. Consequently, she expected considerable questioning. Because of Pearl's past, with which Mimi was familiar, she wanted Pearl out of the house. "It seems to be the only decent thing to do. Will you keep her for a week or two until things die down? I will, of course, continue her wages and reimburse you for her food."

"You've come to the right place. I can always use another servant," cooed Mimi. "Do let me know the denouement..."

"I'll keep you informed. Just keep Pearl busy," cried Consuelo, throwing her friend a kiss.

Once again home, Consuelo collapsed in a kitchen chair. Her first objective had been achieved.

CHAPTER NINE

Consuelo doubted that Bart realized a weakness in his defense. True, he had not intended to kill his first mate, but he had. As a captain, he had become accustomed to supreme power, which he might feel would afford him some measure of security now—if he could only speak his piece. In Key West the prestige of his family, as a backup, was a long way off. Furthermore, he was in an outpost where a good many righteous people were struggling to establish law and order. They would view this case as one to set an example to their hometown rowdies. Judge Thomas Boynton, one of the youngest men ever appointed to a bench in the United States, had just succeeded Judge William Marvin, a towering intellect. Boynton would be anxious to prove himself. Judge Marvin, while on the bench, had published "A Treatise Upon the Law of Wreck and Salvage," which had become a standard authority in the admiralty courts of England and the United States. Consequently, Bart's position frightened Consuelo more than she dared disclose. And now, another even more personally unsettling question loomed: Was Anne-Marie alive? If Bart were acquitted, would she lose him to his wife?

Abruptly, Consuelo's meditations were interrupted by a loud knocking. Deliberately she shrieked, "Just a moment, please!"

107

The cry was unladylike, but Bart had to be alerted. She gave him time to descend into his hiding place, fumbling with her buttons as she answered the door. Again it was the sheriff, with two new assistants whom she recognized. "I'm so happy to see you, gentlemen. Have you found anything? Please come in." She waved them to chairs.

"I haven't been able to sleep a wink. You have no idea how frightened I am." One dainty hand crossed to her heart as she batted her eyelashes. Her voice lowered. "Having already endured one tragedy in my life, I thought that would do me. I would not want to lose a treasured friend or to find my trust abused if the captain is a murderer." She touched a handkerchief to her cheek.

"We realize that, ma'am, and please feel assured of our protection. Did Captain Ramsden leave any belongings here?"

"Why, yes, he did, but not a sufficient quantity, I fear, to warrant his coming back for. You may see for yourself." She spoke, nodding toward the stairs, but not rising, apparently waiting instead for the next question.

"He was a friend of yours?" continued the sheriff.

"I've known him for at least five years. Two or three times he stayed here while loading and unloading his ship. He lost his wife not long ago. He was extremely distraught. The poor girl was washed overboard while only the first mate, Brian Delaney, now dead—killed, you say—was on deck. Their child was also lost in her arms. Do you know what transpired between the two men? Did they quarrel? They had been friends for many years."

"Then he mentioned no bad blood between them to you?" pressed the sheriff.

"I had no chance to talk with him, sir. He brought his luggage here and then left. Come upstairs with me and you may inspect his things."

They all ascended the stairs. The doors to the bedrooms were all open to the hall. The shutters were closed, so the rooms were darkened and noiseless. Consuelo threw open the shutters in the guest room, admitting a bright shaft of light that almost exploded into the room. The bed stood neatly made. Bart's satchel, closed and locked, rested on a stand nearby. No other personal belongings were there. Unobtrusively, the men searched the other rooms.

Consuelo swallowed hard, fighting down wild fears that some giveaway noise or overlooked detail—such as a warm bed—would be discovered. But outwardly, she was serene. Finally, taking Bart's satchel, they descended the stairs and, apologizing for the intrusion, departed.

Consuelo lingered on the veranda, watching them round the corner, and then reentered the house. She looked down at her hands, too long steady, now trembling. Weak-kneed, she climbed the stairs to meet Bart standing in the doorway. His looming figure startled her, but steadied by the banister, her composure returned. "My heart has been in my mouth. I knew you were sleeping, but I didn't think I had time to run up to warn you. I held them downstairs until I was sure you would have heard our voices."

"You don't need to worry. I'm used to catnaps," he replied. He could decide to sleep for ten minutes and awake as if by the clock.

Calmly, Consuelo said, "Now that they're gone, I'll change my clothes and go look for the *Sea Witch* and Tim Clayton." Slipping into a street dress and ducking to look into a mirror as she popped on a feathered hat, she surveyed her flushed face. "I feel like a wild woman," she said, dabbing her nose gently with a powder puff—the badge of a wicked woman, the ladies would say if they knew. "Keep your fingers crossed." With that she was off.

It was not going to be difficult to locate the *Sea Witch*, Consuelo thought. Nevertheless, her instinct had been to run, but carefully she restrained it, knowing that anything other than a leisurely pace would attract attention.

She was forced to halt and greet several old and wordy friends, including John White. "Old John," who owned the general store, was one of the wealthiest men in Key West. He not only managed a large business, but bought real estate, built and rented houses and had an interest in almost everything in town. He commenced his rent collecting rounds at an early hour and greeted his dilatory tenants with the cry, "You're sleeping on your rent." With those on time he gossiped. Consequently, he was not a man to be ignored. Old John was hauled slowly around the streets at a snail's pace in an old buggy drawn by an even older horse, gossiping as he went. To Consuelo he called, "I'll be glad to give a lovely lady a ride," his keen eyes peering above a short grizzled beard.

"I need to walk," replied Consuelo, "but I thank you anyway." Any other ride might have been welcome, but she knew she could walk faster than his horse even if she were blindfolded. She smiled her ladylike thanks.

When she finally reached the *Sea Witch* and introduced herself to the captain, she learned that Tim had been given a forty-eight-hour leave. Her heart sank.

"He may come back to the ship to sleep, madame—and then again he might not." He paused awkwardly for want of words appropriate to explain to a lady. But the captain seemed to be a nice man, so Consuelo pressed her case.

"One of your colleagues is in trouble, sir, the captain of the *Catherine*. I know you must have heard of the incident by now. Captain Ramsden has disappeared. However, being wanted for murder, he may lose his ship before the case is resolved. I believe Tim Clayton can give evidence that may clear Captain Ramsden. He was on the *Catherine* when Captain Ramsden's wife and child were washed overboard. For that reason I'm trying to find Mr. Clayton. I would be much obliged if you would put him in touch with me."

The pathos in her voice reached the captain, who kindly promised to see that Mr. Clayton would get her message.

There was nothing to do but return home. Having no idea what Tim Clayton looked like, she could hardly search him out on the street or in bars. There was no hurry about arranging purchase of clothes for Bart as he could not leave until he had a beard and papers. The whole situation was so untidy! Why did men get themselves into such trouble?

Now feeling the effects of the lost sleep and the harrowing early-morning hours, Consuelo's head throbbed. Depressed further by the unproductive visit to the *Sea Witch*, she made her stately way home. Bart would be eagerly anticipating her arrival, but she was returning unsuccessful in her mission.

Dreading his disappointment and aching with fatigue, she stumbled into the house.

"I'm tired—exhausted," she said, crankily, on seeing him.

"They couldn't have sailed so soon?" he asked. His voice seemed flat or his disappointment too artfully controlled.

"No, he has a forty-eight-hour leave and heaven only knows where he is. But I have been up all night and I feel as though the ball is over and the wine has gone flat and the cake is stale. You must let me sleep so that later I can go out and conquer the world or at least accomplish something." She tossed her hat on her dressing table, freed her hair and threw herself onto the bed.

"As soon as I've had some sleep I will tell you every bit of minutiae—every bird that chirped and every sailor's leer, that I really didn't even notice now that I think about it. It was just a promenade. Believe me, if anything important happened, I would tell you now."

"You poor dear! I'm so sorry," replied Bart, stretching out beside her. "Go to sleep. Don't worry, the slightest noise will awaken me. Then I'll have no choice but to get you up."

Hours later, after a parade of strange, disjointed dreams, Consuelo awakened. Her movements, although quiet and measured, brought Bart awake. She prepared a supper tray for them both, mostly composed of leftovers cooked for the night before—which now seemed like days ago.

Rested and nourished, the world seemed a much more hospitable place.

"Before we go any further, I think I should see Mr. Magbee, my lawyer," she said. "He's clever. . . . He often had rather sage advice for my husband and he has kept many thieves out of jail or what we call the 'Sweat Box,' the city lockup—it's the caboose of a wrecked ship at the foot of Duval Street. The man is apt to bleed one dry, they say, but I'll drop by his office on the ruse of talking to him about a property deal that has been hanging fire a long time. I may be able to engage him in a conversation and learn something that may be helpful without giving him the whole story. I don't want him to smell my interest—or money," said Consuelo.

"Good luck to you, but tell him everything if you have to."

"I may be able to throw out a little bait," she said rather mysteriously. "I'll have to play it by ear and you'll have to trust me, I'll be back as soon as I can."

Mr. Magbee was still at his desk, although his clerk had mercifully departed, when Consuelo entered his offices. She had dressed carefully in one of her most becoming suits, one that had been designed to please men, not merely fashion. She had selected a matching hat, which she wore at a rather rakish angle. Magbee sat before a heavy rolltop desk, the lines of which were echoed by the roll of his belly. He was pleased to see her. "You grow more beautiful every day, Consuelo. How has a wealthy, attractive widow like you managed to stay unmarried?"

"Well, you've never proposed, Mr. Magbee," she smiled.

"Ha! You'd be the death of me," he responded. "Too young for your husband or me. But seriously, what can I do for you?"

Consuelo went into the small matter that had been her excuse for calling, which they quickly dispatched. Then she said, "I'm sure you heard of the terrible thing that happened yesterday— the captain who killed his first mate and then vanished. What will happen to his ship? I know the captain, you know."

"Oh, I'm sure that's been confiscated. It will be auctioned right away. Were you thinking of investing?"

"As a matter of fact, it did cross my mind. My money is pretty well tied up for a while. Will the auction come up soon?" Consuelo hoped her manner was casual.

"Probably right away," he replied, his voice rising. "A large vessel like that can't just sit in the harbor without a crew to watch her. Suppose a storm were to come up? From the captain's runaway absence the court infers and presumes his guilt."

"Strange, isn't it," replied Consuelo fighting to hold her composure, "how fast the mills of the gods can grind sometimes and then at other times how interminably long one waits for a legal decision."

"Maritime law, my dear. Another set of rules. I hear they've found guns aboard. A bit late to do the South any good."

"Really?" she replied. "I know Captain Ramsden to be a Unionist. I wonder if those guns had anything to do with the killing? But Mr. Magbee, I've taken too much of your time already," said Consuelo, ready to run from the room. "And I must dress for dinner. Please take care of that little matter for me and I hope to see you soon."

"Always a pleasure, my dear," he replied, rising to see her to the door. "Are you sure you can get home all right? It will soon be dark."

"Of course. Thank you for your time."

Consuelo no sooner reached the walk when she met Euphemia Lightbourne, headmistress of *the* private school in town and one of the most active members of St. Paul's Episcopal Church. Every moment of her time out of school hours was devoted to community affairs. Euphemia had no end of projects in which she wanted Consuelo's involvement; they ranged from choir practice to tending the afflicted.

Twenty minutes later Consuelo escaped this pillar of insistent benevolence and hurried home.

"This has not been our day. Your emissary is a failure." Bart smiled at her woebegone wail. She related the details of her visit with Magbee.

At the mention of guns, his jaw dropped. "Don't worry, I'm resigned to losing the ship. The presence of guns comes as a shock. So Brian was smuggling contraband and sticking with me, protected because I ran a clean ship. I'm going to have a hard time fighting my way out of this, girl."

She silently agreed.

The next morning Consuelo again left early, making her way toward the harbor. There was always the possibility that the captain of the *Sea Witch* would forget to give her message to Tim Clayton and at that moment nothing was so important as getting his statement before the appropriate authorities.

A resplendent sun bathed everything in a clear crystal light that bounced back and forth from leaf to leaf, stone to stone, as if reflected in a thousand mirrors. People moved jauntily, catching the excitement of a dancing, still-cool morning breeze, bringing everything in its path to life. Suddenly, the breadth of the port opened to Consuelo's shocked search. The berth of the *Sea Witch* was empty. A few tiny white caps swirling as bits of foam on the glistening surface of the water played before her. Tim was gone. It was impossible! Perhaps the ship had simply changed berths, but a second glance confirmed the first. A ship that size could not hide. Her heart sank.

Fernando Moreno, an underwriter's agent, strolled to her side. Courtly and polite, he was to be seen every afternoon taking his constitutional on a pacing pony, out to the bush and the South Beach. He was deaf and carried a silver ear trumpet, which strangers often took for a cornet.

"Mr. Moreno," cried Consuelo, "have you seen the *Sea Witch*?" He looked shocked. She repeated her question, but this time he put the trumpet to his ear and seemed greatly relieved. His distinguished manners prohibited him from saying that he thought she had said "sea bitch," but his shock and delay in answering unnerved Consuelo. The *Sea Witch* had set sail before dawn.

It would not be easy to return bearing this news. One by one, doors seemed to be closing in front of Bart.

Her instinct was to slip quietly into the house. Then she realized this might frighten her refugee and drive him unnecessarily into the black shaft. So she carefully shuffled her feet at the door as she fumbled for the key before easing it into the lock. . . .

"She's gone. It's unbelievable, but true. The *Sea Witch* is gone. What can I say?" Under Bart's stoic gaze she felt cold as ice. "Don't look at me as if it were my fault," she cried.

"Here, here, my dear, you misunderstand. I'm not blaming you. I'm angered at myself for all the trouble I've caused. All this will take longer than we thought, that's all," he replied meekly.

"I feel as though I've let you down terribly. You have counted on me and I've failed. I should have sat there at the wharf and waited or asked how long the ship would be in port." Consuelo was ready to weep, but the tears would not fall. Their bathing release would not come so easily. . . .

Soon after, in the small wooden courthouse, a dozen or so gentlemen bid on the *Catherine* at auction. A sealed bid proffered by the owner of the *Sea Witch* was the highest.

The news made Consuelo visibly ill. She should not have

talked to the captain. He deliberately whisked Tim out of the way so that no defense testimony would interfere with the sale of the *Catherine*. Bart had left everything in her hands and, slowly but surely, she was ruining him.

Consuelo attended the auction, feeling helpless, but certain it was important to be present. The second highest bidder at the auction was Ben Baker. Unknown to Consuelo, he was a frequent guest of Don Miguel at Los Claveles. Baker was considered the king of wreckers in Key West. He owned a large two-story house at the corner of Whitehead and Caroline streets, diagonally across from the Stone building, where the United States court tried the salvage cases. He also owned a plantation on Key Largo where he raised pineapples. Tall, hook-nosed and hawk-eyed, he was in those days nearly always the master wrecker at every wreck on the reef. In this depressed moment, he was the last person Consuelo felt like chatting with and yet he called to her. "Consuelo, how are you? It has been a long time since I've seen you—regrettably."

"I'm very well, Ben, and I hope the same for you," replied Consuelo, rising to the occasion.

"I'm sure you saw, I was beat out. I really wanted the *Catherine*, but she brought a good deal more than I think she's worth."

Muttering something to the effect that often price has little to do with value, Consuelo got away from Ben Baker as fast as she could. The thought of a group of men, like vultures, feeding on misfortune was almost too much to bear with civility....

Bart took her news about the sale of the *Catherine* in a way she had not expected. "I'm not married to one ship, dear girl. But every vessel of mine has been well maintained and others know it. Slowly, I've bought bigger and better ships and sold them for a profit. If I can clear myself of this present mess, the court will award me the proceeds of the sale, so all is not necessarily lost."

"You are an eternal optimist," said Consuelo.

"Perhaps. But there is one point on which we can take heart. The captain of the *Sea Witch* will soon be back. I doubt that he has gone further than Tampa. He saw an opportunity to pick up the *Catherine*, and it was not such a dastardly one at that. Tim's testimony a few weeks later will be just as good. Meanwhile, the captain got his hands on a much better ship than the *Sea Witch*. Probably for weeks Tim has been telling the captain what a great ship the *Catherine* is, so with inside information about what he was getting, he could afford a high bid. Knowledge of a ship is a tremendous advantage. Temporarily removing Tim from the scene only inconveniences me. You know, I might have done the same . . ."

His words were reassuring. But they both understood that Tim's testimony would not be sufficient to clear Bart of murder *and* gunrunning. Some magistrate would need a good deal of assurance that Bart's actions were warranted and that he was not guilty of gunrunning before he would release the thousands of dollars in the city's coffers from the sale of the *Catherine*. It might be a long fight. Furthermore, unless new evidence could be found, it would be hard to prove that Bart knew nothing of the contraband aboard.

Roger Bains, the steward on the fateful voyage, would be hard to find. Bart was not free to search, and Consuelo could not recognize him if he happened to come into port. So Bart would have to escape.

There was nothing to do but proceed with the plan to get Bart off "The Rock" with false papers. Clothes still had to be purchased and his beard was not more than a scruffy virgin coat.

Getting the false papers took her back to one of the waterfront bars which a number of unscrupulous characters were known to frequent. The owner of one, named Wooleye because of two large cataracts that were slowly obscuring his vision, owed a favor to Consuelo.

Wooleye was obviously surprised to see Consuelo and drew upon courtesies long out of use to greet her. "I don't see too well now, ma'am, but your figure in the light of the doorway caught what sight I have left," he said, his smile revealing a stubble of broken brown teeth.

"May I talk with you a moment?" she asked, feeling considerably ill at ease in his establishment.

"I'm honored," he replied, leading her to a closed door.

116

"I could use seaman's papers—six feet, one hundred eighty pounds, age twenty-six or thereabouts, American, blue eyes, fair-haired—the rest is up to someone's imagination," she told him. With that she reached into her bosom and pulled out a few crisp bills which she pressed into his hands. He fingered the notes carefully.

"You'll need more than this."

"That's for you, Wooleye, to insure no leakage. How much more will you need?"

"How about a hundred?" he replied, bearing forward to see her, almost suffocating her with a beery breath.

"Come, come, Wooleye! He hasn't that kind of money."

"But you're most generous, ma'am, yourself..."

"You overestimate my generosity. And I just might want to keep that young man around, you old scoundrel! Seventy-five and no more, payable when the papers are in my hands."

Wooleye seemed to be thinking.

"When can I pick them up?" asked Consuelo.

"Give me about a week. It's not so simple any more. 'The Scribe' has to be careful with the numbers and he has to be sober."

"So, it all comes back to you anyway, doesn't it?" noted Consuelo, shaking her head and smiling an exasperated smile.

Two other questions, unasked, hung in her mind. But to ask them would be exceedingly dangerous. Both would surely pinpoint Bart and leave them both open to blackmail. The first: Who dealt with guns for the Confederacy? The second: Is there any truth to the rumor that a young girl was picked up on the keys? Moreover, the thought of an affirmative answer to the second question chilled her, for it revealed an inner conflict that filled her with shame. So she did not ask her questions.

A small wave of disappointment clouded Bart's face when she told him the papers might take a week to prepare, but it was soon erased. "I guess it will take that long to get my beard in shape," he offered dryly. "I'm also ready for a change of clothes, as soon as you can handle it."

"I can tend to that right away," she said. Then she told him that she had almost asked Wooleye if he knew who had been

117

dealing in guns. "But having let my big mouth go too far once, this time I kept it shut. It would not be too hard for the old coot to put two and two together. Blackmail is surely one of his trades."

Bart concurred in her judgment. "You're brilliant, Consuelo. I'm in awe of you. Besides, I'm not ready to concede yet that you made a mistake in talking to the captain of the *Sea Witch*. A kick is sometimes a shove in the right direction. Time will tell."

Consuelo's spirits were lifted by his approval, and so with some relief she went out to buy him a change of clothing. A secondhand clothing store frequented by the poor in the Louvre seemed just right. A sign that read We Buy Only *Clean* Clothes proved an overstatement. Still, she picked through a table of men's pants and shirts until she found a suitable combination.

"My yardman ruined his clothes working on my trees," she told the proprietor, "so I thought I'd try to replace them. It seems like the decent thing to do, don't you think?"

He, of course, agreed, and with the clothes wrapped in an old newspaper she returned home.

Bart was surveying her purchases when they heard a determined knocking at the door. They looked at each other with frozen stares.

"Quick, hide! Leave the clothes on the paper just as they are," said Consuelo.

Suddenly, she noticed a tray on the bed with two plates, two glasses and two sets of silver. Snatching one of each article, she ran to the kitchen, deposited them in a cupboard and then went to the door, feigning calm.

The sheriff and two of his men stood there, a search warrant in hand.

Wordlessly the men moved through the house, room to room, looking under beds and everywhere a man could hide.

Slowly, shock and worry gave way ostensibly to indignation and anger. The sheriff pointed to the unwrapped men's clothing. "And pray tell," he asked, "who are these things for?"

"They're for my yardman. You have found nothing incriminating in this house and you won't for there is nothing to find! I would appreciate it if you would leave immediately." Her eyes left no doubt as to the sincerity of her words and sheepishly the men departed.

"That was close," said Bart. "Obviously, they watched you buy the clothes and knew you visited Wooleye. Now we know for sure that you are watched—and that's something. We might have gotten careless, you know."

"Now I'm worried about picking up the papers."

"We'll think of a way," he reassured her.

Within a few days there was another knock at the door. Again Bart sprang into hiding. With every step Consuelo braced herself for the dreaded encounter. A vagrant selling sponges stood at the door. "I have the sponges you wanted, ma'am," he said.

"I'm sorry, but I don't need any sponges," she countered, almost closing the door in his face. "Now, please, go away."

"I have reason to believe that you do. This one is seventy-five dollars," he replied. "Take a minute to examine them," he cautioned.

Suddenly aware of the man's intention, Consuelo pretended to examine several, playing the game. "Please wait just a moment. I'll get the money."

Returning, yet hiding just inside the door, she carefully extracted a small roll of paper that looked as genuine as a diamond. Then she slipped the money into the small slit in the sponge and returned that sponge for another. "I think I'd rather have this one," she declared.

"Thank you."

The "vendor" departed and within seconds two deputies were at her door. This time they did not search the house, but carefully examined the sponge. Finding nothing but their own chagrin, they departed. A furious Consuelo tamped down her anger, but it took every ounce of self-control she had.

She then made a quick visit to Mimi's to delay Pearl's return. "They are harassing me, Pearl, you cannot imagine what it is like! But I think it is coming to an end. I have to get you back soon before I either starve to death or just plain die of dirt."

"I'm worried about your washing, ma'am."

"Don't be. You know I have plenty of things. I'll come for you when the underwear runs out!"

Consuelo turned to Mimi. "As long as the sheriff is bouncing into my house with a warrant and searching every inch—even the attic—I don't think Pearl should be there."

"Nor do I. You're under a strain and I doubt that you've been eating well. You must come to dinner tonight," insisted Mimi. Consuelo had no chance to refuse under Mimi's imperative tone. "We'll expect you at eight."

Difficult as the evening would be, Consuelo knew that to accept would be a good idea. Among all her friends she was most at ease with Mimi. Still, she hated to leave Bart.

Now that many of the details of Bart's escape were falling into place, Consuelo became increasingly aware that she was deeply in love with him. He was strong—that was the great thing. He was shrewd, but at the same time kind. But his appeal to her lay chiefly in that he remained marvelously young. His boyishness colored his most profound statements, his every movement, his appetites and his lovemaking. It was this that captured her imagination and led her down this strange path with him. His strengths brought out strengths in her—an invigorating sense of her importance and self-worth. Then there was the wild appeal that had nothing to do with thought. Daily her love for him grew, bringing back her youth to match his, raising her to heights she had forgotten.

All the little fears, the moments of abject terror were nothing compared to the joy of his presence—his smile, his tender caress, and the compliments that were bells ringing. She dared not think of the future without him. This love, this extraordinary feeling, had begun to spill over, taking charge of her life. It filled her, stirred her blood and rocked her soul.

Spontaneously her arms would lift and find their way around his neck, drawing him to her, binding him to her. Still, all the time she knew that the bonds would not hold. The inappropriateness that bothered her—her age—did not bother Bart. Love did not bother him. He took and he gave. For the moment, for the hour, for the day, they were made for each other. No two people could have needed each other more. To expect that

120

this would last forever was to expect that the sea would not erode the beach or that the wind would not topple trees.

The unspoken word that separated them was the name "Anne-Marie." Bart knew that name could cut off Consuelo's support and unswerving devotion. Having once related Tim Clayton's story, he never referred to it again; yet the thought had been planted in them both that possibly she was alive. Bart feared disappointment, and in any case, could not search yet. Like a ghost, Anne-Marie rose to haunt Consuelo. There could be no real lasting consort between Consuelo and Bart unless and until the matter of Anne-Marie was put to rest. Anne-Marie still held his heart.

Bart immediately recognized the value in Consuelo's dinner invitation.

"I hate to leave you," she murmured.

"I appreciate that, but you must not allow me to interfere with your normal activities. Also, until this town gets its own newspaper again, social events are one means of learning what is going on."

"You're right," conceded Consuelo.

The evening was not difficult. Consuelo was paired with Lieutenant W. H. Livermore of the United States Army Engineer Corps, who had recently purchased the salt works, an industry that had been suspended the year before due to the death of the owner. Livermore was already having problems with inefficient and irresponsible free Negro labor. A second topic was that of growing unrest in Cuba against Spain. Several Cuban cigar manufacturers were looking for business property in Key West. The consensus of opinion was that Key West could expect a migration of Cubans. Consuelo also picked up a few amusing anecdotes which she later related to Bart. . . .

"Now you see," said Bart in bed that evening. "It was a good idea that you went. Soon you yourself must begin to entertain. I'll survive up here until I can leave."

Indeed, the time when Bart could leave was approaching. The papers were now in their hands, and his beard was slowly flourishing. He had seaman's clothes. They had now simply to wait for the proper ship.

Daily, Consuelo began going to the wharves to see what

ships had come in and when they were departing. It was not extraordinary that Consuelo appeared in this part of town. She and many of her friends volunteered their services at the Marine Hospital on Emma Street at the foot of Flemming. The fish, turtle and crab market and the blacksmith's shop were also in this area. The information she needed had to be sought casually. They needed a ship whose captain would not recognize Bart and one that would be short of hands so that a last minute berth could be obtained.

Consuelo saw that the *Catherine* was being painted gray. Her new name would be the *Greyhound*. She carefully related to Bart every detail of her waterfront forays.

"You are my eyes and ears," said Bart. "Once I can use my own again, I hope they're as good."

They were lying together in semidarkness discussing the day's activities. Her excursions on his behalf were always complemented with a few of her own. She had errands to run, sick friends to visit and charities to attend as part of her daily life, which he enjoyed sharing. She felt his hand move slowly and caressingly upon her face, then tugging impatiently at her hair. She loosened it so that it flowed freely about her pillow, tumbling to her shoulders. Having attained their minor goals, they felt more relaxed than they had in days. Only a sense of his impending departure was left to upset the equilibrium.

"Did you hear any comments about the weather today," he asked, massaging her arm in a firm affectionate way.

"No, should I have?"

"It has struck me as strange, that's all. There's something brewing, I'm sure."

At that moment a strong breeze bathed them, a pleasant change from the oppressive summer heat. She played with his ear and moved closer, drawn by a rapidly growing need. Their hands took on a new, more forceful purpose. He kissed her neck and then his lips made a burning trail to meet her parted lips. Shivering with apprehension, she felt his fingers free her bosom. Suddenly he was kissing her breasts. A great surge of arousal engulfed her and with it an overwhelming sense of love. Like a vise almost crushing in its intensity, it went beyond passion, being some great human need. The sweep of emotion

122

seemed to have nothing to do with the sense of touch or tactile sensations rippling the surface of her body, but stemmed from a great inner core of feeling ready to explode throughout her.

"I love you too much," she said abruptly.

"One never loves too much, Consuelo. The only dangerous love is self-love and we are not guilty of that."

"You're an incredible man."

"And you are an incredible woman—the greatest I've ever known."

His words brought on a resurgence of emotion. "I'm greedy. I want all your love," she cried out in desperation.

"At this moment you have it all. The love I have for you no one can take away."

"Separating is trying to us both."

Adroitly he had managed to tell her that he also still loved another.

Consuelo fell into a fitful sleep, but soon Bart awakened her. "The wind is picking up sharply. I've gone through the house seeing that the shutters are secure, but I don't dare go outside to bring in the porch furniture. It's so light that it may be blown about."

"I'll manage it," said Consuelo. "I always have." Quickly she slipped into slippers and a robe.

"I feel like an ass, leaving you to do that work." Flashes of lightning momentarily lit the room, revealing the stress on his face. "Had I not been shut up in a cocoon, I might have seen the storm coming."

"We've been too preoccupied. I'll get a neighbor's help if necessary. Think no more about it."

Consuelo opened the door, admitting a gust of wind strong enough to be alarming. One by one, she began bringing in plants and pieces of furniture that had begun to skitter or roll out of place, carried by the wind. The wooden swing was the most difficult to handle, riding high on the chains attached to rafters on the porch roof. As soon as she had it on the floor, heavy as it was, she had no trouble getting it into the living room. She pulled and the wind pushed!

Bart could do little but stand inside opening and closing the door for her, which was a great help. The wind, descending now like a beast, whipped her clothes and twisted her hair into her face. Suddenly, the rain started, carried in horizontal torrents. With it came all manner of light debris. Leaves and twigs came flying into the now crowded living room, where they scurried about like animals. The heavy drapes shuddered and flapped each time the door was opened, beating against table-tops, knocking all loose bric-a-brac to the floor. Finally, they knotted the drapes together, bringing them under control.

Now water was coming down like a river. On the windward side of the house, it came in under and around the double-hung windows, gushing and gurgling as the mixture of wind and water met the sash. Once inside, steady little streams flowed from the windowsills to the floor. Bart opened a window on the leeward side to equalize the pressure on the inside and the outside of the house to prevent a vacuum from forming that could take off the roof or blow the glass windows outward. Outside the wind howled like a pack of wild beasts, tearing off tree limbs that snapped and twisted and then cracked against anything in their path. Inside the wind whistled through the house, trilling and tweeting in a strange song—a chorus of woodwinds without meter. High, eerie shrills rose in a crescendo and then subsided only to be resumed from another corner.

Consuelo and Bart moved about in the semidarkness, checking strange rattles and crashes as debris and wind beat against the house, causing the wooden frame to creak and groan under the onslaught. Tongue-and-groove boards imperceptibly rubbed against one another, protesting the nails that held them fast. Great flashes of lightning periodically inflamed the sky. In the strange light they could make out pieces of roofs and picket fences flying through the air like kites.

"God, we're lucky," said Consuelo. "The roof and shutters seem to be holding."

"What sort of luck do we have? Do I bring it? On top of everything else, now a full-fledged hurricane!" Bart stood listening to the wind howling about them, doing its best to ravage everything in its path. "I feel as though I'm a plague of locusts to you."

"Munching away at the rafters of my house," replied Con-

124

suelo, laughing. "Thank goodness you are here. I would have been terrified with only Pearl here. Powerful as you are, I don't believe you brought this storm."

Bart moved about with a bucket, wringing out towels used to sop up the water on the sills and floors. Certainly, it would have been a miserable experience for two women.

The first light of dawn brought a rapid abatement of the wind. "It's the lull," Bart cautioned. "The wind will soon return from the other direction. Let's hope the other side of the house holds as well and that the next wind will be a dry one."

Together they moved the towels, sheets and rags to the openings on the opposite side of the house.

A few people appeared in the street, particularly young boys, surveying the damage, scavenging, looking for loot. Within a half hour, however, the wind commenced again almost at once full force. This time, as Bart predicted, it came from the opposite direction, driving everyone back to the safety of any standing building. Bart's hope was realized; the wind was drier. They opened as much window as they dared—only a few inches—to let the wind push into the house and out again; it created a mess but it was preferable to having the house battered.

Dirt was everywhere. Sand from the outside mingled with dust inside to form gray streaks on everything—now drying to a crust. For a couple of hours the wind held strong. This time it was less ominous because of the daylight, yet the noises remained. The well-constructed house screeched and screamed under the attack, but it had been built of native virgin pine, so tough and hard that the carpenters had to rub soap on the nails before they could drive them into the wood. Outside, trees bent almost to the ground, returned to an upright position, and then bent again as the gusts continued. Finally, as if bored with the game of destruction, the wind stopped.

Again, people flocked to the streets to survey the damage. Consuelo, now dressed, went out as well, leaving her prisoner gazing at the unholy mess inside. The open shutters that would allow the house to dry out meant that he would have to restrict his movements, lest he be seen.

Trees were down everywhere. Poorly built houses were

either toppled like dominoes or gone. Small boats were in the streets. Seaweed, dead fish and debris littered the town. Piles of jetsam—furniture, boxes, barrels and timber—were being picked over by people running about like vultures. Those not foraging stood numbly under trees denuded of leaves, standing limply askew.

The harbor saw the most damage. Ships lay on their sides or had sunk to the bottom; only their masts and spars revealed their resting places. Small boats had been carried inland hundreds of feet until they were lodged or pinioned against whatever held. Consuelo noted a rowboat in the branches of a tree.

All normal life ground to a halt. Women sat on their steps weeping. Slowly, curiosities satisfied, the damage ascertained, the cleanup began. Furniture, curtains and rugs were hauled outside to dry in the sun that now beamed down upon the tattered earth. In lower houses close to the water, people shoveled out mud and seaweed.

Consuelo walked about, taking in the destruction and fighting down anxiety over the problems that would arise as an aftermath of the storm. Would she need to house some of the homeless? It would not be the first time that she had. What could she do with Bart there? And what about Pearl? The mess that her house was in would recall Pearl—no possible excuse could prevent that now. Bart's presence would have to be revealed to her.

Fortunately, the damage the hurricane had wrought was probably enough to make the sheriff forget about the case. Looters would draw all his attention. The real problem lay in finding a ship to get Bart out. There wouldn't be a seaworthy ship within a hundred miles, so heaven only knew how long that would take. Bart was getting more and more restless. He would be more and more inclined to do something foolish; a hurricane was the last thing in the world she needed.

Tiredly and painfully doing her best not to stumble, Consuelo began to make her way back to the house. Suddenly the thought dawned on her that Pearl might be there already. It was stupid to have left! She dared not run, yet her legs were ready to spring, loose as a rabbit's, powered by a hammering heart.

As it turned out, she arrived home before Pearl. Bart had made a pot of coffee. Temporarily postponing the massive cleanup necessary, they sat in the kitchen. She described the destruction everywhere. "This kitchen seems to be the only place on the island with a little order in it!" she said.

Bart sat hunched over the table. The beard had effectively transformed his appearance. Suddenly seeing him with new eyes, she noticed that he had grown thinner; his hair was much longer; his skin had lost its ruddy glow with the fading of his tan; and the strain of the previous night with its frustrations and dangers bore down upon him. In only a few weeks he seemed to have aged ten years.

"I feel so useless," he said, "and there's so much to be done. If you ever needed a helping hand, it is now, and there is so little that I can do without making myself known. If only I could trim your trees, repair your fences, even sweep your porches—you know that I would! I can only stand in the shadows watching you work. That will be real torture. . . ."

"Horse biscuits! None of that talk. Pearl will soon be trotting back—there's no avoiding that—and in a couple of days, no longer, the house will be in order. We simply have to hope that your ship will come in—and I don't mean to be funny!" she said, laughing at her own pun.

"Yes you do and I appreciate it. But, you know," he said pensively, "the storm may prove a blessing in disguise. Carpenters will be needed for repairs so that fewer seamen will be looking for work at sea. Take heart. You may be rid of me sooner than you think."

"Your indomitable optimism astonishes me. How do you do it? I'm literally ripped apart, you know—on one hand hating to see you leave and on the other hating to have you imprisoned."

Fatigue and unsureness flattened her voice to a moan. Bart took her hand in his and gave it a gentle squeeze of encouragement. They looked up to see a startled Pearl in the doorway.

"Good morning, Pearl. Draw up a chair," said Consuelo. "I have some explaining to do before we tackle the house."

Having Pearl in the place again raised Consuelo's spirits. She had grown accustomed to having someone prepare her meals, clean the house and attend to her clothes. Together they threw themselves into major enterprises—which included cleaning up after parties or a storm. As Consuelo predicted, with Bart's help, the interior of the house was settled into shining order in a few days. The yard, however, would bear the scars for a long time.

Consuelo kept Bart abreast of goings-on at the waterfront as ships were righted and pumped out and others pulled in. No newspaper was being published in Key West, the *New Era* having gone out of business in 1863. News had to come from Tampa and was distressingly slow in arriving. Finally, some papers arrived with devastating news. The *Sea Witch* had been caught by the hurricane and had gone down. A few survivors' names were listed; these men had managed to strap themselves to a floating mast and were finally picked up by another ship. Tim Clayton's name was not among the survivors.

Consuelo knew this would be a terrible blow to Bart, but there was no way for her to keep the news from him. Daily he had sent her out looking for a paper. This was the last straw, the end of a rocky road that led nowhere.

"I can't believe it. Tim was lost at sea." Bart groaned, then dropped into a stony and persistent silence. He lived mechanically. His body performed all the required motions, but his mind was closing in on itself and he was becoming irrational.

Consuelo was convinced that he had to be out and active soon. The commotion caused by the storm had quieted down and the sheriff would soon resume his search. Pearl would come under the sheriff's scrutiny and Consuelo doubted that she could sustain interrogation.

Consuelo prayed for strength.

Fortunately, a ship had put in and a notice had been posted for a hiring. But Bart seemed not to care. His disinterest provoked a crisis.

"Damn it!" Consuelo cried, approaching him and beating him on the chest, her eyes flashing sparks of anger. "We're not going to give up now!" It was a cry from the heart. The urgency in her voice caught him up short and he pulled her into focus. Visibly stiffening, she shook his shoulders and screamed at him. "We are not going to give up now! Do you hear me?"

"You're nearly deafening me! All right," he replied, clearly jarred by her outburst. "Not so loud." He turned away from her.

Enraged, lowering her voice to a whisper and ready to slap his face, she renewed her attack. "We will defeat this yet. It will take longer than we thought, but that's no reason to throw in the towel. Do you have any idea what prison is like? Do you want to be manacled to a moldy wall in a stone chamber, whipped, given wormy food—and little of even that? Do you want to live with vermin, smell nothing but human feces? Would you let that happen to me? Answer me! Haven't you seen Fort Jefferson with your own eyes? Now stop this! You are still a young man with a life ahead of you to be lived. Do you hear me? To be lived!"

By the time she finished, tears of rage and frustration poured down her cheeks. But when he turned to her, she saw that she had reached him. He took her into his arms, holding her fast, drawing upon her inspiration and rebuilding his resolve.

"Consuelo. Consuelo. Consuelo," he repeated, as if her name were magic.

That night he spoke openly of Brian's death. "I don't believe that any man has the right to take the life of another. I didn't intend to kill Brian, but I wanted to make him near enough to the gates of hell to hear the unending agonized cries of the damned. I wanted to mutilate that sweet face, to mash his nose flat so that everyone who saw him would quail before his ugliness and no one would ever again be fooled by his handsome face. But fate deprived me of that. I stood there looking down at him and watched the life go out of him. And believe me, Consuelo, I would have given anything to have him brought back. I wanted him to live a miserable hundred years. He was a jealous, cruel and greedy man. He was truly evil."

"I don't understand how he fooled you for so long."

"He was clever. Anne-Marie read him like a book. There

were aspects of his job that he handled superbly and he knew just how far he could go with me. I knew his hot temper needed a tight leash. I applied it. For a long time we made an unbeatable team, but I never saw his true character. Strange as it may seem, that's the truth. There was something else. Once when we were young boys, he saved my life. I slipped and fell between two good-sized boats belonging to my father. He held them apart until help came to free me. The wind was high and it took every ounce of strength he had. I determined to help Brian, and, I guess, for a long time I did. Later, I was too happy with the profits and too blinded by love of Anne-Marie to see her as a good judge of character, unable to see what I really did not want to see."

Consuelo shuddered. Knowing how proud Bart was, she realized how far he had come to admit these shortcomings. He had been duped. Not only had he lost his wife, child and ship, but in his own eyes he had become a fool. Blustering bravado had carried him for a while, but this too had broken down.

"You may hate me one day and feel bitter believing that I have used you. *I have*, in fact, used you. But you must know that it has not been deliberate, and that in many ways I truly love you and admire you. But more than anything in the world I love and have loved my wife—from the time that she was only a child. That I cannot explain except to say the love was always there. Next to her, there is you. But please don't ask for more than I can give, for I would almost rather cut my heart out than hurt you."

"Oh, don't ask for so much understanding. I am a woman in love—hopelessly so. Please don't trust me. I don't trust myself. Let's not talk any more because these soul-searching discussions tax one's honor, and mine is already worn thin. Don't ask for nobility; my supply of that is running short. Like Brian, I'm greedy."

"You have a capacity to make me greedier than hell. You make me want the world and you too." He reached for her. She felt the warm sticky wetness of his kiss pressing hard upon her lips. Her body moved to accept him. "Oh, what an adorable witch you are," he groaned. "Consuelo, what are we to do?"

"Make love," she replied. "What else is there?"

*　*　*

The following morning Consuelo found his ship.

That evening, stealthily he slipped from the house to join a schooner, the *Dasher*, bound for the West Indies. His name was now Frank Kelly. His pay was twelve dollars a month. For that sum he had to supply his own clothing as well as his labor.

For days Consuelo could not believe the emptiness in the house. Suddenly she was free to scream her lungs out if she wished, but she didn't. She could answer a knock at the door without fear, but hoped no knock would come. She could come and go and entertain as she pleased without explanation or anxiety, but she left the house only by necessity, for the most part. She had never known such loneliness.

Once, driven by a new boredom to a rare promenade, she sighted Wooleye. Because he was alone, she joined him, falling in beside him as he walked along the street pushing a cane in front of him.

"Thank you for your help," she said. "You are a gentleman."

"Always a pleasure to be of service, ma'am."

"Tell me something. How could one go about establishing that a first mate on a ship was smuggling guns unknown to the captain?" she asked.

Shuffling along, looking blindly ahead, he replied, "It would mean finding the connection. The price would be enormous. I can't help you there."

"Thank you, Wooleye. It was just an idle question."

"I know, ma'am," he agreed, crossing the street.

There it is again, thought Consuelo. The closed door. The other question would go unasked as before.

CHAPTER TEN

The summer of 1865 was as hot as the summers of the past had been. Mosquitoes followed the rains with unyielding ferocity and remained until the wind that brought them from the nearby swampy keys reversed and blew them away. When the mosquitoes came, they were unlike anything Anne-Marie had ever seen. They came in black clouds. For the days that they persisted, smudge pots were burned everywhere—almost as obnoxious as the pests themselves. Cheesecloth screens went up at the windows, but still they managed to enter and bite. The only safe and comfortable place was in one's bed under the mosquito-netting tent draping the bed. Whenever it was necessary to step outside for a moment, Anne-Marie and the women could be seen vigorously fanning the air with shawls and skirts, swatting their arms and faces in a usually vain effort to beat off the attackers. The rapacious insects left irritating welts that were easily infected, and they itched for days. Relief came when a change of wind, aided by the thousands of birds drawn to a bountiful meal of mosquitoes, wiped out all but a few stragglers. As suddenly as they came, they went. The worst infestations followed the otherwise beneficent summer rains. Rains filled the cisterns, fattened the limes and broke the obsessive heat.

"Must we always be between the devil and the deep blue sea here?" groaned Anne-Marie, piteously regarding the festering bites on her legs and ankles.

"This climate does take some adjustment," admitted Don Miguel, remembering his own initial reaction to the venomous pests.

Still, there were many pleasant nights when sea breezes were enough to keep down mosquitoes and sand flies or no-see-ums and Anne-Marie and Don Miguel could walk along the beaches.

"Be very quiet and you will see something fascinating," said Don Miguel one ideally beautiful evening. He took her hand and pointed toward the sea.

Anne-Marie could see something, a lump rising from the water. At first it looked like a human head, a dark protuberance surrounded by water shimmering in the moonlight, but then she heard an odd hissing sound.

"What is it?" she gasped.

"Sh!" he remonstrated. "A she-turtle. If she hears anything she'll leave for another place," he whispered, his excitement now infecting her.

Slowly and cautiously the giant sea creature emerged from the water, crawling up on the beach only a few feet from them. Finding a suitable spot, she began digging with her hind flippers, scattering sand several feet. When it was deep enough to satisfy her, she began depositing her eggs one by one. Glistening white, they rolled from her in an almost constant stream until she had laid at least a hundred, each the size of a small hen's egg.

"Once the female starts laying, nothing will deter or disturb her," said Don Miguel, leading her closer. Indeed, that was so. Within minutes a possum scurried to the nest and, ignored by the laboring mother, began feeding upon the freshly laid eggs as they were being ejected. Having its fill, the ratlike possum waddled away.

Anne-Marie watched with astonishment. The turtle, which must have weighed over three hundred pounds, continued her task. When finished, she covered her eggs with sand still warm from the day's sun and crawled back to the water, leaving them forever.

"I never saw anything like that in my life," said Anne-Marie, awed.

Don Miguel marked the nest so that on the following day some of the turtle eggs would be harvested, but not all. "The species must be allowed to thrive."

"I hate to think of taking any of them," said Anne-Marie.

"Nature seems to have taken account for people as well as for perpetuation of the turtle," said Don Miguel, obviously pleased not only with the little drama provided them, but for the opportunity to continue the education of his bright little Anne-Marie. Superbly educated himself, he welcomed an opportunity to broaden Anne-Marie's knowledge, reveling in their growing companionship.

The next morning the sun beat relentlessly upon the garden in a way that was debilitating when one was forced to move about, but restorative when one could sit in a breezy shade watching the play of light on every moving thing. But it was not breezy now; the air was still. Anne-Marie sat trying to concentrate on the Spanish grammar book in her lap, but her attention was continually drawn from the printed page. A parade of ants at her feet seemed extraordinarily busy, not carrying food, but communicating in some strange dance, jerkily detouring to nearly touch a fellow ant and then hurrying back into line. The blue jays that normally squawked in defiant defense of their territory were strangely silent. Squirrels, which usually scampered about the giant live oaks braving the overseer's gun, had retreated into the bushy hammock. All the natural noises were stilled, and an oppressive calm settled on the land.

Anne-Marie could see Don Miguel and several other men a few hundred yards away look up at the cloudless sky. They then returned to their conversation, intent upon each other's remarks. Finally, in long purposeful strides, Don Miguel approached, his expression one of some concern.

"The men feel there's a storm brewing," he said, watching the pale blue sky shade into a growing dusty-orange hue. "They

135

have their own ways of predicting changes in the weather. Prior to a hurricane the sky is different. The color of the water changes and there are exceptionally high tides. The pressure of the air also drops. I can even feel the heaviness in my heart."

Breathing shallowly and rapidly, he waited for her response.

"That's odd," replied Anne-Marie, displaying eagerness and amusement. "I noticed that the animals and insects seemed to be acting abnormally. The noisier animals have grown quiet and all seem to have disappeared. There's not even a lizard about. Even the ants are giving notice of something."

"Everything that's loose out-of-doors will have to be brought in," he told her. "We'll secure the sloop to both sides of the inlet on the more sheltered bay side. Everyone on the property will come into the big house. Although it's calm now, the winds will start picking up soon. You'd better see that there is oil in all the lamps and consider what you would like done inside. We'll nail some timbers against the persiennes on the ocean side."

"I'm glad you know just what to do," she said as she picked up her chair to move toward the house.

"I've been through many of these," said Don Miguel. "You don't have to be frightened. The house will stand as it has done for many years."

She sat the chair down. "I wasn't frightened until you assured me that the house won't blow down. Will it blow like a typhoon?"

"It's not often that strong, maybe only once in a generation. You may be too busy to be afraid, even if it is a bad blow. Water can leak through a pinhole." He started off and then called back to her. "Have someone roll up the rugs and see that buckets and mops are handy." Then he went quickly to see that the most pressing precautions were taken outside the house. She moved to follow instructions.

Throughout the next few hours the wind picked up considerably. Two of the newer men, doubtless from the North, volunteered to stay on the ship, but Don Miguel would not have it. "If it turns out to be a really bad storm, you could neither walk nor swim to the safety of the house. There would be nothing you could do except needlessly lose your lives. No ship is worth that. We will simply make her fast as we can with allowances for a higher tide and hope that she holds."

By now the whole heaven was a luminous frosty yellow, the classic hurricane sky. As the men finished their tasks outside, they came in, bringing their few possessions, including sleeping pallets, just in time to beat the rain. At first they seemed shy and self-conscious, but gradually they relaxed, helping themselves to the plentiful food Don Miguel had ordered put out. Although the wind howled outside and a little water came in, it was rapidly mopped up and no one evidenced concern. Still, it was stronger than any northwester Anne-Marie had ever experienced.

"You can tell by the sound of the wind that it is not too bad," said Don Miguel. "Branches will be snapped off and we'll have a lot of debris to clean up, but I think we are only getting the fringes of this one."

Old-timers concurred with Don Miguel and relaxed with their banjos and harmonicas, making a hurricane party. By midnight the hardest winds had subsided.

"It doesn't look as if she hit us," said Don Miguel. "The eye missed us. We only got the fringes."

"It was enough for me. It was the worst storm I've ever seen," decided Anne-Marie, remembering another on her wedding night, so long ago and far away. But then she had been alone.

"I wonder if she hit Key West?" murmured Don Miguel to draw her from her reverie.

The following day was spent getting everything back to normal. Jardinieres, resplendent and overflowing with plants, were back in their familiar places. The chaos within the house was cleared. Outdoor tables and benches awaited their spreads and cushions. The vegetation hung limply, tired after a thrashing, but not destroyed. The animals reappeared, squawking and scampering, reclaiming their territories and mischievously investigating nature's bashing.

Anne-Marie was fascinated by the animal life on the key. The strange birds especially engaged her attention. Often the sky teemed with brilliantly colored birds in flight to their feeding grounds. The loud flapping of wings and sharp calls—in flawless unison—were unlike anything she had seen and heard.

On the Gulf side of the key, where mud flats ran for miles, the birds were plentiful and almost tame. There were sometimes a hundred egrets or herons wading up to their knee joints in search of small crabs or fish. The birds she had known in the North were small and colorless compared to these southern cousins—the pelicans, flamingoes and whooping cranes—and often totally unfamiliar to her. But there were also possums, turtles, horseshoe crabs, beautiful transparent blue bubbles that were the poisonous Portuguese man-of-wars, the omnipresent prehistoric roaches, rats as big as cats and panthers as small as cats. Anne-Marie, at first alarmed by their numbers, found they ignored her and she came to enjoy watching them.

One of the most pleasant pastimes was a morning swim in the ocean with Don Miguel. Under his tutelage her swimming progressed from a comical dog paddle to a gliding crawl. The exercise firmed her muscles and the cleansing action of the sea and sand made her skin glow. He insisted that they abandon the full-dress bathing costumes of the day and swim nude. At first she was utterly shocked. But, as he said, she would learn to swim sooner unhindered by long sleeves and ankle-length skirt.

It was swimming that reopened their sexual contact. In teaching her to swim properly, it was necessary for him to touch her body. True to his promise, he did not handle her bosom or try to arouse her in any way. At first she clung to him in fear. Later she became playful and cavorted with him. Facing him, wrapping her legs around him in the warm water, suddenly she was painfully aware of the hard muscular promise of his body against hers. Casting inhibitions aside, it was she who found his lips, her mouth taking possession of his, ravaging him, compelling a response. Delighting in his sea nymph, Don Miguel's lips met hers; mesmerized and enchanted, he responded as the waves danced about them. He caressed her, and finally it was she who forced his body into hers, she who worked it until they were both spent. Later she felt humiliated by her attack, shocked that she could be so easily aroused.

"I wondered how long you would be coming to this," said

Don Miguel, smugly, she thought. "You are a passionate woman, and you should not deprive yourself."

She blushed, ashamed that her body had been a traitor to her mind, as she did not love Don Miguel. He had become a friend and protector. What now? "Believe me, I have not felt deprived. But, I see as long as we can't be better strangers, we should be better friends," she said, teasing him. They both laughed until he kissed her soundly.

Don Miguel never told her where he went or what he was doing other than managing his business. There were comings and goings of ships in the basin with occasional strange faces along the wharf. Only captains came to the house. There were dinners not unlike the first, inevitably with only men present. There was always sufficient notice that preparations could be made; the heavy silver service plates, the ornate goblets and French tableware, all decorated with the motif of carnations, could be newly polished. There was time for a hunt to shoot venison, empty the crayfish traps, and collect the turtles from their crawl.

Tall, beak-nosed Ben Baker was due this night and Anne-Marie hastened to dress. Don Miguel looked forward to Ben's arrival for more details on the storm; eagerly he walked to meet the *Rapid* as she slipped into the inlet.

"Greetings, Captain," said Don Miguel, extending a line to a sailor and then a hand to his guest. "I'm glad to see the storm did you no damage."

"That was a piece of luck. Key West was hit very hard. I'm sure you can imagine the devastation in the harbor. The *Sea Witch*, bound for Tampa, was caught in the storm as it veered north. Almost all hands were lost including the captain." Baker went on to elucidate other damage.

"Do you know a Northern ship, the *Catherine*? Now and then she used to put into Key West." Don Miguel's casual question belied a wild thumping in his chest. It was a question he had dared not ask earlier.

"Strange that you should bring her up. She's been the talk of the town. Her captain, a Bartholomew Ramsden, murdered his first mate. He has not been caught. The *Catherine* was confiscated, auctioned, and bought by the captain of the *Sea*

Witch, who did not turn out to be as lucky a man as we all thought. He had a buyer for the *Sea Witch* in Tampa. He was taking her there when the storm hit. And, maybe the ship had been too well stripped to weather a hurricane." Baker shot Don Miguel a knowing glance. "The *Catherine*, now the *Greyhound*, is a fine ship."

"I had thought the *Catherine* was lost at sea," murmured Don Miguel, fighting for composure and turning from Baker as an animal in danger would try to hide.

"*Catherine* is a rather popular ship's name. For a man living on an isolated island, you manage to keep remarkably abreast of everything going on in the world."

Baker turned to issue a few orders to his men as Don Miguel looked to the balcony of his home, where Anne-Marie was standing. She waved to him and he could almost see her smile, so strongly did he feel it. A great possessive surge directed toward her engulfed him, and for a moment he hated the distance between them, wanting madly to hold her to his chest. Slowly he raised an arm to respond to her.

"Captain," he said finally, "my wife is expecting. And, as you know, she is quite young and has tender sensibilities. Considering her condition, I would like to protect her from knowledge of disasters. I would appreciate it if within her presence we keep the conversation on a pleasant keel..."

"I understand fully."

"Until the child is safely delivered, we will remain here in a quiet, salubrious atmosphere, leaving the rest of the world to its troubles."

For the rest of the evening Don Miguel did not want to talk. He wanted to be alone so that his thoughts about the future would overpower his thoughts of a living Captain Ramsden. His urbane fluency left him and Anne-Marie was forced to hold forth at length on the animal life of the key, none of which was news to Ben Baker. Still, her charm and childlike delight were captivating.

Anne-Marie became more visibly pregnant. This pregnancy proved entirely different from the first. There was no recurrence of the dreaded morning sickness; her diet of fresh foods, exercise, rest and fresh air had its health-giving effect. She felt so good, in fact, that she forgot the fact of her pregnancy; moreover, her entire past life was receding into flimsy shadows, easily erased by the strange cry of a bird, the whistle of the wind and the crystal brilliance of the world about her.

By leaps and bounds, under Don Miguel's tutelage, Anne-Marie's Spanish improved and the musical sounds of the spoken language wafted through the house. Don Miguel was tender, solicitous and conveyed only his adoration. Far from prompting rejection, her swollen belly elicited his attention and concern. Never had she been so pampered. Her health and well-being were paramount to their lives.

August brought a new threat. Anne-Marie and Don Miguel were strolling among the lime trees when suddenly he deliberately and violently shoved her aside into the thorny bushes. A small snake, banded in black, yellow and red, no longer than a foot, lay threatening at his heel. With his heavy, gnarled walking cane he struck it, beating it into a rock at his heel. It twisted in its death throes, but not until it had hit its mark. Terrified, Anne-Marie picked herself up and rushed to Don Miguel's side. His face blanched. Hastily he pulled off his belt, making a tourniquet below the knee. Then, falling to the ground, he took a small knife from his pocket and made a deep cut across his leg.

"Squeeze out the poison or suck it out and spit," he begged, being unable to do it himself. His blood flowed freely and Anne-Marie sucked and spit and sucked and spit until Don Miguel's face blackened and she knew that she must have help. She screamed again and again. Within seconds two men came running. Quickly they carried the unconscious Don Miguel into the house. For hours he lingered at death's door. But after the application of countless poultices during the night, the crisis passed. Still barely breathing, he slept.

He had been bitten by a coral snake, Anne-Marie was told. Such bites are usually fatal, they said; prompt and proper treatment had saved him. He was days recovering. Concepción and Anne-Marie took turns nursing him around the clock.

Dear Concepción, What would I do without you? she found

141

herself thinking over and over again. With this incident came the realization that she was bound to Don Miguel. She had become an integral part of the household. She had no doubts about her position.

There it was. No legal formalization of the marriage was necessary.

The incident, however, brought a sobering secret to light. Anne-Marie guessed it as in her panic she had pressed her head to Don Miguel's heart to seek its beat. Instead of a heartbeat, the sound was of blood squishing through his chest. It was unlike any heartbeat she had ever heard before. When Dr. Burbury arrived from Key West, he confirmed her discovery, telling her that for some time Don Miguel had had a seriously impaired heart. Don Miguel was aware of it and carefully paced himself. Deliberately, he led a very quiet life.

The possible or even probable loss of Don Miguel was a shock to Anne-Marie. That he had been bitten saving her— that he would have given his life for her—moved the earth under her feet! How she had misjudged him. Twice he had saved her life. She had allowed her Puritan upbringing to come between them. The "real human values" that Don Miguel had spoken of required a total commitment that would enrich both their lives—if he would only live.

She sat by his bed praying, holding his hand, virtually willing new life into him.

As he recovered, a new peace entered the household as if blown there by the storm. Her devotion to Don Miguel endeared her to others in the household as nothing else could have. Their love and loyalty had always been for him; the strength of the bond between Don Miguel and herself was now apparent to all and they silently acknowledged her as mistress of the house.

Having settled the important things, there was little to do now but await the birth of the baby. Dr. Burbury returned to examine Anne-Marie, an examination performed through layers of clothing while she was completely dressed.

"The baby is in a good position, so we don't have to fear a breech birth," he reported to Don Miguel.

Fortunately, one of the help, an old black woman, had considerable experience in "birthing" and she, of course, would be on hand as midwife. Because this was a second child, it was not expected to be a difficult birth and it wasn't.

On November 6, 1865, eleven months after her first child was born, Anne-Marie gave birth to her second child; a resounding squall heralded a healthy daughter.

"What shall we name this child?" asked Don Miguel.

"Samantha," replied Anne-Marie with a finality no one could question.

"Then Samantha she is," he replied.

Her choice of a name had not come without thought. She remembered Don Miguel's words, long ago. "You could erase another face, not half so pretty or so gentle, but one that I once cared for."

Only this little face known as Samantha would forever wipe out the memory of another with the same name. Thank God, thought Anne-Marie, And I love him too much to be reminded myself of that other Samantha with him.

CHAPTER ELEVEN

Like the first baby, Samantha favored her mother, but there any resemblance between the two infants ceased. An entirely different set of planets favored this child as generously as they had plagued her lost sister. For Samantha it was as if a benevolent Jupiter, energizing Mars and a beautiful Venus had come together to bestow force and vitality upon her. The power in her lusty lungs in protest of any bodily discomfort could bring six people running. As soon as she was old enough to smile, her happy gurgling and cooing brought rapturous adoration. This tiny, powerful, magnetic presence, lightening and brightening, changed the whole focus of life in the house on the key.

Anne-Marie's deepest thoughts were no longer tied to other times and other places. Once again, she had something harmoniously her own. This world was largely of her own making; the feeling of having been tossed about by fate or the will of others receded into a nearly forgotten distant past.

She no longer grieved for Bart, even though the romantic memory of him remained as that of her great lost love. The thought that he might be alive somewhere never occurred to her. Bart, the all-powerful, would by now have found her, she vaguely supposed. This was a private tragedy that she was proud to have buried. The funeral was not marked by any one date, but by a series of events associated with the flourishing development of Samantha and the overriding pleasure she afforded.

Don Miguel was infinitely more interested in and intrigued by Samantha than Bart had been with his child. The first baby had been a slightly divisive entity in their lives, drawing Anne-Marie's time and attention from Bart. Because of her ill health she had become an inconvenience that was borne good-naturedly enough and sensibly by Bart, but still, he had missed his wife.

Anne-Marie also had feared that Bart would have preferred a son. In addition, Anne-Marie had felt guilty for having delivered a puny baby. Because she had carried and nourished the child and had given birth prematurely, she felt she was the one who had been at fault.

Don Miguel was totally involved with this child. To him she was "the world's most perfect creation." Nothing Samantha did inconvenienced or annoyed him. The entire household felt the same. "A baby in the house—a perfect example of minority rule," pouted Anne-Marie, who occasionally was reminded of her New England upbringing, which did not cultivate spoiled children.

From the moment that Don Miguel laid eyes on Samantha, she took command like a queen. Nothing was too good for her. Under all the attention, she flourished.

Instead of being a divisive force, she became an endearing one. Anne-Marie was proud and grateful for Don Miguel's appreciation. To Anne-Marie, he became more than an intimate friend and in many ways she loved him. His kindness, his generosity, his appreciation of her worth and his love for her guaranteed a harmony that was enhanced by his love for the child.

Don Miguel had been born in Spain, a bastard sired by a man in an unimportant noble family. His mother was Irish and it was from her that he had learned English as his first language. When he was ten his mother died and he was taken into his father's household.

That he was the brightest and handsomest of all his father's

146

children only made his life difficult. In time, he determined to get as much education as he could and strike out on his own in the New World as soon as he became of age. When that time came his father gave him a sound sum of money and his blessing.

His position in his father's household, where stepbrothers not only taunted him because of his birth but also resented his obvious superiority, had firmed a resolve to acquire a fortune and standing. Opportunities in trade for a young man with some capital abounded, and Don Miguel's fortune grew by leaps and bounds. He became very rich. His surefootedness in commerce, however, was not matched in his choice of a wife. He married a titled but spoiled and selfish fortune hunter who made life difficult by hating every place they lived or went together. After a few years of misery with her, he packed her off to Europe, where with an adequate settlement she eventually procured an annulment. "To perdition with titles," he swore. "From now on, I am 'Don Miguel' as both first and last name and that is it."

After a season of healing, Don Miguel met and fell in love with a lovely quadroon. She and their child were murdered by a berserk servant. In his grief he retired to the lonely key. Then, a serious heart condition made his quiet life in this outpost not only wise but quite to his liking. He was prepared to live out his days there, forswearing female companionship— until he found Anne-Marie on the beach.

Consequently, Anne-Marie found herself with a man infinitely wise in the ways of the world and deeply understanding of her predicament. But a lonely and insecure heart can be a shrewdly tenacious one when it comes to a new love. Even the birth of the baby and her apparent affection for him had not lessened his insecurity. Don Miguel was determined to keep Anne-Marie. He now lived one day at a time; and one day at a time he kept her.

When Samantha was a few months old, Anne-Marie told Don Miguel that she was writing her family explaining her situation. "They have thought me dead for so long. I can't leave them with that sorrow any longer. I'm sure they will be

147

understanding of my long silence and happy to learn of you and the baby."

Her words brought no visible reaction other than a meditative smile. "I suppose if you must, you must. I'll see that the letter is taken to Key West for mailing."

But he did not; he burned it. After three months, when no reply came, Anne-Marie mentioned the letter.

"I, too, should have thought that you would have a response by now," said Don Miguel. "Surely, they were happy to receive the news that you were alive, but you must also consider that they are probably displeased that you are living with me and not married. This may be their way of expressing it."

"No, you do not understand my parents," said Anne-Marie, raising her eyebrows so that she almost revealed the depth of her irritation. "I was brought up in an understanding, loving household. It was not an overly religious one. My people are not intolerant. They would be displeased, but their joy to learn that I am alive would overcome their displeasure."

Secretly she wrote a second letter, again telling her story and also mentioning the first letter. She held it until they had guests. Catching a moment when Don Miguel was out of the room, she asked Ben Baker to post it for her. "I'll be glad to mail your letter," he said, taking it. However, he was clever enough not to do such a thing without first privately mentioning it to Don Miguel.

"I would prefer that this letter not be mailed," said Don Miguel, taking it from his friend's hand. Then and there he touched a match to it. Only a few ashes fell to the deck of the *Rapid*, carried by a capricious breeze.

Ben dismissed the incident as being typical of a marriage between a young woman and a middle-aged man.

Anne-Marie wrote no more letters. A curtain had come down.

Don Miguel's health was perceptibly failing. There were some days when his color was poor and his breath short; at such times he moved only when necessary and then slowly. On other days he seemed in excellent health; he would sit for hours playing with Samantha, watching her grow. Her thick coppery hair was just like her mother's and as her baby fat disappeared, she resembled Anne-Marie even more. "She also has eyes like her Irish grandmother, God love her," said Don Miguel.

"Blue eyes were a rare thing in Spain. My mother was a wonderful horsewoman. I think you would enjoy riding, Anne-Marie. I'm going to get you a fine horse. We can make a bridle path and it would be good exercise." As he spoke, enthusiasm grew in his eyes.

"I would love it," said Anne-Marie, expectantly. "I haven't ridden in years and I don't ride well, but you could teach me."

"Yes, I could. Would you be willing to start from scratch so that I could teach you properly?"

"Of course, but I don't understand," replied Anne-Marie, looking puzzled.

"I'd want to start you bareback, the way cavalry and Indians learn. You'll have to have some riding pants made—a skirt would be impossible. And it will go slowly at first. You'll be very sore," he warned, watching for her reaction.

"If I'm going to learn, I might as well learn thoroughly. This is a good private place to look like a fool, and you must promise not to laugh at me too much."

"I hear a man in Tampa has some Justin Morgans. This would be a good horse for you." Don Miguel went straightaway to his desk to order the best two mounts the man had.

"I'll tell you why you should make a good rider. You are a very sensitive person. You will know your horse and be so understanding of him that you and he will function as one being. That's why I want you to start bareback—just as my mother taught me. She called me her little centaur—a horse with a man's head and brain—or, if you prefer, a man with the speed and strength of a horse."

The horses arrived and the lessons started.

"Learn to feel with your hands, your knees and your seat what the horse is doing under you," said Don Miguel. "Sit always in balance with him, maintaining your position without holding his neck with your hands or squeezing his sides with your legs." All this he advised as she mounted.

With a long tether, either Don Miguel or the overseer would stand as a pivot in the center of a circle, leading her horse around.

"Don Miguel! You're...asking me to perform a...a miracle," she stuttered, slipping and clutching, gaining and regaining her balance, then slipping and clutching again.

"You will get it. Don't worry," he replied.

Just so they continued for many tiring days. Her sore legs were a trial, but she persisted. Her determination surprised Don Miguel; she spent hours struggling with unaccustomed muscles and it was always the horse that was tired first.

"You are truly good," Don Miguel kept repeating and the encouragement spurred her on. Finally he insisted that she learn to ride standing on the horse's haunches.

"I will not!" she cried. "Are you training me for a circus? How could you expect me to do that?"

"You are as lithe as a young boy. I expect you to be the best rider in the country. You've come so far and now you want to quit."

His words were infuriating, but they made her persevere. Time after time she felt herself falling and expertly landed on the ground, soft sand cushioning her fall. "You are cruel to impose this on me," she cried resentfully. But she continued and mastered the art.

Finally, one day he surprised her with a saddle. Eagerly she took her seat and moved off beside him as he joined her on his own mount. "This is so easy! There's nothing to riding now," she called to him, the pride of accomplishment shining in her eyes. Only then would Don Miguel permit her to ride for pleasure—and still with limitations.

"Don't try to swim your horse across an inlet. An untrained animal, unused to swimming, will attempt to rest his forelegs on any object near him. So any person near the horse's chest will be struck and forced underwater," cautioned Don Miguel. As he spoke Anne-Marie felt his gaze searching to meet her eyes, but this she avoided. The message was all too clear: He had not given her a way to leave the key. She could ride around half of the key because of the inlets. From the tip of the island she could look across to an adjoining key and another beach just like their own. The sight of that other land was, indeed, tantalizing. But in any case, the cut was impossible to cross. The riptides between the keys were notorious. However, to try would be pointless for she well knew that there was nothing there, nothing to escape to. That island only led to another, all inhospitable.

She did try another tack with Don Miguel. "Samantha has never seen another child. She has never seen streets. Soon she should learn that she must make adjustments to people and places. Here she is the center of her world. It is not a healthy situation. Can't we take a trip?"

"She will have plenty of time for that. I don't know a healthier place in the world. There's no disease here, no yellow fever..."

Rebuffed, Anne-Marie was silent for a moment, then she plaintively cried, "I'm bored, Don Miguel. It's not Samantha. It's me! I need to see *people*. The help here gets off the island. Why can't I?"

"Soon," he replied, closing the matter.

It was more than she could combat. Had he refused point-blank. She could have argued, but instead he ended the discussions with "Soon."

"Make me some jumps, some hurdles, then—so that I can enjoy something new. I loved the challenge of learning to ride, remember?"

"That's a fine idea," he replied. "For jumping, the horse will have to be trained also, so it may not come as easily."

"As easily? Did you call all that easy?" Chagrin crossed her face.

"Certainly, you're ready. You can ride at walk, trot, slow gallop and fast gallop without using reins or stirrups. Now we'll see if your horse will jump."

Don Miguel immediately put the men to work making jumping standards. When the first was finished, they commenced.

The beginner's bars were placed parallel on the ground, so they amounted to no jump at all.

The horse responded beautifully and Don Miguel's eyes shone with pride. "I think you've got a good jumper in the making," he said.

151

Soon Anne-Marie was mastering jumps eighteen inches high. "It's great fun," she said. "I love this." The oneness with her animal, the conquering of her fears and the sense of achievement combined to make her spirits soar.

Don Miguel always sat watching, vicariously enjoying her accomplishment. "You know, you're really very good. I think I've never seen a better natural rider," he said finally.

"Given some expert teaching by a patient teacher, and a superb horse," she added graciously. "But I thank you. Your compliments always inspire me. Now, once more around."

The physical strain and the concentration burned nervous energy that had become harder and harder to control. For a few more months Don Miguel's "soon" was easier to bear. She felt certain that only the riding kept her from madness.

Then one day the bad fall came.

She had fallen many times, of course, but had always escaped serious injuries. This time her leg was severely broken. The pain was so great that she fainted when they carried her into the house. No doctor was available on the key so Don Miguel splinted the leg himself after dressing it as he had been taught by his doctor to do, knowing that one day such a casualty would occur. At once they set off to Key West in the boat to have the leg properly set. Without expert medical attention, Don Miguel knew Anne-Marie could be crippled for life. Worse still, if infection set in, the leg might have to be amputated.

Much as Don Miguel wanted to hold her, it was not at that price. Morphine made the trip bearable, but barely so. Extruding bone had punctured the skin, and surgery was necessary to set the leg properly, Dr. Burbury told them. He also told them that it was imperative that she remain in Key West until the wounds healed and the bone knitted. This would take a number of weeks, and he suggested that they rent a house and remain where medical attention would always be available. Infection, even gangrene, was common in open wounds suffered in horse spills and contact with the soil, he said.

There being no other course open to him, Don Miguel complied without hesitation. A suitable house was found and Don Miguel, Anne-Marie, Samantha and two servants moved in— Anne Marie on a litter.

Having escaped from one prison, she now entered another, this one even more constricting. With infection and high fever, delirium set in; twice a day the anxious doctor came to tend the wound and check her condition. Some weeks passed before the infection finally came under control. "Only her excellent physical condition has saved her," Dr. Burbury told Don Miguel. "Let's hope our luck holds."

Don Miguel stayed by her side, sponging her face, bathing her, forcing her to drink water and fanning her when the breeze hushed. At night he catnapped in a lounge chair when she slept briefly. Clearly, she would be many more weeks recuperating, but the doctor advised that she should not be moved. "It would be foolish to take a risk. A roll of the boat and a sudden movement could undo all we've done. It will be at least a couple of months before she can bear weight on that leg and even then a trip might be dangerous. Crutches are impossible on boats."

Feeling certain that Anne-Marie would be incapacitated and unable to attempt to leave him, Don Miguel complied with the doctor's orders. He began to make trips back and forth between Key West and Cayo de las Matas to carry on his business while Anne-Marie made a safe and quiet recovery.

But Anne-Marie's convalescence slowed. Though physically improved, she was despondent. It seemed to her incomprehensible that fate could be so cruel. She had gained her wish to leave the key, only to find herself in another prison. The pain had been excruciating; now far less, it remained a constant discomfort. She was still unable to walk. There was nothing to do but lie alone in bed with now even fewer people to talk to. Samantha's presence in the room—the child exuberantly moved about and frequently tried to be near her mother and touch her—was frightening. The child might forget and touch her leg or climb onto the bed, tilting it. The doctor's visits made the only break in the everyday monotony, and even these calls were marked by some pain. Often Dr. Burbury found her weeping.

"Here, here, now. That pain can't be that bad," he said. "The leg is doing beautifully."

He put on his best bedside manner as he relaxed in the easy

chair, to tell her some of his little jokes to distract her. He knew that she needed this, but she was not distracted. Her smiles were weak and soon disappeared altogether. After some days of this he decided that she was genuinely depressed. His opinion was confirmed by Concepción. "She no talk. She no eat," the woman said. Further questioning revealed that Anne-Marie cried a lot.

On his next visit he prescribed some company for her. "I know one or two young women in this town whom I'm going to send around to offer you a bit of female companionship," he told her flatly. "I believe that you are lonely."

His words unleashed a flood of tears, an unexpected outburst. His perception and understanding opened the locks on her frail sensibilities. Covering her face with her hands, she sobbed as she had not in years. Her wails brought everyone in the house running to her door, only to be dismissed by the doctor with a wave and a nod. "Now cheer up. There's nothing like a good cry, and I think I've hit upon the proper medicine for you. Tomorrow afternoon you will serve tea here in your room. Now, I must go and invite your guests."

Leaving the house, the doctor reflected on how much truth that breakdown had expressed. "How stupid of me not to have thought of that before," he said to himself aloud. And so alone on that key for so long! Methodically he began ticking off patients and suitable acquaintances of her age and station. None quite filled the bill.

Dr. Burbury would have preferred to have discussed this recent turn of events with Don Miguel; however, the man was not in Key West and time seemed of the essence. Don Miguel would not want him to delay any treatment he thought necessary, he judged. For some time now he had been treating Don Miguel and the doctor knew the seriousness of his condition. Obviously, Don Miguel was satisfied with his own company. Of his personal life he knew nothing except that he had a young and beautiful wife whom he obviously adored and a beloved small daughter.

The doctor had often wondered why Don Miguel always came to Key West alone, leaving his wife on the Cayo de las

154

Matas. He had supposed that she preferred life on the key. Evidently, this was not the case.... Nor was it, he reminded himself, his business.

His steps took him by chance to the house of Consuelo Lamar. Having rejected the young women on his list as possible companions for Anne-Marie, he decided to drop in on Consuelo for suggestions. She knew everyone on "The Rock" and he enjoyed talking to her. Fortunately, she was home and able to receive him.

"Dr. Burbury, to what do I owe this delightful visit? I'm sound as a dollar," she said, showing him to her most comfortable porch chair.

"I can see that you are," he replied. "But stick out your tongue." She stuck out her tongue, but not for professional examination.

"No," she said. "You are not here for my health. Do tell me, at once."

"I have a slight problem and I thought in passing that you might be able to help me with it. Our roles are reversed. You are to do the treating, if you will," he added a bit sheepishly. "Besides, it is always good to see you."

"As long as it's not midwifery, Dr. Burbury, I'm at your service."

"Lord, no, Consuelo," he replied, trying to retain his laughter. "I have a patient, hardly twenty years old. She lives on one of the keys in virtual isolation except for her family and servants. While riding, she had a terrible accident. Fell and broke her leg. It was one of the worst breaks I've ever handled—and handled successfully, I might add. Her husband, Don Miguel, is an older man, wealthy and powerful, comes and goes on business. But she knows no one in Key West. She's confined to her bed with no one but a couple of servants and her small child to talk to and she should have some company. I'm not suggesting that you should be the company, but I thought you might know someone—among your 'Rising Stars,' 'Daughters of the King,' and so forth. Or one of their daughters, perhaps..."

"Why, I'm flattered you thought of me," replied Consuelo. "I think Mimi's daughter would be perfect. She's one of our idle rich, and I'm sure she could use something worthwhile to do. I'll speak to her today."

"That's terribly good of you, Consuelo. I promised to send someone by for tea tomorrow, and only after I'd said it did I realize perhaps I'd taken on more than I could handle."

Don Miguel was not entirely unfamiliar to Key Westers. He was known to be rich but otherwise he was a mystery, apart from the few who knew that he had servants and workers or associates. But no one that Consuelo knew knew him—or would discuss knowing him. The name alone was enough to pique her interest.

"They have rented the Fitch place." Dr. Burbury looked at his watch and bid her a hasty farewell. "Thank you. You are an angel of mercy and a great relief to me as well."

Wasting no time, Consuelo headed for Mimi's house. Mimi's daughter Suzanne had been educated in France, and, because she was lively and fun like her mother, she would be an ideal friend for the young woman, Consuelo thought as she walked up the steps of her friend's house.

"Mimi, do forgive me for not sending a note first. I hope this is not an intrusion, but it seems urgent," she said rapidly.

"You know you are welcome any time of the day or night," replied Mimi as they exchanged kisses of greeting.

Suzanne, glancing into the parlor, saw and greeted Consuelo and then moved to leave, but Consuelo called her back. "You're involved in this too, my dear, so please don't go."

Seated, Consuelo began her story. "You know how curious we've been about the people in the Fitch house—so reclusive. Well, today Dr. Burbury told me about them. It seems the house has been rented to Don Miguel—of all people. His wife, about Suzanne's age, had a terrible riding accident and has been in bed for over a month with a badly broken leg. She's terribly lonely. To clear her depression, Dr. Burbury promised to send some ladies to tea tomorrow. Then, of course, he couldn't think of anyone and came knocking on my door just as I'm knocking on yours."

"You'll go, won't you, Suzanne?" asked Mimi.

"Well, I did have plans, but nothing so important," replied the lovely young lady.

"You are a darling," responded Consuelo. "Take some friends with you if you can and report back everything. Your mother and I have been dying to know what's been going on in that house. Some of the older women have left cards but have simply *not* been received."

"It would be nice to have an interesting new friend, even if she is married and on the shelf, wouldn't it?" joked Mimi. "Suzanne gets so bored in Key West—and I'm so bored when she's away!"

"Yes, I'd say the more friends the merrier," added Consuelo, noting the hesitation in Suzanne's face.

"All right, Tante Consuelo. I'll do it for you. But next time, please find some charming young gentleman in need of company. Nothing too debilitating—or contagious," she replied, laughing.

Consuelo gave Suzanne a loving pat. "Dr. Burbury does not often call upon me to find amusement for his patients. Boils, carbuncles and scurvy coming in on boats make up the bulk of his patients' ills, and the rest of those with two legs walking around Key West you have already picked over, my sweet."

To Mimi Consuelo observed, "With both a naval base and a fort here, wouldn't you think they'd have enough men to choose from?"

"They're spoiled," replied Mimi comfortably.

"I've taken enough of your time. Remember to report." Hugging Mimi and Suzanne, she departed.

The following day at three, Suzanne and a willing friend, Mercedes Carmona, were received at the Fitch residence and were ushered into Anne-Marie's room, where a splendid tea was set. They curtsied to the young woman propped up in bed and gave their names. "Mine's Anne-Marie," the hostess said. "Please don't be formal and do sit down." She gestured toward the chairs. "It is sweet of you to come. I'm so tired of being alone—not to mention lying in this bed."

Neither of the young ladies could have imagined the flurry of preparations that had preceded their visit. A table was dressed with exquisite linen, an enormous silver tray held a matching tea service, and plates of dainty open-faced sandwiches and cakes were placed invitingly about. A great bouquet of anemones dressed a smaller table. For the first time in months Anne-Marie labored with her hair and toilette. She wore a lovely bed jacket imported from France, but it could hardly disguise how thin she had grown. Dark circles under her eyes underlined the severity of her illness.

"We heard that you had a terrible accident and we're so sorry," said Suzanne. "How did it happen?"

"You know, I hardly remember," replied Anne-Marie. "I understand *not* remembering bad accidents is rather common. I was jumping my horse—not even over the highest bar. I heard a crack and touched my leg and felt the bone sticking out of it. Then I passed out—I guess from the pain."

"How perfectly awful," said Suzanne, paling at the thought of the ordeal. "I can't endure pain. I simply collapse."

"She collapses most dramatically," added Mercedes. "One, there is always an audience present—particularly some handsome young man. Two, she goes into a slow reel—if you know what I mean—gently floating arms and all, then a slow knee failure, sort of revolving levitation because she never hits the floor. Three, at some inner signal, she collapses."

"The signal is some man taking me by the elbows, if you must know," replied Suzanne, looking her innocent best.

With that, a chorus of laughs echoed through the house that heretofore the servants had described as silent as a tomb.

"Don't make me laugh so, please," begged Anne-Marie. "It is so funny, but it hurts!"

Still, they continued to laugh together.

"My gifts are small," said Suzanne, defending herself and grasping her bosom. "I'm forced to use them very well, very discreetly. Consequently, I've made a charming little reputation, they say." Mercedes threw Anne-Marie an amused look of feigned disapproval.

"What do you girls do?" queried Anne-Marie, still smiling. "Tell me and pour yourselves some tea, please."

Mercedes and Suzanne's eyes met questioningly as if to say, "What does she mean, what do we *do*?"

"Do you go to school? Are you married?" asked Anne-Marie, sensing the ambiguity of her question.

"I suppose, if you want an honest answer, we are shopping for husbands. We do this by attending and giving a series of dull parties—dances, promenades and so forth, always seeing the same old faces. Schooling is finished. We are two eighteen-year-old spinsters!"

"I know Mother looks upon me as an old maid," said Mercedes dourly. "Do you get *that* look, too?"

"Constantly," Suzanne replied. "I simply haven't chosen the man who will choose me," she said, helping herself to a second petit four.

"Have you always lived in Key West?" continued Anne-Marie, genuinely interested.

"Born here and I'm dreadfully afraid we will die here," answered Suzanne. "Her mother is Spanish and mine is French. Our fathers were English. We were both sent to finishing schools in France where the nuns 'finished' us. So now we're filling our hope chests and collecting recipes.

"Mercedes's hope chest is in her bodice," quipped Suzanne. "She never touches a needle." Again, laughter rippled about the room.

"As small towns go, there are worse places than Key West. We do have the naval fueling depot plus Fort Taylor for a supply of eligible young men. The town is full of colorful old characters, too. They've come from all over—Bahama wreckers, Englishmen, Irishmen, Dutchmen, Swedes, Norwegians, Hindoos, Russians, Italians, Spaniards, Cubans, Canary Islanders, Canadians, Scotchmen, South Americans—world wanderers who've knocked around all over and finally settled here. You'll see, as soon as you're well. I promise you, you'll like Key West," said Suzanne.

"We must go. We've stayed too long and we don't want to tire you," said Mercedes.

"It has been the best time I've had in months," said Anne-Marie. "Please come back." The pleading note in her voice was unmistakable, and the girls promised that they would. "We can bring Louisa Tatine and Petrona Martinelli and Lizzie Browne for a little variety."

"I once knew a Lizzie Browne from Key West," said Anne-

Marie pensively, "at St. Mary's Hall." Her eyes brightened. "I had quite forgotten."

"We'll be back," Suzanne and Mercedes chorused, departing.

Reluctantly, but somewhat fatigued, Anne-Marie rang for Concepción to see them to the door.

Outside, the girls parted. "Thank you for helping me do my good deed for the day," said Suzanne with a wave.

"I quite enjoyed it," said Mercedes, meaning it.

Suzanne, as promised, stopped by Consuelo's house.

"And how did you find the young lady?" asked Consuelo, sitting down by Suzanne on the porch swing. The air was cool and lovely and Consuelo settled down for a nice chat.

"She's very sweet," replied Suzanne. "You can tell she's been quite sick. There are dark circles under her eyes."

"Well, go on . . . was her husband there?" asked Consuelo.

"The only other person we saw was the maid."

"Well, where does she come from?"

"I don't know," said Suzanne, looking baffled. "Now that I think of it, I learned nothing about her. She plied us with questions. There was no chance for ours. We laughed a lot. She is charming, but she didn't say anything except that she fell off her horse jumping. I gather that she's an excellent rider. She certainly didn't brag. And, oh, yes, she attended St. Mary's."

"Well, she comes from a good family, then," remarked Consuelo, now rocking back and forth on the swing. "Indeed, she must be a charming person, not going on about her pain and keeping the conversation on you. I'm sure she is clever. It was sweet of you to go and I know Dr. Burbury appreciates it."

"Oh, I enjoyed meeting Anne-Marie," replied Suzanne.

Suddenly, the motion of the swing stopped. Consuelo appeared startled. "That's her name?" she asked, regaining her composure.

"Yes," answered Suzanne. "It didn't strike me as an unusual name."

"Of course, it isn't," replied Consuelo, suddenly propelling the swing with a sharp kick of her foot. "In fact, it is a rather ordinary name."

The name had hit Consuelo like a blow. From the moment of the impact she felt suspended, teetering, then paralyzed, as if she were a marble statue accidently bumped and about to fall.

"As a matter of fact," she said, trying to cover her agitation, "it's a common name. You will note, when you get a little older, that certain names have a strange way of recurring in your life over and over again, sometimes as friends, rivals or runaway children. The same names come back to startle you because they bring back memories long forgotten of other people, places and events."

"I know what you mean," said Suzanne. "Once you really dislike someone, it ruins the name for you. I never knew my father, but when I was small I would often find my mother weeping over the loss of him. I hated to see my mother sad and so I began to hate his name. Even now that I am old enough to see how unfair this is of me, I still have to overcome an initial antipathy when I meet someone by that same name."

Suddenly Consuelo wanted to be alone to think. For a few minutes Suzanne prattled on while Consuelo pretended to be listening.

"We're going back to see Anne-Marie and next time I'll try to learn more about her," said Suzanne apologetically.

"Oh, don't worry, I'm really not that interested. We're only doing Dr. Burbury a favor, you know," replied Consuelo.

For Anne-Marie the afternoon's visit was the nicest thing that had happened to her in months. The two carefree girls were a stark contrast to anything in her life. Even the girls she had grown up with seemed more serious. I guess it is what they call Southern charm, she said to herself. Perhaps I have always been too serious. She knew that Suzanne and Mercedes would be back, and she wondered how long it would be before they would be asking questions and not understanding the answers. More importantly, she knew that Don Miguel would resent her new friendships. If she did not tell him about the visit, the servants certainly would.

When Dr. Burbury made his evening rounds, he was delighted to find her so improved. "You look as if you've had a pleasant afternoon and I don't think it tired you too much," he said, examining her leg.

"Dr. Burbury...I have a feeling Don Miguel will not be too pleased by my having company," she said with hesitation. "I have always been kept so isolated. Because *he* is satisfied with so much solitude, he evidently thinks that I am too. I love my home, but sometimes I need to get out. Please, please talk to him and convince him that I need some diversion that doesn't come from a book. It may or may not be hard to do. I really don't know my husband. This may strike you as strange, but it is true."

Dr. Burbury listened carefully, covered her leg with the sheet, and gave her a gentle pat. Don Miguel was old enough to be her father. He had outgrown his youthful need for fun with others. No wonder there were problems. Here was a woman hungry for life, caged and isolated by Don Miguel. At the same time the doctor felt sympathy for Don Miguel. Beauty is always powerful and coupled with unpredictability it is fascinating, he thought. After a long silence he looked up into her eyes, regarded her with a slow, reluctant smile, and said, "Of course, I'll talk to Don Miguel. If you remember, I was the one who sent the girls here, and I hope he won't be displeased." He paused a moment and seemed to be viewing the flowers. "Has he told you that his life may be short? I feel this fact explains a lot about his behavior. You should be aware of this and when he does go, you should have friends that you can turn to. I'll make that point to him—if necessary."

Anne-Marie shuddered and a lost, bereft look widened her eyes. For a moment she envisioned death, an obscure figure with a sickle, stalking the house. The doctor was speaking as if Don Miguel's death could come momentarily. An old apprehension suddenly became a bright new fear. "I have noticed that his health has been failing," she said. "I think that if he felt well, he would be here now. He paces himself very carefully. That is all part of my problem. Distressing him or angering him could bring on an attack and possibly his death. I

162

would not want to be responsible for that just because of a bit of loneliness on my part."

"You need have no feelings of guilt, my dear," interjected the doctor. "You have already prolonged his life. He would not be alive today had it not been for his interest in you and the child. I'll take the responsibility for the visitors and I will make it clear to him that a lengthy depression can be as deadly as an infection. Have a restful night and I'll see you in the morning."

The next day Don Miguel arrived and Anne-Marie haltingly told him about her visitors. He sat next to her bed, Samantha on his lap, running his fingers through the child's hair, playing with the back of her neck. He seemed hardly to be listening to what Anne-Marie was saying, so absorbed was he with his daughter, but Anne-Marie knew that he had heard every word. Finally he said, "Your company seems to have done you a world of good. I hope they return soon." Then he took Samantha to her room and was gone a long while as he told her a story.

Men, said Anne-Marie to herself. I will never understand them. When Don Miguel returned she was almost asleep. He bent over her and kissed her forehead. She raised her arms to embrace him and murmured, "Take care of yourself, dear heart." Slowly he pulled himself from her arms, painfully aware of her sleepy reluctance to let him go. That seemed to be so much of what life was about: giving up and letting go. That was the hardest part. When he left the room to retire he felt as if he were performing a small secret heroism without promise of reward.

"I must return to Los Claveles today," said Don Miguel the following morning.

"Why so soon?" asked Anne-Marie, both surprised and disappointed.

"Some important visitors are coming in tonight and I must be back to meet them. I'm leaving you some money in this drawer as a reserve," he said, placing a small cash box with her other things. "This money in your night table is for you to use for food and spending money."

"That looks like quite a lot."

"Well, I expect you will have to pay the doctor something and the servants will need wages."

"Come back as soon as you can. I'm getting deathly tired of these splints on my leg. I'm going to have to learn to walk all over again and I'll need you to lean on. I've discovered that I don't have any little well of private courage to draw upon, Don Miguel . . ."

Catching her winsome, plaintive smile, he kissed her good-bye. The woman didn't know her power.

CHAPTER TWELVE

Bartholomew Ramsden, now Frank Kelly, found a last-minute berth with Captain Stiles on the *Dasher*. The job proved to be different in every way from those he had previously occupied, but he was determined to be a good sailor. He did not shirk work and enjoyed the respect and friendship of the other men. Many times he had to stifle the urge to issue an order when he knew that one was called for. But by quietly doing the job himself, others soon followed him, a natural born leader, though without rank. Within a short time he had made a reputation as a good man.

After an uneventful voyage to Boston, they quickly unloaded and took on a cargo for California, a voyage of over one hundred and fifty days around the Horn. It was an arduous journey, during which many of the men became ill due to exposure and malnutrition, which overworked those who remained well. Finally, they came to anchor in the spacious bay of Santa Barbara.

For many days Captain Stiles had seemed very much out of humor for no apparent reason. He found his food unsatisfactory and quarreled with the cook; he had an outrageously unreasonable and public dispute with the second mate and threatened to throw him in the brig and later even to the sharks.

This he would not have done, but the heat of his ire was unsettling to the crew; each feared he might be next on the blacklist—if for no better reason than the color of his eyes. The fact that each able-bodied man outdid himself made little difference; the captain remained unreasonable. In the end, his displeasure settled on a crewman named Sam Lightfoot, a West Indies native.

Sam, although a trifle slow, was nevertheless a better than average sailor. He had not joined the sick and had shouldered more than his share of the work. He was a big, burly man, part black, and often—because of his native patois and a stutter—difficult to understand. At times his speech briefly failed him totally when excited.

Captain Stiles settled his general displeasure on Sam too obviously and eventually without cause or reason. The manifest injustice of this provoked not only the interest of the crew but sympathy for Sam.

Stoically, Sam bore the unwarranted attacks; the journey was almost over.

The captain had ordered the first mate to ready the gig to take him ashore and was about to depart when Bart heard a scuffling in the hold, where many of the men were at work. He could hear the captain bellow, "Will you ever give me any more of your jaw?"

There was no answer and then Bart could hear the question repeated: "Will you ever give me any more of your jaw?"

"I ain't never meant to give you jaw, sir," stuttered Sam, halting and half-choked.

His reply only infuriated the captain more.

"That's not what I asked you. Answer my question," screamed the captain.

There was only silence and Bart knew that the more upset Sam became, the less able he was to speak. Already Sam had spoken his piece.

"Answer my question or I'll spread-eagle you," roared the captain. "By God, I'll flog you!"

Still, he was met with Sam's painful silence.

"I'll give you one more chance to answer me and I'll teach you who is master of this ship," said the captain, flinging off his coat. Enraged by Sam's silence, he ordered the mate to seize Sam up, repeating, "Seize him up, I said. Make a spread eagle of him. I'll teach him to answer me." The captain, now yelling at the top of his voice, shook his fist as he turned to climb up the hatchway.

The crew and officers followed, muttering their displeasure with his order. They too were defying him, he screeched. Only after repeated orders, Sam, without resistance, was placed against the shroud and made fast, his jacket off and his back exposed. The captain stood on the break of the deck only a few feet from his victim. In his hand he lovingly caressed a bight of thick, strong rope and began the beating.

Sam writhed in pain, but issued no sound as the rope rose and fell in deliberate, numbered, cracking reports, one after another. The man's body might have been a post or a tree buffeted by a storm. The captain was a big, powerful man and two lashes landing in the same place could cut deep into a man's flesh. Slightly misplaced lashes could break a man's back.

Bart stood back, his teeth clenched in anger, fighting for self-control, wincing inwardly with every unjust stroke. Finally, with the tenth lash Bart forcefully interjected, "You know that man can't speak, sir?" Possibly the beating had already gone on too long.

With that the captain turned on him. "I'll broach no interference," he roared, his eyes flashing and his face blood-red with anger. "Seize *this* interfering sailor up now!"

When the mate remained where he was, his mouth open in astonishment, the captain roared again, "Seize him up!"

The mate, obeying the order, met no resistance.

"I'd like to know why I'm being flogged, sir," said Bart. "Have I ever refused duty? Have you ever known me not to do my work?"

"You're being flogged for interference with the captain and asking questions!" shouted Stiles, readying his rope for Bart's back. He began the lashing.

"No one speaks on this vessel but me," the captain screamed, dancing as if imbued with the devil. As he went on his passion increased. "I'm flogging you because I love to do it. Do you understand me?"

"Yes, sir," replied Bart, now writhing under the pain. Sweat poured down his face and body as the welts appeared and his back was bloodied. But the captain's stroke had weakened with exhaustion in his violent beating of Sam, and when the mate finally cut down Bart he had received only seven lashes. Doubled over with pain, he went down unaided to the forecastle. Sam, unconscious, was carried below.

There had been no recourse open to the crew. If a sailor resists, it is mutiny; if the sailors together resist and take over a vessel, it is piracy; when a sailor resists the captain, he is breaking the law. There is no lawful response but to bear it.

From the forecastle Bart could hear the captain, still on deck. "Do you see what it means to interfere with me?" The crew did. He continued to harangue them, and Bart could visualize the men standing stiffly at attention throughout the tirade.

Long after the captain quieted, Bart and Sam went aft and asked the steward for salve or balsam to spread on their backs; crisscrossing stripes and welts were oozing blood and had begun to swell. Overhearing their request, the captain roared, "No. Put on your shirts. You're going ashore. No more men are going to lay up on this vessel."

Because neither Bart nor Sam could bend their backs to row, others pulled them ashore with their belongings and reluctantly left them to their own devices on the captain's order.

At least ashore they could get medicine to prevent infection. They took care of one another while their backs healed.

"Stay in California," Bart told Sam. "It's a land of opportunity. I'd stay myself, but I have some things to clear up." Bart pressed enough money in Sam's hands to hold him a few weeks.

By Christmas of 1866 Bart was back in Key West knocking on Consuelo's door.

"Who is there?" she asked before opening it.

"Frank Kelly," he replied.

Frank Kelly! Thrusting open the door, there stood Bart—dear Bart.

"Knocks on the door at night still give me a turn," she cried, falling into his outstretched arms. "I'm so glad to see you. Can you feel my heart tripping? Look, even my hands are shaking."

"You say that to all your sailor friends," he laughed.

"Oh, indeed, I do—to all the Barts and Franks and Tom, Dick and Harrys who come to haunt me like lost ghosts."

"I'm back like a bad penny."

"More like a legacy. Come into the kitchen. I know you're hungry." His face was thinner, but otherwise he looked good.

"Sailors don't exactly eat well. Knowing your kitchen, I haven't eaten all day. Getting used to the food was my biggest adjustment."

"Eat this chopped fruit while I heat up some pork roast. You can also tell me where you've been. I'll make a tray and we'll go upstairs."

"Don't touch me until after I've bathed. My self-control has limits—and I'm not exactly perfumed." He attempted to distance himself and failed.

"I hadn't noticed," she replied. "It had been so long I almost gave up ever seeing you again. But you left a lot of money here, remember?"

"I left a lot here," he replied, looking into her eyes. "It's been one hellish trip. I make a much better captain than sailor, I'll tell the cockeyed world."

When he had finished eating Consuelo took the tray downstairs. In the kitchen she attempted to marshal the facts of his situation. Since he had left, precious little had been accomplished in his behalf, despite the many months. Her lawyer, James Magbee, was now a judge of the circuit court so he could no longer handle her legal affairs. They would have to start over with another lawyer. The most disturbing fact, however, was her fear that Don Miguel's "wife," Anne-Marie, was Bart's wife, now living only a few blocks from her home. This thought was intolerable.

Consuelo could hear Bart in the bathing chamber as she climbed back up the stairs. She undressed and lay down on the bed in the dimly lit room. Finally, he appeared. "I feel like a bride," she said. "Isn't that ridiculous?"

"I'm rather excited myself. It has been a long time." He sat

169

down on the bed. Somewhere in the night an Obeah ceremony, the voodoo brought from Africa with the slaves, could be heard, like the thumping of her heart, beating out a dance. Witchcraft!

"Hear that," said Bart, listening to the strange rhythm that reverberated over the island, a low, heavy, jungle beat.

"It's the darkies. Now that the curfew is over we hear them more often at night. They're making magic," she replied, looking into his eyes and touching his arm.

"The magic is all in your touch," he said, bending over her to press his lips to hers and running his hands down her shoulders. Her body trembled slightly under his touch; her creamy skin glowed in the soft light. "You have no idea how I've missed you," he whispered, stretching out beside her as she closed her arms about him, drawing him to her.

Her hands ran down his back and then abruptly stopped. Easing out from his kiss, she whispered, "My God, what are those ridges across your back? I know every inch of you. They weren't there before."

"No, they weren't. I'll tell you later. Don't make me talk now," he urged, breathing the warm wind of his words into her ear. He felt her shiver as one hand caressed her breast. Then the undulating waves of her body beckoned him. A desperate wanting seized them both and he kissed her hair, her eyes and her face and then let his hands work down her body, stroking the softest skin. Rhythmically, he raised her to a feverish pitch of desire, until her body beat against his, pleading for his entrance. Holding back no longer, he began the plunges. Wave after wave of ecstasy washed over and through them until one great quivering shock, pulsating on and on, carried them to heaven's heights. The emotion was more than Consuelo could contain. Tears streamed down her cheeks, an aftermath of inexpressible release, let loose as if by floodgates opened.

"What have I done?" cried Bart, feeling her tears.

"You've come back. I'm nearly furious about it because I had almost learned to live without you. I'm so happy, though, I'm afraid I'm going to die."

"I don't pretend to understand you. You're talking in riddles, but if you're happy, that's fine," he said, kissing her again.

"And those ridges across your back?" she could finally ask.

170

"They're the relics of a beating I took from a brutal captain. But one day he'll get his just deserts, if only to be locked up as crazy."

Neither could really sleep well throughout the night, reaching out to each other, entwining and releasing, slipping in and out of consciousness, aware and unaware, finding and losing, until they finally synchronized and, locked together, found a second release.

The following day was spent reliving the past year, for Consuelo was hungry to hear everything that had happened to him. Another surprise later in the day, however, was to open the past in a more welcome manner. Consuelo and Bart were in the kitchen when there was a knock at the door. "I don't think it is anything," said Consuelo, putting down a momentary fright. "Listen, and if it is, flee out the back."

Consuelo answered the door to find a stranger—tall, well-dressed, her age—tipping his hat. With a decided British accent he said, "Pardon me for the intrusion, Madame. My name is Timothy Clayton." Consuelo was struck speechless, giving Bart time to emerge from the kitchen, his face abeam with delight, his arms wide open, rushing toward Tim.

"Come in. Come in," cried Consuelo, finding words.

Inside, the two men embraced, radiant at the sight of each other.

"We thought we had lost you on the *Sea Witch*. Your name wasn't on the survivor list."

"Well, here I am," replied Tim, grinning from ear to ear. "You see, that greedy captain was so anxious to get his hands on the *Catherine* that he had no interest in supporting any information that could quash the sale. So, he didn't give me Madame's message until we were at sea. I was furious, so much so that I skipped ship at Tampa—otherwise I might not be here today."

"We might have appreciated hearing that you were alive. You put me through a lot of grief," said Bart, cocking an eyebrow and giving him a wry smile.

"Grieving widowers are easiest consoled," replied Tim, smiling at Consuelo. "There was no point hurrying back at that point. But I did have reason to get back to England to pick up a small legacy that was grinding through the courts. Of course, that took much longer than I thought it would or I would have been here sooner. And you?"

Bart briefly told his story. "Consuelo hid me until I could get some false papers. My name is now Frank Kelly. I've been to California and got back only last night. I still have to clear my name some way. We hoped your statement might do it."

"You know I'll do everything I can," replied Tim. "How do I start? That's why I'm here."

"How long will you be here?" asked Consuelo, gripped by inner turmoil. Changes were in the air and the future loomed uncertain. It was nothing she could quite put her finger on, this unsettled feeling, but she could feel Bart drifting away from her.

"I thought I'd stay, if you Key Westers don't mind. I plan to buy a little house. I liked this town the minute I saw it."

"We'll see a lawyer tomorrow," said Consuelo. "Bart must still remain hidden, for your statement might not be enough— or soon enough. It seems the *Catherine* was carrying guns, but I've been told that to prove that this was Brian's private little enterprise is well nigh impossible. But now, let's bring out a good bottle of wine and drink to your good health!"

"What a sight for sore eyes you are," added Bart, taking the wine bottle from Consuelo's hands to open it.

"I presume the beard is part of your disguise; you're hardly the type to be sitting for holy portraits. But seriously, contraband guns aboard your ship is like the pox."

They talked long into the night, the men mostly, going back to days they sailed together, days when Bart was riding the crest, in control of his own ship, immune to beatings and humiliation, beating out slower, poorly run ships for the prize market money. This clever, capable man was now reduced to hiding in a damp, dark shaft.

Somewhere a dog barked, mellow, sad, far away. Consuelo found herself overwhelmed with an incredible sadness. I'm overtired, she thought. It's the wine.

When, eventually, Tim left and she and Bart climbed the stairs together, Consuelo's feelings of estrangement returned

172

without overt action or speech on Bart's part. Seeing Tim again had honed his memory, dislodged the rust and sharpened the realization that Anne-Marie might still be alive. He undressed, totally unaware of Consuelo's presence. She knew that he meant nothing rude, but he had wrapped himself in a cocoon of thought that excluded everything else. Indeed, Anne-Marie was now back in his mind so constantly that it was almost as if he were looking at her in some other setting transposed upon his view. Tim had been the catalyst, bringing back the old world. Much of what she had with Bart, his confidence, his trust and company would now be shared with Tim. She felt her stature diminished, usurped by Anne-Marie and Tim. Finally, she slept, but both she and Bart spent a very restless night.

The next day Consuelo and the rejuvenated Tim walked to lawyer Leeds's office. Falling into an easy stride with him, made easier by taking his arm, she began telling him what could not be said in Bart's presence. Surprisingly, today she felt remarkably at ease with Tim. The previous evening's jealousy was gone. Tim could prove an ally, worthy of her confidence, and she knew she needed some help.

She explained that she had learned that Brian had instigated Bart's beating, but that when Bart returned with Brian after a pleasant and successful voyage, she had lied to him. "Perhaps it was wrong of me, but I felt terribly sure Bart wouldn't believe me. This is important evidence that we need in writing. I think this can be bought."

"It was probably a mistake to lie to him," said Tim, "although I can only speculate on what might have changed. He might have dismissed Brian, for one thing. I'm sure that once he gets out of this jam, he'll forgive you. You've been extremely good to him." Tim looked down, giving her a reassuring glance.

"Remember, Mr. Leeds can't know that Bart is here in Key West. Our story will be that we are trying to clear his name at the urging of his family. It is important that you report that he was in a blind rage when he left you to find Brian and that circumstances prevented your returning earlier."

With Tim fully briefed, they addressed Mr. Leeds, a rotund, kindly gentleman wearing a pince-nez.

"Mr. Leeds, we're here to ask you to take on the defense of Captain Bartholomew Ramsden, accused both of murdering his first mate, Brian Delaney, and smuggling arms on his ship, the *Catherine*, recently confiscated. I am acting for his family," Consuelo said.

"I'm somewhat familiar with the case. It is one of the most serious in Key West in many years," replied Leeds. "I know the ship was auctioned."

"Until this gentleman, Timothy Clayton, returned to Key West yesterday, we did not have one voice in his defense. Mr. Clayton, however, is an important witness," said Consuelo. "His statement should explain Captain Ramsden's actions. He was aboard the *Catherine* on the fateful voyage."

Leeds listened attentively while Tim told of having overheard that a young girl had been washed up alive only a few days after the captain's wife was lost. "I relayed this information to Brian Delaney, the first mate, who promised to inform the captain," said Tim. "Immediately, I put out to sea. When I returned a few weeks later, I happened to meet Captain Ramsden and asked him about the message I had given the first mate about the woman washed ashore." Tim then described the captain's reaction on receiving the withheld information. "Realizing that Brian Delaney had acted maliciously and deliberately, he flew into a rage."

Tim went on to explain that even more damning information had come to light through a statement of the steward, Roger Bains, while in the West Indies. Bains had heard the mate lie, but fearful of retaliation, he did not come forward. "The hours of searching for the wife and child had been pointless," concluded Tim.

Consuelo then related information from her source that the first mate had instigated an attack on the captain.

Mr. Leeds took careful notes and suggested that they try to get an admission by the captain's attacker that the dead man had hired him to commit assault and battery. "Do you think you can get the attacker's testimony?"

"Yes, for a price," Tim replied. "And I will assure him that he will not be charged for his attack."

"Well," replied Leeds, "you can't give him immunity from prosecution, because that's up to the prosecutor. He has, after all, committed a crime, and will be confessing it. However, it is a relatively minor one compared with that of which your friend is charged—murder. If the man is willing to confess that Delaney paid him for the attack, I think I can persuade the prosecutor to look the other way. His testimony would show that Delaney bore the captain ill will which he carried into action.

"If Bains can be found," continued Leeds, "to testify that Delaney stood by and silently let the wife and child be swept overboard, and that he lied about that, it would surely be an ameliorating factor for Captain Ramsden regarding the fight in which Delaney died. Moreover, possibly Bains could help your friend in establishing that Delaney was the smuggler. Otherwise it will be difficult to prove that the captain knew nothing of it and should not have been charged. A lucrative smuggling business may have been Delaney's motive in all this. It would appear that he wanted to put Ramsden out of business and to take his place as captain. Who knows? Find Bains if you can. Meanwhile get the admission from the captain's assailant. Then we shall see . . ." The lawyer peered over his pince-nez while Tim and Consuelo looked to each other. "I wouldn't advise the captain to come back to Key West until we know where we stand. That is, if you have any idea where Captain Ramsden is," added Leeds, looking back to his notes. "You never know how these things will turn out."

Consuelo felt the blood run from her face and fought for poise. "We have a lot to do. Mr. Leeds, thank you. We'll take no more of your valuable time today. We'll do our best to do as you say."

Tim accompanied Consuelo on a second visit to Wooleye, who seemed glad enough to see her despite the problems she inevitably brought.

"What do you need old Wooleye for this time?" he asked,

175

smiling at Tim, while straining to get a good look at him. "Are you her bodyguard?" he interjected quickly. "She needs one."

"Sounds like a good job," replied Tim.

"Wooleye, I need the name of the man who assaulted that captain a while back," said Consuelo. "What's his price and what's yours?"

"I can't promise you anything, you understand?" he said finally. "But I'll be in touch with you."

After leaving Wooleye, Consuelo and Tim walked down to the waterfront, always in a foment of activity when the fishing boats came in. The sun was a brilliant gold and it would perceptibly grow redder and redder as it lowered in the pink mackerel sky. The water turned from a flaming, uneasy phosphorus to the color of oxidized mercury or mauve-lemon light. A deep melodious percussion of the fading afternoon formed a background to their conversation.

"How magnificent this world can be," said Consuelo, gasping at the light, "and then how hard. The life of subterfuge that Bart is living breaks my heart. I can't bear to look at scenes such as this without thinking of him cooped up or slaving on some miserable ship with only a deck to walk."

"I know what you mean."

Suddenly, she turned to face Tim and said, "Can I trust you with something? Will you swear to secrecy until I relieve you of your promise?" When he hesitated a moment she added, "I must confide in someone and I need help." Her plea had its effect.

"All right, if you insist, I promise. What is it?"

"There is a young girl living in Key West whose name is Anne-Marie. She is here only because of a badly injured leg. She led a very . . . ah . . . abnormal and reclusive life, it appears, until she came here. Her description fits that of Bart's wife."

"Well then, for heaven's sake, let's go see her," cried Tim, his eyes alight.

"Tim, she's married to another man—a very powerful, wealthy man. And they have a child. Were I to tell Bart, he would rush over there, exposing himself to apprehension—and suppose she isn't the right girl? Or suppose she is and she's happily married to her present husband? We don't know what has happened, do we?"

A half-formulated reproach died on Tim's lips. "Maybe you're right, but just remember, no good deed goes unpunished—that's an old Hawaiian saying. However, sooner or later Bart will discover that there is such a woman in Key West. I'm sure she is gossiped about—even the sailors at sea will probably have heard of her as 'the rich mystery woman.' If Bart ever discovered her presence here he would know that you knew of it also and didn't tell him what he had a right to know. You are his friend . . .

"But, perhaps you are right," he continued. "He might go off half-cocked and do just that. Perhaps you should wait until we've had a chance to find his witnesses. Then would be soon enough. Meanwhile, he's talking to no one and won't hear of her."

"I hate myself for burdening you," she added, looking at him.

He consoled her. "Uneasy people seem to have a mania for self-justification and seek a rationale for their actions. It leads to some strange thinking. But anyway, they say a burden shared is a burden halved, or something like that. Now, dear lady, have you any more secrets up your sleeve?"

"Yes," she said impulsively, "I'm in love with Bart." She plunged ahead recklessly. "If and when he finds and returns to his wife, it will be the end of me. I have no more secrets."

Tim maintained his composure. "They say there's no accounting for the human heart."

"But I'm supposed to find the wife . . ." Suddenly, she regretted having made the last revelation; she could have sworn Tim was disappointed. Perhaps he felt she had deliberately withheld information, or had moved too slowly. Her actions could have been self-serving.

Finally he said, "My dear lady, you have your share of troubles and at this moment I do not judge you. Also your last secret is not very well kept." Now he was smiling down at her and she felt much buoyed by that smile. "Come, let's get back to Bart and tell him what we have accomplished today before curiosity kills him."

"Remember, we can't tell him about the visit to Wooleye or he will know that I deceived him once before. I have never told him that Brian hired his attacker."

Long after Bart expected them, they returned. "I had forgotten how interminably long one waits, first to see a lawyer, and then how they have to take down every detail," he confessed. "Still, I'm heartened by your progress. It is disappointing to learn the process will take many weeks. Heaven only knows what can happen in that time. We seem to be so near and yet so far. I would go mad sitting around here, so I'll ship out on the next ship bound for anywhere but China. Can you find me a berth, Tim? I hate to shove off so soon after finding you again, but I think it's for the best."

"In light of what we learned today, I would say so, too," replied Tim grimly. He dared not intrude upon Consuelo in that moment with even a glance.

Three days later Tim had located a ship bound for Boston and back. The timing was perfect. As a crew member of the *Annabelle*, Bart left Key West.

CHAPTER THIRTEEN

During the next few days Tim was a frequent visitor to Consuelo's house. They dined on her patio attended by Pearl, no longer fearful of intrusion by deputies looking for Bart. Consuelo was helping him in finding a house. Though Tim would have a few pieces of family heirloom furniture from England shortly, she promised to help with furnishing of the place as soon as he could take possession. The making of curtains, selecting linens and dishware would be a welcome distraction for her, and Tim knew very little about housekeeping and furbishing and welcomed all suggestions.

The pace of Consuelo's life that had for so long been reduced to a crawl was now moving into a gallop. Events were pulling her along, but to what destination? Foremost in her mind was the problem of clearing Bart. Perhaps I have accepted more than I can deliver, thought Consuelo. For the moment there was little that could be done until she heard from Wooleye and learned more about the mysterious Anne-Marie Miguel. At least, in Tim she had an ally.

One afternoon as she was discussing various problems connected with Bart's case, Tim sat regarding her, listening, but also doing some thinking of his own. Finally, he said, "Do you know what I think you should do? I think you should pay a visit to Anne-Marie yourself. You've been sending out boys to do a man's work." He was referring, of course, to Suzanne and Mercedes.

"I've had a feeling about her all along, but didn't want to accept it, Tim," admitted Consuelo. "She's the mystery woman of the island. She *has* to be Bart's wife."

"Go find out for yourself," he advised.

It was with considerable trepidation that Consuelo dressed to visit the woman she regarded as a rival for her lover's affections—unless, of course, Anne-Marie no longer wanted him. Afternoon tea had become a frequent "at home" in Anne-Marie's bedroom; Suzanne and Mercedes brought in other young friends who were also curious, sympathetic and concerned about the interesting new resident. Anne-Marie's prosperity alone was bound to receive a good measure of attention. After all, she wouldn't be laid up forever, and it was easy to envision Anne-Marie as a lavish hostess and one of the most sought-after guests.

Louisa Tatine and Josephine Ximinez had also called this afternoon, Consuelo discovered, but had left early. Consuelo was well-received, but it did not take her long to discover that Anne-Marie had become highly adept at evading questions that touched on her past. Consuelo could establish nothing definite without revealing that she knew Anne-Marie's husband, if Bart were indeed he. In her evasions, Anne-Marie was utterly charming. Within the flick of an eyelash she could gracefully turn any question away from herself, adverting to a compelling current event, the elegance of one's hat or the price of tea in China.

Consuelo herself was adept in asking questions and artfully steered the conversation to regional social customs to provide an opening to ask Anne-Marie where she had been born. Bearing her best smile, Anne-Marie responded, "Oh, no place anyone has ever heard of! But where were *you* born?"

The moment Consuelo replied, Anne-Marie was off on the subject of Key West. Accepting defeat in this game, Consuelo

180

turned her thoughts—though not her rattling tongue—elsewhere.

The most disturbing thing was Anne-Marie's beauty. Consuelo felt instinctively that if Bart had not been a husband in love with her, he now, within five minutes, would be. Hers was not a superficial beauty, but beauty that ran deep, one of character.

This elegant and sophisticated woman was far from the naive, innocent, girlish beauty that Bart had described and had married—and certainly carried as a picture in his mind. Those God-given attributes, the mass of coppery hair, the planes of her face, the long exquisite neck and luminous eyes were a part of the picture, but altered. Here was a woman who could become the mistress of a king should he lay eyes upon her. A pity there was not one in Key West...

Consuelo stood by the bedside night table as Anne-Marie opened a drawer to show Consuelo a sample of unusual lace. Consuelo glanced down and saw what appeared to be a drawerful of emeralds. "My heavens, Anne-Marie!" exclaimed Consuelo. "Aren't you afraid of thieves?"

"I just discovered these this morning," said Anne-Marie, pulling a necklace from the drawer where it had been hastily dropped instead of into its velvet case where matching earrings and a bracelet still rested. "This was a lovely surprise. I'd like to share it, but dared not with others present who might be inclined to babble freely about their worth. You, obviously, would not." Anne-Marie held up the most magnificent emerald necklace Consuelo had ever dreamed existed. Anne-Marie put it on, pulling the bed jacket aside to reveal one solitary emerald on a fine gold chain. Over it now lay perhaps fifty emeralds laced together by a delicate filigree of gold. The magnificent arabesques and scrolls filled the V of her neck and bosom. "Isn't it exquisite?" asked Anne-Marie. "And here are the matching earrings and bracelet."

"Your husband loves you very dearly," said Consuelo. "It is quite the loveliest jewelry I've ever seen—and perfect for you. Emerald must be your birthstone," she probed, hopefully.

"Why, I suppose it is," replied Anne-Marie. "I'd never thought of that!"

"And you must soon get well to wear these to balls and to the opera in all the capitals of the world. I'm afraid that here you'll make everyone envious."

"Perhaps not, but anyway I shall not wear them here. They are only important to me for the love they represent."

A maid knocked and entered. Consuelo inferred that her presence meant that it was time for some sickbed routine, and she quickly made her excuses.

"Please do return," begged Anne-Marie. She smiled, lighting Consuelo's departure like the green fire of the emeralds.

At the earliest opportunity Consuelo related to Tim the account of her visit. "I feel free in telling you this because I'm certain it will go no further," said Consuelo, "but when she pulled out an emerald necklace and put it on top of another emerald she was already wearing, I thought I was looking at all the emeralds in the world!"

Consuelo's excitement kept her from noticing a startled expression on Tim's face. How often he had seen that solitary emerald around Anne-Marie's neck! He almost blurted out that this fact confirmed that the girl was indeed Bart's wife, but checked his tongue, feeling there might be a more appropriate time to reveal it when he could do so gently. Quickly erasing his surprise he replied idly, "Jewels—the orators of love."

"And it is obvious she loves her husband dearly, Tim," added Consuelo.

It was only a few days later that Consuelo received a note from Wooleye. She and Tim were to visit him the following day at four. "It has to be important news," said Consuelo, "or he wouldn't have called for us."

It was with some trepidation that they wondered what the price would be—and not necessarily in money.

Again they were ushered into the private chamber. They had expected to see only Wooleye, but seated at a table with him, with a glass of rum in his hand, was the ugliest man Tim or Consuelo had ever seen. His face was a ruin, a horror mask. Consuelo, struck speechless, gladly let Tim conduct the meeting. "I understand, sir," said Tim, "that the first mate on the *Catherine* hired you to assault the captain—at least, I believe that's why we're here."

"As you can tell by the looks of me," he replied.

"I'd like your statement to that effect, and I'm willing to pay for it. The captain was a friend of mine who, I'm sure you know, later killed the mate."

"I don't exactly bear your captain-friend any love, mister. I'll carry this face to me grave!"

"What's done is done. We all bear the consequences of our acts, some more visibly than others. What's the price for a sworn statement?"

"Five hundred dollars," the man replied curtly.

"That's a lot of money."

"That's me price," he said flatly.

"Then come. We may not even need your testimony, but it could speed things up. We'll visit the lawyer now. No dillydallying or the deal is off," said Tim, his voice carrying a convincing tone of finality. Consuelo knew that it was a bluff and that Tim was taking a huge gamble, but it worked. Consuelo put a one hundred dollar note in Wooleye's hand and, with Bart's assailant in tow, they left.

Lawyer Leeds proved adroit in handling the assailant, Richard Shuttele.

"I wasn't to kill him, sir, I'd never agree to that, but I was to put him out of business."

"You were to use a knife?" queried Leeds.

"Yes, sir," was the reply.

"Mr. Shuttele," continued Leeds, "do you have any idea why the mate was so anxious to get rid of the captain?"

"No, sir."

"He never told you the captain was a bad man—mean, or anything like that?"

"No, sir."

"I can certainly attest that he wasn't," interjected Tim.

"That's already in your statement, Mr. Clayton," replied the lawyer. "I do want that point in Mr. Shuttele's deposition, however. We don't want it to look as if the captain had this beating coming to him."

They waited while Leeds carefully formulated Shuttele's statement, which was then signed and witnessed.

Once outside, Tim put the money in Shuttele's hands, slowly counting out five hundred dollars. "If you can gather any information or evidence that the first mate was smuggling guns, I'll pay for that too," said Tim.

"That's out of my line," replied Shuttele, walking away.

"We could have subpoenaed that man and gotten the story out of him for nothing, but you would have been finished with your underworld friends," said Tim.

"Don't be superior," Consuelo sniffed. "Had it not been for my underworld friends we never would have found this man."

"We made rare progress today," said Tim, sniffing his Chianti over a celebration dinner at Marcus's place. There was only one respectable restaurant in town, owned by Marcus Oliveri, known only as "Mr. Marcus," a handsome, tall Italian. He was a typical independent Key West merchant. When someone foolishly complained about the food or service, he would reply curtly, "Go somewhere else. I don't care a shucks for your patronage." Since there was no place else to go, the rebuked diner usually blushed and remained. The food was usually good; the service was uncivil. Tim and Consuelo did not notice.

"You were wonderful today with Shuttele. My heart is lighter than it has been in a long time," said Consuelo, her voice ringing with sincerity.

"We had to get him down there fast before he had time to up his price," said Tim. "I've handled a lot of rough characters in my day. 'What's in it for me?' generally means 'How much will you pay?' If you surprise a man by paying his price without haggling he will take it and do as you ask..."

As Tim spoke his voice dwindled off. Suddenly he saw Consuelo and her situation in a new light: He was now conscious of her as he had never been before. Having felt she belonged to Bart, a man with enough troubles, he had taken a back seat, and as a point of honor would not have courted Consuelo. But now, he saw her as a lovely creature about to be hurt. Bart would return to Anne-Marie, he felt certain.

Consuelo's perfume and the one rose on the table mingled to assault his nostrils with a delicate sweetness. As she raised her wineglass to her lips, gently swirling the ruby nectar, then daintily sipping it, her womanliness smote him.

Meeting his moonstruck gaze with kindly affection, Consuelo suggested, "Let's have coffee at my house. It will take so long here."

Tim paid the bill, and they left, both somewhat bemused. As they walked, a light, cool evening breeze touched Tim's face, and, thinking that she might feel it too, he drew her light shawl over her shoulder, soft as a rose petal.

Embarrassment flushed his face. "I thought you might be cold," he said. Consuelo gave no indication that she had noticed his expression or his explanation because indeed she hardly had. Her thoughts were of Bart. Tim seemed to her like a brother. As they entered the house, a not too far distant bell tolled.

In the parlor Pearl set out Meissen cups and a silver coffee-pot warming over a gold-tipped azure flame. One lamp cast a warm protective glow about the room, a soft, relaxing light.

Instead of seating himself to be served, Tim walked about, his hands nervously jammed into pockets too small to contain them, while Consuelo filled their cups, adding his two lumps of sugar. Uncharacteristic of his usual good manners, with one big swallow he bolted it down.

"You seem terribly nervous," she observed. "Is there something you haven't told me?"

Suddenly, Tim pulled her to her feet and as quickly took her into his arms. "There's a lot I haven't told you," he replied and pressed his lips to hers.

For a moment she struggled, pushing him away, but to no avail. "Tim, please, don't. Let me go!" she said. "This is wrong."

"No," replied Tim. "You ask too much of me."

"Tim, asking you to unhand me is not too much. Be reasonable," she pleaded, not wanting to offend him, and yet . . .

"I love you, Consuelo," he replied thickly, caressing her shoulder under her gown.

Straining for release, foreseeing his intention, she gasped. "Please, Tim, stop and think what you are doing!" By now she was hammering on his chest, but she was no match for his powerful arms.

"I want you, Consuelo. You're not for Bart, but for me."

Consuelo was not a woman who could be raped—nor was Tim a rapist. He thought no further than the joy of the moment. Still, the nearness of her and the wine that loosened his inhibitions combined to trigger him. He held her as if she were life itself and continued to kiss her as if she were his sole salvation. Finally, seeing that her protestations did no good, she responded, at first as if aware of a friend's need. To her astonishment the caresses and embraces became pleasant and comforting. Like igniting sparks that found a prepared hearth, his kisses leapt into a flame. In the end she said to him, "Let's go upstairs. I hope you know what you're doing."

"I do, Consuelo—better than you think." With that he followed her upstairs to make love to her willing body. At first she was coolly unresponsive, the time involved in undressing having given her second thoughts, but finally, to her embarrassment, she found herself cooperating.

Afterward, she turned to him. "This may shatter your friendship with Bart," she said curtly.

"No, it will not. Believe me it won't or I would not have taken you. Bart is still in love with his wife and I know that she is alive. It is you that I'm thinking of. You will bear the loss of Bart easier with me around. I'll play second fiddle—for a while."

"Tim Clayton, you act as if I *liked* loving Bart. It is the greatest cross I have to bear," she cried. "For one thing, I'm ten years older than he is. He wants a family. Don't think I haven't been tormented by this."

"I'll wait for the rebound," he replied. "Also, I'm going to tell him how I feel about you and he can flatten me if he chooses. Don't think I haven't seen the damage his fists can do."

"You act as if you can cut me up, divide me, like a pie!" cried Consuelo, now angry.

"Nothing of the sort. I don't want to see you hurt by anyone. Neither would Bart want it."

"Please don't feel that I'm not flattered that you care for me. And I'm really not angry with you. I can't be. But what in the world am I going to do with my crazy heart? Why must we all be so tortured?"

"I have no answers. I only know that I want you and I believe that I can make you love me one day," he replied.

Consuelo donned a robe, seated herself at her dressing table and began brushing her hair. She could see Tim's face in her mirror as he was dressing to return to his home, and it was thus that she talked to him. "What do you think that we should do next?" she asked, scanning the mirror for her answer.

"I'd like to talk to the sheriff," replied Tim. "We just may be able to get his sympathy. We should find out whether or not there were any arrests for gun smuggling in either Boston or Key West. If there have been, it might lead to something. If you have any other suggestions, I'd like to hear them."

"I'm afraid I've been so rude to the sheriff that he would never help me. But you are a fresh face—and it is a kind face you wear, Tim," she added. He bent, placing a kiss on her forehead.

"Good night, love," he said, departing.

The following day, Tim paid the sheriff a visit. The man listened patiently as Tim concluded, "It is entirely possible, sir, that the wife of Don Miguel is one and the same person as Anne-Marie, Captain Ramsden's wife."

The sheriff disguised his interest. "I'll see what can be done to achieve justice, but Captain Ramsden is still a fugitive and it will take a court order to change that. I'll let you know if any gun smuggling operations come to light," promised the sheriff. "The war is over and so is that business, for the moment. Of course, there's always a little gun trade to Cuba."

Tim left the sheriff's office, not particularly satisfied with the meeting, but unable to put his finger on the reason why.

The minute he left the station, a watch was put on the Fitch place.

The sheriff's friend, Don Miguel, was also notified that a person or persons in Key West seemed to believe that his wife was the wife of Captain Bartholomew Ramsden.

CHAPTER FOURTEEN

As Anne-Marie's spirits improved as a result of her afternoon teas, so did her physical condition. Dr. Burbury's visits dwindled, imperceptibly at first. Time no longer dragged.

Her first steps were frustrating and exhausting because her mind, restless and swirling in need for action, could not accept the slow pace her jellied muscles demanded. Laboriously, step by step, the process of learning to walk again began.

"How strange it is to be a toddler," Anne-Marie told her friends. "After so long being powerless and limited, four steps across the room seem like a hike to New Orleans. Coming downstairs is a day's journey."

"Don't worry, Mama, I'll help you," assured Samantha, joy mingled with fear on watching her mother struggle with crutches.

"I can't go far. My underarm aches within a minute. I never dreamed of that problem. The cane stage will seem like a trot and just plain walking a gallop."

Her love for Don Miguel had grown as true love does. Love at first sight, she knew, is for youngsters, captured by a yellow curl or a dashing moustache. She had wondered whether her love for Don Miguel was grounded in pity, but this she dismissed. He was not a pitiful figure. His masculinity tempered by gentleness and kindness was his attraction. Their pleasure in each other was clouded only by the fear of losing him in death. Her suspicion about his business, possibly nefarious, was obscured by all she felt for him. Now she accepted his silence about many things as an irrelevance in their relationship.

Once in Key West, Anne-Marie had soon learned that the business of wrecking was one of the prime occupations of the area and that it was carried on with the full approval of the law. Bart had never explained the worthwhile legitimacy of the Key West wrecking business to Anne-Marie—nor had Don Miguel. Anne-Marie had to learn to speak Spanish and then she learned from Concepción that wreckers were "good men." Men on the coast who deliberately wrecked ships were no less than pirates, and naturally gave the business, which was salvage, a bad name in many people's minds.

Anne-Marie learned from Suzanne and Mercedes that the richest cargoes of the world—laces, silks, wines, silver and articles of commerce—reached Key West legitimately in this manner. Sale of these goods brought speculators and insurance underwriters to the town. The wrecker's life, sometimes dangerous and hard, was often jolly and carefree. Their craft were well-stocked with food and well-equipped. Typically, wreckers spent the night in safe anchorage. By day—nearly every day—they cruised along the reefs, on the lookout for vessels in distress—and there often was one. Then there was a shout, "All hands to work." And they did work, night and day to relieve the ship lest heavy weather drive the ship further onto the reef or cause her to bilge. When that occurred, men worked either waist deep in water or diving in an all-out effort to save the cargo, awash in whatever the ship carried: molasses, sugar, perhaps even guano.

At the time that Anne-Marie landed in Key West, the wrecking business was in its heyday. Before the treaty that ceded Florida to the United States, salvors from the Bahamas and Cuba would rescue vessels on the Florida reefs and then take their salvage claims to Nassau or Havana for adjudication. To prevent this, in 1825 Congress passed a law prescribing that the claims for salvage work in United States waters be brought to a port of entry within the U.S.—greatly increasing custom revenues. In

1847 Congress further stated that wrecking must be licensed by a judge of the U.S. District Court and that salvage vessels must be seaworthy and sufficiently equipped for the work. The wreck master was required to be innocent of fraud or misconduct—a far cry from Anne-Marie's first impression.

This newly acquired knowledge caused Anne-Marie to reexamine her feelings about Don Miguel. It had taken her a while to realize that he was a complex personality. Now, when she began to learn to walk again, she realized that she was starting life anew.

Each step that she took was a victory, sweeter because it would please him. As she sat at her dressing table, brushing her hair, highlighting her cheeks with a whisper of rouge or applying a tinge of lip salve, each gesture was designed to delight her Don. His sudden arrivals and departures marked her life like a sundial; his absences were nights unrecorded, his presence measured by the swiftly passing marks of the day.

One day she realized that she had never told Don Miguel that she loved him. But surely he knows, she thought. He can surely read it in everything I say. But she determined that when he next returned, she would put the matter right.

Hearing, finally, his footsteps on the stairs, she called out to him, "Is that you, my love?" knowing full well the answer. As he stepped into her room, her musical tones filled the room. "Oh, my love, you are finally here. I have missed you so..."

Blind now to everything but her open arms and the cadence of her voice, closing his eyes as if to protect himself against seeing something that would destroy the moment, he reached for her. Stumbling, she fell into his arms.

"I love you," she whispered hoarsely.

"Say it again and again," he cried. "I can never hear it enough." The moment had been a long time coming. It had been almost three years since Anne-Marie had been picked up by him on the beach, another man's wife.

Don Miguel eased her to the bed, loosened his clothing and pressed his flesh down upon her. Coaxing her body with sure, powerful hands, her trembling met his own. In a frenzy, Anne-Marie was borne along, buoyant as if floating in a stream, carried past marvelously shimmering images that caught her and then released her, and then held her again...

"I have come to care for you so much," she whispered later as they lay together looking for words to match the fulfillment of their bodies. She saw that Don Miguel was looking at her with tears of admiration in his eyes. Then he embraced her again, not passionately, but as if his soul had finally, after years of wandering, found a resting place, secure and content where he wanted to be.

Now it seemed to her so silly—so wasteful—that she had not allowed herself to reach this point earlier. Don Miguel had been waiting for her, patiently.

Anne-Marie's analysis of Don Miguel's state of mind was not entirely correct. Their lovemaking had drawn the color from his face. He had gone out to her unreservedly, and, in the spirit of the moment, he was on the brink of making a clean breast of what he knew, utilizing her avowal of love to cushion the news that Bart Ramsden was alive. Had he been a younger man, surely he would have given way to the urge, but Don Miguel had grown cautious. He could not risk losing her now, and so the faltering moment passed.

Knowing the decision was morally wrong, he was pained, but this pain was infinitely less than what the pain of losing her would be.

"We have so many things to do," he said. "You should attend some fancy balls and the opera in Europe..."

"Once those things seemed so desirable. Perhaps knowing now that I can have them makes them seem frivolous and unimportant. With you I will be happy anywhere. I would not trade a month of operas for five seconds of your life. Don Miguel, I'm terrified of tiring you or straining you or doing anything—even making love with you—that might spend the precious energy that keeps you alive." As the words tumbled out she turned to him again, burying her head on his shoulder, feeling the comfort of his warmth and daring to think no more of the emptiness of a life without him.

His visits never lasted more than a few days. He never offered information as to the nature of his business, and Anne-Marie never asked, not wanting to risk the harmony between them. She knew that the plantings on Cayos de las Matas absorbed him, especially new crops such as sisal; he had always been interested in introducing new plants. Keeping the tender cuttings alive over the long journeys was a great problem. Further, once on the key a little too much sun or wind often made their precarious voyages in vain. These enterprises, however, could hardly account for the wealth that Don Miguel possessed, nor could the business of wrecking, which she felt sure he controlled. She could not permit herself to believe that he could do anything wrong. Earlier misgivings about him receded. What existed was only what she saw and touched. Nothing else mattered.

Understandably, once Anne-Marie was on her feet, her first arduous task was standing for a dressmaker's fittings. "It's high time for a new wardrobe," declared Anne-Marie.

Don Miguel readily agreed. His warm dark eyes lent approval to the bolts of fine fabrics slowly shaping into ruffles and flounces that caressed each curve of her body.

"Don Miguel, do you like it?" she asked, referring to a dress that had just been delivered. She was standing before a mirror, smoothing the glowing apricot silk over her tiny waist, eyeing herself. "Please tell me the truth."

"I'm the wrong person to ask. I think a flour sack would become you—if it were properly sashed, of course."

"You're no help," she chided. "People judge a man not by his clothes, but by his wife's clothes. Don't you know that?"

"I can see my esteem in the world rising like a hot air balloon. Do you think I can handle all the worldwide approbation?" he queried.

The altered light in which she saw Don Miguel illuminated all the corners of her life. For the first time she saw herself as a composite human being. Life was no longer an unhealed place where accidents, diseases or storms took their toll. So it was in this peaceful climate that Anne-Marie began daily excursions into the world outside her home. At first it was only an exhausting walk around the block. As she grew stronger, she ventured further away, usually with Samantha, who by now knew her way about the city, having walked with the maids every afternoon.

The waterfront was naturally the most compelling and lively sector and Anne-Marie gravitated there like a mermaid. Occasionally, she was there when the cry went out, "Wreck ashore," which electrified the usually slow-moving population. As if on a signal, sails were hoisted, and groups of three or four vessels slid out of the harbor.

One afternoon, in a bright and blinding sun, while walking in this sector, Anne-Marie looked up to see what at first she imagined to be a mirage. The intense light had washed the blue from the sky, and a slight breeze skimming across the surface of the water made the sea look silver. Only close to the wharves did the water pick up the blue against a glistening, shimmering background. Blinking her eyes to adjust to the reflected light, she looked again. Clearly she saw the *Catherine* pulling in.

The men aboard her looked like ants scurrying about. She shook her head as if to clear cobwebs shrouding her senses. Steadily she looked again, but nothing had vanished. The *Catherine* was still there.

The full impact of that sight struck her and her heart began to hammer. Slowing her pace, she walked as if in a trance, oblivious to everything and everyone except the ship. Bumping into people, hastily and numbly begging their pardons, she pushed on. Finally, she saw the name *Greyhound* and the hammering in her heart subsided and once more she could breathe.

Of course, it was a sister ship, undoubtedly built by the same shipyard, and painted gray, not white, she decided. With considerable relief, she recovered from the awful shock. Still, she waited as if irresistibly held. She had no idea how long she stood there, transfixed. For a few moments she was catapulted into the past. Long forgotten memories, sensations, crowded in upon her. Wordlessly, they slowly revolved and then picked up speed and sound. The sounds grew louder and louder as the pictures, the forgotten scenes, one after another, came faster and faster. Finally, their force caught her breath and she gasped for air. The noisy intake in her throat brought her back to the present.

The crew was made up of men who were strangers to her.

194

Eventually, as their work drew to a halt, some of the men noticed her and made obvious comments, their fresh remarks being readily discernible without being audible. When they were free to leave the ship and disembarked one after another, she stopped one man who by his attitude seemed a little more genteel than the others.

"Who is the captain of this ship, mister?" she asked with no little hesitation in her voice. The strangeness of the name he gave was for an instant reassuring. "The ship looks so much like the *Catherine*, I was taken aback. I thought I would know the captain," she added, catching a questioning look on the sailor's face. Then she realized her words probably made little sense as the man still stood there.

"She used to be the *Catherine*," he said, felling her.

"I...I...thought the *Catherine* was...lost?" she stammered, the world turning again.

"No," he replied. "But it's a sad story. The captain murdered his first mate. No one knows why except that he must have been deranged. He had lost his wife and child not many months before. Then the captain disappeared. They never caught him."

Anne-Marie stood, her mouth agape, her eyes widening and burning with the blinding white light his words had fueled.

"Are you all right, ma'am?" the man asked, an arm extended, but not daring to touch her. "You look as if you don't feel well."

"I'm quite all right," she replied with more certainty in her voice than she felt. "Just shocked. Please tell me, then what happened?"

"That's simple. The *Catherine* was confiscated and sold at auction. A new owner took over and there's a new captain."

"You have no idea then, what happened to...Captain Ramsden?" she continued, her eyes hungrily focused upon his.

"Swallowed up by the earth, ma'am. There's no telling where he could be. It has been a long time, you know..."

"I'm relieved he's alive," she said finally.

"If you'll pardon my saying so, you look as though you've seen a ghost."

"Perhaps I have, but thank you for your information."

There being no place to sit down, Anne-Marie turned. She

retraced her steps, feeling the heaviness of her feet somehow dragging her body in a homeward direction.

Inwardly she wailed, Oh, dear God, what am I to do? Oh, what am I to do?

She was met by a household relieved to see her. "I walked too far and had to stop to rest," she told Concepción, trying desperately not to reveal her distress. Haltingly she stumbled upstairs. Only the anxiety in her maid's face kept her from crawling. Closeting herself in her room, she fought for composure. "I must have time to think," she cried aloud, throwing herself on the bed. "What can I do?" She wept.

Hearing cries that sounded not unlike a wounded animal, Samantha came crashing in. "Mama, Mama, are you all right? Did you fall again? Did you break your leg again?" she asked anxiously.

"No, my little one," replied Anne-Marie, diverted for a moment if only because she was startled by the child. "Mama just got too tired, that's all. You've been too tired sometimes, haven't you? It hurts, doesn't it? Run along now like a good girl and let Mama rest. Eat your supper." The words were abrupt, and the toneless voice did little to pacify the girl. Reluctantly, she retreated.

Concepción wisely brought up a tray with a light supper that Anne-Marie ate, scarcely noticing it. Still, she had been ravenously hungry. She felt as if she had been struck a mortal blow and yet she was still alive. She thought she had endured just about all the emotional adversity life could offer, and now this.

The man she loved had deceived her terribly, inconceivably. He had told her the *Catherine* was lost with all hands. He must have known this was not true, maybe not at first, but certainly later. Her only comfort was that Bart was alive, that his young life had not been snuffed out. But where was he? Too easily he had given her up. By now he was probably married to someone else. Possibly, too, he had other children. And Don Miguel had lied to her and stood by and watched her suffer, letting her grieve, knowing all the time. It had been cruel. Heartless. Needless.

She had been a plaything, a doll to dress and caress. It was all too wicked. Yes, *wicked* was the word. And, after making

196

her love him, he was hurting her again, hurting her by disappointing and disillusioning her with his baseness.

Now, dry-eyed, she sat twisting a handkerchief, twisting a handkerchief just as her poor mother always had. The thought of her mother opened a new set of wounds. Her poor, proud parents! How they had also needlessly suffered. In that moment she knew for a certainty that they had never received her letters. Undoubtedly, all these years they had also grieved. Surely, they would have learned that Bart was wanted for murder—bad news travels fast. He would not have returned home a fugitive from justice. Never. He was too proud for that. So they had suffered that too.

"Thank heaven Don Miguel is not here," said Anne-Marie, "much as I need someone to talk to and much as I need help, he could help least of all. I need to think."

Her most rational thought in some hours was interrupted by the sound of Don Miguel's footsteps on the stairs. Just the thought of him brought a flush of anger to her face. "Dear God," she prayed. "Keep me from crying. Don't let me break down."

Slowly he opened the door and, seeing her still dressed, a great smile crossed his face as he moved to embrace her.

"Don't touch me," she hissed, turning from him.

"To what do I owe this wifely greeting?" he asked, withdrawing, his eyebrows knotted in a frown.

She rose from the bed, turning sharply so as not to look at him while grasping a chair-back for support. Her hands clenched the top rung, steadying her. Her eyes now slanted like those of a cat ready to spring.

Don Miguel had never seen her in such a rage and, baffled, said, "I'd like to know what brought this mood on?"

"This *mood*," she cried, spitting out the words. "Do you think this is a *mood*? Well, I'll tell you, it isn't!"

"I'd thank you to keep your voice down. Samantha is sleeping and there are servants about."

Her fury ebbed for a moment, then returned, but infinitely better contained.

"I walked down to the waterfront today," she said slowly, deliberately, "and do you know what I saw? No, you couldn't.

I saw the *Catherine*! It did not sink! It is now the *Greyhound*. You lied to me. You let me grieve. You seduced me! You choked me with kindness and destroyed the letters to my mother. I know you did. Don't deny it!"

Don Miguel visibly paled. Slowly he sat down on her bed, his shoulders stooping. He seemed winded by her blows, crushed by her righteous wrath.

"By that time your husband was wanted for murder," he replied. "Your letters would have alerted the police. They would have watched us in looking for him. My dear girl, you would have been the bait."

Anne-Marie's eyes never left him. "Your motives were not entirely altruistic, I'm sure. This has shocked me almost as much as anything in my life. I'm happy to know Bart is alive, but I'm utterly crushed and disillusioned by you. I had learned to love you and now I find that you are a basely wicked man. I am devastated!"

"I admit, Anne-Marie, I acted wrongly. I was selfish, desperately lonely. I fell in love with you the moment I looked at you and thought only of keeping you. You were held like a prisoner—I can't deny that. But as soon as I could, as soon as I felt that you would not leave me, I set you free."

"You did not set me free. You bought me a *horse*!"

"And it developed you. It gave you a sense of accomplishment. But I, too, have suffered with your pain. Believe me." His eyes, sweet and doelike, pleaded for forgiveness, but Anne-Marie stood unyielding, though softened somewhat, for who could deny a love daring such risk. She hated her weakness, her ability to be touched, but this time she could not offer forgiveness so easily. The shock of the day had been too much.

"Don Miguel, I do not want to discuss this with you any more, especially not tonight. I want to think," she said, gathering strength. "I think that you still know much more about Bart Ramsden's plight than you have told me."

"That I deny. Of course, I learned that the captain of the *Catherine* had killed his mate and was wanted for murder. It was the talk of the whole coast. But he escaped, and to my knowledge he has not been seen since. Believe me."

198

"I wish I could, but I learned tonight that I cannot," she replied firmly, her eyes lowered.

"Tonight you learned of a crime several years old," he retorted. "Put that in perspective!"

"There may be something I can do to clear his name. I could make a statement about the first mate that would turn your graying hair white." Fire flashed from her eyes as she remembered Brian's gaze while, surely, he had seen the monstrous wave approaching. "He stood there impassively looking on as the baby and I sat helplessly, and then he saw that wave coming as I could not and let me stand to take the full brunt of the mountain of water. I had forgotten it all, Don Miguel, in my shock. But I remember it all now very clearly. That man stood by coldly watching me and my child die and never lifted his voice, much less a finger. He knew that I could drown with the child—and I almost did. Can you imagine that behavior from a seaman? They never turned and came back, breaking one of the first laws of the sea."

Don Miguel sat thinking of what she had said, knowing that he, too, would have crushed that man's skull at the first opportunity. He thought of the moments of wretched terror that she had buried—later allowing only her innate sweetness and gentleness to come through. He thought too of her idealism, her naive world that admitted to no cruel flogging, keelhauling or walking the plank. How fine she was . . . "I think you should make a statement. It would be the honorable thing to do. It may not help because there were other charges. The *Catherine* was smuggling guns. You may not have heard about that," he added.

"Bart did nothing illegal. He was an honorable man. That I know." Her tone implied that Don Miguel was not an honorable man.

He flinched. "I don't know how far you want to go with this. I think you should consider your child. Moreover, Bart Ramsden now probably has another name, perhaps a wife and even another child. You are also acknowledged to be my wife and a respectable woman. For Samantha's sake, you must consider that. My days are numbered on this earth. I'm here tonight because I feared that I was getting down to hours, not days.

199

I never thought that I would live to see the outcome of this. I never intended to take even this much of your time."

By the time Don Miguel finished speaking and rose slowly, his face was ashen, and Anne-Marie knew that he spoke the truth. Never before had he used his failing health as a ploy. She regretted her rage as she would have regretted a gun aimed at his chest.

"Don Miguel, at this point I have no idea what I want to do. Believe me, you have only reminded me of responsibilities I have considered without making a decision. Today has been a baptism of fire. I will not do anything hastily. My love for you has been shattered, and I swear it is more painful to me than it is to you! Now will you please go and let me rest. I am exhausted."

Sadly he left the room.

Anne-Marie did not sleep, but rose to pace back and forth in her room. She had been a prisoner; now she was chained. Despite what she had said in her rage, her love for Don Miguel had not been destroyed. It had been struck a terrible blow, but not necessarily to the death, she now reflected. She had lived with suspended judgments, notwithstanding her early suspicions of Don Miguel. Her superior, holier-than-thou attitude with him now perhaps had been a mistake. She had spoken in violent anger. If only he had not come home when he did, but had instead given her time to take stock or to do some constructive thinking, she might not have behaved so badly. As he said, it was all water over the dam.

If she were to leave Don Miguel, she knew he was powerful enough to take Samantha from her if he wished. He could buy every judge in the state if he should choose to do so. That thought was embarrassing. She knew that he would never put the child in such a battleground. Was she no more honorable than he? Furthermore, his power could be used to clear Bart. No matter if Bart had replaced her; they both owed Bart that. She had been unthinking. Her violence having subsided, she was left in a limbo, alone and miserable, not knowing what to do or how to do it. There was no one to talk to except Don Miguel.

She stepped to the window and looked down into the night flooded with the light of a full moon. A strong breeze persistently rustled the tamarinds in the yard, stirring the shattered prisms of reflected light into thousands of shimmering beams so that she could see as clearly as if daylight were already upon them.

Suddenly she saw what appeared to be a misplaced tree trunk; then she made out that it was really the still figure of a man. He was looking up at her, silhouetted against her dimly lit room. She could see two eyes. Then the eyes and the stocky figure disappeared. Was he looking for Bart, or had the police been alerted by her questions on the wharf and put a watch on her?

Determined to find out, without stopping to put on slippers, she slipped down the hall to Don Miguel's room, where the door stood ajar. Don Miguel had not remembered to close the shutters and the room was bright in the moonlight. Stepping into the room, pressing her nose to the mosquito netting that encompassed his bed, she looked down at him. His face, ashen in color, lay still and expressionless. He was deep in sleep. Turning abruptly, furious that he could lie there sleeping while she suffered, she returned to her room.

Finally, she fell asleep, but to a series of nightmares. She was whipped by strange ugly forms wearing frightening masks. When, at her begging, the masks were removed, even more terrible faces were revealed. Before dawn a more steady sleep overtook her. When she awakened, much later than usual, Don Miguel was gone.

This fact was in itself maddening. Had Don Miguel remained, they could have had a quieter, more rational discussion and might have come to some sensible conclusions. She might have gone to the prosecuting attorney's office to make a statement. This she hesitated to do without speaking first to Don Miguel. She certainly did not want to appear and swear under oath that Don Miguel had lied to her. So unless she did, they would ask why she hadn't come forward earlier? There seemed nothing to do but wait for his return...

It was now apparent to her that the house was being watched. Some stranger was always hovering about the street. Her comings and goings were reported either to Don Miguel or the sheriff or both. The days wore on, each more empty of solutions than the last.

The unpleasant state of affairs proved so distracting that Anne-Marie found it impossible to talk to anyone for more than a moment or two. Afternoon teas and light chatter with her friends were choking and irritating.

By his absence Don Miguel was giving her the time she had asked of him. He could not know that she needed him. So she suffered. Her wait was made more difficult by a drooping Samantha who missed her father. As long as Don Miguel came and went, the child was happy enough in Key West, for the first time meeting and playing with other children. Now she spoke longingly of Los Claveles.

"Mama, I miss my other house," she said, laying her head in Anne-Marie's lap. "When is Father coming?"

"Soon, dear."

"He's been gone for so long. Our beach is much nicer at Los Claveles, Mama."

"I know, I know, dear. Now let's have a cup of chocolate."

Anne-Marie drank the chocolate from a trembling cup, living in the privacy of her own mind, making only temporary excursions into the child's world and then as a command performance. She looked down at Samantha and began absently playing with the child's hair that was so like her own. Suddenly, she realized that Samantha was speaking to her. "What's that, dear?" she asked guiltily.

"Mama, don't you ever listen?" replied the child.

"Mama is sorry. I, too, wish Father would come for us." It took her a moment to realize what she had said. Then she let the thought go. What did it matter? Anything would be better than this incredible loneliness, made even more uncomfortable because it was essentially her own doing.

She began a letter to Don Miguel and planned sending it with a servant, but the written words seemed embarrassingly mawkish. She ended by tearing up the paper. Then she thought of talking to Consuelo; the woman was older than most of her friends and worldly; but Anne-Marie hardly knew Consuelo and the whole problem was so personal and so dangerous that she dared not confide in her. The whole story of her life with Don Miguel would have had to be revealed. It was too humiliating—too complicated. Finally, she simply told the servants to get word to Don Miguel that she and Samantha wanted to return to Los Claveles.

The servants would manage it.

CHAPTER FIFTEEN

Bart returned to Key West, his arrival, as always now, being announced by a few pebbles thrown at Consuelo's window. Instantly awake, she slipped excitedly into a robe and went flying down the stairs to unbolt the door.

He took her in his arms as he always had, but the passionate kiss was replaced by the words, "Is there anything new?"

"Any day now," was all she could reply, still clinging to him.

"Tim has been to the sheriff. If it weren't for the fact that the judge's decision will cost the city a few thousand dollars, I think everything would have been settled by now." She looked into his eyes, laying her heart bare before his, but meeting eyes that were strangely noncommittal in return. "You don't seem to be overwhelmed to see me. Is anything wrong?"

"No, Consuelo," he replied, again drawing her to him, cupping her head in his hand. "I'm just disappointed, that's all. I'd so hoped to have a decision by now."

Arm in arm they walked to the kitchen, where Consuelo heated some food for him. "This fresh bread tastes so good," he said, tearing off a piece and cutting a slice of cheese. "Forgive my manners. Forgive my intrusion. I come in only to mess up your life and you take it with such grace. I'm truly humbled."

"Bart, for heaven's sake! I love you. How could I do otherwise?" she replied, scanning his face. His life of hiding was getting to him. Never before had he returned in such a depressed state.

"You must not care so much," he said, and then, looking at her, added suddenly, "Who knows what will happen to me?"

She had caught the brief, revealing pause and sensed that he had been about to say something but had changed his mind.

Once upstairs, however, their familiar relationship was resumed. Consuelo was very skilled in the art of making love when the situation called for it. She knew the gentle art of dalliance and delay, the spells that a woman could weave. Soon all initial reluctance to play the role of the great lover vanished, and once again Adam bit from Eve's apple. Together, as if caught in a whirlwind that neither could stop or control, they were carried upward and away, tossed about by waves of animal emotion. With Bart, pure instinct sufficed. Her face could have been almost any pretty face, her body, any pretty body. Not so with Consuelo. She truly loved, and the act was a consummation of that love. So absorbed was she in her own giving that she could not have noticed his lack of total surrender. It was not that Bart wanted, simply, to move on. He wanted the relationship to change, to ease. Subconsciously, he believed that Anne-Marie was alive and that he was still in love with her. Not wanting to hurt Consuelo, he could not tell her this. There was no way to formulate the painful words to put the relationship into proper perspective. It did not mean that he did not love Consuelo, but only that he loved Anne-Marie more. On a long-term basis, which was what this now was, Consuelo deserved more. As an interim consolation and savior of his sanity as well as his body, he would always be grateful to Consuelo in a way that was not in the least demeaning. But she did not claim his whole heart, as much as she might have deserved it. This he could not change.

Perhaps as a means of escaping the romantic web that Consuelo had woven, Bart occasionally left the house in broad daylight now and walked about the streets, hardly caring whether or not he was detected. This terrified Consuelo.

"My God, we're so close, don't be foolish!" she told him.

"Our evidence has reopened your case. If they had forgotten about you for a while, they haven't now!"

Despite the obvious anguish these excursions prompted, Bart continued to slip out.

"So, I go to jail. My patience has worn too thin, Consuelo. Maybe I want to be caught, if only to move things along. Don't ask me to do what I can't do any longer."

If he were gone more than fifteen minutes, Consuelo was almost beside herself with anger merged with fear. He seemed to forget that he could bring her down too. But the sight of him here, safe, calmed her and the gale in her heart dissipated as fast as it had gathered.

Bart never loitered, but walked purposively as if bent on some important destination. A small crowd, such as a funeral party, was often a cover. He was often drawn, then, to the city cemetery, to the northeast of Passover and Windsor Lane. It lay in a well-peopled part of the city. Several times he joined a group of mourners walking from a church and hovered in the background. In poor families only the immediate family dressed in black, so his casual white apparel was inconspicuous. By the expressions on some of the faces, he decided that he was often not the only interloper present, that these sad little pageants had a way of drawing the curious and perhaps some who had no focus for emotions of their own. The epitaphs on some of the tombstones spoke eloquently to him. He was drawn to one stone that read:

WHO SLEEPS BELOW? WHO SLEEPS BELOW?

IS AN IDLE QUESTION NOW.

When he returned to Consuelo's house, she could always tell him who had died and why, together with bits and pieces of their lives. His excursions did prompt distracting stories and even fables. It was on one of his walks that Bart caught sight of a child who for a brief moment reminded him of someone. She was a copper-headed girl, firmly held by a negro maid. She skipped along, pulling the servant this way and that to explore one fascinating interest after another.

Just so had Anne-Marie looked and behaved when he had first seen her, a small enchanting neighbor. His first view of this child came from behind them so that he could not see her face, and this

207

he must see, he thought. So he followed them for some distance, even stepping up his pace to come a little closer. The nearer he came, the more smitten he was with the child's resemblance to his wife. It was only when he feared that perhaps the servant had noticed a follower that he held back. In doing so he lost them in a cluster of mothers and children, baby carriages and dogs. For quite some time he walked around searching for them, so he was gone much longer than usual.

He returned to find Consuelo distraught. Her eyes were puffy from tears and her voice was hoarse and choked with emotion. "I've been worried sick," she cried. "This perverse behavior will not only ring down the curtain on you, but will incriminate your friends as well. Can't you see that?" she raged, her face now white.

What she had said was, of course, true. Bart stepped to her, took her in his arms, an act that never failed in its desired effect. "I'm sorry, Consuelo. Truly, I am. It has been very unfair of me. Even though I don't give a damn about myself, I have jeopardized both you and Tim. That was foolish of me. I promise you, I will not do it again."

"Thank you. Thank you," she said. "Not for my sake and Tim's, but for your own. Believe me, this will not go on much longer. Please take heart."

"There's always an end of the rope someplace. Every now and then I think I have reached it. Then, all of a sudden, there's a splice . . . right below my nose."

It seemed to Consuelo that his wavering had subsided and that once more he was on a steady course. Tim was there to dinner that night, always a welcome presence for Bart.

"I'm hoping to entertain you in my home soon," said Tim. "I'm practicing my cooking. To have you there to dine right now would be nothing less than a crime."

"I'll bring my first-aid kit when I come," replied Bart, "and a few leeches."

"You'll need a litter bearer, too," said Consuelo. "I cruelly accused Bart of trying to hang us both today," added Consuelo, "so obviously, the two of you deserve each other. Just don't kill me!"

"Something strange did happen today," said Bart, abandoning the humorous track. "I went out for one of my occasional brief walks, and I saw a little girl who reminded me so much of Anne-Marie as a child that I was stunned."

Tim and Consuelo sat listening, intent and still as if suspended in space, unable to breathe, not daring to glance at each other. "I followed them for quite a while. Our little girl would have been just that age by now, I guess, not knowing much about children. I got closer, hoping to see enough difference to dispel this similarity. Instead, I found just the opposite, an uncanny resemblance."

"And then what happened?" asked Tim.

"Well, nothing," replied Bart. "What was supposed to happen?"

"Oh, I don't know," replied Tim. "Haven't you met someone that you know you have seen before, only to discover that your paths could not possibly have crossed?"

"We see what we want to see," said Consuelo.

"I suppose it is natural that seeing a child would make me wonder what my own little Samantha would look like now."

"As you said, we see what we want to see," echoed Tim.

Consuelo could not escape his stinging words. It had been unfair of him to have put it so. Bart noticed nothing, apparently lost in his own reverie. Finally he said, "I suppose you are right, but it never happened to me quite this way. Never with such an impact."

Tim stared at Consuelo. His eyes seemed to be saying, Can't you see? He will never care for you as you would like.

Then, remembering his promise to Consuelo, Tim came as close as he could to breaking the news without actually doing so. "I believe Anne-Marie is alive," he said, "and the child may be too."

Startled, Bart turned to him. "What do you mean? Are you holding something from me? Do you think that I am some sort of an animal that must be held on a leash with information stingily parceled out? Can't I be trusted with information you have?" Anger was rising like a cloud around him, flushing his face, sharpening his tone.

"I said what I believed," replied Tim. "I personally have no evidence. I spoke of intuition. I offer it simply as encouragement, for whatever that is worth. But don't put your insecurities in my lap or tell me what I feel or think. I know that better than you." His friendly tone softened the harshness of his words.

Consuelo was furious with Tim, a feeling all the more infuriating because it had to be concealed. She was then startled when he deliberately forced her hand. "We must find a woman named Anne-Marie who wears one solitary emerald on a gold chain," he said, looking straight toward Consuelo.

"Or a breastplate of emeralds," replied Consuelo, gathering her wits, "which is just as likely." Her voice seemed to fall with the words and she shivered. "Bart, I'm growing a little chilly. Would it be too much to ask you to get me a shawl? I left one on my bed."

"Of course not," he said, marching off.

"What in the devil are you doing?" hissed Consuelo, as soon as Bart was out of earshot.

"What I think best for all concerned," he replied. "For two people I love."

"Don't pretend that you care for Bart," said Consuelo in a seething whisper. "He is a rival you would throw to the wolves, and you pretend that he is a friend, encouraging him with a dream of Anne-Marie to separate us! I see right through you, Tim Clayton."

"No you don't, my dear," said Tim just as Bart returned with the shawl.

Consuelo was inwardly shaken, however, with the information that Tim had only then confided to her that Anne-Marie wore an emerald. Was it true, or had he picked up that little tidbit from her in order to shake her confidence and to falsely convince her that her acquaintance was really Anne-Marie Ramsden?

When Bart returned, the atmosphere in the room baffled him. His eyes followed Consuelo as she poured the coffee and then cognacs, put on and took off her shawl, ignored Tim one moment and engaged his attention the next. She was nervous.

Consuelo did her best to hide her feelings under Bart's scrutinizing gaze, but inwardly she trembled. The whole earth seemed to be shaking, and she looked up half expecting to see

210

the pictures dancing on the wall. She would have excused herself, but she dared not, not knowing what conversation would follow.

Obviously, Tim was no longer allied with her despite his protestations of love. Bart had distanced himself from them both, possibly no longer trusting either of them—and possibly with reason. He seemed tired of their love affair, but also irritated with Tim.

Tim was aware of Bart's withdrawal and excused himself. The old German adage, "Coming events cast their shadows forward," came to mind as he thanked Consuelo for dinner and departed.

"You and Tim seemed to be having something like a lover's quarrel tonight," remarked Bart. They lay in bed. The room was dark but he was not asleep, and he did not believe Consuelo was asleep but thinking fast and hard. Immediately Consuelo arose and lit a lamp.

"I don't want to talk about such things without being able to see you," she said. "Do you mind?"

"Not at all."

She sat facing him at the foot of the bed. "He tells me that he loves me and he tells me that you do not."

"It seems that all Tim and I have done tonight is put words in one another's mouths. I knew something was going on between you, and, frankly, I'm relieved that it does not bear on my problems, because I did feel that you two were keeping something from me. I did not know what—an unfavorable decision, some new information, who knows? I don't feel that I am a child who needs to be protected from a bit of bad news. As for Tim, I think he would be a wonderful man for you."

His words hit her like a slap in the face. "Don't you understand, I'm in love with you? What can I do about it?"

"I fear, lovely woman, that your heart is out of hand. I have absorbed so much of your time and energy that your feelings are temporarily misplaced."

"Temporarily misplaced! My God," she said, stemming the flood of reproach still on the tip of her tongue.

"It is true that in many ways I love you, Consuelo. I have

been your lover, but I have always felt that above everything we have been friends, loving friends. I owe my life to you. I would die for you if need be. But what you really want from me, some great commitment and exclusive love, I cannot give you. It belongs to another."

Consuelo turned her face to the wall with an abrupt, desolate movement. Her fingers covered her welling tears. Bart put his hand to her shoulder and said, "Consuelo," very softly. "What is it?"

"Oh, leave me alone," she said roughly, and then was silent. There were no words of consolation he could give.

"I'm sorry, so terribly sorry. Believe me. If I am going to grieve you so, I will leave Key West and leave you in peace to find that you do not love me in the way that you believe. Your sympathy for me in my troubles has led you to give me more than you should."

"No," cried Consuelo. "I only want you and I see that is impossible—and it hurts." It was easy for her to see, through her tears, that he was deeply distressed. He had tried not to hurt her. He had told her long ago that his love for her was limited; and she knew that he still grieved for Anne-Marie. It was then she decided, for better or worse, to tell him all she knew.

"There is a red-haired woman in Key West named Anne-Marie. She has a daughter named Samantha who sounds very much like the child you may have seen," said Consuelo dully.

Bart sprang from the bed. "So, this is what you were keeping from me! Why haven't you told me?" he cried, grasping her wrist.

"Because she is married to another man!" said Consuelo, spitting out the words. "She is very happily married to a wealthy man who apparently adores her. Besides, I wasn't sure she was your wife until tonight."

"And what made you make up your mind tonight, pray tell?" Bart asked sarcastically.

"Tim told me tonight that your Anne-Marie wore a solitary emerald. So does this woman. You told me tonight that your daughter was named Samantha. This woman has a child named Samantha."

Bart was stunned into silence. Anne-Marie alive! But married happily to another man although she was still married to him! Why? Why hadn't she looked for him? And Consuelo was still protecting him. She could not have told him his wife had abandoned him, even though she had suspected that the woman was his lost wife.

"Has Tim seen her?" he asked.

"No."

"Does he know where she lives?"

Again, the answer was no.

"What made you suspect that she was my wife?"

"Nothing except that she was a very beautiful, tall, red-haired woman named Anne-Marie. You must admit, that is not much to go on..."

"Have you met her?" he queried.

"Once," replied Consuelo. "That day I did everything I could to learn something about her past. She seemed to evade every question. There was simply no way to learn anything about her. Nor did anyone else discover anything about her, although many tried."

"That's hard to believe."

"But true."

Bart was thoughtful. "Could she be suffering from amnesia?"

"I'm not a doctor, but the woman seemed perfectly sane to me. I only know one other thing about her! She is an expert horsewoman. She takes her horse over every conceivable hurdle."

"That does not sound like Anne-Marie," he said, slowly falling back on the bed, deep in his dwindling hope, leaving Consuelo to the mercy of hers.

"There's one thing I want to know. Why didn't you tell me your suspicion sooner?" He looked at Consuelo with eyes cold as ice.

"Because I only learned it while you were gone on this last trip. I knew that you would react exactly as you have. I thought you might go running into the street to find this woman—who might *not* be the same Anne-Marie—and this woman is guarded by police around the clock."

"What?" Bart exclaimed. "That's incredible!"

"But so. You would have been apprehended before I could snap my finger," said Consuelo. Feeling for once on safe ground, Consuelo spoke further, defiantly. "You would not be able to get past the gate to that house."

"The beating I took on the *Dasher* was nothing to what you have handed me tonight," he said finally.

"I don't think either of us has been particularly kind, despite our best intentions," retorted Consuelo. "Perhaps wrongly, I thought you needed to be protected from yourself—from flying off the handle when you could do yourself irreparable harm. That was treating you like a child and for that I apologize." As she spoke she brushed away an imagined piece of lint from her nightdress and avoided his eyes. Gathering words slowly, she continued. "I knew you would have to be told all this sooner or later, but I hoped I could do it without hurt to you. But chance defeated that hope." She stopped to take a breath and then pushed on. "There is something else I must tell you. The Anne-Marie that I met is no sweet, simple, naive little girl whom you may or may not have married. She is an exquisitely beautiful, sophisticated, wealthy, powerful woman—in my opinion a clever manipulator of people. I don't believe she has lost her memory. If she is the right woman, don't feel that you can simply move in and pick up life where the two of you left off. She will not be the same person."

"Christ! I don't feel that I'm the same man," replied Bart, bitterly glancing toward Consuelo with a look that was sullen and as hurtful to her as her judgments had been.

"Don't look at me like that, Bart Ramsden," said Consuelo. "Because I know that you would have upset the apple cart and there would have been more pieces for me to pick up to try to glue back together again. You have been patched up for a long time now, but the glue hasn't really set. Suppose this woman is your Anne-Marie and suppose she refuses to come back to you. What then?"

"You are not talking about the girl I married. I'm sure of it. We took those vows: for richer or poorer, 'so long as ye both shall live.' Anne-Marie would abide by them."

"I'm glad you're so sure. I'm not," replied Consuelo. "It has been a long time."

"There's no need our arguing. This is all speculation."

"I'm not arguing. I'm trying to keep you from going off on an emotional tangent so that if you find your Anne-Marie again, you will not lose her."

"That's the kindest thing you've said tonight and I appreciate your interest," replied Bart coldly.

"I told you, you bloody idiot," said Consuelo, "that she is happily married. Now prepare yourself for that! And if you don't mind, I want to go to sleep."

With that, Bart took himself from the room. For a moment or two Consuelo sat frozen, fearful that he would leave the house, but he only moved to another bedroom. His clothes remained in her room, and as long as they were there he would not be able to go anyplace.

This was their first serious disagreement, and she felt shattered. She had been hard on him, but at least the whole story was now out. Nothing was withheld to come back to trip them, severing forever their relationship, whatever that was. There was no way to anticipate how Anne-Marie would feel or what she would want to do. Consuelo knew enough about women to know that.

She also knew that Don Miguel was considered an attractive and powerful man who would not easily give up a lovely young wife.

But Bart had also changed over the years. The loss of his family, his ship, his status in the world—and above all his freedom—had profoundly affected him. Among those he cared about, Consuelo and Tim, he felt secure. She wondered about his self-respect. Had it been shattered by the years as a fugitive. Perhaps not. Perhaps he had simply matured and grown in stature. In any event, both he and Anne-Marie were different people today.

Consuelo tossed and turned, invariably coming back to her relationship with Bart that had suddenly changed, leaving her the loser. She had never really envisioned herself as his wife, but more as a partner of prime importance to him. That would never be. What was there had peaked and retreated. That there would not be more left her with a great inner ache and sense of loss. She lay huddled in bed, wrapping her arms about herself as if they might give comfort. Outside a cat howled, piercing the night with its painful need. Another voice followed and then another. The fight that ensued made sleep impossible. Now she could hear Bart shuffling about, then descending the stairs. Knowing that he was probably hungry, she slipped into a robe and went downstairs.

She found him in the kitchen. "I thought there was a thief in the pantry," she said, smiling while catching his sheepish grin.

"Christ! A cat fight—tonight of all nights," he said, groaning in disbelief. "I'm so glad to see you, woman. We've never had such words. How could you expect me to sleep?"

"We need a plan. I don't believe Anne-Marie would admit to me who she is despite the fact she found me *simpática*. Too much in her life would be at stake. You should not appear either, for all the unpleasant eventualities that there is no need to remind you of. However, you could send an emissary. Tim would immediately recognize her—and you said she liked Tim. Would you be willing to let him talk to her? That way you would not expose yourself and you could learn how she feels."

"In my fight with my pillows, I had come to that idea myself. Strangely, it is a difficult thing for me to do. Are you sure that she won't feel that I'm a coward?"

"Better a smart coward than a dead hero," said Consuelo, pouring two bowls of hot soup from a large pot that she had been absentmindedly stirring as they talked. "Perhaps Tim should only take one step, that of determining whether or not she is the person we're looking for. If she isn't, he wouldn't mention you. He would not have to say that you are here in Key West, you know . . . even if she is your wife."

"I would not want to put a muffler on him. Tim is smart. I think I'd rather he played it by ear. I trust Tim—he has an excellent mind. I wish you could appreciate it," he added, meeting her eyes.

"Let us not get into the human heart again tonight. I now declare it out of bounds."

216

At the single window in the room a white curtain moved softly like a sail. The room was full of the aroma of soup. They ate wordlessly with the embarrassing hunger that follows a deathwatch, both drained of emotion, having spent too much for one night. Consuelo reached out to him, at first touching his shoulder, massaging it as if it ached. Her hands then moved charmlessly to his face, pinching his chin, and then moving on to press the tip of his nose. The fingers were like those of a blind woman seeking a secret panel that would slide back and reveal some hidden cache. Bart rose slowly and then lifted her to her feet. Taking her into his arms, he gave her one long hug and they retired for the night, a modicum of peace reigning.

The next day Consuelo went to Tim's house, not knowing what sort of a reception she would get.

"To what do I owe this unexpected pleasure, Madame?" queried Tim. "Allah, Zeus, our Lord or the devil himself. I feel some very powerful force had a hand in it."

"How right you are. It was Bart." Her smile, however, put the meeting on a friendly basis, which he, too, was happy to accept.

"I'll get you a cup of coffee," he said, moving toward the kitchen. He returned almost immediately with two cups in hand.

The room was beautifully furnished, thanks to Consuelo's unfailing taste. His fine English pieces, which included several paintings, were balanced about the room. Dark, heavy, upholstered furniture had been recovered with lighter fabrics appropriate to a tropical clime. The general effect was one of repose and charm without being in the least feminine.

Consuelo accepted the coffee, but then almost sputtered. "My God! Pardon me, but do you call this coffee?"

"I made a big pot a few days ago exactly like I've seen dozens of ships' cooks do. I thought it tasted fine," he replied in a most apologetic tone.

"I've never tasted such coffee in my life and I can't imagine how you did it, but never mind. I came to tell you that I've told Bart everything I know about Anne-Marie. The slate is clean. As you can well imagine, he was upset. We were up almost all night hammering it out. He's willing to take a rational course."

"You did work on him!" replied Tim. "So far it sounds good. Now, what can I do for you?"

"For one thing, you can determine if she *is* Anne-Marie Ramsden. The rest is up to you. Bart wants you free to tell her whatever you think best. You see, she might welcome you with open arms, or she could throw you out. We can only guess. She may be a victim of amnesia. Other than Bart himself, you are the only one who can do this."

Tim sat quietly digesting her words. "Christ," he said finally. And them, "Well, as Pope said, 'What can we reason but from what we know?' I'll think of some excuse to rap on Madame's door and let's just hope that I can see her. I'll let you know right away what happened."

"It's good of you, Tim."

"A stranger's kindness often exceeds a friend's," he replied, smiling, "but I'll do what I can. Also, I'll look forward to your gratitude."

"If I didn't need you, I would hate you!" said Consuelo.

"Right now it is a luxury you can't afford," he said, smiling smugly.

She left, her anger rising with every step. Tim stood in the doorway, fighting to keep his smile from bursting into laughter as he watched her march down the street, ready to kick anything in her path.

"He is absolutely infuriating," said Consuelo, entering the house and ripping off her hat, which she tossed like a discus into a chair.

"You mean he won't go?" asked Bart, a look of surprise flashing across his face as he stood immobilized before her.

"Of course, he'll go," she said, shaking her head with disdain. "Let's not talk about him. Talk about something pleasant."

"I'm sorry, I didn't know he was unpleasant. I never found him so. Remember, the winds and the waves are always on the side of the ablest navigators."

"You sound just like him. There's nothing to do now but

wait, my dear. He will be here as soon as he can—he knows you are anxious. I need some coffee. One sip of his almost poisoned me."

"He has probably been reheating that same pot for a week," Bart said, knowing that Tim's coffee was probably made exactly as it was aboard a merchant ship—a strong and bitter brew, seeded with dregs.

Before many minutes they found themselves pacing the floor, each making little circles, hers marked by a swish of her skirts, his by a clenching of fists or a hammering of hands. Every few minutes their eyes met.

"How long do you think he'll be?"

"How would I know, really? Sit down, you make me nervous—pacing back and forth like that."

"I haven't noticed you napping," replied Bart, obediently taking a chair.

For a while they faced one another. The air seemed suffocatingly still. Little drops of perspiration dampened Consuelo's upper lip and temples. She picked up a fan and began a series of short flaps that sent the loose hair about her face dancing in staccato as the moisture rapidly disappeared.

Bart watched this most avidly, the little distraction of her presence becoming a balm. She was hardly aware of his scrutiny. "We'll know something soon," she said, talking to herself.

Looking at Bart, she felt a great pang of sympathy for him, for his weaknesses and for his strengths, and for the dreadful entanglement in which he found himself. The situation was one that seemed more bearable for a woman than a man. There were no dragons to slay, no outlets for the physical energy and strength that he possessed, no heights to conquer; waiting was a woman's game. Finally, the suspense of less than an hour ended and Tim stood at the door.

His face was blank. For a moment he simply stood there, hat in hand across his chest like a shield. Then he stepped into the room and quietly said, "She's gone."

"What do you mean?" sputtered Bart, not daring to believe.

"Just that. The house is closed—tighter than a vault."

"Did you speak with any of the neighbors?" Bart asked, still hungry for words of clarification.

"I asked them all," replied Tim. "That's why it took me this long. No one saw anything. They left during the night, a day or so ago. What more can I say? You have it all."

"Does anyone have any suggestions as to what we should do now?" asked Bart, dejection all over his face, his shoulders slumped, his voice colorless.

"How about a good drunk?" replied Tim.

"Not without first putting him in irons," said Consuelo, nodding toward Bart and smiling a smile of relief.

At least for the time being, the terrible tension was over. She was unwilling to admit that they had made no progress; it had been nothing like what they had hoped for.

"There's something I need to tell you," said Tim, looking at Bart, but also throwing a glance toward Consuelo. "I want to be open and honest with you. . . . I know that you and Consuelo have had a very close relationship, but you should know that I love Consuelo. My love is unrequited. I want you to know that I am going to do everything in my power to find your wife because it just might give me Consuelo."

"You'd make a wonderful pair," declared Bart. With that he ducked as a book came flying through the air toward him. Consuelo turned sharply and left the room.

Bart and Tim broke out into laughter that to her mind was damnably cruel.

CHAPTER SIXTEEN

As the sloop carrying Anne-Marie and Samantha pulled into the inlet on Cayo de las Matas and approached Los Claveles, Don Miguel stood waiting on the terrace. His thin form was bathed in brilliant sunlight, so bright it was impossible for them to make out his features. In the background and in the shadows of the house the faces of the servants could be made out. Samantha danced about the ship, joyfully jumping up and down and then scampering back and forth and getting in the way of the men, which they took good-naturedly enough.

With hands on his hips, Don Miguel approached the wharf, his face a steady beam to guide Anne-Marie into his arms. For a moment they stood holding one another until Samantha came crowding up from under, forming a wedge between them to reach her father's embrace. "I have missed you so, both of you," he said, looking down at Samantha and taking her hand to lead her to the house.

Talk was quite impossible with Samantha unwilling to surrender her father. As if through a wordless agreement between them—he signaling his entrapment and Anne-Marie her acquiescence—Don Miguel turned his attention to the bubbling child and Anne-Marie to greeting the servants and looking over her house. There would be time enough to talk. Her return was in itself a capitulation. She was there with him, ready to be his wife in spirit if not under the law. She would see to it that it would be a pleasant life, devoid of the passion of a few weeks earlier, perhaps, but not one of grudges or anger.

To mark their return, a special dinner was planned with only the best from Don Miguel's larder. Assorted fresh shellfish followed by roast duck à l'orange and sweet potatoes were prepared to perfection. A melange of vegetables newly picked from the garden was delectable; the French wines were superb. It was clear to Anne-Marie that the meal had been planned long in advance and had only waited her arrival to be put into execution. It was on the one hand annoying that he was so certain that she would return to him, yet flattering that he would have made such an elaborate welcome. A gift marked her place and Samantha's also. This evening the child was allowed to dine with them. A tiny, but exquisitely worked gold cross on a delicate chain with matching ring and bracelet were Samantha's gifts. To Anne-Marie's delight, hers was a watch set in a band of emeralds and a magnificent emerald ring. The gifts bore the mark of a famed Parisian jeweler.

Anne-Marie could do little but sit and smile at him, sighing over his generosity and obvious adoration, while Samantha chattered. His gifts had always been lavish, not at all appropriate for Cayo de las Matas, Key West or even Atlantic City, but suggested a very different sort of life either in New York or abroad—even in court circles. She had thought about this and had finally decided that such extravagances were simply Don Miguel's idea of what gifts should be.

When dinner was over and a sleepy Samantha had been led up to bed by Concepción, they could begin their own talk. Anne-Marie bravely launched it. "I waited a long time for you to come back, Don Miguel, then I decided you never would," she said with no humiliation in her voice and no acknowledgment of defeat. She waited for his reply.

"You should not have made such assumptions, my dear, for you should know that I would choose a position of strength rather than that of a beggar. It is far better this way. You have made a choice of your own free will."

222

The evening air was redolent with night-blooming jasmine. Recumbent in the massive antique chairs, they faced each other, wanting to put into words the root of their feelings, yet not wanting to offend or alienate.

"I am here," she said. "That should speak for itself. I could not have come had I not wanted to. I believe that I belong here with you." He reached for her hand. Taking it gently, he pressed a lingering kiss upon it and searched her eyes. "Do you want me or do you want my help?" he hazarded.

"Are they not the same?"

In that moment his whole body seemed to lose poise and strength. He shrugged. "I think that depends upon how long you intend to stay."

"I intend to remain with you always," she said, smiling tenderly. "I don't use people. I must be honest and confess that I want your help in making a statement that may help clear Bart Ramsden, but I have no intention of ever leaving you. I need your help, but more than anything else, I need your presence. I simply need you," she said, lowering her eyes.

Her utter womanliness, that perfected femininity was Anne-Marie's great power. She knew just when to yield and when to stand just out of reach. It was never a total surrender, but a giving and then pulling back. "I would have made a statement earlier, before coming here, but I would never admit to a court that I had not done so earlier because you had lied to me. I'm too proud for that. I need your help in a statement, but more than anything else I need you beside me, not today and to-morrow, but every day." Tears welled in her eyes, a small visible reflection of her recollected hurt. The effect upon Don Miguel was profound.

"I will help you," he said, rising and pulling her into his arms.

"I've come home, Don Miguel," she whispered.

The weekend followed and Don Miguel insisted that she get back on her horse. Together they rode, starting slowly along the beach.

Don Miguel had always loved this ride for it evoked his sense of ownership of land, so unlike his childhood rides when position and property had been denied him. Side by side they rode, and Don Miguel spoke of improvements under way, and other neutral subjects which interested her, but were really much more his dominion. It was the first time she had been on a horse in almost a year. At first she was mildly frightened and this was reflected in her tense stance.

"I may have to throw that saddle away and start from the beginning with you," said Don Miguel.

"No, just give me a few minutes," she replied. "I don't do anything in a hurry."

"That is true," he replied, giving her a knowing glance.

Gradually she relaxed. "My muscles have lost their tone. A long ride would cripple me. Let's go for a swim!"

"In no time you'll be back in shape. I think as long as you live you will feel the need to come back to Los Claveles to regain strength," he said.

Don Miguel tied up the horses and they undressed. They walked ankle-deep in the surf, slightly out of reach of the waves, shells, sponges, sea fans, and brown ribbons of seaweed collected in serpentine walls, flung ashore marking the tide. Walking deeper, hand in hand, they met the surf head on. The water slipped by their bodies, polishing skin until it glistened, splashing about them in great thunderous waves as the sand beneath their feet slipped away. They cavorted like children, tossed here and there, losing and regaining the bottom under their feet. Finally, the pounding sea won and they found themselves tossed ashore.

For a long time they lay spent, Don Miguel brown and muscle-hard, she creamy white and soft. Then she leaned over and kissed him full on the mouth. Like soft breathless stabs she continued her attack, until finally she rolled over him and while the rising tide of the warm sea broke and sluiced around them, they pressed their bodies together and surrendered to the pounding of their hearts locked into one.

Wordlessly, but having said it all, they slipped into their clothes and rode home.

The following day they took the sloop back to Key West. With Don Miguel at her side she gave a statement to the court detailing the manner in which the first mate Brian had calmly stood by to let her drown. It was firmly established that the first mate had not cried "Man overboard" nor had the *Catherine* circled.

Because Don Miguel knew Judge Boynton there was no problem in obtaining a private hearing. They spent the night aboard the sloop and returned the next day to Los Claveles.

Within a few days Mr. Leeds received notice by post from the prosecutor that the murder charge against Captain Bartholomew Ramsden had been dropped. Leeds immediately sent his clerk to Consuelo's house asking that she come to his office.

On receiving Mr. Leeds's message, Consuelo hastily donned a hat and gloves while Bart hovered by. "What do you think it means?" he asked, his brows knitted anxiously.

"I have no idea. What do you think? It could mean anything or nothing. I'll be back as soon as I can. I'll try to find Tim to get him to accompany me—should I faint."

"I can't imagine that, but it's probably a good idea."

"Fainting?" she queried.

"No, taking Tim. You *are* rattled!" he replied, shaking his head.

Tim was not at home so Consuelo went on alone. She found Mr. Leeds in good spirits. "The murder charge against Captain Ramsden has been dropped. I trust you will be in touch with him soon. Here's a copy of the letter as well as copies of the testimony of individuals who came forward. I thought this would please you." Consuelo's mouth dropped open and she sat blinking, hardly able to believe her ears as Mr. Leeds pressed the papers into her hands. "You can study these," he said hastily.

"I'm sure he will be delighted—and I can't thank you enough. This has been a long time coming. An innocent man has suffered considerable hardship."

"You must excuse me," said Leeds. "I have a hearing in five minutes, but I will talk with you soon."

Bidding Mr. Leeds goodbye, it was all Consuelo could do to contain her joy, but at the same time her trepidation. Once more the stability of her world was threatened. The future loomed strange and uncertain. The familiar walkways which she knew so well blurred before her. Finally, she looked up to see her house and knew that she was home. Inside Bart and Tim sat waiting for her, two faces without bodies, tense and expectant.

"Would someone be good enough to pour us all a drink?" she asked, handing Bart the sheaf of papers and taking a place beside him. Tim busied himself with a bottle and glasses while Bart fumbled through the pages.

"Let's see what we have here," he murmured, reading.

"It seems the murder charge against me has been dropped. Your statement is here, Tim, as well as one from Shuttele admitting that he was hired by Brian to work me over. I certainly didn't get the truth from you there, did I, Consuelo?" Suddenly, Bart blanched. "Here is a statement by Anne-Marie Ramsden naming Brian as an attempted murderer! Where in the hell did this come from?" asked Bart, his eyes now spitting fire.

Consuelo and Tim were shocked into silence. The disbelief written all over their faces was unmistakable. They sat stunned. Bart's icy stare moved from one to the other and back, gleaning nothing but empty stares in return.

"What?" they cried, almost in unison.

"What have you two been up to? Will you finally level with me once and for all?" he shouted.

"We would like to," replied Tim, "but I, for one, don't know what you're talking about."

"Nor do I," added Consuelo.

"Well, here's a statement sworn to by Anne-Marie. . . . Explain that!"

"I know nothing about it, absolutely nothing. I swear. I haven't seen her or communicated with her since the day she disappeared," said Tim.

"Leeds didn't tell me about this," said Consuelo, shaken. "I don't know anything about this either. Who then has approached Anne-Marie for a statement?" asked Consuelo, looking first to Tim, then to Bart and back to Tim.

"I don't know or I'd tell you," replied Tim. "At this point, Bart, we have nothing to hide. Believe us, for Christ's sake!"

226

"My God," said Bart, shaking his head. "Where are we? Just where are we?"

"Let me look at those papers," said Tim, reaching for them and greedily poring over the sheets. Finally, he looked up into mystified eyes. "There is no mention here of the gun-smuggling accusation. That still stands. This may be a trap." Another stunning silence swept the room. "I'm sorry, but that's what I believe it is. Perhaps you see it otherwise."

"That's a strong statement, Tim," said Consuelo. "The truth is, we have offered no evidence to clear Bart of that charge. Without a trial in which the state proves he was guilty or can't prove it, I guess no one would go out on a limb. Furthermore, Anne-Marie made her statement only three days ago. We know she has not been in her house. Where is she?"

Bart rose and stumbled about the room. Tim and Consuelo looked at each other, trying desperately to read something from the other's face, but drew nothing but blank stares.

"I feel as though we are back to the beginning—back to Genesis," said Bart.

"No we're not," said Consuelo defiantly. "We've just learned a lot. Listen to me. Anne-Marie is alive. She knows that you are alive, Bart. She is simply unwilling to come forward, or can't, which is more likely. She has tried to clear you of what she could. Obviously she could not testify on the gun-smuggling charge. I think she is an honest woman and I doubt that she would lie about something she knew nothing about. But she may have seen . . ."

"What address did she give?" asked Tim.

"The Fitch house," replied Bart. "We know that house has been closed." He sat slumped, his head in his hands, staggered by Consuelo's words. "Well," he said finally, "does anyone have a plan?"

Consuelo played with her glass of sherry. "Another conference with Leeds is called for. He could not talk with me today because of another hearing. Then we should try to get Anne-Marie and Bart together for a talk. I don't think this is a trap, but Bart must remain hidden. I see nothing to do but wait until Anne-Marie returns to the Fitch house. Does anyone else have a suggestion?" Bart looked inquiringly at Tim. "The applause is overwhelming," said Consuelo, rising. With an angry swish of her skirts she left the room.

"I can't better her suggestion," said Tim, "but I have an interim suggestion. This morning I was out buying a boat. That's why Consuelo couldn't find me. Why don't you and I take a little sail? We can cast off at night when you would not be detected, do a little fishing and hunting, and let the air cool a bit. What do you say?"

"It's the best idea I've heard in months!"

Consuelo returned to find the atmosphere in the room completely changed. When she heard their plans for the sail, she exclaimed, "It's a beautiful idea, perfectly beautiful!"

"I think she's glad to be rid of us," said Bart, affecting a dazed expression as a joke.

"I don't think Anne-Marie will be back right away—the house is closed too tightly—so you are not losing any time and the change will do you good."

"I fully agree," said Bart with a newfound cheer.

The full realization that Anne-Marie was, indeed, alive and that she had come forward for him suddenly struck Bart, making his spirits soar. His high spirits were infectious and Tim jumped to his side. With that they began to dance together about the room—making their own music—just as they had learned to dance as sailors aboard ship when there were no women as partners. It struck Consuelo as one of the funniest scenes she had ever seen. Finally she joined in the clapping, the slapping of thighs and stomping until all three dissolved in laughter.

The comic episode provided a moment of much-needed relief. The rest of the day was spent compiling a list of what the men would need. Carefully they organized Tim's shopping for the following day. Fortunately, Tim's appearance on the scene had meant that he could purchase some additional clothing for Bart.

"I can't help you with the shopping, Captain," said Bart facetiously, "but I'm a good, hardworking sailor, so get what materials you may need together to get your ship in order and I'll work."

"I don't know that I relish the change of roles," said Tim. "I might just be the owner and let you be the captain."

After so many weeks of gloom and despair, their laughter was a welcome relief to Consuelo.

"We could take you along, Consuelo. Would you like to come?" asked Tim.

"As a sailor? I know only the front and back end of a boat."

"You don't even know that! Anyway, I was thinking of a cook," said Tim.

"As sailor and cook? What nerve!" Consuelo laughed. "I don't even cook in my own house. No thank you, I'll stay here."

The following evening, while deep, midnight blue water lapped against the *Pretty Lady* in a perfect high tide and a gentle moon rose steadily in the sky, they slipped out to sea, leaving a shimmering phosphorescent silver wake like a visible echo of laughter that Consuelo could see and hear for miles.

Consuelo's first errand the next morning was to visit Mr. Leeds.

"I rushed out of here," she told him, "so excited with what appeared to be a complete victory only to get home to discover that it was not. There is no mention of the gun-smuggling charge."

"I didn't tell you that we had a complete victory, my dear," said Leeds. "As you remember, we offered no real evidence refuting this, only a blanket denial. I'm sorry, my dear. It is only one step, but it is a good one. I must say, I was also surprised to see Mrs. Ramsden's statement. She apparently doesn't intend to return to Captain Ramsden. That's a strange state of affairs, isn't it?"

Consuelo allowed that it was.

"I would suggest that we petition for another search of the *Catherine*, now the *Greyhound* and see what we can learn. That's all that I can suggest at the moment," the lawyer continued.

"Please go ahead with that," said Consuelo. "It would be nice if we had that in hand when the *Greyhound* returns, as I assume eventually she will." She left, discouraged by the painful slowness of the process of exonerating Bart.

At least twice a day Consuelo made sure that she passed the Fitch house, looking for some sign of life within. The shutters remained closed and bolted, and the porch tables and chairs had not been returned to their familiar places. The house stood sealed like a great white tomb, the entrance of which was marked by two Grecian urns spouting hardy, feathery ferns.

The absence of Bart and Tim gave Consuelo respite so that she could freely reenter the activities of the town and more successfully continue the double life she had been living. She had not realized what a strain Bart's presence had put upon her. It was not that the civic responsibilities took so much time that they could not be continued, but that her state of mind foreclosed them. Also, she lived in fear that some careless statement would slip out that could not be explained. Even her walks past the Fitch house were enough to cause remark because of their frequency. Still, she made her pilgrimages, but the house remained empty.

Massive and elegant it stood, possessor of secrets and eerie because those secrets affected her life. The closed doors and windows, the uncut roses, the still air and brooding silence touched her with frightening intensity. Yet, there the house stood, uncaring, empty and idle, a great whiteness. Before it, the varying greens of each tree stood out, singled and emphasized by the bright sun, like guardians. Some were lacy, wavering slightly in the breeze, others stood stiff and unyielding, heavy with wax.

She should be, she thought, done with the need and hope for Bart by now, but the invisible bond remained, persistently tightening its hold upon her. Despite a series of awakenings, the lingering dreams continued, coloring her days as well as her nights, so that she was never free of it. She had marshaled the strength to pursue his cause, but it was her pride that was forcing her to do so. Pride sustained the excruciating wait. The union that she craved hung uncompromisingly out of reach.

Then one day—with the suddenness of a shot—the house was opened. Not daring to stop to consider what she would say or how she would say it, fearful that her courage would desert her with even a moment's hesitation, Consuelo marched to the door and rapped. Within seconds a servant was there. With Anne-Marie herself standing in the background, no escape or retreat was possible.

"Excuse the intrusion, but I was passing by and saw that you were back and I wanted to welcome you," said Consuelo, looking past the maid to the smiling but surprised woman beyond.

"Consuelo, how nice! Come in. Excuse this disorder," she said, waving an arm, "but we just arrived."

Some order appeared in the living room, but Consuelo could see beyond into other rooms where white sheets still covered chairs and tables.

"All of Key West will be excited," said Consuelo. "How are you? You don't have to say—you look absolutely wonderful." She went on mouthing amenities in a nervous feminine chatter sustained only by her genuine admiration for her rival, whom she could not help but admire. Much as she would have liked to hate this woman, such a feeling was impossible. All she could muster was a full-blown case of acute envy.

Anne-Marie ordered coffee and, when no one was within earshot, Consuelo said, "May I speak with you confidentially? It is something rather important."

Guessing that this conversation would involve Bart, Anne-Marie suddenly distanced herself. Consuelo felt her stiffening and drawing away as rapidly as she herself was softening and dissolving, as if Anne-Marie were sapping her energies and resolve.

"I mean no intrusion, Madame—" said Consuelo.

"But I fear you may be doing just that," interrupted Anne-Marie, "especially if you are going to refer in any way to my past."

"I'm not thinking of your past, Anne-Marie, but Bart Ramsden's future."

Finally, it was out—the dreaded words. Now Anne-Marie could have her thrown from the house if she wished.

Anne-Marie appeared surprised. "Then you know him?" she asked, her voice thin, drawn as if through the eye of a needle.

"For many years, first through my husband and then several years of trying to clear him."

"I did what I could to help him," said Anne-Marie. "He was a part of another life. I live very happily now with a man to whom I owe everything. Twice he saved my life. He is not well. Like all couples, we have been through some storms together, but we love each other dearly." Her open sincerity colored every word, every phrase. "I see no point in opening old wounds. My commitment to Don Miguel is too great."

Their conversation ceased for a moment while a maid brought a tray with coffee, but resumed when she left.

"Then you will not see the captain?" said Consuelo.

"I would prefer not to. I think it would displease Don Miguel and it would change nothing."

"Do you know that Bart has not been totally cleared?" asked Consuelo.

"No," said Anne-Marie, looking surprised. "Then it would also be risky for him to meet me."

"He was cleared of charges in the death of his first mate, but not of the smuggling charge. We have never been able to refute that. The contraband—apparently a considerable quantity of guns—was found in the captain's cabin. Bart is not in Key West now. I really don't know where he is at the moment, but he will return. He is determined to see you and I fear, knowing how headstrong he is, if he tries, and against your will, he will do something foolish and land in prison. That's why I've come to ask you to see him. He will never believe it when I tell him you will not leave your husband."

"But, my dear, that is the case," replied Anne-Marie, looking directly into Consuelo's eyes.

Clearly, Anne-Marie's firm stand was a painful one. To Consuelo it also seemed to be one that had been anticipated and resolved in advance.

"If I could arrange a reasonably safe way for you to meet with Bart for only a few minutes, would you be willing to?"

"Let us put it this way. If you think that merely my words can convince Bart and that this conviction will stop him from doing something foolish, I will try to meet him, but unwillingly."

"That would be good of you," replied Consuelo with relief. For the first time in some minutes, she felt able to breathe. And also, perhaps there was a chance for her with Bart after all, but she dared not think further of that.

"You must remember," said Anne-Marie, speaking in a voice so low that it was almost a whisper, "my husband always has bodyguards. You say the police are looking for Bart. It adds up to a tight net to slip through. But if you can do it, well..." She shook her head. "Don't think me hard," she continued. "I am not. I once loved Bart with all my heart— and he was my first love, a memory that I cherish. But now there is another man in my life. Surely, I don't have to tell you that people change. I don't believe in 'the great love,' although I did for a long time. I believe that what I have now is more stable, and more enduring. I would not dream of hurting Don Miguel and upsetting the life of my daughter."

"You will hear from me with a plan," said Consuelo. "And, by the way, Tim Clayton is with Bart." Hearing Don Miguel's footsteps on the stairs, Consuelo hastened her departure. "Thank you from the bottom of my heart."

Consuelo left the house and began the replay of the conversation, reviewing everything that had been said, reconstructing every word, facial expression and gesture, looking for hidden or misunderstood meanings, implications and connotations, for what might be revealed, and for what was not said. Misgivings showered about her like meteorites exploding in the night sky. Anne-Marie had been very sure of herself, almost too sure. She had spoken like a much older woman— like one whose life was behind her, and yet she was only what? Twenty? Her breathless beauty had not yet reached its zenith. She was invincible in her unwillingness to hurt Don Miguel and yet willing to hurt Bart. Was it only because he had been pushed back in her mind, now a half-remembered figure, a mere shadow, perhaps now a stranger?

When Consuelo lay down to sleep, it occurred to her that she was sitting on a keg of gunpowder and that Anne-Marie was holding the match. At this point there was nothing to do except wait for Bart and Tim's return. Although she had a plan for getting Bart and Anne-Marie together for a brief meeting, Bart would have to approve. There would be conditions. He had said he was fed up with being a puppet, putting his life in other hands, constantly being manipulated one way or another. She would need his promise to gain Anne-Marie's co-operation. Also, she would need outside help. Notwithstanding some uncertainty as to how to achieve all this, she drifted into sleep.

Two days later, Bart and Tim returned, full of their adventures and skill at hunting and fishing, but first, most anxious to hear her report.

It was late when they arrived, dirty, tired and disheveled. Sprawled on the floor to protect her fabrics, they appeared much more relaxed than they actually were. For Consuelo it was going to be difficult to tell Bart what Anne-Marie had said without being cruel. First she told them briefly about her visit with Mr. Leeds, leading slowly to the meeting with Anne-Marie.

"Bart, she told me she will not leave Don Miguel, I'm truly sorry to say. I told her that if she did not, I feared that you would do something foolish. I told her that you seemed to be at the end of your rope. With that, she said that she would see you, but unwillingly." Bart's face, at first expressionless, seemed ready to crack as tiny fissures rippled down his face. One large throbbing vein bulged across his forehead. Consuelo fought to assuage his pain. "She told me that twice he had saved her life and that she would not hurt him. He is unwell. Don Miguel has obviously been very good to her. She spoke of her love for you as a memory from another life, not this life she is living now. She will see you for your sake, not for hers. Maybe you can't understand that."

"No, I can't," he muttered faintly.

"If I arrange a brief meeting in such a way that Don Miguel's bodyguards and the police will not be alerted, she will tell you this herself. But I must have your promise." With that, Consuelo looked to Tim for support.

"Well, that's quite a story," Tim said, smothering a nervous cough.

234

Bart remained silent and withdrawn, too wounded to respond. Never in his wildest dreams had he considered this. Slowly he rose and retreated to the darkest corner of the room.

"How do you propose to get them together," asked Tim quietly, "providing, of course, that we get Bart's cooperation?"

A slight nod directed her attention to Bart.

"I thought of a carnival party in costumes and masks. With Lent coming up, it would be appropriate. It would be a large party, a Mardi Gras, with music and decorations and everyone in town invited, including, of course, Anne-Marie and Don Miguel."

"Anne-Marie would come in one costume and then go upstairs to my room to change to another. In this new outfit she could escape the party and go to your house, Tim. Bart would meanwhile slip into your costume to meet her there, while you would wear his costume and stay at the party. They would have about fifteen minutes together, no longer, while I hold Don Miguel's attention outside in the patio. Anne-Marie would then come back here to change to her original costume. What do you think of it?"

"I think you're a genius," said Tim. "An incredible genius! But why do Bart and I change costumes?"

"Remember, everyone will be in costume and masked. However, the bodyguards and the police may know what costume you are wearing. They wouldn't expect Bart to be in it should they notice it leaving the party. Anne-Marie presumably would be lingering in my room upstairs," replied Consuelo.

Bart sat quietly regarding Consuelo.

"Now mind you," continued Consuelo, "I don't have Anne-Marie's approval yet on this. First I wanted to present the idea to you, Bart. If you will agree to the conditions, I will try to get her consent. She is also taking quite a risk. Otherwise, my dear friend, you will simply have to take my word for what she said."

"It appears that I have no other choice if I want to talk to her," said Bart. "I believe that she can be swayed, despite everything you say."

The determination in his tone sent chills down Consuelo's

235

spine. No one loves a messenger with bad news and now she was being forced to bear the brunt.

"We had practically no time to talk," said Consuelo. "The conversation could have taken only five minutes at most. Then Don Miguel appeared."

"Big decisions are never drawn out," said Tim, "or they become little decisions." His face stony, he abruptly changed the subject.

"Something rather interesting happened on this trip," he said. "We were sailing along on the Gulf side in the direction of Cape Sable. One desolate island after another lay to port. On account of the mud flats, we were several hundred yards from shore. Suddenly, we saw a beautiful red-haired girl on a horse riding along the beach. We followed her, but when she got to the northern tip of the key she rounded it and disappeared. We tried to round the key too, but there must have been a riptide and with prevailing breezes from the ocean, we were too slow. By the time we could sail outside, now southward, the girl had vanished. Heaven only knows where she went. This was the most desolate stretch of land one can imagine."

"Are you sure she wasn't a mirage?" asked Consuelo.

"No, I saw her too," confirmed Tim.

"Well, it *could* have been Anne-Marie," said Consuelo, knowing that was what Bart had been thinking. "But you know, many wreckers live along those keys—and live very well."

Consuelo listened to Bart's tale, only half-conscious of his words. Apparently, he did not like her plan for a party. She determined to drop the idea then and there, since without his full cooperation such a scheme would be dangerous. He could not be pushed into anything; she might just as well try to persuade a penguin to fly.

Then abruptly Bart said, "Have your party, Consuelo. I'm already looking forward to it. I meant to tell you that a minute ago, but I was distracted by the mirage."

Startled, Consuelo looked to Tim, but caught only his surprise. Bart must have grimly come to terms with Consuelo's findings and, like a good captain, adjusted to the new situation as if the old had never existed.

CHAPTER SEVENTEEN

Key West, as the southernmost point of the Florida keys, was a mecca for adventurers—a lively, hearty and on the whole youthful lot—whose backgrounds pointed chiefly to the Bahamas, England, Cuba, Spain and the British colonies. There were also a few educated men from Virginia, France, New England and the West Indies. Some brought their wealth with them; others had been rescued from wrecked ships and were brought to Key West penniless, but they chose to remain. In this exotic community they found a place for themselves. Because of the lack of social barriers, the brightest and hardest working rapidly rose to prominence.

Key West's natural harbor had been on record for over two centuries so that sailing vessels from many nations as well as pirate craft entered the old Nor'west Channel in need of fresh water, fruits and a wide miscellany of ship's supplies. Consequently, the steady influx of colorful characters never ceased. Those independent thinkers typically chose to remain in the Union throughout the Civil War, though actually they were sympathetic to the South.

Settlers soon took on the mantle of Victorian propriety, but because of Key West's semitropical climate, few chose to wear that mantle continuously. Consequently, the town was not an overly religious community in an overly religious era, and social standing meant economic standing combined with civic responsibility.

Those of Spanish descent were predominantly Catholic; the English, protestant. But there were also Jews, Orientals and Moslems; religion hardly interfered with one's capacity for pleasure and therefore the requisites of a good party were plenty of drink, food and music.

With this and other matters in mind Consuelo proceeded with dispatch to organize Key West's biggest party since before the war.

Having obtained Bart's sworn agreement that he would behave and not jeopardize Anne-Marie during a brief meeting, Consuelo then presented her plan to Anne-Marie.

"If he simply *must* hear it from me, then I will tell him," said Anne-Marie, "but I won't leave Don Miguel. I know that I appear to be heartless, but long ago I stopped thinking about appearances. The costume party is a wonderful idea," she added, breaking into a smile. "What would you suggest that I come as?"

"Why not a veiled woman?" asked Consuelo. "Then in my bedroom you will find a soldier's outfit to change into. I would feel safer if you were dressed as a man. A pillow under your belt will create a potbelly that you do not have. As a man you can walk freely to Tim's house without raising eyebrows. Also, at my house, Tim and Bart will exchange costumes for the meeting."

"It sounds like a terribly exciting evening," said Anne-Marie, now obviously looking forward to it. "And what will be Bart's costume so that I will recognize him?"

"He will come as the hangman," said Consuelo, rising to leave, deliberately not looking at Anne-Marie, who she sensed had paled. "And, by the way, during this brief encounter, I will be entertaining your husband in the patio. Please don't overestimate my ability to amuse him beyond the time, and dally."

"I can't imagine such a thing overtaxing you, of all people," replied Anne-Marie in honest appreciation. . . .

Consuelo reported to her conspirators Anne-Marie's ac-

238

quiescence to the plan, and so the preparations for the party began.

Invitations had to be delivered as soon as possible so that those invited would have time to get their costumes ready— clearly stated as mandatory. Consuelo's guest list drew from a wide range of soldiers of fortune and arms as well as an equally broad spectrum of women. Ages from sixteen to eighty were included as were whole families, in accord with the custom in Key West for such an important social event.

"It's going to be quite a party," said Tim. "How shall I dress?"

"You must be someone elegant—perhaps a Spanish grandee! Now get yourself down to the tailor and have something made," said Consuelo. "We can handle your costume here, Bart. Tim's black suit will fit you. I have a black cape you can borrow. It will be easy to make the black hood with just two slit openings for your eyes. Then you have only a rope with a noose to carry for the full effect!"

"You're going to turn me into a spectacle of horror," said Bart sarcastically, "so I'll be noticed."

"Come now, dear. Your costume has to be noticed so that Tim's disguise will aid yours when you leave to court your wife, of course," she added acidly. "But heaven only knows what I shall wear—something exciting! Should I be a belly dancer?" Consuelo's eyes were bright as she wriggled and swayed with anticipation. "Or perhaps I should be a Spanish dancer?" she mused, switching into a tango rhythm, snapping her fingers like castanets. . . .

Bart was appointed head of a decoration committee of one. Tim purchased colored papers for the cutouts which, when strung together, made garlands. Bart then spent hours with the scissors and paste, folding and cutting out multicolored forms that would open like an accordion and festoon the room.

"I feel as though I'm back in primary school," cried Bart, "playing with my paper dolls! What is this, Consuelo? Are you trying to drive me mad?"

"Help him with the paper dolls, Tim. We don't want him to go daffy now," said Consuelo, laughing.

Musicians were hired, and a large order was placed with

the baker. Consuelo also arranged for women all over the island to prepare dishes for her, particularly foods that could be easily eaten with the fingers. It was, without doubt, to be the largest private party ever held in the city. People talked of nothing else.

"I might as well invite everybody," said Consuelo, "since I know those not invited will be gate crashers. There's no way to control who comes when you can't recognize your own friends. Exactly what we want, isn't it?"

Dutifully following Consuelo's instructions, Tim visited the tailor to have his costume made. Because he and Bart were the same size, there would be no problem in exchanging clothes, but Consuelo wanted Tim to have an elegant costume. Because she had not specified its details, Tim felt free to design his own with the expert help of the tailor.

Unknown to Tim, however, or to Consuelo, Don Miguel, hastened by Anne-Marie, had visited the same tailor for the same purpose. The tailor, suddenly overwhelmed with work already and anticipating even more as awareness of the party spread, silently considered his problem. There would be no harm in two similar costumes, he thought. He would thus save both cloth and time. Only the details needed to be different— perhaps strikingly different hats.

All over the city nimble fingers were sewing and fitting costumes in attempts to outdo one another in fantasy. What each would wear soon became a well-kept secret lest it be purloined.

The usual wallflowers for once would not be recognized, so potential gossips and parents would be too busy keeping track of their daughters to notice who else might be involved in some irregularity. However, to add a bit of spice to the evening, it had occurred to many young girls to exchange their costumes in order to assure their own anonymity.

"If you see my old dining room curtains behaving indiscreetly," said Mimi to Consuelo one afternoon over tea, "I do hope that you will alert me. I'm holding you responsible for this whole affair."

"Holding me responsible!" cried Consuelo, firmly putting

down her teacup. "If you have brought up your daughter properly, you have nothing to worry about."

"This is a devilish event you have contrived. Behind your fine Italian hand there must be some scheme under way, but I can't figure out what it is," sighed Mimi.

"Must you always look for ulterior motives?" asked Consuelo, laughing. "Can't I just have a little fun? You must admit, this is the most exciting thing to hit Key West since the last hurricane . . ."

"Indeed, I do. But this is costing you a pretty penny and I would bet my grandmother's pearl brooch that a man is involved that you have designs upon," replied Mimi, throwing Consuelo a knowing but affectionate smile.

"Mimi, my dearest friend, talking in such a manner. I'm ashamed of you."

"Go ahead, be ashamed. But like everyone else, I wouldn't miss the evening for the world," replied Mimi. "I would be there on a litter, if necessary."

"And I'm sure you will have a wonderful time. You know I have neglected my social obligations. I felt something spectacular was required to put me back on the map socially," said Consuelo, laughing to herself.

"Hardly," replied Mimi, not fooled for a moment.

Finally, the appointed day arrived. The living room had been cleared for dancing. The entire ceiling was decorated with Bart's bright, colorful garlands crisscrossing one another, imposing their festive air over the whole house.

Torches in the patio, in the garden and around the front porch—beacons of hospitality and cheer—blazed brightly; tables in the garden and dining room were heavily laden with food. Mimi had sent over all three servants to aid in the preparation and service. Then the musicians arrived with their guitars, accordions, fiddles, flutes and horns; their disparate tunings metamorphosed into music•when the stream of guests began to flow in.

In groups, they came, and finally in droves, excited, spirited and madly incognito, cautiously probing to discover friends, lovers and enemies.

Consuelo had dressed as a gypsy. She moved from guest to guest, firmly taking the hand of each to scrutinize its shape and lines—and thereby recognizing many—telling, or promising to tell, their fortunes. Her natural wit and keen eye produced many an outrageous fortune to the delight of all in earshot.

Her first customer was Mr. John Ziriax, who kept the foremost bakery and whose rotund belly and soft white hands could hardly be disguised. Ziriax had built the Stone Building out of wrecked cement and wanted it called the Ziriax Building, but the name would not stick. "What you have made is turning to stone," foretold Consuelo, leaving Ziriax to wonder whether she was talking about his building or his baking.

Mr. Moreno's silver ear trumpet gave him away. "I know you are going to give us a concert," said Consuelo jokingly to the deaf man, but unmusical Moreno did not hear, fortunately....

Just as Consuelo was approaching panic that Anne-Marie and Don Miguel would not appear, a heavily veiled Arab woman arrived with a Renaissance nobleman wearing a magnificently plumed hat. They danced one dance and then strolled out to the patio. Consuelo, having noticed them, hastily dropped one client's future in thin air, having prophesied for her four children with no mention of a husband, and followed Anne-Marie and Don Miguel.

To Consuelo's consternation, the hangman asked the Arab woman to dance. Don Miguel looked startled; unseemly haste could be taken by Don Miguel to be a challenge. Aware of his jealous protectiveness of Anne-Marie, Consuelo shuddered and kept her eyes open. Thank the Lord, she thought as she watched him speculate and then relax.

Anne-Marie stiffened slightly on hearing the invitation to dance, but then, as she also noted a nearly imperceptible nod of Don Miguel's elaborate plume, graciously bowed her consent. The couple swept out of sight.

Bart's unscheduled liberty was not necessarily dangerous in itself, but it added to Consuelo's discomfort. The costume party, a perfect cover for Anne-Marie and Bart was, by its very nature, enormously difficult to keep under control. She felt like

242

a playwright whose actors were changing the script, jumping from Act I to Act III, as well as changing the time-setting and costumes on her. Clowns, knights in armor, ballet dancers, cavemen, tramps, barmaids, priests, nuns, witches, princesses and princes frolicked about, appearing and disappearing, engendering a confusion far beyond what Consuelo had anticipated. No one seemed patently recognizable. Fighting a rising panic that was heightened by the rousing music, Consuelo followed Bart and Anne-Marie into the house.

Bart and Anne-Marie had joined the dancers.

"I don't believe you are here, Anne-Marie," said Bart. "I don't know how you feel, but I feel as though I am in the middle of a vivid dream. After all these years we are dancing together in a madhouse!"

"You must know," she replied as loudly as she dared in order to be heard over the pounding music, "that I thought you were dead."

"I was," he replied and waited silently as she spoke, as if to interrupt a flood of questions.

"Please, please, don't go into a lot that will make this harder for me. I said that I would meet you alone later and I will try to explain then." Her voice was unsteady and trembling. "The girl you knew is also dead."

"I don't believe it," he said gruffly and though his hold was firm, at that minute a clown asked Anne-Marie to dance, whisking her off. Bart would have protested and pursued her, but he knew that he would see her alone soon and retreated to a relatively safe position at the edge of the dance floor.

Both Don Miguel and Consuelo had watched with relief the separation of the pair and Bart's apparent absorption by the stag line.

As soon as she could, Anne-Marie detached herself from a clanking armored knight and searched out Don Miguel. Arm in arm they moved to the garden, seeking and finding a secluded spot, one tiny area hidden from casual view by a tall shrub.

"What a difficult dance that was," whispered Anne-Marie

to Don Miguel. "Dancing with that knight was like dancing with an armadillo!"

Don Miguel, unsettled, managed a wan smile. Anne-Marie seemed unduly nervous.

"I hope you are having a good time, dear," she said, anxiously searching his eyes.

"I'm fine," replied Don Miguel. "I'm not able to dance as much as I'd like to, considering that my partner is so light on her feet, and that this is the first chance that she has had to dance for a long time."

"If you mind my dancing with others, I won't," she said in a sweet tone. Above all, she wanted Don Miguel at ease.

"Of course, I don't mind," said Don Miguel. A tinge of indignation provided a vent for a small release of emotion.

In that moment a couple vacated a nearby garden bench. "Come, let's sit down while we have the chance," said Anne-Marie, reaching for his hand. "You can gather strength to dance with me." Her touch and smile were placating.

Consuelo then appeared in the garden and was relieved to see Anne-Marie and Don Miguel together. She knew that Anne-Marie would have needed to soothe his anxious spirit and apparently she had done so. Telling a few amusing fortunes, Consuelo worked her way toward the pair. "Gypsy-lady, give the grandee a reading and a magnificent fortune while I run upstairs for a moment, please. In exchange, I will give you a warning," continued Anne-Marie, taking Consuelo's hand in hers and gazing at the lines in her palm. "Beware of a dancing knight in armor. His arm plates will pinch you. He cannot glide, but will stomp and stand on your feet."

Consuelo and Don Miguel broke into laughter.

"I must seek out a needle and thread to repair the knight's damage to my hem or I would stay to hear your prophecy. You seem to be delighting everyone." With that Anne-Marie departed.

"I hope my fortune will be good," said Don Miguel, his tone conveying a smile, "but at least it will come only one day at a time," he added pensively.

Consuelo took his hand in hers, studying it. There was something about the tips of his fingers, a hardening, and an

244

irregularity of his fingernails that struck her. Don Miguel did not work at anything that could harden them. For a moment she was shaken, but then she had to think of other things.

"You are wearing a magnificent hat that describes your ancestors as your accent does not," said Consuelo, thinking quickly. "You are a powerful man with great wealth, and you have taken many chances in your life. You are a very lucky gambler—although not necessarily at the gaming tables. One tragedy struck you," she said, only guessing, "one devastating tragedy." She was safe in this statement, knowing that would be true of anyone over the age of thirty.

"That is so."

"There was a dark woman in your life." This was another guess, but Consuelo was safely inferring that at least his mother was a dark-haired woman. Don Miguel's eyes lit with no little surprise.

"Not too dark," he replied. "She was a quadroon." His face saddened. Consuelo congratulated herself on her lucky choice of the word "dark."

He is still sad in recollection, she thought. She is probably dead. And as a quadroon her life cannot have been easy for her. Consuelo took another chance. "Tragedy involved this woman," she ventured, "but it was so terrible I don't want to think about it. But otherwise you have been blessed with luck."

"You're really quite good at your fortune telling, Madame. Can you read the future as well as the past?"

"Sometimes, but I'm not infallible. You are in control of your life. Your life is what you make it. Do you understand me? Some people's lives are controlled by others, but not yours. You rule. You were born to rule other men. The only great problems in your life have been with women."

This was a logical guess. Consuelo presumed that such an adventurous and attractive man would attract many women. A man with his easy confidence would be interested only in a woman who presented a challenge. Women who threw themselves at him would not have intrigued him.

"Tell me more," said Don Miguel, obviously interested and amused.

In the dim light, his face crisscrossed by even deeper shadows, Consuelo could visualize a small smile curving his lips. Nervously, she wondered how long she could hold his attention. Until this moment she had been lucky. Suddenly she felt her power compromised by her inability to see his eyes, and to use her own. She felt like a woman who wields her fan to hide her eyes even though she knows her eyes are her greatest attraction.

"You have been through a difficult period that eased suddenly and spectacularly." She paused and then added, "You have a serious health problem." It was then that, unaccountably, Consuelo felt the icy cold of an impending death—and not her own. She shivered. Fortunately, she thought, he could not see her consternation. Borrowing calmness from some inner source, she said to him, "You must see a doctor."

"You are a perceptive gypsy," said Don Miguel, who had not recognized Consuelo.

Realizing that she could no longer keep up the pretense of telling his fortune or entertaining Don Miguel with idle chatter, Consuelo knew she had to escape to gather strength. Don Miguel was, indeed, a very ill man.

"Will you excuse me? I left my shawl someplace in the house. I don't want to lose it," she said, departing.

She entered the house and immediately washed her hands as though that act would expel the weight of a heart-rending discovery. Don Miguel was obviously unaware of how sick he was. How insignificant it made the little drama now being acted out by Bart and Anne-Marie.

She entered the living room where she could see the stairs. A potbellied soldier whom she recognized as the disguised Anne-Marie was resolutely ascending the stairs, her rigid back and step signaling anger rather than the dreamy softness of romance.

Consuelo, her gypsy power again alight, knew immediately that Bart had offended her, and greatly. To confirm this she could only wait patiently for Bart's appearance and his explanation. Meanwhile, she looked for Tim, knowing that at this moment he would be dressed as the hangman. But finding him proved difficult. The candle-lit house and garden were packed with moving and turning people. None were recognizable. Many were dancing, their positions constantly changing.

Romping couples slipped in and out of dark corners. Teasing giggles exploded with cascades of laughter like volleys of buckshot landing anywhere and everywhere, attracting and distracting her search. Fractured statements echoed about the grounds in a background of music, flowing and ebbing through one area to another as she walked.

Instead of rooms filled with friends, masked strangers paraded before her eyes dressed as ghosts, buccaneers, demons, gypsies, soldiers, geishas and goddesses—as if on a wild merry-go-round. Everyone seemed to be circulating, laughing riotously, flirting, playing, and, alas for the proprieties, even pinching each other. With identities hidden behind masks and costumes caution was thrown to the wind. Squeezing through the crowd, Consuelo was unexpectedly seized for a few bars of a reel. She managed to extricate herself only to be snatched away again and cast into the dance. Her guests were obviously having a marvelous time, but because she could find none of the actors in her own drama, she began to panic.

In planning this she had not foreseen the total confusion that could result from misplaced identities. Even her house seemed no longer her own. Then to her immense relief the Arab woman materialized dancing with, thank heaven, the Renaissance nobleman in his marvelously plumed hat. They were dancing totally in accord. Consuelo heaved a sigh of relief. Whatever had happened between Anne-Marie and Bart, there was no trouble now between Anne-Marie and Don Miguel. Consuelo could hear Anne-Marie's lilting laughter. Both she and Don Miguel seemed to be having a wonderful time. Now she wanted to find Bart and Tim, who might be upstairs changing their costumes.

She ran upstairs. Two bedrooms were bolted from the inside. She tapped lightly on each and was told both times to "Go away." Shrugging, she examined her own room. The soldier's outfit and the pillow, hurriedly discarded by Anne-Marie, lay on the bed. There was no sign of either of her friends or their garb.

Consuelo hurried down the stairs, inspecting the dancers in the living room. Recognizing no one except the Arab woman and the Renaissance nobleman with a decidedly spectacular hat, she therefore assumed that under it was Don Miguel.

At the back door she found Bart, dressed as a hangman.

"It's been one helluva night," Bart raged, glaring at her.

"What do you mean?" asked a surprised Consuelo, bracing herself for his attack.

"You know damn well what I mean," he replied. "Anne-Marie did not show up."

"She did too," Consuelo bristled.

"Are *you* telling *me*? I suppose you were there," Bart continued sarcastically, his curt behavior crushing her.

"I'm mystified. I did nothing but tell Don Miguel's fortune while Anne-Marie became a soldier and disappeared according to plan. I don't know what you're talking about," she defended, now hotly taking offense at Bart's unjustified abuse.

Suddenly they were interrupted by an eavesdropping masquerader and looked up to see a familiar Renaissance nobleman in an undistinguished plumed hat. "I believe it's the witching hour—midnight, when we all may remove our masks. Madame, it has been a most illuminating evening," said a strangely familiar voice, but one sounding different than expected. With that, the hat was removed. It was *not* Tim; the masquerader was Don Miguel himself. Bart and Consuelo stood frozen in shock. "I have had a delightful time, my prescient hostess and friend of my dear wife, but I must now claim her and retire. Thank you and adieu."

With that he left the patio to find Anne-Marie dancing with a Renaissance nobleman in a magnificently plumed hat. "We can now trade hats again," said Don Miguel to Tim. "I'm tired, dear. Do you mind if we go?"

"Certainly not," said Anne-Marie, looking inquisitively at her husband. To Tim she said, "Thank you for a pleasant dance. It was good to meet you."

"The pleasure was mine," Tim replied.

When they departed, the sheriff and two deputies dressed as priests stepped up to Bart, softly informing him that he was under arrest. "I would advise you to come quietly," said the sheriff. "We don't want to spoil the party, do we?"

Offering no resistance, Bart complied.

The stunned hostess found Tim. "Bart has just been arrested."

"How?" he whispered.

"By the sheriff dressed as a priest. They left by the back way so as not to break up the party. What happened? What went wrong?"

"I found out just now, dancing with Anne-Marie," Tim explained. "When Don Miguel came to take her home she behaved as if she did not know me; but before that she had a chance to tell me something. Anne-Marie left this house intending to meet Bart at mine, exactly as planned. She arrived at my house and looked in the window. Seeing my costume, she thought the man in it was Don Miguel. She thought it was a trap and that Don Miguel was waiting for her—set up by you. She returned in a rage.

"Bart waited, and when she did not come he came back here, also in a rage. Don Miguel must have been suspicious that something was going on because when I appeared, he insisted that we exchange hats. He took my hat and then did not wear it. What a sly fox!"

"Now that I think about it I remember that I noticed he was not wearing a hat!" said Consuelo, sick at heart.

"Anne-Marie insisted that I dance with her so that she could explain a little," continued Tim.

"What a disaster! Bart will never forgive us now." Consuelo looked about at the dozens of guests, all unaware of the drama in their midst, continuing to eat, dance and frolic.

"Take heart. We've escaped from worse messes than this. Bart is no longer fighting a murder charge. I don't think they can hold him long," replied Tim, not thinking.

"Where did we go wrong?" Consuelo moaned, though she knew the answer as she asked.

"Only in going to a tailor who made two similar costumes," he replied, shaking his head sadly. "That we could not have foreseen. We weren't clever enough. See how quickly Don Miguel's suspicions were aroused when he saw my costume and how quickly and quietly he took action."

"Clearly he's a master of intrigue," lamented Consuelo, "as we are not."

"Is Mr. Leeds still here?"

"Let's try to find him," said Tim, pushing through the crowd of now unmasked guests. Leeds was not to be found. "Apparently, he slipped out earlier—with no recognizable hostess to thank at the time."

"By the time Don Miguel left, he had figured me out," remarked Consuelo.

Guests were now departing and courtesy demanded that Consuelo stand at the door to bid them good night and receive their thanks. The torches outside no longer burned. Inside, what little food remained was being put away. Tim started to leave, but Consuelo stopped him.

"Don't go. I can't face this house alone. Sit here and talk to me a little longer—until I gather my wits."

"Your wish and it shall be done," said Tim, tossing his hat in a corner.

Last to leave were the musicians. Tim and Consuelo were left alone to face each other and the house, in shambles. Tim poured her a double rum. "I think you need this. I'm sure you've had nothing to eat or drink all evening. As a matter of fact, I'm hungry too."

Consuelo took the glass gladly, eager for escape, but then put it down. "First some food. It has been a strain," she quavered. "I had imagined a very different end to this evening, although I don't know quite what. I thought and secretly hoped that Anne-Marie would convince Bart that she would not leave Don Miguel. Then our lives would quiet down."

"The future to you is the day after tomorrow, Consuelo, not next month or next year, and that's where your planning goes awry."

"Years ago I promised to help Bart and see him through this," she replied, setting out some cold chicken.

"And you have," interrupted Tim. "And I am committed as well to helping Bart, perhaps as much for you as for him, because, as you know, I love you."

Consuelo's eyes met his. "I have tried to be fair and warn you of the risks. You know that I like you enormously. I would like to love you."

Tim rose and, pulling her to her feet, took her in his arms.

His forceful kiss pressed her lips into silence. The strong rum had taken hold and she felt the room slowly turning about her. Tim's arms held her, steadied her, offered a soothing comfort and release, an escape into an unmindful existence. Suddenly he swept her into his arms and carried her up the stairs. Offering no resistance, she felt his fingers loosen the full blouse and laced bodice of a gypsy fortune-teller. The full skirt and petticoats fell to a heap on the floor. For a moment he left her, but within seconds she felt the warmth of his bare body as he was back beside her.

"You've been so marvelously patient with me," she whispered. "I think had I been in your shoes, I would have sent me packing, but you haven't. I have been so grateful for that."

Another kiss sealed her lips, but then he said, "Great loves never come easily. They're hewn and hacked from stone. They have lasting power. I love you, but I have lusted for you, knowing that you were with Bart. I believe that together we can build a great love, and I hope you are beginning to see it too."

As he spoke, his hands drew her nearer and nearer and deeper and deeper into his world. Then his powerful embrace locked her to him. An overwhelming sense of oneness engulfed her. That Tim, loving only herself, was now returning to her, was a beautiful gift.

She had wondered if it would ever happen again, that sense of true mating. But perhaps it would. . . . Just maybe it would. Easily and gently Tim led her down a path, and then suddenly he was drawing her along with him, faster and more forcibly. As they moved she felt her skin tingle with a burning flush as if some current, some heating force, were flowing through her, enlivening her. His throbbing tempo then caught her so that her whole body ached for the wild, unfathomable satisfaction that only he could provide. Finally, the great sensation came. With soaring speed it crushed down upon her, threatening to press her to oblivion.

"You will never escape me, Consuelo," said Tim a few minutes later. "When the parties are over, I shall be here," he warned.

"I don't want to escape you," she said, sitting up and pulling

251

a sheet around her. "If we build something together, I want it to be permanent. We already have a friendship that is a great foundation to build on. I simply don't want any lingering passion for Bart to diminish it. You don't deserve that, Tim. You deserve a love that . . . a love that is all there is. That's why I have tried to hold you at a distance. I know it now."

"For the first time I feel as though I'm truly advancing with you," he told her.

"You are," she allowed. "It was nice to have someone around who brings no problems, who only helps me solve mine. For this reason, I'm frightened of using you. I won't do it."

"It's nice to be needed, you know," he remonstrated.

"Of course, I know that. I've often wondered how much of a role that has played in the way I felt about Bart," she said.

"I notice that you put that in the past tense. That's interesting—and gratifying, too."

"Don't misinterpret," she cautioned. "But things do change, don't they? We must go to sleep. Tomorrow we must visit Mr. Leeds. If we think about everything we should we'll never get to sleep."

The next morning Consuelo awakened Tim early. "Hurry and dress. There's a little breakfast downstairs. Close your eyes to the shattered house. Pearl will do wonders while we're gone."

"You must believe that all sailors are incredibly tidy. I can face facts, in any case," he comforted.

"All sailors I have known were tidy. They had a passion for everything in its place," said Consuelo, applying a powder puff.

"You have only known captains, who gave the orders, not those who carried them out. Now that I have my own boat, I see seamanship in a different light. But once my feet are on dry land, other basic urges take over. I want to make love, have fun, sleep late. I've done yeoman duty. Now, thankfully, I leave it to others."

Mr. Leeds was more than cordial to his favorite client. "Last night was a memorable evening. I doubt that Key West has ever enjoyed such a party. You did yourself proud, Madame."

"I'm so glad you enjoyed yourself. However, after you left, a friend of mine, also your client, was arrested. Please make haste and see that Captain Ramsden is released. You know, as well as I know, that the charges are ridiculous."

"The charges are very serious, but I'll get over to the sheriff's office now to see whether I can post a bond for his release. I'll be in touch with you right away."

Dismissed, Consuelo and Tim returned to her house.

"We could walk down to see whether he's in the sweat box," suggested Consuelo, referring to the city lockup.

Tim agreed.

They walked to the foot of Duval Street, but the jail was empty.

"That's strange," said Consuelo. "I wonder if he broke away?"

Tim was also baffled, but soon they had the answer from Mr. Leeds. "Captain Ramsden has been turned over to the military. It is now a new and totally different case," he said ominously. "Smuggling guns during wartime is a federal offense. He could be court-martialed for treason."

CHAPTER EIGHTEEN

Anne-Marie had dressed with unusual care to attend Consuelo's party, where she would see and speak to her lawful husband for the first time since the sea had parted them. She would be most beautiful, she resolved, in the diaphanous, exotic robe of an Arab princess. This costume would contrast sharply with that of the potbellied soldier that Consuelo had chosen for their meeting. I guess that's just as well, thought Anne-Marie, considering what I have to tell Bart. It seemed to Anne-Marie as she stood before her mirror, a glittering figure awash with gold, that she was in an intolerable position, locked between two irreconcilable loyalties.

A dozen thin gold bracelets jangled on her arm, raised now to adjust her hair, which had been rinsed black for the ball. Were the selfish interests of wealth, power and position tipping the scales in favor of Don Miguel? Or, had her love for him become so great that she could not turn from him? Indeed, the gold bracelets seemed weightier than the solitary emerald.

Have I changed—much? wondered Anne-Marie. Or is it this strange dark hair and a role to play in Consuelo's drama that have given me stage fright? Unfortunately, none of this could be discussed with Don Miguel. She would have to act without his sage advice. She would do as Consuelo asked, even though she had little capacity for deception.

Still, she wondered if she could trust Consuelo. Obviously, Consuelo had taken great risks for Bart's sake. As an accomplice she would face a jail sentence if Bart were arrested. It was logical to assume that Consuelo cared deeply for Bart or she would not have been a party to such an unlawful act as harboring a criminal. Furthermore, the charges against Bart were so confused and complex that she wondered how severe the penalties might be. What if Bart and Consuelo were executed? It wouldn't be the first time that justice miscarried. The thought was devastating. Through all of this, Bart had Consuelo, but did Consuelo have Bart? With her, Anne-Marie, safe with Don Miguel and out of the way, she might. With that, Anne-Marie believed she saw Consuelo's motive and decided that she could trust Consuelo.

Don Miguel's rap at her door and his appreciative smile drove her worries away for the moment. "You are spectacular, my dear. You are right out of *A Thousand and One Nights*."

"Seamstress Clarke has apparently succeeded again—if you're pleased," she replied nervously.

"I presume the dark hair will be gone tomorrow. You're not yourself . . . but I realize it is appropriate," he added.

"If it rains, I'll be a horror," she laughed. "The color will wash right out, but not, I hope, tonight." She shuddered.

Together they walked the short distance to Consuelo's house. The moon was out, and the stars shivered with brightness. "It looks as if there's no chance of rain," said Don Miguel. "You can relax."

Anne-Marie was glad he thought so. She was of a different mind. Her first shock came when she and Don Miguel entered the patio and Bart asked her to dance. This had not been planned. Only her awareness of Don Miguel and her intense concentration on his reaction took her out of herself enough to present a calm facade.

The few minutes that they had together were totally disconcerting. Bart's impetuosity alarmed her, and yet she saw how in the boisterous confusion of a costumed world he had taken advantage of an opportunity. She should have expected it. This slight deviation from the plan was no reason for her not to go through with her part.

At the appointed hour she excused herself, and in Consuelo's boudoir she changed her costume to that of a paunchy soldier for her meeting with Bart at Tim's house. While she dressed she reviewed what she wanted to say. Don Miguel had saved her life twice and he was an ill and doomed man. She could not leave him. Moreover, she had grown to love him for his kindness, his thoughtful care of her, his interest in teaching her to broaden her life and to appreciate it for her own future happiness. His wealth and power were not factors in her love for him. Above all, she knew she must resist any temptation to fall into Bart's arms. To touch him again would mean entering a new torment. She must remain aloof, not only for her own sake but for Don Miguel and Samantha. Samantha—dear God, what a problem; Bart would think she was his child and she was not. Still, she had made a bargain to speak with him, and for this one night only she would keep it. After tonight, should his actions be his undoing, it would only be by his own choice. A noose of the law hung over his head. Without Don Miguel at her side, she was powerless to help Bart. With Don Miguel possibly she could help him! This was something Bart might understand whether or not he could accept her other reasons.

Fear rising with every step, she descended the stairs and walked out into the night. With frantic haste she walked the three blocks to Tim's house, remembering twice to adjust her walk to a masculine gait. The streets were deserted, but the music from Consuelo's house rose like a cloud over the neighborhood. She stopped at the small well-groomed cottage. Cautiously, before entering, she looked into the window and saw Don Miguel sitting there! Obviously, it was a trap.

She could not believe it. Had Consuelo and Tim double-crossed her? It was inconceivable—and yet there Don Miguel was. Infuriated and losing no time, she returned to the party and re-dressed as an Arab. During the evening she would discover what had happened, she promised herself. She tried to maintain her composure in what now seemed to be bedlam. Mad people in masks danced about her like demons. Perhaps it is a nightmare, she thought. I'll soon wake up. Yes, that's it. Soon everything will be back to normal.

She braced herself for an encounter with Don Miguel. Obviously, he had learned of the assignation. This would hurt him, but she had not kept it, which would please him. He might attribute this to one of the vagaries of the female mind, which he pretended not to understand.

In the melee she spotted Don Miguel coming toward her, hurried and determined. Quickly she looked for an unattached male as a possible dance partner, one who could for a moment offer escape. There was none. She would have to face him now. There was no time to swallow her fears.

Don Miguel suggested that they dance, and the moment he touched her she knew the touch was not his.

"Don Miguel?" she stammered.

"No, Anne-Marie, I'm Tim. Don Miguel insisted on exchanging hats with me. But are you all right? Don't faint!" He pulled off his mask.

"So, that explains it. I thought Bart, waiting there for me at your house, was Don Miguel. How was I to know that you and Don Miguel had the same costume? It is too ridiculous after such careful planning to fail by a coincidence. Bart will be furious. What can we do, Tim, but dance and hope that Bart appears so that I can explain to him? It is terrible to laugh, but the only alternative is to cry."

"Don Miguel and I obviously went to the same careless tailor. If Don Miguel knew, he would have the man's hide."

Together they laughed, and when Don Miguel walked up to them they appeared to be having a marvelous time.

"I hate to take you away, Anne-Marie," said Don Miguel. "You seem to be having fun, but I'm exhausted."

"Of course, you are. How inconsiderate I've been to leave you for so long. I'll thank Consuelo tomorrow. Good night, Mr. Clayton." With that they left to walk home.

"Consuelo had a very interesting party," said Don Miguel casually.

"It was lively enough," replied Anne-Marie placidly. "Consuelo has great imagination."

"She also has courage, my dear. She fights for what she wants. She was the one of your friends I thought best for you."

"Don Miguel, you talk to me as if I were a child," said Anne-Marie, not bothering to disguise her irritation, stepping up the pace toward their home. She would have liked to remain at the party, but fearing Don Miguel was overtaxed, she had gracefully allowed herself to be led home. Now, childishly she was resenting the "imposition."

"I was pleased to learn that you had no interest in an assignation with your former husband," said Don Miguel coolly.

Anne-Marie felt her blood run cold. What had Don Miguel learned and how had he learned it? She would make no explanations. Evidently, she had made the right decision in not entering Tim's house. Nevertheless, he seemed satisfied with the evening and satisfied with her. She was grateful for the darkness. But she could not hold her tongue.

"I think I've made myself clear on this point several times," she replied in a friendly and even voice.

"Unfortunately, now I feel obliged to get your ex-husband out of jail one way or another, but that is neither here nor there. I would have preferred not to have been involved with that," Don Miguel lied.

Bart in jail, he had said. If that were true, then Don Miguel had put him there, she thought. Deftly, he would have had his rival put out of the way. Then, because he had learned that he could trust Anne-Marie, he would see that Bart was freed and gain her approval. Don Miguel had not realized that she was unaware of Bart's arrest. She fought to remain calm.

"I do hope that you will do all that you can to get him out. He has had enough trouble and some of it my doing. His loss of a wife was not only my doing but yours. We both owe him help."

"I'll see what I can do, of course."

"I would appreciate it," she said, finding his eyes in the darkness. "It is unlike you to be small or petty."

The night enclosed them in silence. Even the revelry at Consuelo's could not be heard. Only their footsteps echoed on the footpath. Anne-Marie felt estranged. Don Miguel reached for her hand, which she gave him, irrationally hating him and at the same time, marveling at her own duplicity.

They were met at the door by Concepción. The maid then helped Anne-Marie undress. "It was a big and fine party. Everyone had a wonderful time," Anne-Marie murmured, knowing that the maid expected her comment and would have been distressed if she had not had a good time. Concepción was well aware of her mistress's elaborate preparation for the party and her excitement. "I guess you could hear the music. It was sweet of you to have waited up."

"*De nada, señora. Buenos noches*," the maid replied, smiling and content.

Anne-Marie knew that no good night was in store for her. She must review her concerns. Meeting Bart again had had an impact she was forced to acknowledge. Bart would feel that she had let him down, and, of course, she had, despite her good intentions. The sense of oneness with Don Miguel had evaporated when she remembered the walk home and their talk in detail. She had a strong suspicion that he had had a hand in Bart's jailing, but she could not prove this—and why should she want to? She could also imagine Consuelo's disappointment at the failure of her well-orchestrated plan. An enormous amount of preparation had gone into the party and a considerable expense. She had failed the others. Tim had been sympathetic, but then he alone knew all the facts as she did. It had been nice in that brief moment to talk with him; he was such a kind man. Her old feeling of being buffeted about by the manipulation of others added to her frustration. I guess I have become what mother would have called a weak person, thought Anne-Marie sadly as she finally fell asleep without having resolved a single dilemma.

As promised, the following morning Don Miguel visited the sheriff. He had felt himself a victor when he heard Captain Ramsden's own words that Anne-Marie had not shown up for some planned tryst; he had been certain that something was in the air. Lately, he had thought he had a strange new awareness. Sometimes he supposed it came with a sense of impending death, for he knew his health was failing rapidly. Death had stalked him for so many years that he had become familiar with its footsteps. He was prepared, but not yet dead, he trumpeted to himself. What you know must happen will happen and you can't draw back, thought Don Miguel with the instinct of an old fighter. Now he felt good. He never should have doubted Anne-Marie.

It was with no little sense of power that he entered the sheriff's office the day·after the party.

"Good morning, sir," said the sheriff, proffering a hand. "You'll be pleased to know I turned Captain Ramsden over to the military."

"You *what*?" asked Don Miguel, disbelieving.

The sheriff repeated himself. In an overzealous effort to please his benefactor Don Miguel, he had turned Captain Ramsden in to the federal East Gulf Blockading Squadron. In this area Don Miguel had no influence whatever.

"I . . . I thought you'd be pleased," stammered the sheriff, seeing Don Miguel's flabbergasted expression.

"I can't believe that you would do such a stupid thing," hissed Don Miguel. "No one plays with the federal government. This was to be a little joke, a little lesson . . ."

"But I thought . . ."

"You're not paid to think," said Don Miguel, now hurrying out, his rage like a cloud gathering for a hurricane.

Immediately he headed for the naval base and asked the officer of the day to announce him to Commander McKean. McKean, nursing a colossal hangover earned at Consuelo's party, was not available. "I have no idea where the commander can be found. Where he is, is none of my business," replied the officer stiffly.

"I'll wait," said Don Miguel.

Don Miguel was painfully aware of the full implications of the sheriff's actions: Bart would be given a stiff sentence and his own effort to free him would fail. Nevertheless, he would try.

When Commander McKean returned, he was in no mood to stretch his authority. Having nothing but distaste for the accusation of consorting with the enemy, he refused to act. During the next few days a traveling federal judge, then in Key

West to hear almost a dozen cases of varying import, would decide the captain's case, necessarily with dispatch.

"I see no need to interfere," the commander concluded.

Don Miguel could do nothing but report the sad state of affairs to Anne-Marie. "He must face court-martial and there's nothing that I can do, as much as I would like to—believe me!"

She was stunned. Still, he was not yet convicted. What could his defense be except a clear denial? Poor Bart!

A visit to Mr. Leeds by Consuelo produced the following information: McKean's principals in Washington, now under President Johnson, had voiced radical sentiments and Johnson's own words were, "I say that a traitor has ceased to be a citizen and in joining the rebellion has become a public enemy.... Treason must be made odious and traitors must be punished and impoverished."

McKean's advancement would depend upon favor from Washington. Bart would be allowed counsel, but he would have to stand court-martial for treasonable acts during wartime. There was no recourse.

Throughout the Civil War, Key West had been designated as the headquarters of the East Gulf Blockading Squadron commanded by Flag Officer W. W. McKean. It was the sole port in the South held by the Union throughout the war, and consequently, a very important command. Two hundred and ninety-nine captured blockade runners had been brought to Key West, depriving the Confederacy of much vital material. Courts-martial dispensed military justice rapidly and the three hundredth case would be coming up. Guilty prisoners were promptly transported to Fort Jefferson where they were to serve sentences varying from one year to life.

"I'll do what I can," said Leeds, "but the best that he can hope for is a light sentence. The fact that any number of people had access to the captain's cabin is a very weak defense. He was accused of murder so his record is hardly spotless. He also has been a fugitive from justice."

"How can the military try a private citizen?" cried Consuelo. "They can't!"

262

"My dear woman, if that were the fact, two hundred ninety-nine others would be set free. I can make the motion, but you don't need me to tell you how far it will go. But, we can hope for a light sentence. As soon as the *Greyhound* comes into port the investigation can be reopened. Possibly we can prove that access to the cache of guns was through the first mate's cabin. If that is the case, through congressmen and influential friends we can work for a presidential pardon. This would be the most direct route."

Despite Leeds's eloquent argument in Bart's behalf, he was found guilty. In a sentence believed to be lenient, Bart was sentenced to three years in a federal prison.

Within the week he was transferred to Fort Jefferson, situated on Garden Key, an isolated island sixty miles west of Key West. Garden Key is the largest of ten islands that comprise a group known as Dry Tortugas on the extreme tip of the Great Barrier Reefs of Florida. Garden Key could not be more different than its name implied.

CHAPTER NINETEEN

Over the years, Bart had made numerous trips to Fort Jefferson, bringing in construction materials for the mammoth building, a combined fort and federal prison. Still, he had not been inside since he was a boy.

The giant citadel had been created out of the heart of the mighty waters of the Gulf and appeared to be adrift in the sea. The enormous bastions led to dizzy heights, walling in sixteen acres in a six-sided building, and offered such a display of architectural effect that many were numb on seeing it for the first time. Built by means of cofferdams of magnificent brick-work—possibly the finest in all America—it was laid out on a tremendous scale. It had taken twenty years of construction to produce this architectural masterpiece, an accomplishment that vied with the Great Pyramid in grandeur. This incredible work of art would be seen only by a few seamen, a small garrison and America's worst criminals.

Originally, it had been intended as a naval supply station and as an arsenal to command the Gulf of Mexico. When the Civil War broke out it was still unfinished in that not one gun was in place. Congress, realizing the importance of the fort as a stronghold for the federal government, immediately appro-priated five hundred thousand dollars to place the fort in commission as soon as possible. But instead, it became a prison, housing hundreds of hardened criminals. It also contained deserters—regardless of the circumstances—captured officers and innocent men such as Bart, all of whom suffered alike.

Escape was prevented by the open sea and a sixty-foot shark-filled moat fronting upon the fort's only entrance.

The events of the last few days before his conviction had been so astounding, Bart could hardly believe what had happened. His only saving thought lay in his confidence that his friends would soon have him free. How, he had no idea, but three years of incarceration were impossible to comprehend. In this dazed state, he was transported to the fort; the trip took the better part of a day.

Along with a dozen other men, their hands in chains, he and his fellow prisoners were unloaded like cattle being driven to a slaughterhouse. Then, before they could begin their walk, one prisoner became unruly. Without warning he was shot and unceremoniously tossed from the boardwalk into the moat's shark-infested waters. Shocked into stony silence, the men marched into the fort, aghast at their prospects.

Fortunately, Bart had learned a lesson under the hand of the capricious captain of the *Dasher* in Santa Barbara. He would not protest. He knew that the least breach of regulations, even of prison "etiquette" as defined by the guards, could cost him his life. For the next few days he barely spoke and the others decided to do the same. Silently the men moved about their dungeons. During the day they worked in silence; at night they were locked in their cells and confined their speech to murmurs.

The day following his arrival, Bart was assigned to duty at the prison hospital as an orderly. Also working in this hospital was a convicted traitor, Dr. Samuel A. Mudd. Mudd had set the leg of John Wilkes Booth, who had shot President Lincoln, and for this "crime" he was here.

It was clear to Bart from Mudd's manner that here was a kind and gentle man, but he had become so thin and worn after two years that it was almost impossible to imagine how he might have looked when he arrived in 1865. He had lost his hair and he hardly had the strength to move, much less to sprinkle sand and sweep down six bastions every day as he did. A diet of coffee, bread and butter—and only an occasional potato or onion—had taken its toll.

"My God, is that what I'll look like after three years here?" muttered Bart, finally daring to speak in a whisper to another inmate when, for a few minutes, no sentry was in earshot.

"If you live," was the grim reply.

To wait and endure was to survive.

The prisoners worked from sunup until sundown, with most of the work falling to the new arrivals because they had more strength. Out of simple humanity Bart assumed a major share of the tasks assigned to Mudd and himself, thereby making a friend of that frail figure.

"Don't work too fast," Mudd cautioned, "or they will only give us more to do. After a while you learn to pace yourself here, so that the work and the time come out even."

Another sort of brute, however, stalked prisoners and guards alike. Yellow fever had begun its march across the tropics. A number of cases were reported in the *Key West Dispatch* and soon it was a topic of discussion among the garrisons. The news sifted down to the prisoners.

The summer of 1867 began unseasonably wet and warm, like the summer of '64, when an epidemic of yellow fever hit Key West, forcing the Navy to move the base to Tampa for the summer. This was done when the death rate reached fifteen persons a day.

"I shudder at the arrival of any new men," Dr. Mudd told Bart. "Yourself excepted, of course. This place remains unusually healthy, but the arrival of vessels and steamers from infected ports means a constant threat."

Indeed, within only a few days they stood looking at a single vessel moored at one of the wharves. Not a soul aboard stirred. A large flock of black frigate birds, gregarious as vultures, hovered about or perched on the booms.

"They look as though they smell death," said Bart.

"They probably do. They eat carrion. That vessel is in quarantine. All hands aboard are sick with fever of some description, possibly yellow fever. Several have died, I hear, and there's not one person well enough to nurse the sick. No volunteers from among the prison garrison go to them, so their chances of survival are small."

"I suppose if a prisoner did volunteer there are enough sentries here to see to it that he would never come back to the fort anyway, as if he carried the fever in his pocket."

"But he might be doing just that," advised Mudd. . . .

Later that day Bart saw a reeling man drag from the vessel two bodies that he managed to drop overboard. As soon as he could, he told Mudd about it.

"Just hope that the wind holds from the right direction or we'll get the stink and it will be enough to gag us all."

"Have you ever tried to escape?" asked Bart, thinking of taking the doctor and sailing away in the quarantined ship.

"Oh, yes," the doctor answered, "but I was too well known and they caught me hiding after only ten minutes. They were so happy to catch me that four others got away in the excitement. After that I wore chains and drew hard labor."

"Would you try again?"

"No, I have determined to remain peaceable and quiet and allow the government the full exercise of its power. If I were to take French leave, I could never return to my country. I only attempted to escape because I heard that my family was reduced to begging. Soldiers seeking revenge ruined my farm."

"And all because you set a man's broken leg."

"Booth fled Lincoln's box and in so doing tangled himself in the flag and broke his leg. He had a horse waiting at the stage entrance and escaped into the night." Mudd paused and then continued. "It wasn't pure chance that he came to my house. He had been in the area once before and had knocked on my door wanting to buy a horse. I sent him to my neighbor, also a farmer. But Booth had noted that I was the Charles County physician. On that fateful night he was looking for a doctor and a water route to the South. My farm was on that route."

"You didn't recognize him?" asked Bart.

"Heavens no. He was in disguise. He seemed a complete stranger to me. I put his leg in splints, and because he was too weak to move, I kept him through the night and saw him leave in the morning. Of course, I had no idea the president had been shot and that this man was the murderer. When a search party arrived, I described my patient and even went upstairs to produce the boot I had cut off in order to set his leg. His name was in the boot. With that, I became a conspirator."

"And then you received a life sentence?"

"You have the story," said Mudd. He turned his tired and weakened eyes away from Bart. "I should have been imprisoned in Albany, but the tales of the horrors of this place had already reached Washington, and, desiring to break my spirit and health—because I would never confess to guilt—I was moved here."

"You have no more valid reason to be here than I do," exclaimed Bart, shaking his head. A long silence weighed upon the two despondent men.

"I'm sure in the great scheme of things, there is a reason for my being here," said Bart. "For one thing, I helped build this miserable place. I made considerable money hauling material here. Perhaps I'm being punished for that. However, as to the charge of treason, based upon gun smuggling, I am completely innocent. I was a Unionist."

"I must admit to having a good deal of sympathy for the South. I was brought up on a plantation. I saw the evils of slavery, but was caught in a system. It took slaves to run a plantation and I treated mine well."

"Any people—such as the Northerners and Southerners—who no longer have anything in common save greed for money and a fear of failure deserve to be united for all time," said Bart sarcastically. "I see that now and I have been as guilty as the next man. But it doesn't make me less bitter."

"One soon grows bitter here," replied Mudd, shaking his head. "You have no idea how many times in the last two years I have examined my conscience, searching for some clue, some intentioned wrong, some dishonesty that could have brought about this dishonor, and always my mind is as blank as that wall."

Their conversation abruptly ceased as a sentry approached. Quickly they picked up their buckets and began to mop.

"Get moving, you two," said the sentry. "Any more lip exercises and you'll be wheelbarrowing sand."

They speeded up their work and dropped their voices.

"A man came in on a ship from New Orleans today," said Mudd, "who I believe is ill. He stopped a few times as he walked over the moat. All the prisoners were pushed along, but he stood out. A brute of a guard might have shot him, but the one on duty didn't. He could have yellow fever." He shrugged and squeezed his eyes shut as if to wipe out the vision.

The following day, August 28, 1867, yellow fever visited the island and began thinning out the ranks of both prisoners and soldiers.

"The kingdom of death knows no borders and no laws," said the doctor.

As fear grew on the island, so did extreme measures. Refusing to work or to obey an order was punishable by summary shooting. If one of the prisoners was noisy or unruly he was immediately shot by a sentry. Instead of meeting rebuke, he was commended for his conduct. "The man who did that may one day regret the loss of those two able hands," prophesied Mudd. "We are in serious trouble."

Meanwhile, an infestation of mosquitoes added to the misery. Dr. Joseph Smith was the fort surgeon. Mudd requested a meeting with him which the doctor granted. "I know you realize the seriousness of the situation, sir," said Mudd. "If I can be of any help to you, you may count on my assistance."

"I may have to do that. The fever seems to be due to the wet woolen clothing the men are wearing. I'm ordering the removal of these shirts," said Smith.

Removing the shirts exposed the men to more mosquitoes and within a short while Dr. Smith himself came down with the fever and died. It would be many years before mosquitoes were found to be the culprit in spreading the disease.

The first case had occurred in Company K, which was housed over the unfinished moat. At low tide offensive odors rose like a stinking fog which Dr. Smith thought might be the cause of the fever. The company was moved and the portholes were ordered closed to prevent the deadly miasma from entering. At this time Mudd was working temporarily in the carpenter shop and aided in barricading the portholes and partitions. Still, the fever followed along the rows of beds, passing through boarded partitions, the planks of which were loosely nailed.

"Bart," said Mudd, "I think the poison of the disease is carried in clothes, such as a cloak, because of the movement of the disease."

Upon the death of Smith, Mudd was called into the commander's office. "Some time ago I volunteered my services, sir," said Mudd. "I will be glad to work as fort physician."

"Because of the desperate circumstances, I am going to accept your offer, but you will still remain a prisoner. You understand?"

"I understand," said Mudd. "Please give me Captain Ramsden as an assistant. He's a hard worker and I can depend on him as long as he remains well."

"Granted. Now go to work," replied the commander.

Before long, nearly every man on the island became infected, including the commander, shirts or no shirts. Five hundred men at one time would not cover the sick list.

A headache and rapid pulse marked the onset of the disease. Soon the pulse slowed, the tongue became furred and nausea and vomiting followed. This was accompanied by jaundice, muscle pains, and hemorrhages. Delirium, convulsions and a coma marked the end. At first, as soon as a man was taken ill, he was placed in the prison infirmary, the only facility for the sick. When that filled, which was soon, the sick were taken in a small boat to a neighboring key where an emergency hospital had been established. Mudd told Bart, however, that he feared exposure to the elements in the small boat only exacerbated their illness.

"We seem to be rowing in the dark, traveling in circles," groaned Bart wearily. "Keep them here and they die. Take them there and they die. The sand is easier to dig into there, that's the only difference I see."

"All right, then we'll just bury them there," said Mudd impatiently. "I don't know any more about this disease than you do!"

"It may mean a little less rowing," replied Bart, glancing at the waning sun, his hands, too sore to place on his hips, open before him. Soon the whole fort was to become a hospital.

The next morning a small rain cloud came up with a steady wind which blew the miasma and a black cloud of voracious mosquitoes from the hospital on the neighboring key toward Company M. That night half the men in the company were attacked by the fever. Wild alarm and confusion prompted the closure of six casements nearest the hospital, but still the disease spread. When the sick became too ill to brush the mosquitoes away, the insects bit and moved to the healthy, who themselves became sick. Yet, even then, no one suspected them as carriers.

For more than a week there was a death almost every hour. The small rowboats took off and often did not return. The men preferred fighting the mighty Gulf Stream to returning to certain death.

"You have your chance to escape, Bart," said Dr. Mudd.

"Don't think I haven't thought of that. Two things keep me here. As you said, I might carry the disease in my pocket, and I would not dream of infecting some people that I know. There are others that I would love to kiss if only I could give them this sickness. But I can't desert you. If I live through it, I'll have to live with myself."

"I'm grateful," replied the doctor, placing an arm around the younger man and fighting to smother emotion and even his tears. Fatigue had them both on a short tether. For days they had worked virtually around the clock, snatching mere minutes of sleep when they could.

One morning only ten soldiers answered roll call. Every officer was dead or dying. Three additional hospital areas had been set up, but in fact the whole fort was a hospital. Yellow bodies, not yet dead, turning gray, lay begging for help or raving in delirium. The stench became so unbearable that Bart wore cloths around his face. To obtain more ventilation within the prison walls he reversed Dr. Mudd's decision and ordered the gun ports broken out. Dr. Mudd no longer cared, for now he had the fever. Escape would be easy, but the few remaining well and able could not bring themselves to desert.

The few remaining men gave of themselves as do heroes in war. Here all were heroes, for they could have left.

The rains that had brought mosquitoes had also filled the

cisterns underlaying the emplacements and bastions. Water seeped down into the cisterns from parapets, through brick and sand filters, making fine drinking water for the parched lips of the dying. Bart and those others who remained well moved about with cloths and buckets of water. Dipping the cloths in the water buckets, they then squeezed it into the mouths of the sick.

When Dr. Mudd became ill, Bart moved him to the officers' quarters. Eighteen sets of these rooms stood empty. These were quite different from the dank, dark airless dungeons below. Here innumerable ornamental arches, beautiful fireplaces, sweeping staircases, doors of marvelous grillwork, even ornate sliding doors had been built. Ceilings were high, decorated with plaster as if in a palace. The marvelous brickwork, the granite lintels—many of which Bart himself had transported from Concord, New Hampshire—the sills of Vermont marble and the handsome well-made furniture contrasted sharply with the damp stone and iron cots below. In this area there were few mosquitoes, so reinfection there was less likely, although no one knew that.

Bart and a handful of others ministered to the sick. For some time now, there had been no way to bury the dead. Bodies were simply dumped into the sea. Becoming convinced that isolation was helping the doctor, Bart ordered those who were well to take separate rooms. As a man who loved the sea, Bart always slept where he found a breeze, thereby possibly saving his life. Mudd had become ill in October. Early in December the epidemic had passed.

New officers arrived from Washington and the officers' quarters were vacated. Dr. Mudd had survived and now went back into chains on orders from Washington. Imprisonment became even more painful and odious. Bart drew up a petition, signed by all who survived, describing Mudd's devotion to duty, seeking the president's pardon. Instead of a reward, he was assigned even more menial tasks.

"I would refuse to believe the injustice of this world had I not seen so much of it with my own eyes," said Bart. "Sweet Jesus, was one shot ever fired at an enemy from this miserable place?"

273

"Not that I know of," replied the doctor, "except possibly in training. Look at that forlorn lighthouse tower, a sentinel of horror."

Then Bart realized that undoubtedly Tim would have sailed around the fort looking for some sign of him. He had been so busy caring for the sick that he had forgotten that light, a beacon marking hell on earth. Certainly it had been a nightly reminder to those he loved if they could see it. The thought made him incomparably sad. He knew that Tim and Consuelo in Tim's boat would have spent untold hours looking up at the red bricks above and the yellow bricks below, staring into the hundreds of vacant arches under elaborate bracket work looking for a face they now would hardly recognize. Behind that beautiful exterior they could not possibly imagine the horror within.

And Anne-Marie. . . . What would she be doing? He could not guess. His wife and friends had all been pushed from his mind by the immediacy of more compelling concerns. What he had been through was simply too loathsome, degrading and intolerable to communicate. They were all part of a world that encompassed love—something he dared not think about.

Bart had not written one word to anyone, allowing the monster of a fort to swallow him alive. Pride forbade it. He could not let those he knew realize that such a vile place existed, and that he lived in such devastating conditions. Perhaps one day he could tell them, but he doubted that. He wanted no pity. Better that they thought him dead. Dr. Mudd felt differently.

"My wife and family have been subjected to such hardships and harassment as a result of my actions, I feel they need to know that I, too, suffer. I know that my wife hoped that I would escape, but escape is generally believed to be an admission of guilt."

"I have been at sea with captains who were brutes, but this has been an inferno beyond comprehension," replied Bart, speaking under his breath. "A man could always leave a ship. Here we are chained."

"President Johnson has promised my wife his pardon, but for the time being his hands are tied. To pardon me would insure his impeachment. Your chances are much better. Don't give up hope."

274

Bart gazed at his humiliated and despondent friend, desperately wishing that he could cheer him. Only Mudd had made existence at Fort Jefferson bearable.

"I'd give anything to make you laugh, old friend," said Bart, wanting his friend to come out of his misery.

"Laugh!" said Mudd. "I almost don't know the meaning of the word. As a doctor I did like to laugh at myself now and then, but that's not been possible here. A whimpering doctor is a bad doctor, so I can't even allow myself the luxury of a good cry. Forgive my ill humor."

Bart's eyes met those of his friend. "There's nothing to forgive. We've survived, you and I, but it was easier when we were fighting night and day. I noticed you worked as hard to save the scum as you did those we knew were good men."

"No, that's not quite true, although I tried not to judge. After all, we don't know why people act as they do. And even brutal men and hardened criminals become different people as they lie dying. Have you noticed that?"

"Of course, but so often it appears to be divine retribution, or so I thought until you became ill." As he spoke, feelings of powerlessness and incapacity overwhelmed Bart. He turned and left his friend, slumped in a chair.

Mudd's ill humor proved to be catching, and on this most despondent of nights Bart's thoughts turned to Anne-Marie. The thought that she had refused to leave Don Miguel was unbearable and caused his mood to shift from one of self-pity to burning, jealous hatred of Don Miguel. Once he heard Mudd cry out in sleep that was apparently as painful as the waking hours, and he jumped to his feet. Just as Anne-Marie could not desert Don Miguel, he could not have deserted Mudd. With this thought rage retreated somewhat and he found sleep.

CHAPTER TWENTY

Only after his two visits on Bart Ramsden's behalf to the sheriff and to the commander on the naval base did Don Miguel turn to his own concerns. For some time he had been aware that there were changes in his body not attributable, he had now concluded, to his heart condition. These new symptoms were not of the same kind, although at first he had tried to believe that they were merely manifestations of progressive heart failure and poor blood circulation. As time passed, with even more new symptoms, a pattern became too evident for him to ignore, though he had tried. But the events of the past few days had spurred him to seek either denial or affirmation of his fears. Consuelo had seen something when she read his fortune. Others less perceptive would soon do the same.

So sure was he of his self-diagnosis that he felt as if he had stepped from some peaceful mountaintop where he had been omnipotent and omniscient into a valley where a war was raging. He felt compelled to fight, as if his defenseless presence might affect the outcome, though if his suspicions were correct, he knew it could not. He wanted only to speed it up. He could no longer stand by and wait. Hence his visit to Burbury.

Dr. Burbury was not surprised to see Don Miguel. He had been treating him for years, and this time he was happy that at least it was not necessary to journey to Los Claveles. His bills had reflected this inconvenience, yet they were always paid promptly without complaint. He offered Don Miguel a cordial smile.

"Come right in, friend," said the doctor, beckoning. "I hope you're not having pain. How's the old heart been doing?"

"I can't complain about that," replied Don Miguel, taking a seat and gathering will to speak. "Something has gone wrong with me, doctor, slowly, almost imperceptibly, and I'd like you to see if you can find out what it is."

"Well, let's take a look. That was quite a party Consuelo gave last night. It must have been Key West's largest affair in years." Dr. Burbury reached for his stethoscope, but Don Miguel pushed it away, meeting the doctor's startled eyes.

"No, put that down," said Don Miguel. "Look at my fingernails, the peculiar way they are growing. Patches of my skin are prickly as if needles were sticking into them and other spots, as on my toes, are growing numb."

"Pull up your shirt," said Dr. Burbury, a shaded, somber note creeping into his voice.

Carefully he examined Don Miguel's body despite his instant recognition of the minutely fine red spots, as small as if he had been dusted with red powder. Finishing his examination of Don Miguel's body, he hastily pulled down the shirt as if to hide the skin.

He then felt Don Miguel's earlobes. They were slightly thickened and hard. His hands moved to the bridge of his nose where tear glands in the corners of his eyes had thickened.

"Is anything different in the way you feel?" asked the doctor.

"Yes," replied Don Miguel. "A new general weakness has troubled me. I can't ride as I could—which is usually very easy for me."

Dr. Burbury remained silent, but continued to feel Don Miguel's face, noting the ridges forming in the skin. Gently he turned Don Miguel's face to the light, looking for the emergence of the leonine visage.

"Would you take off your boots, please, Don Miguel. I would like to examine your feet." Carefully he examined Don

Miguel's toes. With a small instrument he poked the flesh. "Does this hurt?"

"Not at all," replied Don Miguel flatly. Dark, impenetrable eyes turned to those of the doctor.

For a moment the doctor preserved a natural composure. Then he rose and pulled from his shelf a bottle of disinfectant and splashed the full strength liquid over his hands. The gesture was a reflex action—not one of decontamination—born of a sudden need for strength to combat mankind's cruelest scourge, acknowledged so since biblical times. The chemical assaulted his nostrils, yet the doctor drew in the essence as if to enhance its efficacy and momentarily distract from the painful workings of his mind. Slowly he gathered the power to speak, now returning to his friend.

"Don Miguel, it is painful for me to tell you this," said Dr. Burbury, still drawing the pungent air into his lungs, air that no longer bit yet mildly stimulated. "I think you are in the first stage of leprosy."

"Do you think or are you sure?" asked Don Miguel.

"I am sure," replied the kind doctor sadly, dropping his hand to his patient's knee.

Instantly there passed through Don Miguel's bowels a ferocious burning, a stroke of revulsion that seemed to resound throughout his whole body. For a moment he shunned the eyes of the doctor, then he slumped in his chair. Dr. Burbury reached for his patient's shoulder. Then the hands closed firmly in a wordless, compassionate, strength-giving gesture. Don Miguel's hands on his own thighs moved back and forth as if he thought they too needed stiffening; he squeezed the flesh as if testing his sense of feel, which he was not doing. He was quite unaware of the movement.

Death alone he had long been expecting. It was to come like a package delivered to the door that had been ordered and paid for in advance. But this was something else, an ordeal that could go on and on. Moreover, it was a heinous ignominy that would brand his family. Then he realized that the doctor was talking to him and struggled to concentrate upon what he was saying.

"Don't worry about having given this to your family. Despite common belief, it is the world's least contagious disease. It is so hard to get that I can't imagine how you got it, except that we get everything in Key West," said Dr. Burbury.

"That is, of course, my worst fear," said Don Miguel. "But I have recently spent very little time with my family."

"There's not much in the way of treatment," warned Dr. Burbury.

For a moment Don Miguel remained silent. He would have to pick himself up out of the chair and move, but he did not know where the strength would come from.

"I would appreciate it if you would not report this," he said finally, "at least not until tomorrow because tomorrow you will not have to. I will contaminate no one, but go immediately to Los Claveles where I must put some papers in order. The utmost secrecy is required. Will you trust me and will you promise me that no one will know?"

Dr. Burbury, stricken by his certain knowledge of his patient's intent, promised. He did not know whether he would keep that promise or not. He knew what a tremendous sacrifice for Don Miguel it would be not to see his wife and child for the last time. He felt Don Miguel's burden moving to his own shoulders with its stifling incredible weight of sadness.

"You must make plans to come to the key tomorrow. I will send the boat back for you," said Don Miguel, gathering a new power from his resolve.

"All right," said Dr. Burbury.

There was no longer any need for anxiety or qualms about his future, no longer any need to fight to hold Anne-Marie or to fear pain and death. He felt free, freer than he had felt in the years when death was something intolerable. Now it was sweet escape, not only for himself but for all others, whether or not they knew it. The strength was there now to stand straight and bid the doctor good afternoon.

"I hope that you know how I appreciate the care and consideration you have given me for so many years," said Don Miguel, adding, "and for your friendship," realizing that he had just imposed a burden on that friendship. But, nevertheless, now he felt brimming with energy and determination with important work to be done.

280

The change in Don Miguel was immediately apparent to Dr. Burbury, who suddenly felt he understood him. Understanding brought with it a sense of envy by the doctor. Could he have had the courage to resolve the problem so bravely had he been in Don Miguel's place? He was awed by this valor.

"Don't be concerned about Anne-Marie and Samantha. They will be all right," said Don Miguel. "Anne-Marie has great strength, which surely will be imparted to Samantha. Anne-Marie doesn't know it, but she will be the richest woman in the state of Florida, or even in the state of New Jersey, where she comes from. She is young, beautiful and intelligent. She will have a new bright future.

Unable to reply to this, Dr. Burbury said gruffly, "I will see you tomorrow, that is, unless you would like me to accompany you on any errands or down to the sloop."

"That's kind of you," Don Miguel hastened to answer, "but I would prefer that you didn't. There are some things that I would like to think about, to remember to do without the need of talking. I don't even want to see a priest. A priest can do nothing for me now. It is too late for me to repent and too early for him to condemn, much less to dissuade. I have already asked forgiveness from those to whom I have given pain. Trouble the kind chambers of your heart no more with my problems. For the first time in months, I am not suffering, but to be with me, you might needlessly." With that Don Miguel left. . . .

For some minutes Dr. Burbury sat stunned. As a doctor, he was legally bound to report this disease, but no one could benefit by the knowledge except himself, if he remained the family physician. In any case, there was no effective treatment for leprosy. He would keep the secret.

Despite a great quantity of rum, Dr. Burbury passed a restless night. Early the next morning a sailor in the employ of Don Miguel was at his door to take him to Los Claveles. Dr. Burbury had assembled a number of packages to take with him.

Before they pulled into the inlet, he knew what he would see. The household stood distraught before the house, the women weeping and wringing their hands in their aprons, the men forlorn.

"You're too late, doc," said the overseer. "It wasn't his heart. Apparently it was a hunting accident. He must have stumbled, setting off his gun."

The men already had been working, constructing a wooden coffin. It would be covered in black felt as usual. They had assumed that the body would be taken to Key West for burial and said so.

"He told me yesterday when he visited me that he wanted to be buried here on the key," said Dr. Burbury conclusively. "I feared his death was imminent—he could not have survived another heart attack. When his man came for me I feared I would find him dead. As soon as the coffin is ready, I will seal it. I don't want his wife to see him."

When the last nail was in place, Dr. Burbury ordered everyone who had touched the body to wash their hands well. "The fever is still around, you know. I realize that you men have done a lot of sailing back and forth between here and Key West in the last day, but you had better go there now for Madame and a priest. I'll wait here, as she may need me."

Dr. Burbury also needed time to gather his wits, as he had not decided how much to tell Anne-Marie about her husband. So little was known about leprosy that there seemed to be no point in telling her about that. It would only worry her for years, both for herself and for the child. A horrible stigma was attached to the disease which he knew to be unfounded, but stemming as it had from Bible times, it was yet something for a family to contend with. This was above and beyond the horrible disfiguration.

A second consideration was a sense of guilt that families carried when one of their own committed suicide. This, he felt, was almost a disease in itself. If there had been any recent altercation between Don Miguel and Anne-Marie, she would feel blame and suffer over it for the rest of her life. The humane course seemed to be to prevent her from believing that it was a suicide, despite the gun. He would construct a lie. This would explain Don Miguel's behavior during the last few hours of his life. He decided to say that Don Miguel had yellow fever; he was disoriented from the disease and from the heavy drug given him. Then the man could be buried in peace. . . .

282

That night he was on the dock to receive quietly grieving Anne-Marie and Samantha with Concepción. Almost ten hours had passed.

"Dr. Burbury, you have been so good to us," said Anne-Marie, embracing him. "Let me get Samantha to bed and then we can talk. She doesn't quite know yet what has happened and Concepción has gone completely to pieces. I feel as though I should tend to her too. She was many years in Don Miguel's employ and loved him dearly."

"You've taken the news well, Anne-Marie," he said, a fatherly arm about her shoulder.

"Oh, not really. I suppose it will undo me later, when I don't have other people I must think about. When I was a child and someone died, neighbors came in like a flock of ministering angels. I remember mother telling me about bathing and dressing the bodies and helping with the deathwatches. Women came in and and cooked and greeted those who paid their respects." Anne-Marie realized that she was babbling. She smiled, though her eyes were full of sadness. "I'm so glad you're here, otherwise I should feel so alone."

"I can't stay long, dear. I have my patients."

"Dr. Burbury," said Anne-Marie. "It was very unlikely that Don Miguel died in a hunting accident. He was always very careful with guns. Could he have been murdered?"

Her question brought Burbury up short and he heaved a sigh of relief for the thought he had given the death.

"He came to my office yesterday with yellow fever and I filled him with morphine. I'm sure he did not want to risk infecting you. He felt ill in Key West and had come to consult me. I told him that he had the fever. In any case, he could have withstood the disease for only a brief time. It is an excruciating death—nausea, hemorrhages and delirium. No, my dear, he was not murdered, but he must have felt it wise to secure his gun. It is difficult to speculate on what really happened."

"That sounds very much like Don Miguel, thinking of every detail," said Anne-Marie. "He would never risk infecting me or his daughter. That would have tried his soul. He retreated

283

into his beloved ivory tower to die with the things that he loved—among them his gun. Surely that."

Later, after the household quieted and Anne-Marie had further time for reflection, she turned to Dr. Burbury for help in a way that surprised him. "Dr. Burbury, I want Don Miguel's death to be kept a secret for a while. Is that possible?"

"I must say, that is rather unusual," replied the doctor, stifling a startled expression, not entirely successfully.

"No one in Key West knows other than you. The people on this key I trust. I do have another living husband who has been falsely arrested for gun smuggling. I must continue to use Don Miguel's power in the hope of freeing him. I did not bring back a priest, because I did not want anyone to know of his death—Don Miguel must fight his own battles in the hereafter for a while. I will go through Don Miguel's papers—and I assume there's no need for money—but there will be charitable contributions and perhaps other gifts coming from Don Miguel." She hesitated, then asked, "Is all this possible?"

"I'll have to turn in a death certificate when I return to Key West. It is the law, my dear. If you return when I do, you would have a few hours, not much more time."

The following day she and Dr. Burbury sat down to the eerie task of examining the dead man's carefully guarded secrets. Don Miguel had left his papers in order on his desk where Anne-Marie would immediately find them. He left generous legacies to all the servants. And, as if he knew that Anne-Marie would never leave him, he had placed hundreds of thousands of dollars in cash and securities in their joint names, and all his other property as well. A trust had been set up for Samantha Ramsden. Apparently, no detail had been forgotten.

"I will miss him terribly," said Anne-Marie. "He taught me so many things. He became my dearest friend." As she spoke tears ran down her cheeks. "He picked me up off the beach, half drowned. For a long time he seemed to be keeping me a prisoner, and then suddenly, I knew I was free. Now I can't imagine living without him, not having him any more to be my best company or to comfort me or simply be there. He never forgot to make life seem useful and promising, nor forgot the usefulness of making an effort. I see now that from the first time I met him so much of what he did was predicated upon his knowledge of impending death. It was a driving force. He had to make me strong. He had two lives to mold in so little time, mine and Samantha's."

Her words had cast a new light upon Don Miguel, a man the doctor had thought he knew so well until the last few days. He had given his wife no instruction in how to manage money, trusting that she would learn soon enough. Instead he had chosen to build character, keeping the money that had never brought him health or happiness something of a secret.

"And what of Captain Ramsden?" asked Dr. Burbury. "How do you feel about him?"

"Nobody has ever measured how much love a heart can hold," she replied. Realizing that Dr. Burbury perhaps needed an explanation, she continued, "He is a fine man, but I no more know him today than I know President Johnson. In the year of our marriage we spent less than two months together. The rest of the time he was at sea. A few days ago I danced with him for two minutes. Then I learned that he had been arrested. Don Miguel was trying to have him freed."

"Samantha is..."

"It's a wise child who knows its own father," interrupted Anne-Marie.

"I see," said Dr. Burbury, raising both eyebrows, but with no air of condemnation, simply an acknowledgment of fact. "I find that life has a few surprises when I examine the human heart, especially when I think I've seen everything. Frankly, it is only a lack of nobility that disturbs me. You would be amazed at where I find my heroes and heroines," he added, smiling and patting her hand.

"Tell me, what do you plan to do?" he asked.

"I have a mother and father who have believed me dead for some three years. I must see them and put an end to their grief. Twice I tried to do this, but Don Miguel never let the letters leave the property. I was not ready yet, he said. This is no place for Samantha or me. I'm only twenty."

Her words struck Dr. Burbury like a sword piercing his heart. How difficult life had been for present-day children. At twenty they were still children, catapulted into maturity by one

285

of the century's cruelest wars, he thought, or abused by fates in a young, burgeoning country. The strong would survive, and he was now gazing at one of the most beautiful of the survivors: How strong remained to be seen.

"Don't take too much upon yourself too fast. Pace yourself. You are going to need more time than you realize to recover from the last few days. Certainly, as soon as possible, you should go home. Obviously, it was a happy place for you. There you can best discover your goals."

"Thank you for your kind help, Dr. Burbury. I have needed it more than you recognize."

Outside, a blinding tropical sun focused upon Los Claveles with a burning intensity. On just such a day she remembered walking to the terrace, closing her eyes and then opening them to see below a battered basket. Were she to look now, she would see a coffin. She had come to Los Claveles in grief and so she would depart.

CHAPTER TWENTY-ONE

Bart Ramsden's shock upon being sentenced to three years in a penitentiary was equaled by his friends' horror. "Oh, my God, Tim, how is that possible?" Consuelo moaned.

"It would seem that all things are possible."

"Could we go to Washington and get a pardon?" she asked, looking toward him for encouragement.

"Let's not be hasty. We still know nothing that has not come out in court. I doubt that the president would listen to our pleas now; he has his own troubles with Congress, and the country is full of vengeance. To go there and beg now is probably premature. That will be our last resort."

"I think we have reached that point," said Consuelo flatly.

"Not quite—" replied Tim, his words cut off by a knock at the door.

To their surprise Pearl admitted Anne-Marie.

"Please forgive this intrusion," she begged, "but I've been at Los Claveles and only just now arrived in Key West. I'm anxious to learn what has happened to Captain Ramsden. Don Miguel told me he was arrested."

"Please come in and sit down," said Consuelo. "It is no intrusion. I'm afraid we have only bad news. Bart was court-martialed this morning and sentenced to three years at Fort

Jefferson. Tim and I are trying to decide what we should do next and we'd welcome any suggestions. We are quite desperate."

"How terrible," Anne-Marie quailed, her eyes wide with shock. For a moment Consuelo feared that Anne-Marie would faint. She had stumbled to the chair Tim had held for her and clearly she was terribly distraught.

"Anne-Marie, are you all right?" asked Consuelo. "You don't look well."

Dark circles rimmed her tired eyes, and her figure drooped; she trembled. Her assurance was gone. Neither Consuelo nor Tim had expected that she would be so disturbed by the news, or that she would show it so transparently. Anne-Marie always had so much poise, containing her emotions, but now tears were filling her eyes.

Consuelo shot a questioning gaze at Tim, whose eyes met hers with the same consternation.

"I'm all right," said Anne-Marie, "but the last few days have been very difficult. I have just buried Don Miguel. I didn't want anyone else to know it except you for a few hours. I had hoped to use the time to pressure the sheriff into taking some action, thinking the orders came from Don Miguel. But I see now that it is too late. Bart is far out of the sheriff's hands now."

"Oh, Anne-Marie, we are so sorry. If there's anything we can do..."

"I've known that Don Miguel did not have long to live. Still, it is a shock. I thought I had myself very much under control, but seeing friends, especially with your tragic news, undid me. It is almost too much."

"We may still use Don Miguel's influence," said Tim. "Let's try to force the sheriff's hand. Do you feel up to visiting the sheriff with me? It might be asking a lot of you right now."

"That's why I'm here," replied Anne-Marie, visibly regaining presence.

"We can insist that he put out a wire to all ports to look for the *Greyhound*. Once the ship is located, she should be reinvestigated. I think that we will find that the spaces where guns were concealed originated in the first mate's cabin."

"There would be nothing lost and possibly quite a lot gained," Consuelo interjected.

"It is just my suspicion," said Tim. "Brian was an expert carpenter. I don't believe he would have had the time or an opportunity to make an unobserved entry on the side of the captain's cabin."

"You must stay here with us, Anne-Marie, for as long as you're in Key West. I'll have a guest room readied for you. You should be with friends," said Consuelo.

"That's kind of you. I hadn't thought about my quarters with my house here and our boat. Let's go see the sheriff right now before any more time is lost."

Arriving with Anne-Marie, Tim found the sheriff a thoroughly changed and shaken man. "I don't believe you've had the pleasure of meeting Don Miguel's wife," introduced Tim. "She is completely familiar with all Don Miguel's dealings."

"These offices will do everything possible to aid you," assured the humbled sheriff. "I, too, feel that a mistake has been made in the Ramsden case."

"Please put out a warrant to all ports to look for the *Greyhound*. As soon as she is located, the ship should be searched. I believe that it can be determined that the concealed spaces originated from the former first mate's cabin even though they extend into the captain's cabin," urged Tim.

"You understand that this is of utmost importance," added Anne-Marie, taking on the authoritative tone her husband would have used.

"I'll put out the cables immediately."

That night at dinner Anne-Marie had another project to put before Tim.

"I like Key West and I think that I would like to winter here. Los Claveles is too isolated for me and for Samantha. Would you consider entering my employ and building a house for me, Tim?"

"That might be fun," replied Tim. "I'm not exactly overworked." He looked to Consuelo for a reaction and found her smiling.

"Perhaps before I leave we can find a piece of ground. I plan to take Samantha to visit my parents and then, if necessary, travel to Washington to see if I can gain a presidential pardon for Bart. I guess there's nothing more we can do for Bart until the *Greyhound* is located."

"If I may make a suggestion," said Tim, "as soon as you find a building site, leave Key West for the summer. We are beginning to have cases of yellow fever again and we may have another epidemic. Doctors don't know how the disease is spread, but you and Samantha would be safe in the North. As soon as we hear anything from the *Greyhound*, we'll send you a wire and the papers. You could then proceed to Washington with new evidence."

"Fine. We'll look for some land and I'll give you my requirements for a house. Spare no expense and give yourself whatever wages you would like. I know you will do a beautiful job and I trust you."

Within a few days, suitable waterfront land having been purchased and Tim's work having been laid out for him, Anne-Marie left to pick up Samantha and to travel to her family's home. She left ten thousand dollars at Tim's disposal.

The cases of yellow fever in Key West mounted and as the weeks bore on, more were anticipated. Dr. Whitehurst and Dr. Burbury issued pleas for volunteer assistance.

Consuelo was one of the first to heed the summons, anxious for any worthwhile occupation that would take her mind off Bart's plight. She joined the volunteer nursing staff at the Marine Hospital, caring for the influx of victims who came in ill off ships and had no home in Key West where they could be cared for.

As she walked about the packed wards and corridors, crowded with cots, examining identification tags at the foot of each bed, she found a name she knew: "Roger Bains." Could this man be the steward who might save Bart?

Bains had come in on a ship and soon collapsed with fever. By the time Consuelo found him, he was already in a delirium. As soon as she could get free, she hurried to Tim with the news of her discovery.

"You must come right away and identify him, and then

we'll see if intensive nursing can pull him through. I will do it. To think that he could finally appear in that condition! It's maddening," cried Consuelo.

Together they hurried back to the hospital, hardly daring to hope. He might even now be dead.

Bains had always been a small, fear-ridden man. The drink and his illness had further ravaged his appearance and his ferretlike face so that now he looked like a derelict. His skin was saffron yellow, his mouth loosely agape, his cheeks sunken; his eyes rolled back, sightless.

"It's Bains," said Tim, "but I think his chances are small." For the next twelve hours they worked constantly with the wet cloths to bring down his fever. Finally Tim insisted that Consuelo go home for a few hours' sleep. They would have come to that decision earlier had it not been for other sufferers who constantly pleaded and needed attention.

"You must go so that you can relieve me or all will be lost. No one else is going to pay any attention to him," he worried.

It was true. Moreover, Bains was a specimen of humanity that disinclined others to sympathy.

Exhausted, her workday long past, Consuelo obeyed, but in a few hours she was back to take over from Tim. It was an onerous task, bending and rising, to cover Bains, head to toe with cool wet cloths, too soon heated by his hot body. Between changing cloths it was also necessary to force a few drops of water down his throat. More than a few drops might drown him. Though Consuelo was close to despair, she was determined to save him. She and Tim worked diligently.

The crisis passed and Bains was still alive. Finally aware, when he recognized Tim, a feeble smile crossed his lips and he fell into a restful sleep.

"It will be a day or two before he can talk," said Tim. "We must be very sure that he is fully conscious and cognizant of the questions asked him. Otherwise his statement could be discounted."

"I don't know how to thank you and the lady, Mr. Clayton," Bains finally croaked. "You've been caring for me for a long time, I know. You were always here."

"You'll be able to thank us with a favor when you're well, but don't worry about that now."

When Bains was stronger, Tim explained Captain Ramsden's struggles over the last three years. "As soon as you are well enough to remember and to talk, you could help us mightily with a statement. Don't try to talk now." Bains nodded, too weak to say much, but obviously happy to be able to help.

By the time Bains could sit up to make his deposition, he knew what he wanted to say. Mr. Leeds arrived with his clerk and because Mr. Leeds was frightened of even entering the hospital, Tim carried Bains outside.

Bains had been on the *Catherine* since Ramsden's purchase of the ship; during those months they had made four or five voyages. Bains was "not sure exactly how many" and asked that that point be left so, as it might have to be corrected. "No log should prove me a liar," he said. It was after his third voyage that he returned to the ship one night to make sure that the captain's quarters were completely in order when he heard a strange noise in the first mate's cabin and went to investigate it. There he surprised the first mate, Brian Delaney. Carpenter's tools were scattered about the floor and Delaney was working under his bunk. The first mate rose, furious that Bains had entered. He further swore that if Bains admitted to seeing anything, he would throw him to the sharks at the first opportunity. Bains loyally swore himself to silence for the captain's sake, he supposed, and thought no more about the incident.

It was on the following voyage that Captain Ramsden remarked to him that it was damned peculiar that Bains could not stow his gear as well as formerly.

"You used to be able to put everything away tidily," complained the captain. "Now my space is jammed to the gills."

Fearing the first mate, Bains said nothing, but it was then clear to Bains that the captain knew nothing about the several inches that had been taken by Delaney from his storage space. "Delaney would 'ave killed me if I'd reported 'im to the cap'n. He meant it."

Bains also explained that several times he would have left the

292

Catherine, chiefly because of Delaney, but Captain Ramsden was uncommonly good to him in comparison with other captains.

Bains went on to explain that he had been in the companionway the evening that the captain's wife was lost and that he had heard the lie to the captain about the lady having gone below.

During the course of that afternoon the first mate had given the wheel over to two or three other sailors for a few minutes, but the whole time Bains was in view of the steps. "She never came down 'em," he said.

"But she lived," said Tim, thankfully.

"It seems like a miracle," replied Bains. "She was a lovely lady." Bains then explained that by the time the voyage was over, he was even more terrified of the first mate. The captain had been grieving and drinking too much to rely upon as protection from the first mate. "I'd 'ave done anything to get off that ship." He hid in Key West for several days before he dared show his face. Then as quickly as he could, he boarded another ship and stayed away from Key West and any other ports where the *Catherine* might be.

Leeds's clerk recorded every word.

Within the week the *Greyhound* was examined in New Orleans. Bains's testimony was corroborated; the screws in the dummy partition had all been inserted from the first mate's cabin, a detail totally absent in the previous reports. Once it had been established that Captain Ramsden was a murderer, the authorities had no interest in further investigation of facts bearing on the smuggling charge.

The day finally came when Tim and Consuelo could visit the offices of General Smith, known as "Baldy" Smith, of the International Ocean Telegraph Company, to send a wire to Anne-Marie stating that papers were on their way that would clear Bart. She could take them to Washington for a certain presidential pardon.

While Leeds's offices were assembling the papers, Tim and Consuelo sailed the sixty miles to Fort Jefferson hoping to catch sight of Bart. It was not Tim's first excursion, but the first he had made with Consuelo.

They circled the fort, but saw no signs of life. Quarantine signs stood on the entrance to the boardwalk and on the wharves, but not one face appeared in the hundreds of arched windows. Not a single sentry could be seen on duty, nor did one puff of smoke come from the kitchens. "It's incredible," said Tim. "Usually the inmates are intrigued with the arrival of a ship of any sort—their boredom keeps them watching, you can be sure. I'll admit this is a tiny ship and hard to see, but the quiet is unnatural. We ought to rouse someone. The yellow fever may have killed them all . . ."

"Tim, could that be so?"

"Consuelo, you've seen what it can do."

At one point, Consuelo thought that she had seen a limp body dropped from a window into the moat, but then dismissed the idea as preposterous. For several hours they sailed around the fort, then anchored by another key.

"I don't dare anchor near the prison. If anyone is alive it is too dangerous," Tim had said.

What appeared to be burial mounds swelled the ground behind the sandy beaches of nearby Bird Key, but there was no activity.

"Do you realize that Anne-Marie may be going to Washington to have a dead man pardoned?" queried Tim, morosely facing facts.

"Yes, but she should do it anyway. For his family's sake his name must be cleared. She doesn't have anything better to do."

"That's true," agreed Tim sadly.

"If anyone comes out of that place alive, it would be Bart."

"I hope you are right."

For some time now, Tim and Consuelo had lived as if they were man and wife, though they had maintained enough discretion to keep the townspeople unaware. Consuelo supported charities, attended church and was always available to help with nursing. Tim was always there to help her with problems, not to present her with more, he had said. She soon found herself in an easy, close, dependable relationship that grew stronger and, she now realized, far more satisfying than Bart's uncertain love and his life-and-death struggles.

Now she sat looking at Tim, a magnificent summer sunset

behind him, making the whole western sky a blaze of fire. Silvery mackerel clouds strewn through the blaze softened the reds to pink and so lit the surface of the water that the horizon vanished in the glittering distance. Only the water close to their ship was blue; beyond it it was pure silver.

"When I look at how beautiful this world is with you in it and think of the illness and terror there behind us, I think, no, it cannot be so. We are just imagining it. But those in the prison, too, have eyes. They can look out as we do and see the beauty about them and take some comfort," said Consuelo.

"I'm glad you put me in your beautiful portrait," observed Tim, looking at life more brightly than he had a few minutes earlier. "I've been hoping that you will marry me soon," he said shyly, uncommonly meek.

"I've been hoping that you would ask me," she invited, moving next to him. "I think we both want to dignify our relationship with some permanent and public tie. I have learned to love you deeply, Tim Clayton."

"You know how I have always felt about you," he exclaimed, taking her into his arms.

"It's almost wicked," she said, remembering.

"What do you mean?"

"To be happy so close to this miserable place."

"I know what you mean," he replied, welcoming the darkness.

The night sea heaved at the base of the fort, booming, seething and echoing along the massive walls. They saw only the looming up, like a cliff in the blackness, of the dark shadowy spray. She felt his long light body warm against her and thought of the body that splashed into the moat. Far away there seemed to be a small lament in the distance, but what did it matter? Magically, Tim had abolished loneliness and sorrow. What did anything matter except this triumphant physical experience. "I love you. I love you," Consuelo whispered, dissolved in his embrace.

Later she said to him, "Promise me that you will never be jealous of Bart."

"I'm not the jealous type. Perhaps you should know that I was married once, but not for long. Before a year was out she had died of consumption. For years I suffered, but after I met you, I remembered her gently and bade her farewell. She was gone, and you are my love."

"You have never spoken of another woman, so I was sure that there had been one, an important one." She raised her hand to touch his face and gently ran her fingers through his hair. "Then you agree. The past is past and to be forgotten. Promise me?"

"That's like the desert Hindoos promising to eat no fish," he replied. "Think of a harder vow," he ordered.

"That either Pearl or I will always make the coffee in our household."

"Enough, woman!" he interjected, his voice rising. "Did you ever hear of a man marrying a woman to reform *her*?" he asked, laughing.

"Oh, Bart," she replied with disgust.

"Do you realize that you called me Bart?" he asked, his tone slightly sharpened, at the same time releasing her.

"Yes," she replied. "Now that you mention it. And I may do it again. Especially when I despair! Don't take offense, besides, I thought we just buried that subject?"

"Touché," he replied, taking her again in his arms. "You are absolutely right."

Together they lay enjoying the pure night. Softly the water slapped against the siding, gently rocking the boat like a hammock. They lay in silence with no disturbance possible. Their fire quenched with ineffable communication, close and touching, they slept away the night under a thousand stars, lanterns of the universe.

The following day, after starting early with one more sail around the fort, still seeing nothing, they returned to Key West.

"Should we forgo all the celebrations of our marriage until Bart is free?" asked Consuelo.

"If you really want it so, but I feel it is our day," he replied.

"You're right. We've made enough sacrifices for others. I'll talk to Reverend Herrick tomorrow. I love you," she added.

CHAPTER TWENTY-TWO

Anne-Marie, anxious to see her family, considered taking a Morgan Line steamship which ran between Baltimore and Havana, stopping in Key West; but a northbound ship was not due for over a week. An alternative was to take a mail boat to Cedar Key on the west coast of Florida to meet the terminus of the Florida, Atlantic and Gulf Railroad. This line connected with several others and would eventually enable her to reach Atlantic City by rail. However, much of the way this was a cattle route and first-class accommodations were sporadic. Finally, she decided that the quickest way to New Jersey was via her own sailing craft.

"I forget that I am a rich woman with a ship and a captain at my disposal. Truthfully, I haven't kept pace with the changes in my life and I certainly haven't adjusted to my authority," confessed Anne-Marie to Consuelo.

"It's understandable, but don't worry, you will!"

With the captain, two sailors, a cook, Concepción and Samantha, Anne-Marie set sail for Great Egg Harbor. They stopped in Jacksonville and Charleston for supplies, and to afford the captain some much needed uninterrupted rest. The winds were ideal, but traffic was heavy. Not wanting to risk a collision, the conscientious captain put in long hours himself.

During the first ten days Anne-Marie suffered, but by the last few days of the journey, her gloom lifted. She fought a mounting excitement, not knowing exactly when she would arrive or what she would find. She rehearsed scene after scene. Impartially, she hoped first to see her father. During the week he would be in his offices near the harbor, but if they arrived at night or on Sunday, he would be at home. Then she would have to find a carriage. Townspeople catching sight of her would think they had seen a ghost. Needless to say, her arrival would come as a shock, but also a joyous occasion.

Quite naturally, other thoughts sometimes colored the voyage. One night she awakened and in a half-sleep thought she was back on the *Catherine* and frantically reached for the first Samantha's basket. Not finding it, she broke into a cold sweat. Jumping from her berth, she fled to the deck. There Captain Sands, startled at seeing her in her nightdress, spoke quickly.

"Are you all right, ma'am?"

"It was just a dream, Captain, but I'm all right now," she stammered, feeling as though a careening world had suddenly halted.

"You are in good hands. Don't be frightened," he assured her. He was aware of her earlier tragedy and not surprised that something like this had happened. "Shall I call Concepción?"

"No, I'm fine now," she told him, retiring—but not to sleep.

Fortunately, aboard the ship there was always movement. There was the sound of water surging beneath them. Constantly light and dark shifted about. Unsteadiness pervaded everything, day or night. Because of it, whenever she felt a lurch or pronounced dip she was prompted to grab at the nearest solid object which might serve as a handle to keep her aboard.

Anne-Marie spent hours preparing Samantha for the reunion. "You will meet your grandparents, who will love you and who will try to spoil you," she warned the child.

"Like Papa did!" Samantha said happily. Anne-Marie let that comment ride. To Samantha being spoiled meant being loved.

"You will see where Mama lived when she was a little girl."

"In the olden days, when wicked pirates stopped ships and stole ladies' jewels?" the girl asked eagerly.

"Olden days? Well, yes. But pirates? No," replied her mother. Her parents would enjoy that "olden days" tag for Anne-Marie's childhood only fifteen years before.

The long days of travel in the confinement of the cabin meant that Anne-Marie had to amuse and divert Samantha, a free spirit who had had a whole island to herself. Telling the usual fairy tales had been the custom of Samantha's father. Anne-Marie was forced to draw upon her own childhood for story material. The anecdotes that color the history of every large family, the tricks and the whippings, the threatened "royal" beatings, the favorite pets and the near-tragic accidents that were all part of any family's lore fascinated the child. Fortunately, Samantha wanted to hear favorite stories over and over again. The embellishments grew, but finally by the end of the voyage Anne-Marie felt that the child had been introduced to the new people who would become a part of her life.

Her family would, of course, assume that Samantha was the older child. The thought haunted her. How could she explain? Or should she? She could not. Finally, she decided that the truth would distress them for her loss and for Bart too. After all, this Samantha *could* be Bart's.

When she dwelled upon the recent past, she quailed. The palms of her hands broke into a sweat. Her parents would be shocked enough upon seeing her, and too many pressing current problems, like freeing Bart, deserved their attention. What was done was done. She would have to explain Don Miguel as an eccentric benefactor who held them captive, but she did not relish the prospect.

As it happened, it was almost dark when they landed in the harbor. The captain disembarked to make arrangements with the harbormaster and to secure a carriage for them. Fortunately, the driver was a man she did not know, sparing her a premature reunion and explanation with some old friend.

"To Jason Frazier's. Do you know the place?"

He did.

"Drive carefully, but do hurry," Anne-Marie implored.

Within the carriage, Samantha sat between the two women sharing her hands. Concepción's dark Spanish eyes strained to see this new and different place. The child sat still, relieved to be free of the boat; tired, but aware that something momentous was about to happen. She would see the people in the stories.

Nervously Anne-Marie picked up a comb, once again to preen the child, but Samantha would not have it and clambered to Concepción's lap for protection.

"I don't blame you," said Anne-Marie, laughing. "You've had enough, haven't you? No matter. You look fine. It is just that Mama is excited about seeing her own mama and papa."

After what seemed like an endless journey, the carriage drew into Jason Frazier's wide circular driveway where the stone house loomed before them, a warm glow issuing from its windows. Anne-Marie descended, pressed a coin into the driver's hand and, clutching Samantha and with Concepción close behind, entered the familiar foyer. A soft hum of voices in the dining room continued, uninterrupted by the opening door. So many had free access to this house that Anne-Marie knew there would be no pause until she stood in the doorway to the dining room. Everyone knew the timing within the house, the exact moment to lift their heads to greet the new arrival. From habit alone she turned quickly to the massive pier mirror and saw a surprising picture, an elegant and sophisticated woman, calm in face and manner. This was the woman who had so cleverly parried the questions of her interrogators in Key West. She was in control again when she needed it. Beside her Samantha and Concepción were watching expectantly. Her coppery head high and smiling, she took the few remaining steps and with arms outstretched stood gloriously at the entrance to the dining room, facing her mother at the head of the table.

Emily Frazier looked up and, unbelieving, gave a terrified cry. Startled, Jason turned. Anne-Marie stood so, waiting and smiling, her composure unruffled though her heart was crushing her with its joy. When no one moved, paralyzed in disbelief, she said, "Aren't you going to welcome us?" and drew Samantha into view. That question released them. Her father and sisters moved swiftly to embrace her. Emily alone sat, convulsed by sobs. "My baby. My baby. I can't believe it. Where have you been? Where in the world have you been?"

Only by chance, on that evening Anne-Marie's two sisters,

Kate and May, with their husbands, were there for dinner, adding immeasurably to the impact of the reunion.

"You have no idea how I have dreamed of being here," cried Anne-Marie, tears now streaming down her cheeks. "Here is Samantha, your granddaughter."

"Our prayers have been answered," sobbed Emily to Jason as she rose to embrace her daughter and greet the astonished Samantha, who was enjoying the hugs and kisses of the multitude her mother called her "relatives."

"Why didn't you let us know?" scolded Emily, remembering the years of needless, unremitting pain.

"I tried, Mother, believe me," begged Anne-Marie, a small girl again.

"Sit down," said Jason, pulling up chairs. "Tell us what happened."

"Your father never gave up," interjected Emily. "He never believed that you were lost for good."

"Some of that was for your mother's benefit," confided Jason, his eyes also now wet.

"This is Concepción, my maid," said Anne-Marie, turning to the woman who stood by, brimming with excitement and beaming with delight at Samantha's reception. "She speaks only a little English, but she has been wonderful to me, a pillar of strength." This implied a kind of hardship Anne-Marie had not suffered except at the beginning, and this she meant to convey so that out of delicacy her relations might postpone embarrassing questions. "It will take days to tell you the details, but we were picked up on the beach by a wrecker on a desolate island—a key, they call it. I wrote you, but the letters were never posted. I was held a captive for months, having been told that the *Catherine* had wrecked and that all hands and Bart were lost. You could never imagine the isolation, with no possible escape."

She then told them of what she had learned of Bart's plight and his imprisonment at Fort Jefferson.

"A couple of weeks ago my captor died; but he turned out to be my benefactor because he left Samantha and me a fortune. I could have let you know then that I was alive, but I feared that you would not have believed or understood a telegram. It

301

seemed much better to come here myself. So I came as fast as the wind could bring me, in my own ship."

Turning expectantly to her father, she continued, briskly changing the subject. "Now our task is to free Bart. He is imprisoned in Fort Jefferson. He has friends in Key West who are working on his case. As soon as they have the evidence that we believe exists, we must go to the president for a pardon. We do not know whether Bart is still alive."

"Nothing but terrible news has come from Fort Jefferson. Yellow fever has wiped out almost everyone there, we hear," cautioned Jason.

"I have feared that, Father, but still, we should clear his name," replied Anne-Marie. "Let me go to greet the servants and see that Samantha gets to bed, then we can talk."

There were many things to explain. Samantha was sure to refer to Don Miguel as her father. Don Miguel's power, but also his kindness and her acceptance of it deserved clarification. But she also needed news. Time had not stood still for her family either. There had been marriages and births and deaths in her absence. The next few days would be busy, with a future to plan. She would need her father's advice on investments. The cottage had been rented.

"I had to put someone in there who would take care of it," said Jason. "It would have gone to wrack and ruin standing empty. Your personal things are packed up here."

"I refuse to even think of the cottage," admitted Anne-Marie sadly. "I don't want to see it, unless I have to."

"The tenants have taken good care of the place and there's no need for you to torture yourself. This is a time for rejoicing," added Jason.

When they finally decided it was time to retire and Anne-Marie was once again safely in her old room, she ran her fingers lovingly over the furniture. It was so incomparably sweet to be home, to have relieved her dear, faithful people of their sorrow, and to have found again the strength, solidarity and loving care they proffered. She would have to offer the same to Samantha. All the wealth of Don Miguel could not substitute for that heritage, the outrageous fortune that had been her birthright. A great wave of gratitude swept her as she recounted its blessings in her prayers.

The exertion and excitement of the day finally extracted its toll, and she fell into a deep, satisfying sleep, or so she would think on the morrow.

The next few days were filled with visiting other relatives and Bart's parents, who welcomed their "granddaughter" as an astonishingly healthy "spitting image of Bart," they said. No one else thought so, unfortunately for a guilty Anne-Marie. More fortunately everyone else saw Samantha's strong resemblance to her mother. A procession of friends called both to welcome her and to satisfy their curiosities. Only a concern for Bart remained to quell her delight.

In one long conference with Jason, Anne-Marie placed a series of bankbooks from around the world in his hands. There were stocks and bonds of the Chicago, Burlington & Quincy, Rock Island, Milwaukee and St. Paul railroads; New Orleans and New York street railway stocks, mining stocks from Colorado, gold mines in California—all in great blocks. There were deeds to buildings in Paris and London, plantations in the West Indies and Jamaica, even a hotel in New York. "You may need a better financial advisor than I," said Jason, astonished. "Your benefactor bought wisely. He had great faith in railroads—which speaks poorly for shipping over water, where my interests have been."

"He knew what he was doing. Profit from it, Father," replied Anne-Marie. "You may want to sell out here."

Jason considered this suggestion. Certainly her benefactor had foresight, and in the last three years of his life he had hardly touched his fortune as it grew by leaps and bounds.

"I'm going to build a house in Key West," she said. "You would love that little town, and it doesn't have a bank. When you consider retirement, you and mother might at least give a thought to wintering there."

That night Jason confided to Emily. "Your daughter hasn't done badly for herself the last three years. She may be the richest woman in the country. She's certainly the richest in the state of New Jersey."

"You don't mean it!" Emily cried, wondering how all that money would change Anne-Marie's life. "Money is no ticket to happiness," she pontificated.

"Don't be too sure," he advised.

Within a week a telegram arrived. BART APPARENTLY LIVES STOP PAPERS FOLLOWING SHOULD WARRANT PRESIDENTIAL PARDON FOR EARLIEST RELEASE STOP TAKE HEART CONGRATULATIONS TIM. The years of waiting were almost at an end.

"Now we move," said Jason, as gleeful as Anne-Marie had ever seen him. "Now we don't go begging. With righteous indignation we demand immediate justice! Now you will see how money talks and the power that it can wield." He glanced smugly at his wife. "Dinner can wait," he ordered, underlining his satisfaction with his own sagacity.

"Thank goodness, Anne-Marie, that you thought to bring your portfolio so that I know where your heaviest investments lie. We will begin to talk at once with the presidents of the major concerns where you own large blocks of stock. These gentlemen will have influential contacts and law firms at their disposal. At the same time we will set up appointments with senators, not only those from New Jersey, but also every state where you have sizable interests. We'll bring pressure to bear from every corner. Have no fear, the president will act, pressed by his own party and the opposition as well. He sits in a hot seat right now and this will be a golden opportunity for him. Your case is a political plum!"

Anne-Marie had seldom seen her father so enthusiastic. Only a few days ago a tired old man had turned his face to her as she stood in the portal of his dining room. Since then he had shed ten years. Now the vigorous, inspired and determined gentleman had a new lease on life. It was immensely gratifying that she, who had been the source of so much sorrow, could now put a scepter in his hand. Indeed, as Consuelo had predicted, she would learn to use her authority, and this was the first satisfying step.

Throughout dinner and late into the night Jason composed in his mind the many letters to go out the following day over his signature to influential men across the land, setting up a timetable of political pressure, radiating like spokes of a giant wheel with Washington as the hub.

"Father," said Anne-Marie as he departed the next day for his office, "I know that you have many letters to do today, but perhaps your secretary can arrange for a private railroad car to take us to Washington. Mother would enjoy the trip."

Jason looked startled, but then smiled and pinched her cheek. "It would not have occurred to me, but it is a very good idea. All Washington will know about it!"

During the next three weeks, while waiting for the papers from Tim, there were times that tried Anne-Marie's soul. Her early preoccupation with Bart's problems, the voyage and the entertainment of Samantha and finally a reunion with her family had distracted her from more intense normal feelings of personal loss. It did not take long, however, for the renewal of her familiar childhood surroundings to wear off, leaving her with the thinking habits of over three years, thinking habits invariably entwined with Don Miguel. Her sense of propriety demanded that she sublimate her sorrow. Now she was in Bart's home territory as well as her own, and no one but Concepción could understand her distress.

Fortunately, when she retreated, her family assumed she was suffering, but over Bart; her duplicity added to her discomfort. A thousand times a day, it seemed to her, Don Miguel's name was on the tip of her tongue, only to be swallowed. A thing of beauty, interest or amusement faded sharply with the bitter, poignant remembrance that it could not be shared. Only an extreme exercise of will carried her through the period of waiting for the papers to release her into action.

Emily was as excited as Jason over the travel accommodations, an undreamed-of extravagance that her daughter took for granted. It seemed to Emily that Anne-Marie stepped into the private railroad car as nonchalantly as she would have stepped into an old shoe. Her daughter's apparent serenity was, however, only an outward manifestation of a distanced lonely heart not yet set free, not a careless disregard of money.

Their privately staffed car was furnished with blue velvet carpets, matching silk draperies with white silk curtains. The comfortable chairs were upholstered in gold-colored plush.

Magnificent gilt-framed mirrors reflected the traveling splendor. Provided also were a card table with lounge chairs and a writing desk with ample stationery for letters and telegrams. Four berths for sleeping, enclosed by gold brocade curtains, completed the quarters.

These posh accommodations were matched only by those assigned to them by the hotel in Washington as part of their royal reception. With the papers clearing Bart, the letters of support, introduction and "at-your-disposal" appointments came a flurry of invitations from Washington society. Jason tossed a sheaf of these into Anne-Marie's lap. "You'll have to decide which of these you want to accept, but I suggest that you accept none until we have Bart's pardon in our hands. We don't want to offend anyone and some would be more helpful than others. But at this point, we simply don't know."

Jason's instincts were correct. Washington was a hotbed of political intrigue due chiefly to Johnson's political ineptitude and the dissension of Reconstruction.

Appointments with the senators were followed by one with President Johnson himself. Wind, rain, thunder and lightning colored the morning, but by afternoon at the appointed hour, the storm had abated. The official document was already prepared and signed when they arrived. A worn and frustrated president seemed to find considerable pleasure in meeting the beautiful young Anne-Marie, so much more attractive than most of his petitioners. And he said as much as he placed in her hands the invaluable document with the great seal of the president of the United States.

"A telegram freeing your husband has been sent through the Navy, Mrs. Ramsden. I imagine that by now he has been trasported by the Navy to Key West. It gives me much pleasure to right this wrong."

"I thank you, Mr. President, from the bottom of my heart," breathed Anne-Marie, unable to believe that it was all over.

"Everything did go all right, didn't it? The rain held off, mother managed not to weep..." said Anne-Marie, suddenly remembering uttering those very words over three years before. Only one line, "Brian didn't lose the ring," no longer applied. She shuddered.

CHAPTER TWENTY-THREE

As suddenly as he had been imprisoned, Bart learned that he had been pardoned.

While a Navy vessel waited for him, he stood at the moat bidding farewell to his friend, Dr. Mudd. Being free while his friend remained in prison made his release bittersweet, although better days for Mudd were in sight. Dr. Daniel Whitehurst of Key West had just arrived to take over the medical care of the fort. He was both a physician and an attorney, and he had been a popular mayor of Key West. Whitehurst was known as a gentleman of the old school, traveled and experienced. He had expressed a desire to have Mudd work with him, and the presence of this obviously kind and intelligent man would brighten his friend's days.

"I'm going to work to free you. That's a promise," said Bart, embracing Mudd in farewell.

Bart disembarked at the naval station in Key West to find a crowd awaiting him. Consuelo and Tim, of course, were there and others who knew him and those who knew of him. There were reporters from Tampa papers and from the *Key West Dispatch*, and, as always, where there was a crowd, the city fathers.

The commotion took Bart entirely by surprise. He had hoped

to have clean clothes before meeting anyone. Instead he remained as bedraggled, ragged and scruffy as Fort Jefferson inmates were. Aghast, he was immediately encircled by reporters, plying him with questions. Tim, who had stationed himself where he could reach him most quickly, was with him as he stepped down from the ship.

Tim interceded. "Gentlemen, please," his voice booming above the din. "Captain Ramsden has been isolated at Fort Jefferson. He doesn't even know who obtained the presidential pardon. He knows only that he is free and that he has left the fort. You will have to confine your questions to Fort Jefferson."

"What do you intend to do next, Captain Ramsden?" queried one reporter.

"Get presentable," replied Bart, alerted by Tim's announcement to the fact that he knew even less than he supposed about happenings in the last nine months.

"Of course, I'm anxious to be with my family, but I'm also determined to see Dr. Samuel Mudd pardoned. His imprisonment is a travesty of justice. Since I arrived at Fort Jefferson, I've worked with Dr. Mudd under the most difficult conditions, day in and day out, and I would stake my life on the decency and moral fiber of that man. His is a cause on which the press needs enlightenment. My own cause has been won and is over. If you gentlemen of the press will allow me two hours to repair my appearance and my feelings, I shall give you a story that will circle the world."

Reporters, however, were far more interested at the moment in hearing of Bart's personal life. Anne-Marie, because of her wealth, suddenly had become a *cause célébre* in Washington.

"What do you think of the mansion your wife is building in Key West?" asked another reporter. Again Tim, seeing the surprised look on Bart's face, intervened.

"Gentlemen, please, Captain Ramsden is a modern-day Rip Van Winkle. He's not yet familiar with the family's plans."

Fortunately, at this moment Mayor Henry Mulrennan stepped up to shake Bart's hand and speak his welcome. The press, bound to quote him exactly, was diverted. When the speech ended, Bart quickly thanked the mayor and disappeared into the carriage Tim had thoughtfully provided, leaving the scrambling reporters to await his pleasure.

"Whew," exclaimed Bart, leaning back in the seat beside Consuelo and Tim. "I never in my wildest dreams expected that. For heaven's sake, fill me in, friends. Nine months and I am reborn, ignorant as any other newborn!"

"We have all sorts of great news for you," said Tim, grinning.

"You will be happy to know that Consuelo and I are newlyweds. Also," added Tim, changing his tone, "Don Miguel died suddenly—weeks ago. Because he left your wife and daughter wealthy women, Anne-Marie was able to move heaven and earth to procure your pardon. Now I work for her constructing what will be at least a winter home for you here in Key West." He spoke as they entered Consuelo's house.

"Now let's start all over again," said Bart, finding no better comment. "Give me the details, but first, let me offer my congratulations. I think you've made a perfect match." He looked now to Consuelo, knowing her well enough to read her reassuring look.

"Details over champagne!" said Tim. "How's that?"

"Civilized," answered Bart as his eyes roved appreciatively around Consuelo's familiar sitting room, which, more than once, he had feared he would never see again.

"Let me shave, dress and borrow some clothes," said Bart. "It will give me a chance to digest what you've told me so far. I have a lot of questions on which I'll need your advice. So let me do a bit of reflecting. I'd like to gain perspective..."

"Of course, you need to take everything slowly," said Consuelo, taking his hands as she sensed his mounting anxiety and tried to draw it from him to herself. "There have been changes, but believe me, they're all for the better."

As she spoke, tears of relief and happiness sparkled in her eyes.

Bart gratefully understood, but fearing that he might also weep, he bolted the room.

Tim moved to Consuelo's side, firmly wrapping an arm about her waist. Together they watched Bart ascend the stairs, but not as he used to, two steps at a time. "He's a changed man," Tim reflected.

Consuelo concurred. "I think 'matured' is the word."

"He seemed more interested in Mudd's case than his own," noted Tim, "and I thought he took the news of our marriage very well."

"The old foolhardy cock-sureness and blustering ways—notice the way he climbed the stairs—are gone. Young, impetuous Captain Bart Ramsden has fallen by the wayside."

"He's been through a lot," said Tim.

"Haven't we all?" replied Consuelo.

They talked with Bart throughout the day and night. Clearly, Bart needed convincing that Anne-Marie had not rejected him, but had sacrificed her own happiness through a sense of duty to a dying man. "You are two dear friends, anxious to comfort me, but despite what you say, I feel I must not take Anne-Marie for granted. She will need winning back again. . . . But more importantly, I've seen a lot of injustice that I'd like to try to right instead of simply thinking of my own interests. My goals have changed. Once I thought only of making money and a successful name for myself."

"A natural ambition and not one to be ashamed of," remarked Tim.

"I'm sure there's something better. My immediate objective is to free Dr. Mudd, but this is only a first step. I hope Anne-Marie will help. Perhaps on better acquaintance we will build something new. For now we are two entirely different people from the pair who were separated on that terrible voyage. Anne-Marie loved Don Miguel. I know her and I know that."

"A pardon for Dr. Mudd will not be easy," warned Tim, "even with Anne-Marie's money behind you, and she has a great deal of it. The world hasn't yet figured out the extent of Anne-Marie's wealth, since a large part is in foreign holdings. Your life won't be the same."

"You will see what Tim means when you read the papers," added Consuelo. "But nothing worthwhile ever seems to be easy. I've felt very sorry for Mudd. I think he was framed by someone needing a scapegoat."

310

"You can count on our support," added Tim, nodding toward Consuelo.

"That's a lot. No man ever had two better friends. But, good people, no one ever leaves Fort Jefferson unscathed— even *without* a yellow fever epidemic. You come out bitter and broken or wiser and stronger—if you live."

"Dear Bart," said Consuelo, "I hope you can keep your attitude, because it is one thing to be generous and altruistic in the glow of the first breath of freedom, and quite another to keep that attitude when you encounter the sort of resistance that will be inevitable when you champion Dr. Mudd."

"Bart is no quitter in rough weather," added Tim. "But let's not make any assumptions about what he can or can't do."

Bart rose. "Bed for me, my good friends. I refuse to take the position that I am a saint, and I'm too tired to try it."

"We're all tired," said Tim, "so, see you over hotcakes and catfish in the morning. You will have to see the house. Then, maybe for fun, a sail?"

"Perfect. I'm anxious to be off. There are so many people that I want to see. I want to strain my eyes looking! Would you believe that I'll take a boat to the first railroad?"

"That's quite a shift for old Bart," murmured Tim. As soon as he was out of earshot Tim turned to Consuelo. "Well, how do you feel about him?"

"Oh, why do you ask me that?" she parried, smiling.

"I don't know . . ."

"Do you really want to know?" she pressed.

"I think so . . ."

"I feel very romantic. Will you do something about that?" she asked, reaching for his hand.

Happy and satisfied with her answer, Tim stretched both of his long arms toward his wife and drew a deep breath. "Are you trying to sell an idea to me?" he queried, amiably teasing.

"I wouldn't be surprised," she replied, moving into his arms. Her voice lowered until her words were barely audible. "Let's go to bed."

"What an intriguing idea."

"I can't think of a better one."

Slowly, arms about each other as the clock struck two, they climbed up the stairs.

As they trudged around the rocky building site, Tim pointed out rooms marked by budding walls and foundations. The workmanship was first-class and Bart was astonished by the size of the place.

"Anne-Marie expects to live in splendor, doesn't she?" he remarked, laughing, but recalling his statement that he and Anne-Marie were now two different people. She was not the young wife who was thrilled with her cottage curtains. Would he like her?

"It's magnificent, Tim—and what a view!" exclaimed Bart. Anne-Marie had chosen the site well—with a good rise overlooking the ocean. That ocean! It's varied hues from indigo fading into a milky whiteness, whipped up by a steadily growing southeasterly breeze, stretched miles before them. Above it the sun, a burst of glory, gave it a sparkling brilliance not unlike a wide stream of precious stones.

"It is breathtaking," agreed Consuelo, "so beautiful it guarantees happiness." She smiled at Bart, reaching for his hand to steady her on the precarious terrain. Tim left them to speak with the workmen, but Bart did not release her. Almost stripped of breath, reeling under the impact of her nearness and the first moment with her alone, he stammered, "Consuelo, Consuelo. . . . I'll never be able to tell you . . ."

"You don't have to. I know. Please don't say anything. Only one thing is important, you have survived and are well in every respect. I doubt that Tim or Anne-Marie could ever sympathize with or understand what we have between us. It is there. It never interferes with our love for others now. Let's keep it a sustaining force or a beautiful dream, whatever each of us needs whenever we need it. Think of it as a blank check of love."

"It is signed," replied Bart as she pulled him along toward Tim.

When they returned to Consuelo's house—as Bart still thought of it—a naval officer was waiting for them. A warship

312

leaving that afternoon would take Bart to New Orleans. From there he could travel to his New Jersey home by rail. The speedy departure was fortunate, especially after Consuelo's romantic avowal of friendship. He knew that it was designed to bolster his ego. Tim was also his friend who must not be given cause to doubt it. He was glad to be leaving, as much as he loved them both.

On the voyage to New Orleans Bart thought of little but a reunion with Anne-Marie. Above all, he wanted the time to be with her alone, without family and friends or even onlookers to distract them. Virtual acquaintance would need to be renewed.

On reaching New Orleans, he sent her a telegram. His message, DEAREST WIFE, MEET ME TUESDAY AT THE CONTINENTAL HOTEL IN PHILADELPHIA, was too abrupt—inept. After a moment's consideration he added the word, PLEASE.

Consuelo's earlier caution against presumption prompted a second wire to the hotel reserving a suite rather than a double room a hotel clerk might have assumed. Although he wanted her, in his emotional turmoil he was not sure yet whether he would want her forever. On the other hand, the thought that she might reject him came back again and again to become more and more unsettling.

In 1860, the Continental Hotel, then the largest house of its kind the country, was opened at the southeast corner of Ninth and Chestnut streets in Philadelphia. The Continental had entertained the Prince of Wales, Abraham Lincoln and Charles Dickens, so Bart felt relatively secure in his selection of an elegant site in which to meet Anne-Marie. His suite, ordered for the following day, was immediately available to him, so despite the long journey and the late hour, he fell into the hunter's half-sleep, waking and listening many times that night. Nerves and muscles cramped in apprehension brought him half-dreams of heavy weather at sea. Eventually, he convinced himself that he was in a land-man's bed and he slept. . . .

When a peaked Philadelphia midday sun broke through the

haze, he awakened with a start. He dashed to splash his face and shave off a five-day beard, not daring to take the time necessary with a barber. Twice he stopped to steady his hand, but even then he nicked himself. Giving up a breakfast he longed for, he rushed to a nearby haberdasher for a fresh supply of shirts, socks, underwear, ties, handkerchiefs and a new top hat, all of which complemented Tim's best English wool suit.

The transformation from the previous evening was astonishing. Still, the tinges of gray hair dappling his sideburns and the scars crisscrossing his back tallied four years of physical abuse.

Waiting, he polished his new New Orleans boots until they shone like mirrors. Every sound in the hall, each footstep, each muffled voice, each key in a lock halted his breath until he heard the gentle knock at the door. It was Anne-Marie.

Beautiful woman? Yes. Handsome man? Surely. But neither saw the other so. Suddenly the years rolled back—far back, not a mere four years. With blurring eyes he saw a small girl in a white jumper with coppery hair that could not be contained in pigtails. While she looked fondly at a freckle-faced boy who seemed much bigger than she with very large ears and huge feet and eyes bluer than forget-me-nots.

They, like children, swooped into a child's embrace, laughing and crying, together, beginning again as they had long ago.